LOOSE ENDS

LOOSE ENDS

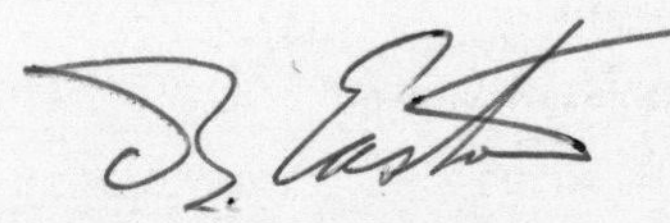

Don Easton

A Castle Street Mystery

THE DUNDURN GROUP
TORONTO

Editor: Barry Jowett
Copy-editor: Jennifer Gallant
Design: Jennifer Scott
Printer: Transcontinental

National Library of Canada Cataloguing in Publication

Easton, Don
Loose ends / Don Easton.

(Castle Street mysteries)
ISBN-10: 1-55002-565-1
ISBN-13: 978-1-55002-565-1

I. Title. II. Series: Castle Street mystery.

PS8609.A87L66 2005 C813'.6 C2005-900168-2

2 3 4 5 09 08

We acknowledge the support of the **Canada Council for the Arts** and the **Ontario Arts Council** for our publishing program. We also acknowledge the financial support of the **Government of Canada** through the **Book Publishing Industry Development Program** and **The Association for the Export of Canadian Books**, and the **Government of Ontario** through the **Ontario Book Publishers Tax Credit** program and the **Ontario Media Development Corporation.**

Printed and bound in Canada
Printed on recycled paper
www.dundurn.com

Dundurn Press	Gazelle Book Services Limited	Dundurn Press
3 Church Street, Suite 500	White Cross Mills	2250 Military Road
Toronto, Ontario, Canada	Hightown, Lancaster, England	Tonawanda, NY
M5E 1M2	LA1 4X5	U.S.A. 14150

To Brenda, my guiding light:
Without you, I would not have survived.
Without you, I would not have cared.

To Mike and Steve:
Even as children, your individual personalities combined to strengthen our unity at a time when it was most needed. You are both extraordinary, and our lives could not have been complete without you.

I love you all.

chapter one

Ben Anderson paused to savour the sweet smell of alfalfa. He had no idea that his world was about to collide with a very different world. A world that would attack without provocation or warning. A world that for all eternity would feed off his soul like starving rats in a war zone. Ben was a farmer. He didn't know this other world existed.

He tossed another bale onto the hay elevator and watched as the bale slowly ground its way to the top before tumbling into the loft above.

It was early afternoon and the sun was hot. The morning shower had done little to cool the air. The sun sucked the moisture out of the ground and the added humidity caused his shirt to cling to his back and chest. The smog from Vancouver, over an hour's drive away, hung in the air. Ben chose not to notice the smog. The smell of cattle and alfalfa was much more rewarding.

He caught a glimpse of Maggie's freckled face and her red hair done up in pigtails as she scrambled to keep up with the bales falling from the elevator and bouncing down onto the loft floor. For a ten-year-old, she was a hard worker.

At two years younger, her little brother was not a lot of help. But no one ever told Ben Junior that. His hair was blonde and his face was well tanned from working on their family farm. Unlike his sister's pressed jeans, his were dirty and ragged over one knee.

Ben Junior looked serious as he swung a hay hook into another bale and dragged it with both hands across the wooden floor. The bale slid easily. The floor had become shiny and polished over the years from bales being dragged to the back of the loft.

Wizard drove the new silver Acura down the highway. He had already switched cars three times within the last two hours, but now that The Suit was with him, his paranoia intensified. He slowed down and watched his rear-view mirror. Cars passed him. A good sign.

At a glance, Wizard's clothes gave him the appearance of a businessman who had taken the day off to go golfing. It was Wizard's face that gave a clue as to what business he was in. His nose had been broken so often in his younger days that the swelling between his eyes had become permanent. Deep creases in his forehead gave the impression that he was much older than his forty-five years. His salt and pepper hair was trimmed short, and his moustache and greying goatee partially hid a scar that traversed his upper and lower lips.

It had taken him twenty years to become president of Vancouver's west-side chapter of the Satans Wrath Motorcycle Club. It had been a long road, and he wasn't finished yet. Satans Wrath had dozens of presidents in charge of chapters in eleven countries. Each country had one national president. Wizard would do whatever it took to replace Damien as the national president for Canada.

Wizard glanced at The Suit's face. The Suit was about his age, but he was skinny and weak. He hated that he needed him. It was Rolly, another member of the club, who had first told him about The Suit.

Rolly had told Wizard that The Suit was a sick bastard. Someone to be shunned. Wizard was more of a businessman. He saw opportunity. It was his idea to recruit him. Not as a club member, of course, but strictly for business. Only Rolly and Damien knew about The Suit. His identity remained top secret. His real name was never spoken, and personal meetings were handled with extreme care.

Wizard played the game well, and Damien rewarded him by assigning him to oversee their most valued business ventures: drugs and prostitution. Many in the club thought Wizard was a genius when it came to business. Some said he had a psychic ability when it came to beating the competition or the police. It was what eventually earned him his nickname. Wizard wasn't psychic. He didn't have to be. He had The Suit.

Ben shut off the machinery and for a moment enjoyed the silence. He put his hands on his hips and slowly arched his back. He was a big man and the work came easy to him, but a heart attack he had suffered two years ago told him not to exert himself.

Maggie's face immediately appeared up above.

"What's the matter, Dad?"

"I think it's time for some lemonade. I'll come up and see how you two are making out."

Seconds later, Ben Junior's face appeared. "Did it break down again?"

"No, Ben Junior, it didn't break down this time."

"Are we finished then?" asked Maggie.

"No, not yet."

"How come you turned it off?"

"Slow down, Ben Junior, I thought we could use a rest is all."

"Yeah, Doodle looks tired. But not me! I'm used to man's work."

Maggie pretended not to care. Doodle wasn't a nickname that she appreciated, but this time she wasn't going to give her little brother a reaction.

Ben climbed the ladder into the loft. Without being asked, Maggie poured three glasses of lemonade from a plastic jug.

She gave her father a big smile as she sat down on a bale.

Ben grinned to himself when he saw her concentrating on holding the plastic glass while extending her little finger. *That's my girl, always trying to be a lady*. His attention to Maggie didn't go unnoticed.

Ben Junior retrieved a cardboard cutout that he had made that morning. It was in the shape of a shark and he had used silver foil to give it extra large teeth. Seconds later, the shark attacked the back of his sister's head in a feeding frenzy.

Maggie swatted at the shark and the silver teeth fell off.

"Daddy! She broke it! I made this for Uncle Jack." He started to wail.

"He started it! I was just —"

"That's enough, you two! Keep that up and you'll both spend your last few days of summer vacation weeding the garden."

The children knew enough to keep quiet, at least for the moment. Maggie pretended to pick particles of hay from her glass. She then flicked her wet fingers in Ben Junior's direction. Seconds later, the children made a face at each other, then giggled, forgetting their anger.

Ben Junior gulped down his lemonade and went to swing wildly on a rope hung from a rafter in the loft.

Maggie saw a yellow jacket walking around the rim of Ben Junior's empty glass. Several other wasps, attracted to the sweet smell of the lemonade, hovered nearby.

She took a small sketchpad and stubby pencil from her hip pocket and drew a caricature of a wasp, sporting a happy face, climbing out of a glass.

Ben leaned over to take a look. "Pretty good, girl," he said. "I think you're going to make one heck of an artist some day."

"Thanks, Dad." Maggie flashed her newly grown adult teeth, which looked out of proportion in her face.

Ben looked at all the bales that had been dragged to the far end of the loft. The children's muscles had not developed enough to stack them properly.

"Okay, I think you kids have earned your keep for today. Check with Mom first. I think she's in the garden. If she doesn't need you then you can go and play."

"Whoopee!" Ben Junior yelled. "Come on, Doodle, let's go!" he said, leaping from the rope and crashing in amongst some bales. Both children scrambled to be first to reach the ladder.

Moments later, Ben Junior raced down the gravel driveway on his bicycle. Muddy water sprayed out from the puddles in some of the deeper potholes. Ben Junior lifted his feet high off the pedals, but not high enough to avoid getting splashed by the mud. Maggie followed behind but kept her distance.

Elizabeth, watching from the garden, shook her head.

"You two be back in time for supper!" she shouted. Then as an afterthought she added, "Maggie! If you want to pick some berries, I'll make your favourite pie for dessert!"

Wizard checked his rear-view mirror as he turned off onto a gravel road. He held his breath and let it out when he saw that the Acura was the only car on the road.

"Where the fuck are you taking me?" The Suit asked.

His German shepherd stuck its nose out of the back seat and licked his ear. He yanked the choke chain around the dog's neck, jerking it back.

"Just a small detail to talk about with Rolly. Will only take a couple of minutes. I'll get you to the motel on time."

The Suit didn't respond. Wizard's business could not be discussed in phone calls. He took a gold cigar case out of his Armani suit and opened it.

A ring-necked pheasant flew up from the side of the road as the car swept by. The German shepherd lunged at the side window. Flashing fangs exploded with saliva as the beast turned its attention to the rear window.

Maggie hung on to her plastic pail of blackberries as she followed Ben Junior around to the front of the abandoned farmhouse. Her skinny, freckled arms hung from her T-shirt and bore scratches from the sharp thorns of the nearby blackberry bushes. Ben Junior's mouth and cheeks bore deep purple traces from the juicy berries he'd already eaten.

The front door of the house, leading into the kitchen, had been kicked open. By the way the big splinters of wood hung from the lock, Maggie figured it had to have been done by a grown-up. Most of the windows were broken, and the kitchen cupboards were only a shell. The grey linoleum was buckled and cracked. It made her think of a giant web.

"Next time, I'm gonna bring my stuff and draw a picture of a big spider on this floor."

"Why?" replied Ben Junior. "I'm sure there's real ones in here."

A pigeon burst from the top of a cupboard and flapped across the kitchen.

Ben Junior instinctively grabbed Maggie's arm but let go as the pigeon escaped through a broken windowpane.

"Scared you, Doodle?" said Ben Junior.

"It scared you too! And if you don't stop calling me Doodle, I'll tell Mom you stole money from her purse."

"It was only a quarter," he said.

"You still stole."

"I just borrowed it. I'm going to put it back."

"Doesn't matter. You never asked, so that means you stole. I should tell Uncle Jack."

Ben Junior paused, then changed the topic. "Come on, let's play grown-ups!"

They entered a room off the kitchen that had once been the main bedroom. Part of a broken mirror hung from the back of the door. Maggie placed her bucket on the floor. She found a rag to rub a circle of grime off the mirror and pretended to put on lipstick.

She did not see the freckle-faced kid with pigtails in the reflection. Instead, it was a pretty lady. *Like the cover girls who advertise makeup. Except I'm not going to be a cover girl. I'll be an artist. A really famous artist...*

Ben Junior nudged in front of her. "I have to shave," he said, sounding gruff.

"Well then hurry. You have to drive over and pick up the baby..."

A car's arrival interrupted their game. They knew the old farmhouse was off limits. Maggie looked at Ben Junior and put her finger to her lips. Outside, a big dog barked.

Maggie peeked through the crack in the bedroom door. She saw two men walk into the kitchen. One carried a blue sports bag. He had a grey goatee on his chin. He also had a tattoo that looked like a couple of words over a picture on his arm.

The other man was dressed in a suit. He was slim, clean-shaven, and had dark, wavy hair neatly trimmed at the top of his collar.

Wizard tossed the sports bag on the kitchen counter, where it landed with a thud.

"I don't have all fucking day. Where is he?" asked The Suit.

Maggie heard another car arrive.

"He's here now," said Wizard, peering out the window.

Maggie looked at her brother. His sparkling blue eyes stared back. He had a devilish grin on his face and tried to push her aside to peek out the door. She grabbed him by the shoulder. He caught the fear in her face and became more sober, stepping back from the door.

Maggie saw the other man walk into the kitchen. He wore a black leather vest and a black T-shirt that partially covered a round and hairy belly. A hunting knife hung from a scabbard on his belt. The end of the handle had a skull on it with ruby red eyes. His balding head and hairless, pie-shaped face and chubby chin reminded Maggie of a plate she had in her dollhouse. The plate had a man-in-the-moon face on it.

"Any trouble finding the place?" Rolly asked.

"Your directions were good," said Wizard.

"So what do ya think?" asked Rolly. "Good place to rent for a grow op."

"Later. What about today's business? Ya get it all?"

"Fifty keys of quick, dead on. Got the French bitch laid down at the Black Water for tonight. She'll be back on the train tomorrow. That the bread?"

"It ain't my fuckin' lunch."

Maggie saw Rolly unzip the blue bag. She could see the crack at the top of his flat bum. He took out a couple of bundles of money, then crammed them back inside. He reached inside his vest pocket and took out a small plastic baggie of brownish powder. He held it out toward Wizard and said, "I brought it if you want to see it."

The Suit yelled "You fucking idiot!" while slapping Rolly's hand. The baggie flew out of his hand and spilled on the counter. "I told you never to bring that crap around me!"

"Relax," said Wizard. "It's only a sample."

"Not this! What about the fifty kilos?"

"You think I'd be drivin' around with that!" said Rolly indignantly. "It's already stashed."

Wizard picked up the baggie. Sunshine illuminated his arm and Maggie saw the tattoo. The words *Dirty Dog* were emblazoned over the head of a dog.

These are bad men, thought Maggie. *Uncle Jack will know what to do with them!* She took out her sketchpad and heard Wizard say, "Make sure the French bitch is on the train tomorrow. Don't want any complaints from back east."

Maggie wrote the word *Dirty* and heard the whine of a dog. She peeked through the crack of the door and saw a German shepherd pad into the kitchen. It sniffed the floor, slowly moving toward her. Its claws made a light clicking sound on the linoleum, zigzagging closer.

Maggie gently closed the door. It creaked slightly.

The men quit talking. *Did they hear me? What if they find us? I bet they'd be mad!* She looked at the broken windowpane in the bedroom and then at her brother. No way to escape.

Wizard reached into the sports bag, wrapping his hand around the shortened stock of a sawed-off shotgun.

"A hell of a *hot* day, isn't it?" Maggie heard Rolly say. She could hear the dog panting.

"Yeah, you can really feel *the heat*," replied Wizard.

Maggie breathed a sigh of relief. *Good. Everything is okay.*

The dog whined.

The mirror in front of Maggie's face exploded into a multitude of broken shards that penetrated her face and neck like porcupine quills. The first blast caught her hand and the side of her ribcage, spinning her around and dumping her on the floor like a rag doll.

The deafening roar of three more blasts followed, but all missed their mark. Smoke and dust ebbed through the rays of sunshine. The sulfuric smell of gunpowder filled the air.

Ben Junior, unscathed, stood staring at his sister. He could see her eyes. Open, but without expression. She wasn't moving. Ben Junior closed his eyes and hunched over.

"Fuck! It's just kids!" said Wizard.

"Good thing. I thought it was the cops," Rolly replied. "Let's get the hell out of here."

"Not so fast, you morons!" said The Suit.

"Nobody has seen us," said Wizard. "We'll just fuck off and —"

"You might take chances; I don't!"

Wizard shrugged his shoulders indifferently, then passed the shotgun to Rolly.

Rolly rested the muzzle of the shotgun on the bump at the top of the spine near the back of Ben Junior's head. The little boy shook and squatted in a fetal position, squeezing his eyes tighter. His jeans turned a darker blue.

Rolly hesitated as the wet stain appeared around the little boy's feet. He lowered the shotgun and looked at Wizard.

"Do it!" The Suit yelled.

"It's time you earned your tattoo," said Wizard.

Maggie's body convulsed and thumped on the floor as she released a gurgling sound from her lungs. She was still alive.

chapter two

Jack Taggart's apartment was on the eighteenth floor and it provided him with a good, if slightly distant, view of the heart of Vancouver. He gripped the railing on his balcony and stared blankly at the street below. Mozart's *The Marriage of Figaro* played through the open door of his balcony. He thought the music would ease his depression. It didn't.

He had joined the Royal Canadian Mounted Police when he was a fresh-faced kid of twenty-three. Fourteen years had passed, and he had long since lost the innocence of his youth. Six years of working undercover on the Drug Section had been followed by a transfer to the Intelligence Section, where he had spent the last five years working undercover on organized crime.

He was a survivor and was good at what he did. His work had not gone unnoticed by a superior officer. Taggart wasn't only good at his job — he was too good. Too good to be playing by the book.

Jack exercised to stay fit, but his dark wavy hair was starting to recede, and plucking the occasional grey hair was becoming a daily ritual. Vanity was not something that he admired about himself, but neither was living alone.

He decided to strike at the root of his depression and strode back inside and reached for his stereo. *The Marriage of Figaro* faded as he dialled his boss.

"Louie, it's Jack."

"How did it go last night?"

"Another shipment arrived in a Winnebago at two-thirty this morning. I watched and met my informant after he helped unload. He confirmed that it's coming from the same guy in El Paso."

"That's good. Put it in the report for Interpol."

"Forget Interpol! I'm going to El Paso myself."

"No. You're not," said Louie firmly. "Wigmore won't approve it. Child porn is low on the list these days."

"But my source says they're linked to snuff films, for God's sake! That's murder."

"I know."

"Does Wigmore know that the El Paso connection distributes to most of Canada?"

"We've been over this. I told him."

"Damn it, Louie! The guy in El Paso has a family and is a leader in his church! I could turn him in about ten seconds. We'd get his distribution list for Canada, not to mention his connection, who is either producing it or knows who is."

"As Wigmore pointed out, the victims aren't Canadian. Pass it over to Interpol."

"The victims aren't, but the goddamned perverts are! We're talking about children being raped and murdered! Who cares what their nationality is?"

"I hear you, but Wigmore wants this handled through channels."

"That could take forever, plus I promised my source I wouldn't burn him. This needs to be handled right. The hell with Wigmore. I've decided to take leave and pay for it myself."

"Forget it, Jack! You go flying off to Texas and he'll have your ass for working in a foreign country without authorization. He's been looking sideways at you ever since Levasseur's body turned up last month. I'm sure he figures you were behind it."

"Levasseur was murdered in Montreal. I haven't been there in years."

"I know. You also look better without a beard." Louie paused a moment, and when Jack didn't reply, he said, "Wigmore's not in right now. Let's meet for coffee tomorrow and talk about it. Maybe I can convince him to cut loose with the funding."

"Appreciate it. Speaking of funding, when am I getting a new partner? It's been three months since Paul was transferred."

"You know Staffing as well as I do. Your guess is as good as mine."

Jack hung up the phone and stared at the cardboard cutouts of fish dangling in his waterless aquarium. A breeze from his balcony made the fish start to spin. Some were sharks with silver teeth. The rest of the fish were bright, colourful, and looked real.

Great kids. Lucky to have been born in Canada. The telephone rang and he picked it up.

It was his sister. She said someone killed both her babies. Her voice was hollow and detached. Ben had gone to look....

*

Jack accelerated along the dusty road. Last Sunday he had been with Liz and Ben. They had gone on a picnic with the kids. He had played hide-and-seek with Maggie and Ben Junior. Later, they had roasted hot dogs over an open fire. Ben Junior had dripped mustard down his shirt.

Jack's car bounced along the gravel driveway leading to the house. He had made the usual one-hour drive to the farm in less than forty minutes. Dust billowed behind, then overtook him as stepped out of the car. A police car, with lights flashing, sat empty outside the house.

Jack sprinted inside.

A uniformed officer appeared in the hall.

"I'm on the job too. This is my sister's house," said Jack, reaching for his badge.

"She told me you were coming. They just left. We've got a car taking them both to the hospital. She's really out of it. I think she broke her nose."

"What happened?"

"She found her kids in an old abandoned farmhouse down the road. She fainted and smacked her face."

"Are you sure the kids are...?"

"I'm sorry. Both dead. That's all I know. Homicide should be arriving any minute."

A police car blocked the driveway leading to the abandoned farmhouse. He saw a uniformed officer talking with two paramedics leaning against an ambulance. Any hope he had was gone.

Moments later, Jack was careful not to disturb any evidence as he walked along the edge of the driveway leading to the house, but the driveway was mostly overgrown with grass and he didn't see any identifiable tracks. He reached the small clearing where the house was located.

A young uniformed officer walked out from behind a mass of blackberry bushes. His white face and the smell from the bushes explained it all.

"Who are you?" the officer demanded.

Jack flashed his badge.

"Man, you wouldn't believe it in there! With this heat and the greasy food I had for —"

"I don't need to hear it."

A voice behind Jack asked, "What are you doing here? Aren't you still on Intelligence?"

Jack recognized Connie Crane. She was attached to the Homicide Unit on the General Investigation Section.

"Where is everybody?" he asked.

"On their way. I just got here myself. What are you doing here?"

"The parents ... they're my sister and brother-in-law."

"Yeah? Oh ... Jack, I'm sorry."

"Thanks."

"You know them well?"

"Very."

"Any problems?"

"Forget that idea," replied Jack. "They're good people. Decent."

"Just doing my job."

"Well let's go in there and do it."

"You're not goin' in there!"

"I'm going in!"

"Like hell you are! You're *not* on GIS, let alone Homicide, so get out of here and leave me to do *my* job."

"Damn it, CC! These kids are family!"

"Forget it. Don't blame me. It's policy."

They locked eyes and neither spoke.

Jack was the first to break the silence. "Have the bodies been formally identified yet?"

"Maybe they didn't see the faces, I heard it's pretty messy in there, but..."

"Policy wouldn't consider that a proper ID. I can do that now. Or were you looking forward to watching their mom and dad do it?"

CC paused, then let out a sigh. "Okay. You win. ID the bodies and then go. Deal?"

Jack nodded, and CC rummaged inside her briefcase and handed him a pair of protectors to slip over his shoes.

CC gave Jack a hard look and said, "Remember, it's not your investigation!"

"I hear you."

CC flicked on a small tape recorder and cautiously entered. Jack stood at the entrance, looking in. He saw a kitchen, with a trail of blood across the floor to an open door on the far side. He resisted the urge to rush in. He watched CC practically hug the wall as she moved through the room, avoiding contact with anything someone else might have touched or walked upon. She talked as she went.

"Blood on the kitchen floor indicates two different sizes of footprints. Appear to be a man and a woman's. Note, must seize the parents' footwear."

CC moved past the kitchen counter and studied the open door leading into the bedroom. "A door leading off the kitchen has numerous chunks and small round holes taken out of it. The pattern is similar to what a shotgun with heavy shot would do. Appears to be multiple blasts, maybe three or four. Entry point is on the kitchen side. No sign of shell casings."

"CC!"

She clicked the recorder off. "I knew you wouldn't be able to keep your mouth shut! What is it?"

Jack indicated where some dust had been disturbed on the counter.

"So?" asked CC.

"Something slid across the counter. There are grains of powder in the dust! Brownish-grey. Bet it's heroin or meth!"

CC bent over for a closer look, then said, "Maybe someone weighing drugs. I'll have it looked at." She then turned her recorder on and said, "Now, facing the entrance to the room off the kitchen. Inside is — Christ!"

CC shut off the recorder and stared into the room.

A voice in Jack's head and an eruption of burning bile up his throat and into his mouth told him to get out of the building. But he didn't listen. He swallowed, then slowly moved to the doorway and looked in.

Sunshine reflecting off splinters of mirror cast bright, rainbow-coloured images. Vibrations from their feet caused the images to dance and shimmer throughout the room. Shards of light flickered across red and pale-white flesh. It looked mystical. Surreal.

He felt the urge to run. To go back to his apartment and crawl into his closet and hide. Hide from Liz and Ben. Hide from this room. Hide from this world.

He paused in his thoughts and found himself staring at Ben Junior's little hand. He thought back to a month previous. He had been roughhousing with Ben Junior out on the lawn. Ben Junior had pressed his tiny hand against Jack's hand and said, "My hand will never be a big as yours, will it, Uncle Jack?" Jack had replied, "Someday. But mine is bigger now!" Then he'd grabbed Ben Junior, who had squealed with delight.

Jack forced himself back to the present. He felt numb as his brain tried to deal with what he saw. *Please don't be sick. Think meat. Maggie and Ben Junior are gone. This is just raw meat. Part of her rib ... No! Part of the rib cage blown away ... blood splatters ... one of her fingers by my feet ... but her body is halfway across the room. She was shot while standing behind the door. But her face! ... Pieces of skull ... she was shot in the face later. Ben Junior ... executed from behind. Oh God! I can't be sick. It'll ruin evidence.... Maggie and Ben Junior ... just meat.*

He studied a bloody imprint of someone who had fallen in the bedroom, knocking over a pail of blackberries. A pattern of bloody hand marks with slender fingers extended across the floor from the imprint.

Blood tells a story. It was all too easy for Jack to read. Easy to read; impossible to erase. The tipped pail, the bloody imprint of an adult body with slender hands...

Liz fainted when she saw ... and awoke next to the bodies of her children. Red streaks, like small railway tracks, snake their way between red palm prints. *Liz was covered in blood.* The fingers point into the room. Speckles of blood are partially obliterated by sliding palm prints. *She broke her nose when she fainted and was dripping some of her own blood as she got to her knees, before crawling backwards out of the room.* The railway streaks from her knees disappear, but red palm prints pepper the floor, along with red scuff marks made by her shoes. *She tries to stand ... feet slip on the linoleum ... falls ... gets to her feet.*

Jack's senses become alive. He is conscious that the hot summer sun has turned up the humidity. *A musty odour ... stifling hot. Rotten wood in the air ... my tongue feels thick. Sound of flies. They're buzzing everywhere. Evil sound.*

Tracks from a workboot cover part of Liz's footprints. *Ben's tracks. First Liz finds the bodies, and then Ben comes to check.* Small red globules of blood are embossed between the thick tread marks left by his boots. The boot prints become farther apart. *Ben is run-*

ning, frantic to protect her from what he saw. He is too late. Too late to protect her — or himself.

Long red narrow streaks against the white enamel paint of the doorframe. *Liz claws at the doorway as she tries to escape from the house.*

A bluebottle fly with a fat hairy body crawled along the sticky blood on the doorjamb.

Jack stepped outside and the fly buzzed around his head, angry at being disturbed. It landed on his lip. He spit and mauled his lips with his fingers. The fly returned to the doorjamb.

I feel like I've tasted death. Is that possible? He spit again. The taste remained. It would remain in the fibres of his brain forever.

Jack handed his shoe protectors to CC. Neither spoke while she placed them in a plastic bag and filled out a label.

She looked at Jack. "Formal identification of…?"

"Margaret Anderson and her brother, Ben Anderson Jr. Yes, it's them."

CC glanced at her watch and made a notation in her notebook. "How they were shot will be hold-back information."

Jack nodded silently, then walked back to the main road as an unmarked police car arrived with two more investigators, followed by a van belonging to the dog master. A wild-eyed German shepherd barked furiously from inside the van.

Jack knew that the bodies of Maggie and Ben Junior would haunt him for the rest of his life. It didn't scare him as much as what he had to do next.

chapter three

Danny O'Reilly looked like he had stepped out of a recruiting poster for the Royal Canadian Mounted Police as he stood outside the main entrance to the hotel in downtown Winnipeg. His red tunic was tailored to fit perfectly, and his deep brown leather riding boots equipped with silver spurs gleamed in the afternoon sun. He was shorter than most police officers, but it wasn't too noticeable when he wore his riding boots.

Danny was looking forward to his transfer to the West Coast. It was no secret that he hated Public Relations. Today he was to open the door of a limousine when it arrived and salute the prime minister as he stepped out. A mannequin could have performed the same function. Any real threat or danger was to be handled by the plainclothes officers. Not that any serious threats had been identified.

He stared at the media and leaned slightly forward on his toes to relieve the pressure points on his heels, then used his brown leather gloves to dab at the perspiration that escaped from under his stetson.

He caught the hand signal of one of the plainclothes members of the VIP Security Detail. Estimated time of arrival for the prime minister was three minutes. *About bloody time.* He glanced at his watch. The PM's flight had been delayed, and it was two hours past the time that he had promised Susan he would be home.

Danny thought back four months to when Tiffany was born. He recently bought Susan a gift certificate for a massage and manicure. As a new mom, she really appreciated the idea. She had booked the appointment for this afternoon. She wouldn't be happy about missing it.

The spurs on Danny's boots jingled when he snapped to attention as the lead cars in the procession of limousines arrived in front of the hotel.

Danny was unaware that fate would alter his life within seconds, plunging him into a world of rules he didn't know existed. A world where the strong murdered the weak. A world where he would have to find out which category he was in.

Jack's footsteps echoed down an empty, antiseptic-smelling hallway as he walked away from the nursing station. Ben and Liz would want answers. He could tell them *why*. No doubt a drug deal. Whoever did it likely heard a noise and thought it was a ripoff, or maybe the cops.

Jack vowed that one day he would be able to tell Ben and Liz *who* did it.

But there was something he was afraid to tell them. If it was a dope deal, more than one person was involved. Defense lawyers would insinuate that the other lawyer's client did it, making any conviction tenuous. They would argue the murders weren't preplanned so any conviction would probably be the result of a plea bargain with the condition of an early release.

He wouldn't tell Ben and Liz that today. Let them go through their disbelief and shock. For them, anger would come later.

He took a deep breath and slowly exhaled as he stepped into the room. *Promise not to cry. They will need me. Must stay strong.*

Ben's and Liz's eyes were windows to their terror. Jack saw their pain. Pain that gripped their throats and made talking or breathing difficult. Pain that no words could cure.

Jack broke his promise to stay strong.

It was a day that would be locked forever in their souls.

Damien squinted at one of the closed-circuit television monitors and saw Wizard looking up at the camera from his car.

Damien's voice was curt and to the point. "I'm out back, at the pool." He released the electronic gate, then walked outside to turn the heat down on his barbecue.

He looked at Vicki's bikini-clad body as she tossed a beach ball back to their three children in the pool. Buck was twelve years old and his two sisters, Sarah and Kate, were ten and seven. She still had a fantastic figure. *So what's wrong with me?*

Vicki returned his gaze and wrapped her arms around him, pulling him close.

"Company?" she asked.

"Business. Won't take long," he answered, gently pushing her away.

"What's the matter, Papa Bear?"

"You know what the matter is."

"You're still brooding about last night? Don't worry. It really doesn't bother me."

"It bothers me! How could it not bother you? I'm fifty-two, but you, you're only thirty-four. You're in your prime."

"Hey, you're still in your prime too. Bet you were just tired. Next time take a Viagra."

Damien sighed, then said, "I did. It didn't work."

Wizard drove up the circular driveway to Damien's estate and parked in front of the four-car garage. Communication antennas and satellite dishes bristled from the roof of the mansion.

One garage door was open, and Wizard caught a glimpse of a new red Jaguar parked inside. The Satans Wrath's emblem of a skull with horns grinned from the gas tank of a Harley Davidson motorcycle next to the Jag.

Wizard smirked to himself as he opened the gate to the back of the mansion. Damien didn't like being bothered at home. What he had to tell him would piss him off even more.

The cobblestone path led to the sound of children's laughter. He spotted Vicki and felt the blood go to his loins. *Yes, Damien has it all.* For a moment he allowed himself to fantasize that Damien was dead. Vicki was lonely and horny. She wanted him to…

The barbecue lid closed with a bang. Damien glared at him and abruptly flicked off one burner. He was wearing only trunks. His arms and legs were exceptionally hairy, and his physique caused Wizard to think that he looked like a paunchy old bear. His short hair had noticeably thinned. *Does he think he can hold on as national pres? He's becoming old and weak. The election is only a couple of months away.*

They walked along a manicured garden path while Wizard gave his version of what had happened that afternoon.

Dark lines formed in the furrows on Damien's forehead and shadows appeared under his eyes. His response was venomous. "You whacked two kids!" Spittle from his mouth landed on Wizard's face.

"Well, actually, Rolly whacked the boy. The Suit told us to do it and —"

"Since when does the fucking Suit give us orders? You were in charge!"

"I was in charge, but —"

"Fucking millions to be made and you pull this stunt!"

"Damien, you weren't there. We had no choice. They were mouthy little brats. Knew what was goin' on and threatened to tell the cops. We had to do 'em. Especially seein' as they saw The Suit. Besides, nobody knows about it or can connect it with us."

"Why the fuck did you have The Suit with you way out there?"

"He was already up the Valley at a meeting all morning. Rolly was looking for spots for grow operations. It just worked out that way."

"Next time, he takes his own wheels to the motel! You do the delivery after he's there."

Wizard nodded that he understood.

"Where is he now?"

"Gettin' his treat at a motel. Rolly will clean that up after. I thought I should come and let you know right away."

"Getting his fucking treat? Killing two kids didn't bother him?"

"Actually, I think he liked it."

"Nobody is to know about this!"

"Rolly earned his Dirty Dog. I sanctioned it."

Damien thought for a moment, then said, "Okay, he gets it, but not a fuckin' hint to anyone about *how* he got it!"

Damien monitored Wizard on camera as he left. His instinct told him that Wizard hadn't been totally honest. He had to trust his instinct. It got him to where he was. *People who lie to me are my enemy.*

"You little shit!" Buck's voice drifted in through the open patio door.

"Buck! Don't speak that way to your sister!"

"Sorry, Dad."

"Don't 'sorry' me. Apologize to her."

"Danny!" said Susan, flicking the brim of his stetson with her finger.

Danny remained at attention but saw Susan as she held Tiffany, bundled up in a cotton blanket, in her other arm.

"What are you doing here?" asked Danny, as his eyes darted toward the arriving limousines.

Susan ignored the question and thrust Tiffany into his arms. She awakened and started to bawl loudly.

"I can't —"

"Be careful, she's still colicky." Susan handed Danny a baby bottle and walked away as the prime minister's limousine rolled to a stop.

The media came alive. The PM stepped out of the limo and smiled broadly at the zeal and laughter of the media, then saw that the cameras were pointed at a policeman who was saluting him with one hand, while holding a baby in his other arm.

The PM knew a photo opportunity when he saw one. Kissing babies was a classic. He gently took the infant from the policeman's grasp. The baby immediately quit crying. He smiled with delight and lifted the infant above his head. *Picture perfect!* The noise from the media drowned out a concerned comment that the policeman made. He brought the baby closer to his face and pursed his lips. It was then that Tiffany chose to vomit.

chapter four

It was the first day after the September Labour Day weekend and Danny O'Reilly's first day as a policeman in Vancouver. He was dressed in a suit and tie. The last-minute decision to have him transferred to Intelligence instead of GIS puzzled him. The reason would soon be clear.

After a forty-minute wait, he was summoned inside the office of Superintendent Wigmore, who was in command of all the Intelligence units in British Columbia.

Danny stood at attention for two minutes while Wigmore sat behind his desk in an overstuffed leather chair, flipping through Danny's file. He wore a tailor-made suit that gave the impression that his shoulders could have belonged to someone who played pro football. His black hair was closely cropped and his moustache was trimmed top and bottom.

Wigmore eventually looked up and said, "Sit down."

Danny sat in a wooden chair across from the desk.

"It's too bad," said Wigmore, shaking his head. "Up until this incident with the PM, you had a good career. A few years in uniform, followed by four years on Drug Section, two years on GIS, and lastly, five months on PR duties. I understand you were transferred from Winnipeg GIS to PR because you blew the whistle. Is that right?"

Danny sighed. "Yes, sir. Two of my colleagues embellished evidence to try and convict a bank robber. They said he spent more time casing a bank than he really did. I told, and Internal interviewed them. They admitted that they may have exaggerated, and the trial was dismissed. It felt pretty uncomfortable working in the Section after that."

"Your actions were admirable. I would expect nothing less from anyone who works for me. But now..." Wigmore made a clucking noise with his tongue before continuing, "After this stunt with the PM, your career is in the toilet. In case you didn't know it, Internal Affairs is contemplating having you charged with neglect of duty."

Danny felt his stomach knot. "I didn't know that, sir."

"Fortunately for you, I have a good relationship with Internal." Wigmore clasped his hands on the desk and leaned forward, staring intently at Danny's face. "You're going to be working with Jack Taggart. Have you ever heard of him?"

"No, sir."

"Good. What I am about to tell you will not leave this room, understand?"

"Yes, sir."

"It's quite simple. I don't trust Taggart, and *you* are going to provide me with every detail of what he is doing."

"Sir?"

"Everyone Taggart works on, criminal organizations that have survived for years, seems bent on self-destruction once he starts to investigate. Ever hear of Project Stop-Watch?"

"The French gang that robs banks across the country? They're notorious!"

"They were."

"They keep crooks outside disguised as shoppers to shoot any officer in the back who might arrive early. A young officer was shot in the neck in Montreal. I think she lived but was paralyzed from the neck. The mastermind was Levasseur. He never entered the banks himself but would pick up his men a few blocks from the heist where they switched cars. It was like he was made of Teflon. Nothing ever stuck to him in court. What does this have to do with Jack Taggart?"

"Two months ago, Taggart somehow got lucky and turned an informant in the gang. Last month Levasseur was murdered."

"I heard that most of the gang was arrested."

"One day Levasseur's men did a job and drove to ditch their car. Levasseur wasn't there. Vancouver City Police were waiting instead. Taggart tipped them off moments before. Word is, when the gang caught up with Levasseur back in Montreal, he said that some guy with a beard car-jacked him at gunpoint as the heist was going down. He said he was let go afterwards."

"Obviously a lie. So he set up his own guys?"

"That's what they thought. His mutilated body was recovered later."

"So Levasseur was Taggart's informant?"

"No. Taggart's informant was some low-level hood. Levasseur wasn't anyone's informant. What I do know is that Taggart had a beard then but shaved it off the day after."

The suggestion made Danny catch his breath. "It might be a coincidence," he offered.

"Coincidence, my ass! He might fool others, but he doesn't fool me! Up until now, I've never been able to prove anything. This time will be different. A perfect opportunity has arisen."

"Sir?"

"Something unexpected that I can use to my advantage. The only family Taggart had was his sister, her husband, and their two kids who lived on some farm up the Valley. Recently the two kids were murdered. Taggart's at the funeral right now."

"That was his niece and nephew? It's in the news…"

"This is the time to get hard evidence on this hotshot. Someone messed with the only family he had. He won't be thinking all that clear. Gain his confidence, if you can, but be careful. Don't get sucked into his world. I want you to stick to him like shit to a sheep's ass. If he so much as jaywalks, I want it documented. You see anything, you sense anything, report it to me."

"Shouldn't Internal Affairs be handling this?"

"They looked into Taggart and got zip. I need someone close to him. Someone he trusts."

"Sir, I don't relish having —"

"You don't relish it?" said Wigmore, pounding his fist on the desk. His chair bashed against the wall as he stood and jabbed his finger into Danny's chest and said, "I bet you relish having a job to support your wife and baby girl, don't you, O'Reilly?"

Danny cringed back in his chair and said, "Yes, sir."

Wigmore slowly sat down and said, "Good." His voice softened and he said, "As policemen, we all have to do things we don't like sometimes. It's part of the job. Just make sure you do your job and I'll see to it that you're looked after."

"Yes, sir."

"In the future, don't go through my receptionist. I don't want any leaks on this matter or anyone to suspect you're talking to me. You're to report to me at home," he said, handing Danny a slip of paper with his telephone number. "I expect a report, say, every Monday night around eight. Call me more often if you think you should. If we need to meet in person, there's a place near my apartment called the Oceanside Lounge. The address is in the phone book."

Wigmore glanced at his door. Danny caught the cue and started to leave.

"Oh, O'Reilly! One more thing." Wigmore waited until Danny turned to face him. "Welcome to Vancouver." Wigmore gave him what he thought was a reassuring smile.

Wigmore's smile became genuine after Danny left. *Child pornography. It's time for Taggart to go. He's too dangerous. A loose cannon.*

Jack stared down at the two small caskets holding Maggie and Ben Junior. Mourners dropped handfuls of earth onto the caskets. He took two envelopes from his suit jacket.

Inside a nearby van, CC watched with binoculars. "What's Taggart up to?"

Her partner, Charlie Wells, grabbed his own binoculars. "He's taking something out of an envelope … looks like paper fish. He's dropping one in each grave."

Jack dropped the cutout of a paper shark. It fell quickly to the earth in Ben Junior's grave. The cutout of a sunfish that he dropped on Maggie's casket made a slight thud. The bullet folded in the fish bounced off the side of the coffin.

chapter five

Jack booked the rest of the week off, but the day after the funeral he called CC.

"Anything?"

"Jack, if we make an arrest, I'll give you a call. Until then, let me do my job."

"Any leads?"

CC sighed. "Not much. But who knows. It's too soon yet."

"What about the powder on the counter?"

"You were right on that. It analyzed as methamphetamine."

"That's good! Every chemist who makes meth leaves what amounts to their own chemical signature in it. The lab can cross-match different samples and you might get a match to identify where it originated from."

"Damn it, Jack. Butt out! Lucy at the lab just explained all that to me."

"So you've put word out to turn in meth samples so the lab can cross-match with —"

"I was going to do that, but instead I'm talking to you! Get the picture?"

Jack allowed himself a glimmer of hope as he hung up. He had his own plan. He called the toxicology department in the crime lab. Lucy was one of the good guys. She would help.

Luigi Grazia was in charge of the Intelligence Section that Danny was assigned to. He was fifty-four years old, and with his greased-back hair, swarthy complexion, and pinstriped suit, he could have passed for a gangster in a B movie. Before he became a desk jockey, he'd had a reputation for solving difficult problems. Some said he was lucky. The fact was, he was cunning.

"Welcome to the section," said Grazia in a gruff voice. "Everyone calls me Louie."

Danny was conscious of Louie's penetrating eyes as they shook hands.

Louie told him he would be sharing an office with Jack Taggart, who would be his immediate supervisor. Danny was glad Jack was off for a week. He wasn't looking forward to shaking hands with his new partner. He discovered, however, that waiting was worse.

Danny reviewed the reports that Jack had recently submitted on an international child pornography ring. When he finished those, he spent the rest of the week reading reports on past investigations about organizations involved in extortion, stolen-auto rings, prostitution, contract murders, drug trafficking, armored car holdups, and more. Louie told him to think of it as a history lesson.

The weekend would have been a good chance for Danny to unpack the many moving boxes that were still piled in his living room, but he felt listless and tired.

"Monday tomorrow," Susan commented over their morning coffee.

Danny's blank expression told her that he wasn't listening.

"What's wrong, honey? You acted thrilled when you first told me you were being transferred to Intelligence. But ever since you started you've been really quiet. You act like the cat that swallowed the mouse. What gives?"

"I'm just tired. I've done a lot of reading this week."

"Tired? I can't remember the last time you worked a week of straight day shifts. I think your new job seems great!"

"Maybe I'm not used to it." He forced a smile.

"Maybe things will be different tomorrow when you meet your new partner."

Danny chose to bite a piece of toast.

"Hope he's someone you like. It's too bad about his niece and nephew."

Danny took another bite.

"You said he was single; maybe you should invite him over for dinner sometime."

Danny was grateful that at that moment Tiffany started to cry from her crib. He left to pick her up.

It was noon when Jack woke up. He was still groggy when he answered his telephone.

"Hi, handsome."

Jack was instantly awake. He recognized Lucy's voice. He held his breath.

"You sound like you were sleeping," Lucy said. "I worked all weekend."

"Not as late as I did. Come on, Lucy! You wouldn't call me at home unless you had something."

"I've got good news and bad news."

"One of the samples I brought in matched?"

"No. None of those three matched. You know, I only had about one-tenth of a gram to work with from the murder scene. But it's close enough that I'll call these a match. I sent a request to all the labs across the country. We got lucky. Four matches. Three out of Quebec and one from Vancouver."

"All made by the same cook?" asked Jack.

"The same chemist brewed all four, or, with what was recovered at the murder scene, I should say all five."

Jack wondered if his heartbeat could be heard over the phone. "Were any of the seizures high-level busts?"

"Two of the Quebec seizures were at the pound level. Both apparently seized from dealers who are known associates of Satans Wrath."

"Satans Wrath! What about the Vancouver seizure?"

"That's the bad news. It was less than a gram. Turned in by a Vancouver beat cop. I talked to the guy. It was night and he took a stroll with his partner down some alley on East Hastings. A woman panicked when she saw them coming and chucked it. Probably a hooker. They never did catch her. The only reason he sent it in was because Homicide put out a bulletin saying they were interested."

"What night did this happen?"

"Same date as the murders."

"Told Homicide yet?"

"Spoke with CC. She said there's not much you can do with it under the circumstances. Guess she's right, but I still thought I should tell you."

Less than an hour later, Jack burst into Louie's office.

"I'm going to do an intelligence probe on Satans Wrath, starting tonight."

"They're involved in your porn file?"

"No. I'm putting that on the shelf for a moment. This is more important."

Louie studied Jack's face, then said, "This is connected with the murders, isn't it?"

"It could turn out that way if —"

"Come on, Jack. I know this means a lot to you, but give Homicide a chance. We work on organized crime. The brass won't put up with —"

"Satans Wrath is the number one organized crime group in this country."

"I know, but what does that have to do with the murders?"

"Our lab cross-matched speed found at the murder scene with speed seized in Quebec connected to Satans Wrath. Now they matched a gram of speed found in an alley off East Hastings as coming from the same chemist!"

"East Hastings? Even Satans Wrath wouldn't hang out in that scuzzball part of town. Does Homicide know?"

"They're who the lab did it for."

"Jack, I understand that this is personal for you, but it's still up to Homicide."

"Come on, Louie! Identical speed connected to Satans Wrath in Quebec is turning up here! There are more members of that gang in this city than there are in any other province. And they're big enough and cautious enough to find an abandoned farmhouse to conduct business."

"They're also one of the most dangerous! Damn it, Jack! This isn't the way we're supposed to do things! What am I going to have to do to educate you?"

"This isn't coincidence! If they're not involved with killing Liz's kids you can bet they'll know who did do it!"

"You're not listening! This is a Homicide investigation. It's up to them to —"

"GIS wouldn't make any progress in that part of the city! They'd stand out like nuns in a brothel. Homicide told the lab that it's not enough of a lead to do anything about it. They're a reactive section, not proactive."

"What makes you think you would succeed? Every operation mounted against them has soured. Years of wasted surveillance, dead informants, wiretaps that turned up nothing."

"I've had a good teacher."

Grazia sat back in his chair, drumming his fingers on the desk. "Some lowly speed dealer from East Hastings wouldn't travel all the way out the Valley to do a deal."

"I know, but someone higher up the ladder might."

"But East Hastings?"

"I've got to start somewhere. I'll come up with bigger connections sooner or later."

Louie paused, then said, "Okay. Check it out. But be careful! The brass wouldn't approve of you sticking your nose into the murder investigation. Wigmore is acting a little kinky these days. He would never authorize funding for us to do street-level drug buys. For now, keep it strictly to surveillance and see what you learn. Forget trying to claim any expenses."

"I know. I haven't claimed any expenses yet."

Louie gave him a hard look. "I didn't really think you took last week off. You've already been buying dope, haven't you?"

Jack shrugged and said, "I wasted my time — and money. Three scores and no matches."

"Jesus, Jack! I don't want you taking risks like that! Policy says you need authorization and a proper cover team if you plan on buying dope. If Wigmore found out, you'd be toast."

"Wigmore won't find out."

"He didn't get to where he is by being stupid. I've got some news for you. Your new partner has arrived. He's been here all week. Seems anxious to meet you."

"Who?"

"His name is Danny O'Reilly. Came from back east. Was in Public Relations but —"

Jack groaned. "Just what I need, my own PR person. I bet he's a pansy."

"He has Drug experience and GIS. I'm told that PR was just temporary while he was waiting to sell his house and transfer out. It was his baby who puked on the prime minister."

"That guy? What a hoot! The way I feel about politicians, I'd rather work with his baby."

"He's a few years younger than you. Acted a little nervous, but after what he went through with the PM, who wouldn't be? Take him with you on surveillance. *Nothing else* until we get grounds to ask for authorization."

"You got it."

"Better come up with a project name."

"How about Project 13?"

"Perfect. One more thing. I have no idea what your new partner is like, so be careful. I mean it when I say I don't want you taking risks. Especially with Satans Wrath. If something doesn't feel right, phone me and I'll back you up. Day or night."

"Thanks, Louie."

"Come on, I'll introduce you."

Later that afternoon, Danny found a private moment to call Susan.

"What's your new partner like?" she asked. "Or can't you talk now?"

"I can talk. He looks like a hood, but actually seems quite nice."

"You sound surprised."

Danny paused, then said, "Sorry, I don't have much time to talk. I wanted to let you know that I won't be home for dinner. Sounds like I might be working late."

"You've already worked all day! I thought we were going to unpack tonight. Speaking of which, the movers found the headboard and frame for our bed. It arrived today."

"Sorry, honey, I have to work."

"Is he making you work?"

"Jack? No. He told me to go home and work with him tomorrow night, but..."

"But what?"

"I need to stick close to him."

"Why?"

"Because it's the right thing to do. I'll dig into those boxes tomorrow."

"Okay. Maybe I'll put the bed frame and headboard together myself."

"Who needs a headboard? It'll just bang on the wall and wake up Tiffany."

Susan giggled. "You're awful. Love ya."

It was getting dark as Danny drove the two-door compact sports car, following Jack's directions. He stopped for an early amber light and heard a slight grunt of disapproval.

"I heard about your niece and nephew. Just wanted to say I'm sorry. Susan and I have a baby girl. It would be hard to imagine anything more terrible."

"Thanks," Jack replied.

"I hope Homicide solves it soon. I wonder if they have any leads?"

"They don't think they do."

Neither spoke for several minutes. Danny then flipped on the windshield wipers and asked, "Where we going?"

"East Hastings."

"Being as we're partners, maybe you could tell me why?"

Out of the corner of his eye, Danny could see Jack sizing him up. He seemed to be weighing his response carefully.

"We're starting what's called an intelligence probe. Project 13. It's —"

"About speed," said Danny.

Jack looked surprised, so Danny continued. "The thirteenth letter of the alphabet. Letter *M*. Stands for methamphetamine. Bikers sometimes tattoo the number on —"

"So you know a little bit about drugs and bikers."

"A little. Spent four years on Winnipeg Drugs. Also saw you at the office going through pictures of bikers."

"Satans Wrath. Ever work on them back east?"

"Not really."

"They have at least eighty-five members out here on the West Coast. In our area they've got four chapters with between eighteen to twenty-five guys in each chapter. Every chapter in the country has a local president and they all report to the national president. He's a guy by the name of Damien who also lives here. They've also got about a dozen strikers."

"Strikers?"

"Probationary members who do a lot of the dirty work for the club and take the risks."

"Sounds like a big group to be taking on."

"It's worse than that. The rule of thumb is that for every regular member of the club, there are about ten hard-core criminals who work for them. Overall, in our area alone, we're dealing with an army of about nine hundred professional criminals."

Danny let out a low whistle, then said, "So what are we up to?"

"I think someone in Satans Wrath is either directly or indirectly supplying speed to the area we're going to. I'm going to find out who. Are you a trained operator?"

"UC? No."

"Didn't think so."

"Why not?" Danny tried to keep the annoyance out of his voice.

"You look too straight for undercover." Jack paused for a moment, then looked at Danny and said, "Actually, that's not altogether true. There is a certain aura about you. You remind me a little of a used car salesman who's trying to sell me a lemon."

Danny chose not to respond. He stared out at the part of the city they had entered. On the steps of a men's hostel, a small knot of men huddled in the doorway. Farther down the block was a small park. A syringe stuck out of the trunk of a dogwood tree.

He drove past several pawnshops. Heavy steel reinforcement bars guarded the windows and doors. One building had been bulldozed, leaving a cesspool of rubble and garbage.

"Turn left and drive slow down the next alley."

Danny did as directed. Partway down the alley, he noticed that Jack paid particular attention to a grey steel door behind one building. A light above the door had been smashed out, but the words *Black Water Hotel* could still be seen in black on the door.

Moments later, Danny parked on the second level of a parking garage that overlooked the front of the hotel. The hotel was in dire need of paint. A sign in red neon lights hung from the front of the building. The letter *T* was burned out so it appeared from a distance as "HO EL."

"Pop the trunk."

Danny watched as Jack took off an ankle holster holding his Smith & Wesson semi-automatic 9-mm calibre pistol and, along with his badge, stashed them both in the trunk. He handed Danny a pair of binoculars.

"Why are you stashing your piece?"

"I find it uncomfortable to wear."

"Really?"

Jack stared at Danny briefly, then said, "Your job, *O'Really*, is to stay here and watch."

Danny wasn't amused. "You're not going down there alone. Policy says that —"

"Policy can get you killed. You're not ready for the Black Water yet. Wait here."

Danny waited until Jack walked away from the car before making an entry in his notebook. No doubt Superintendent Wigmore would be interested. He checked his watch. Less than an hour before he was to call him and report in.

Danny used the binoculars and saw Jack approach the front of the hotel. The red neon lights flared off the hookers' faces as he spoke with them at the entrance. Then he ducked inside.

It occurred to Danny why Jack had left his gun in the car. *That son of a bitch!*

chapter six

Jack discreetly studied the patrons in the bar. A short, squat-looking man sat at a table with a hooker. A steady stream of people came and went. The money exchanging hands under the table made it pretty clear that he was a low-level dealer. Jack heard one of the customers refer to him as "Spider."

Jack knew that trying to order an ounce of speed right away would generate some interest — and suspicion. But the higher he could start up the ladder, the sooner he could reach the bigger dealers. The type who preferred remote locations. He approached Spider's table.

"I'm lookin' to score," he whispered in Spider's ear.

"Who sent you to me?"

"Nobody, man. I'm in the business too. Not hard to spot," said Jack, taking a seat.

"How do I know you're not a narc?"

"If I was a fuckin' narc, I'd have already busted ya for the flaps you got on ya."

Spider stared at him for a moment, then said, "What do ya want? I got everything."

"Speed."

Spider held his hand under the table to show Jack a small piece of paper folded in a flap.

Danny threw his tie in the trunk and unbuttoned the top of his shirt, then slid his holster off his belt and strapped on Jack's ankle holster. Minutes later, the door banged shut behind him as he entered the Black Water.

The smell of smoke and stale beer turned his stomach. It was noisy and crowded. He let his eyes adjust to the darkness. There were no windows in the long room, and the cardboard-tiled ceiling, like the walls, had been painted a flat black. A stage in the centre was brightly lit.

In the dim glow at the back of the bar, he saw some pool tables and the silhouettes of several men with cues stalking the tables before executing their shots. At a right angle to the entrance another door opened and he caught a glimpse of the lobby. The rest of the illumination consisted of a few lights recessed in the ceiling, which filtered a yellowish glow through grime.

He saw Jack slouched at a table, talking with a hooker and a short man who was built like a fire hydrant. Beer bottles and cigarette burns decorated the green elastic tablecloth in front of them. Danny strode over to an empty table where he could watch. *What scum.*

A waitress came by and Danny ordered a bottle of beer.

She stepped back and looked at his shoes, and then slowly worked her eyes up the rest of his body until she stared into his eyes. "You a cop?"

Danny felt the lump in his throat. "No," he said, flashing open his sports jacket to show it wasn't concealing a gun.

"This doesn't look like your kind of place."

"Yeah? Got nowhere else to go. Just lost my job. An hour ago I could've got you a good deal on a '94 Buick. But not now."

"I can't afford a car."

He felt more comfortable when the waitress returned with his drink and gave him a friendly smile. He opened his wallet and gave her a generous tip. More generous, he thought, than someone like her deserved.

He didn't see the waitress eyeball the money in his wallet — or the subtle nod she gave to some junkies at the next table.

Jack looked at the dope in Spider's hand and shook his head. "Not worth my while. As I said, I'm in the business too. I'm lookin' for an ounce. If it's good, I'll be lookin' for a lot more."

"You want a fuckin' ounce just like that! I said I got everything man, but I'm not a fuckin' warehouse!" Spider gave Jack a hard look and said, "I smell a cop!"

"What do ya mean, ya smell a cop?" asked Jack.

Spider looked past Jack and said, "Sittin' by himself over there."

Jack turned slightly in his chair and saw Danny sitting at a nearby table. *Damn it! If he blows this...* He looked at Spider and said, "That guy looks too straight to be a cop."

"Maybe."

"Listen, I'm here to do business." As Jack spoke, he slowly pulled a wad of cash partway out of his front pocket and then shoved it back in.

Spider sat back in his chair. Jack could see him trying to make a decision. Having seen the money, greed would take over. The waitress came and Jack held up one finger.

Danny toyed with his drink and checked his watch. *About time to call Wigmore.* He saw Jack order another beer and knew that he had time to slip into the lobby and make a call.

Spider saw Danny walk to the lobby, then asked Jack, "So, you want an ounce?"

"Yeah, for now."

"What makes you think I want the competition?"

"Relax. I'm puttin' out far away from here."

Spider mulled it over, then said, "Okay. Wait here."

Jack watched Spider slink over to the next table and talk with a woman. She was big and solid-looking but had no fat. She wore a man's singlet white undershirt that looked grey. It was stretched tightly over her bare chest. Her black jeans and knee-high leather boots gave her a certain air of hostility. She had long red hair, but judging by the black roots, Jack knew it had been a long time since she had last bothered to dye it. She had "HD" tattooed on one arm and "Live to Ride" tattooed on the other. A tattoo of a rose was visible on the top of her breast.

She gave Jack a long cold stare, then whispered to Spider.

"Fuck, Red, I talked to 'im. He's all right, I tell ya!" Jack heard Spider reply.

Moments later, Spider returned. "Go to the can and wait!"

Jack entered the men's room and stood by the sink. He glanced at the graffiti covering the wall. Much of it was obliterated with grime. Seconds later, Spider and two junkies entered, and Jack barely had time to look up before the junkies grabbed him by the arms, smashing him back against the wall.

"Hey! What the fuck are —"

Spider clamped his hand over Jack's mouth and said, "Shut your fuckin' trap! This ain't a rip. We're goin' to have a little look-see is all."

His hand tasted and smelled of smoke and stale beer. He took his hand away and ripped Jack's shirt-sleeve back as one of the junkies pinned his wrist to the wall. Spider took a syringe out of his jacket pocket. The syringe was filled to capacity, and Spider hovered the silver tip of the needle over a vein in Jack's elbow. A drop of murky liquid dangled from the tip.

"Don't fuckin' move, man!" hissed Spider. "Don't even try an' breathe! 'Cause if you do, we'll spike you right now. And there's enough in this rig to kill an elephant, let alone a pig!"

Danny checked to make sure the lobby was empty, then he called Wigmore.

"You think he's trying to buy dope where?" Wigmore asked.

Danny repeated the name. "The Black Water Hotel. On a street called East Hastings."

"Bingo! I spoke with GIS today. They said that some drug found in an alley off East Hastings matched the same drug found at the murder scene. I knew Taggart would get involved. I might recommend he be charged with obstruction!"

"Sir? What should I do?"

"Continue to play along. Give him some more time, or I should say rope, to hang himself. Make sure you make notes that he went in there alone and left his gun in the car."

"Already done, sir." Danny hung up the phone and let out a deep breath. He realized that he had a headache. He made another call.

"Hi, honey! You on your way home?" Susan held the telephone with the crook of her neck as she placed some family pictures on the dresser in her bedroom. A portrait of Danny in his red tunic looked particularly handsome.

"Sorry, babe, not yet. I'm stuck in some fleabag of a bar watching my new partner drink beer and chat with some hooker."

"What are you doing in a place like that?"

"Good question. Everyone in here is a degenerate. My so-called partner seems to be having fun. How's Tiffany?"

"She's asleep. Listen, I got the bed put together, but can't find the nuts to the bolts."

"Don't worry about it. I've got my own nuts."

Susan snickered and then said, "But what about me? I don't have any."

"You can use mine whenever you want. Don't wait up. Love ya!"

Spider didn't take his eyes off Jack as he put the syringe down on the edge of the sink before searching him. He started at Jack's neck and worked his way down to his feet. He took his time and wasn't bashful. He found a hunting knife tucked in the top of Jack's boot.

Spider pulled out the knife. "What's this?"

"I ain't in the business of lettin' people rip me off!"

Spider smiled, then looked at his two companions and said, "Okay, let 'im go."

"So what the hell was that all about?" said Jack in a voice he hoped sounded convincing.

"Just makin' sure you're not the heat."

"This is fuckin' bullshit, man! I'm no more the heat than you are!"

"Yeah, well, it pays to be careful. Don't take it personal. Go wait by the pool tables. Should be along in about half an hour."

"Give me my blade back!"

Spider pointed the knife at Jack's eye and used the tip of the blade to flick his eyelashes. Jack slowly reached for the knife. Spider relinquished his grip and Jack shoved the knife back in his boot. He slammed the door as he left, then walked to the rear of the tavern.

Spider left the men's room and went directly to Red. He whispered to her and then returned to his table. The two junkies came out a minute later and left the bar. They had just been given their fix for the night. He noticed Danny return to his seat.

Jack chalked his name on a board to play pool. His legs felt weak and he stood with his hands in his pockets, hoping nobody would notice him shaking. Red went to the lobby but returned a few minutes later.

Ten minutes later, Jack saw Danny get up and go to the men's room. A scrawny junkie at a nearby table gave Danny a long, hard look, and then followed him. Jack hoped his frustration didn't show. *Now what? Blow my cover for some jerk I told to stay in the car? Goddamn him!*

Danny stood at the urinal. He heard someone come in behind him but didn't look up. The junkie took a buck knife out of his pocket and opened the blade. He partially hid the knife beside his leg as he crept up behind Danny.

The pain was instant. Danny briefly lost consciousness when the butt end of the knife slammed hard into the side of his skull. He crashed into the wall and his knees buckled as he slid face-first down the urinal. The junkie grabbed his hair and smashed his face into the drain.

Danny's teeth cut his tongue and he could taste the blood as it ran down the back of his throat. The deodorizer cake in the bottom of the urinal stung his eyes and lips. His left hand was partially pinned under his face, and the junkie held his other wrist high up his back. He felt the sharp edge of the knife on his throat and froze.

"You so much as whisper or blink a fuckin' eyeball and I'll slash yer fuckin' throat!"

For a strange moment, Danny didn't feel fear or panic. A sorrowful calm seeped across his brain. *There is nothing I can do. I am not in control of my life — he is. In a moment he'll find my badge and then I'll die. I'll never see Susan or Tiffany again. It's so sad....*

The door to the men's room opened and he cocked his head and saw Jack. Both Danny and the junkie stared at Jack, who sauntered up to the urinal next to them. Danny heard him unzip and then softly whistle.

The junkie kneed Danny between the shoulder blades, pinning his face harder into the bottom of the urinal. He felt the junkie's hand slide his wallet from his pocket. *Son of a bitch! He's not going to help me! I'm going to die in here like this!* Panic replaced sorrow.

Jack eyed the situation. *How do I help without blowing my cover?* Then he spotted Danny's ring. If the junkie wanted it, he'd have to release Danny's arm.

"Missed his wedding ring," Jack said, trying to sound casual.

Danny saw the blood and water trickling across his gold wedding ring.

"Yeah. Gimme yer fuckin' ring!"

Danny raised his left hand above his head. The junkie released his grip on his wrist and reached for the ring. It was the chance Danny needed. He uttered a panicked squeal while grabbing the knife by the blade. The sharp steel cut through his flesh while he started bashing the junkie's wrist against the ceramic side of the urinal. He drove a sharp elbow into the junkie's ribs and the knife clattered into the bottom of the urinal.

Both men were in a frenzied struggle for the knife. Danny's brain didn't register Jack yell, "Hey! You made me piss on my leg!" Nor was he aware that Jack then kicked the junkie in the head, knocking him off balance. Danny grabbed the knife as the junkie turned to scramble away. Within a heartbeat, Danny buried the knife into the junkie's back — and then recoiled in horror.

A different panic swept over him when he realized what he had done. The junkie staggered to his feet and tried to reach the knife protruding from under his shoulder blade.

"Here, let me help you with that," said Jack, while zipping up his pants. He pulled the knife out and added, "You better split, man, before this guy finishes you off!"

The junkie flopped against the door, opened it, and hurried out.

Danny sat on the floor, gawking at his bleeding hand while Jack rinsed the knife in the sink. Neither spoke as Jack cut off half of Danny's shirtsleeve and tied the cloth around his hand. Jack handed him the knife.

"Stabbing someone in the back. Is that what they're teaching at the academy these days?"

Danny's mouth hung open as he stared at Jack in both shock and disbelief. "We've got to report this. That guy could die! We can't just —"

"Forget that! You're a cop. You'd end up in jail. Only citizens are allowed to panic."

"But what if he dies? You can't —"

"He won't die. A shoulder isn't what you would call a vital organ. If you wanted to kill him, you should have gone for his carotid artery."

Danny looked down at the blood seeping through the cloth on his hand. "I need stitches."

"You'll need a few. There's a clinic about five blocks away. But not now."

"What do you mean, not now?" said Danny, as a combination of fear and anger crept back into his voice. "I'm bleeding."

"I need fifteen or twenty minutes. You can hold off that long. I obviously didn't make myself clear when I told you to wait in the car, so let me explain it to you in your language."

"Huh?"

"The gentleman I was sitting with is lining me up with an ounce of speed. He goes by the name of Spider. A tattooed lady of questionable character is involved. She has long red hair and goes by the name of Red. I want you to watch and see if you can figure out the action."

"Walk out like nothing happened?"

"Yes. This place is not all that genteel. An extra set of eyes might help."

"So now you decide to follow policy?" said Danny harshly.

"Forget about policy. You need to learn the rules … to be educated."

"What rules? What are you talking about? Educated about what?"

"For tonight, two simple things. Lesson one, leave your attitude behind. You look like you think you're better than everybody else."

"I *am* better than anyone in this dump!"

"That attitude will get you killed. Besides, you've never walked in their shoes."

"This is nothing but a den of snakes! Scum! I can see that much!"

"That's the second lesson. If they don't respect you, you'll become a victim."

"I just did!"

"I mean a *dead* victim. Everybody will know what happened. They'll have a lot more respect for you if you stay and don't act like a pansy. Wash up, then go out there and order a beer and drink it slow. Hold the beer in your cut hand. The cold will slow the bleeding. When I leave, don't walk out with me. I'll go out the back. Wait at least ten minutes then go out the front."

"Anything else?" asked Danny, sullenly.

"Yes. Zip up!"

Jack returned to the pool tables. The wounded junkie was gone. A few minutes later, Danny stumbled out of the men's room. The noise level dropped as patrons saw his bandaged hand and the open knife held forth in his other hand. His anger and paranoia was evident as his eyes darted about. Everyone waited and stared. Danny then used his good hand to press the release button and his forearm to close the blade. He dropped the knife in his pocket and then growled at the waitress to bring him a beer. The noise level returned to normal.

A few minutes later, Jack noticed a slim man with a shaved head and moustache walk casually through the bar. He was wearing a black leather vest that had silver medallions for buttons. He gave Red a subtle nod and walked back out the main entrance.

Red went to the rear of the bar and stood by the fire escape door. The door could be opened only from inside the bar. She waited until she heard a rap on the door and then opened it. She was passed something and then pulled the door shut.

Several men, all holding cues, slowly encircled Jack. Some held the cues by the wrong end, gripping them like a baseball bat. They stared into his eyes, defying him to make a move.

The circle parted slightly as Red walked up to Jack. Without saying a word, she handed him a plastic baggie of brown powder. Seconds later, the transaction was completed. Jack pushed open the fire escape door and disappeared down the darkened alley.

Danny showed up at the parking garage on schedule.

Jack held up the plastic baggie of powder. "See anything after I left?"

"Yeah. Red went to where Spider was sitting and gave him a couple of bills. Then she met a guy who just arrived. A minute later they both split for the lobby."

"Bald? Leather vest?"

"You saw him?"

"He cruised through the bar right before the deal went down. I'm sure Baldy is her connection. Bet he stashed the dope in the alley until he checked things out, then went and handed it to her through the back door."

"Recognize him from the photos?"

"No. A club member would never deliver it." Jack saw Danny grimace as he adjusted the piece of shirtsleeve wrapped around his hand and said, "I'm sorry if I was a little snarky in there. I respect how you handled yourself after. You don't listen very well, but you've got guts. If you don't want to be my partner I'll understand."

Danny thought about Wigmore. *Do I have any choice?* He looked at Jack and replied, "I'll still be your partner — for now."

"Good. Then I'll clue you in as to what my plans really are. This is just the beginning."

I'm sure Wigmore will be very interested to hear your plans. Danny stared down at his hand and said, "This is just the beginning?"

Jack playfully punched him on the shoulder and said, "What a pansy. Okay, I'll drive you to the clinic. We'll talk after."

chapter seven

Jack and Danny entered the medical clinic and approached the receptionist, an older, heavy-set woman with short grey hair. Behind her, a younger woman wearing a white lab coat stood bent over with her back to them as she rifled through some papers.

"What can I do for you two gentlemen?" the receptionist asked.

"My friend fell on some glass and cut his hand."

Jack picked up a magazine and sat in the reception area. He heard the receptionist ask Danny for his provincial health card. Jack winced when Danny didn't lower his voice to explain that as a federal police officer, he was on a different health plan. He was glad there were no other people in the office. A moment later the receptionist said, "Doctor?"

The doctor turned around. Jack noticed that she was a petite woman, with a slim figure and long black hair.

"Hello! I'm Dr. Trovinski," she said to Danny in a cheery voice. "Come with me, officer, and we'll take a look."

Jack joined them as they entered a small examination room and stood beside Danny as he sat on the edge of the examination bed.

"And why did you come along?" the doctor asked.

Jack smiled and stuck out his hand as he introduced himself. She reluctantly accepted his handshake but remained silent, awaiting his reply.

"My partner suffers from a phobia about seeing doctors. On the way over he made me promise to stay with him."

"Really?" She looked at Danny, who looked perplexed. "You suffer from iatrophobia?"

"Probably got smacked on the bum too hard by a doctor when he was born," Jack offered.

The doctor gave Jack a furtive look and smiled. Her bright white teeth shone, as did her eyes. She turned her attention to Danny's hand and slowly unwrapped the shirtsleeve that was being used as a dressing. Classical music softly played from a nearby office and she hummed quietly as she worked.

"Fantasy. D-Minor by Mozart," said Jack.

"You know your music," she replied without looking up.

"My favourite is *The Marriage of Figaro*."

"Mine, too, but that CD is scratched." She finished unwrapping Danny's hand and started to wash off the blood.

"Would you like to eat pickled herring in chocolate sauce?" Jack asked.

"Would I what?"

"Would you like to eat pickled herring in chocolate sauce?"

"Certainly not. Sounds gross!"

"Sounds gross to me too. Looks like we have at least two things in common. Are you a vegetarian?"

"No, but I see where you're going with this, and —"

"That makes three things we have in common."

"I'm married."

I'm such an idiot! He looked at the doctor and said, "Sorry." He found the silence that followed more embarrassing, so he asked, "Do you have children?"

"Uh, yes. Three of them."

"You're not wearing a ring, so I thought..."

"Sanitary reasons."

She examined Danny's hand carefully, then looked at Jack. "You told my receptionist that he cut his hand when he fell on some glass."

Jack nodded.

Dr. Trovinski's face hardened. "I don't appreciate being lied to. Do you really think I don't know what a defensive knife wound looks like? Especially working in this neighbourhood? Give me a break! I treated a fellow not even half an hour ago with a stab wound to his shoulder. Believe me, I know knife wounds when I see them!"

"Is he going to be okay?" asked Danny.

"Who?"

"This other guy, who was stabbed in the back."

"How did you know that it was the back of his shoulder?"

There was an uncomfortable silence, then she said, "Yes, he'll be fine. I don't know what happened between the two of you and I really don't care. My job is to patch people up. Most of my customers wouldn't come in for treatment if they thought I would tell anyone."

"Thank you, doctor," said Jack.

She nodded curtly and then turned back to Danny. "I smell alcohol on your breath. I suspect you've had enough to drink that I won't need to waste time administering freezing."

Danny sat upright. "No! I didn't drink that much!"

The doctor pursed her lips into a slight grin as she walked over to a cabinet.

"Pansy," whispered Jack.

It was well past midnight when Jack drove Danny away from the clinic.

"How's your hand?"

"Sore. So's my tongue. I bit it when he whacked me."

"What were you prescribed?"

Danny handed him the small bottle of pills.

Jack examined the label. "T-threes." He tossed the pill bottle into the back seat. "I have better medicine."

At 5:15 in the morning, Danny found himself sitting cross-legged on a seawall in Stanley Park, overlooking the ocean. Jack's medicine was a bottle of Jose Cuervo Gold tequila that they passed back and forth between them.

Jack explained the real reason that he was interested in Satans Wrath and admitted that he didn't have proper authorization or Louie's approval to buy drugs.

Danny felt tense. *Will Wigmore forgive me for stabbing that guy if I come clean with Taggart?* He looked at the half-empty bottle of tequila. *What the hell, at least my hand doesn't hurt. Come to think of it, I can't feel my legs, either.* He rolled over on his side and kicked to untangle his legs. He then snickered when he thought of Jack's awkward pass at the doctor.

"She was pretty, wasn't she?"

"Who?" Jack asked.

"The doc."

"Yes, I noticed."

"You noticed! No shit! I would never have guessed. Too bad she's married."

"She's not married."

"Yeah, she is. Don't you remember? She can't wear her ring 'cause —"

"She lied." Jack paused, then took his first real swig on the bottle. "Not that it matters. She obviously didn't want to go out with me." He passed the bottle back to Danny and added, "I can't believe I acted that way around her. I was a fool. No wonder she wasn't interested."

"What makes ya say she lied?"

"Her demeanour and her eyes."

"Her eyes?"

"Most people's eyes look slightly in one direction when they recall something that is true. Her eyes did, when we talked about music and food. The eyes usually look in the opposite direction when they use the more creative side of their brain to formulate a lie. Her eyes were no different. She doesn't have a husband or children."

"Son of a bitch! What are ya? A two-legged lie detector?" Danny chortled but abruptly stopped. *Hope the son of a bitch doesn't ever ask me about Wigface ... no, Wig...*

"Come on," said Jack. "Time to take you home."

It was 6:25 when Susan awakened to the sound of the key turning at the front door. She saw Danny's figure as he entered the darkened room.

"You're home late. How was your first shift with your new partner?" Susan asked, leaning out of bed and turning on a bedside light.

It took Susan a moment to grasp the situation. Danny was covered in sand and there was blood on his face, shirt, and bandaged hand. He carried his sports jacket over one shoulder. His other arm was half bare with the jagged remains of his shirtsleeve hanging above.

"My God! What happened? Are you all right?"

"Am I all right? Look at me! I bit my tongue. Some son of a bitch tried to rob me! I got whacked on the skull and had my eyeballs jammed into a urinal with a knife at my throat! Meantime Jack comes in and pisses in the urinal beside us.... Yeah, I'm all right."

"Didn't he help you?"

"Help me? Help me! Oh yeah, he helped me all right. Told the guy to steal my wedding ring while he was at it! Did I tell ya I bit my tongue? That's why I sound funny."

"Didn't you call the police?"

Danny stood on one leg as he tried to take off his pants. "Christ! I am the police! Besides, if I had called, I'd be arrested for what I did to the guy."

"What happened? What did you do to the guy?"

Danny hopped sideways three times across the floor on one leg, before losing his balance and falling face-down on the bed.

"I gotta make notes on this," mumbled Danny. "Think I'll be in shit tomorrow ... or today ... or whatever." Seconds later he started to snore.

Susan looked at the picture on the dresser of the man she had married and then at the man beside her. *Is this the same guy?*

Danny snorted as the bed collapsed, then continued to snore. The noise did awaken Tiffany, who cried from the other room.

chapter eight

An hour and a half after Danny's bed collapsed, Jack met Lucy when she arrived in the parking lot of the crime laboratory.

"Another sample?"

Jack handed her the baggie of powder that he had bought from Red.

Lucy looked closely at the powder. "Looks like meth. Good amount this time. We're pretty busy at the moment. Probably take me a week or ten days to compare."

Jack's shoulders slumped. His voice was monotone. "I got it in a bar that backs out onto the same alley as the one that you cross-matched from the beat cop. Tough bar. If this matches, I could be on to something."

"Buy this yourself?"

"Don't ask. Appreciate it if you keep this between the two of us."

"If it does match … what about Homicide?"

"If it matches, I'll let them know in due time."

"Fine by me. It's your neck. I'm just the analyst. I don't know who is running what."

"Thanks, Luce."

"You don't look so good. You better get some sleep."

"I'm heading home now."

Lucy waved to a colleague as her husband dropped her off while two little kids waved goodbye from the back seat. Lucy thought they looked sweet. She saw Jack blink a couple of times, then wipe his eyes with the back of his hand as he turned and walked toward his car.

"Jack!" She waited until he turned around. "Make it three days. I'll have the results then."

Jack picked up Danny and they arrived at the office late in the afternoon. They checked hundreds of pictures of members of Satans Wrath and known associates. Baldy was not one of them. Moments later, Louie summoned Danny into his office.

"What the hell happened to your hand?"

"I fell. It's just a couple of stitches."

"Yeah? Well, your eyes look like two eagles' assholes in a power dive! What were you up to last night?"

"I'm not feeling well. Maybe a touch of the flu."

"You smell more like Jose Cuervo beat the crap out of you."

Danny heard Jack chuckle and realized that he had come in behind him.

"So? What happened last night?" Louie demanded.

"There's a bar that backs into the alley where the gram was recovered from. The Black Water Hotel. Saw a redheaded woman inside with a Harley Davidson tattoo. She looked like she was dealing. Going to see if we can properly identify her." Jack then looked at Danny and added, "At least we'll take another stab at it."

Louie thought Danny's face looked even more ashen.

The next shift was uneventful. Jack watched from the parking garage while Danny slowly sipped on a beer inside the Black Water. Jack wanted to give the impression that he was busy selling drugs elsewhere. Spider and Red were in the bar, but there was no sign of Baldy.

Danny made his beer last a long time. The smell of it didn't help his hangover. He looked at the white band of skin around his finger. Susan didn't mind that he left his ring at home.

She was also a little happier when a sober Danny arrived home before midnight and told her that he had the next day off. Jack had some personal business to take care of, and his next shift wouldn't start until the day after.

Ben quietly walked up to Elizabeth in the kitchen. Neither one mentioned it was Maggie's birthday. There was no need. They also never discussed what to do with the wrapped birthday present hidden under their bed. The easel was too big to hide anywhere else. Ben placed his hands on her shoulders and looked intently at her face.

Elizabeth spoke first. "Jack phoned a few minutes ago. He was going to come out but called to check in case we wanted to be alone. I told him not to be silly."

Ben grimaced. "He shouldn't worry. I'm glad he's coming. It's good to have someone to take your mind off it."

"But if we want to talk about Maggie and Ben Junior, he doesn't clam up or change the subject, either."

Ben swallowed as he stared down at his wife.

"You know," she continued, "I feel sorry for him. He feels guilty that they haven't made an arrest. He needs someone to talk to as well. I invited him for dinner…" Elizabeth's words trailed off when she looked into Ben's eyes. He wasn't really listening.

Ben opened his mouth as if to say something, then closed it and started again. "That's good. What time did you tell him to come?"

"This afternoon sometime. Dinner will be around six."

Ben continued to stare at her.

"What is it, Ben? What are you thinking? Is it just … because it's today?"

Ben took a deep breath and let it out slowly. "I've been wonderin'. Maybe we should sell and move away. This place has got so many … memories." His eyes were watery and his voice cracked as he spoke. Words didn't come easy.

Elizabeth shook her head as tears flooded her eyes. "Memories are all we have. I don't want to lose those, too."

Ben squeezed her shoulders with his big hands. He looked relieved. "I feel that way, too. Today, I see a lot of … memories. I wonder if we shouldn't do something."

"Like what?"

Ben opened his mouth, but then closed it again and shook his head.

"Tell me, Ben! What are you thinking? I know you've been raised that men aren't supposed to show emotion. But you can't keep everything bottled up inside you. It's not good! Your body is like a dam. It breaks if you don't let go sometimes."

Ben paused, then said, "I was wonderin' if we shouldn't do somethin' as a tribute."

Elizabeth nodded encouragement.

"I picked ... I picked a pail full of blackberries."

Elizabeth was momentarily stunned and her eyes brimmed with tears. "Oh, Ben! I'm sorry. I can't. I'll put them in the freezer. But not now. I just can't. I'll make another pie, but not that one, not yet."

"I'm sorry. It was a dumb idea."

"No, it's not dumb. It's just me," she sobbed.

Ben pulled her close to his chest. She continued to sob as she choked out what she wanted to say. "It's strange, there are times when I look at the pictures Maggie drew, or hold the teddy bear that Ben Junior used to drag around with him all the time. Sometimes I feel the need to cry. I think it helps. But I can't make a blackberry pie, not yet. It was Maggie's favourite."

"I know it was," whispered Ben. "I know," he repeated, patting her on the back.

Then she looked Ben straight in the eye and added, "But we sure as hell aren't going to move, either."

They hugged each other tight, and then they both cried.

Jack climbed into the loft and saw Ben sitting on a bale, staring at a rope hanging from the rafters. Jack self-consciously cleared his throat before sitting on another bale.

"Glad you could make it," said Ben. "You're early."

"Thought you could use an extra hand with the hay."

"Rained last night. I'm givin' it another day to dry." Ben was silent for a moment, then said, "Nothing new?"

"Might be connected to drug dealers out of Quebec. I'm working on it."

"Think the murderer is from Quebec?"

"I think whoever did it is from the West Coast. Only a high-level dealer familiar with the area would go to the bother of using a place like that."

"Yeah, it was a real bother, wasn't it?"

Jack choked on his own breath, then stammered, "I'm sorry Ben. I didn't mean…"

"Naw, forget it. I'm sorry. I shouldn't have said that. You've been a real friend, Jack. Probably the best damn friend I've ever had. It's just that today is, well…"

Ben's voice trailed off and both men sat in silence. Eventually Ben gestured at the rope hanging from the rafter and said, "It was only two weeks ago that Ben Junior was pretending to be a pirate and swingin' out on that rope. Maggie was sitting here drinking lemonade."

Jack didn't respond. He didn't know what to say. He felt the gnawing in his stomach. He clenched his teeth to control his tear ducts, then took a deep breath and relaxed his jaw.

"You know, Jack, I'm not a violent man. But if you ever find out who did it … I'd like to see this rope used for a different purpose. I know it won't bring Maggie or Ben Junior back. Nothing could. I just figure somebody should pay for what happened."

"Somebody will pay for this," said Jack tersely.

"I can still see Maggie sitting on the bale drinking lemonade … trying to act like a grown-up lady. Sometimes I walk in the kitchen and expect to see her sitting at the table drawing pictures. Then I remember. I'll never see her again. It makes me embarrassed I could forget, even for a moment, what happened."

"Maybe it's good to remember the good times."

"Maybe. Liz still sees the blood. She woke up again last night, screaming and pushing my head away from her pillow, thinking it was Ben Junior's at … at that place."

Jack saw the tears in Ben's eyes and wondered if Ben was talking to him or to himself.

"I'm sorry, Jack. Shouldn't be talking to you this way. I know you're doing everything possible. There is something I was going to ask you to do for me, if you can."

"Anything, Ben."

"Maggie's little sketchbook. You know the one. She carried it in her back pocket all the time. Just before it happened she was sitting where you are and drew a picture of a wasp on a glass. We want to get it back."

"I'll check with CC. I'm sure it's not a problem."

Natasha Trovinski looked up from her desk as her receptionist walked in and handed her a compact disc with an envelope attached to it.

"What's this?"

"Some cute guy said to give it to you, then he left."

"Who?"

"One of the two Mounties who were in the other night. Not the one you treated."

Natasha examined the disc. *The Marriage of Figaro.* She opened the envelope and read the note:

> *Please accept my apology for lying to you the other night. I also want to thank you for your discretion. If you <u>ever</u> do get married, I hope your husband enjoys this music too.*
>
> *Sincerely, Jack*
>
> *P.S. I also don't appreciate being lied to. Looks like we have another thing in common.*

"Did he ask you out on a date?" the receptionist asked. "Better be careful you don't catch scarlet fever!"

"No, he didn't ask me. Besides, you know I don't date patients."

Jack paid Homicide a visit and spoke with CC.

"Ben asked me for it yesterday. He watched her draw her last picture in it of a wasp on a glass, maybe less than an hour before she was killed. She kept it in her back pocket. Should be in her personal effects."

"I have it. Actually, it was on the floor at the scene. Behind the door. I looked through it. That kid could really draw! One picture looks like you."

"It was me." Jack smiled as he recalled the event. "She made me sit on a log holding a hotdog near my mouth for half an hour for that one."

"Wait here, I'll go to the exhibit locker and get it for you."

A moment later CC returned. "The wasp wasn't the last thing she put in it. She printed the word *Dirty* on the next page. Sign for it and you can take it."

Jack signed the release form and looked at Maggie's last entry. "This doesn't fit. She was really talented. Why would she put that word in there?"

CC shrugged. "Who knows? Kids.... It doesn't matter. Just take it."

"Was her pencil in her pocket?"

"No. It was on the floor. Covered in blood. The parents won't want that."

Later that afternoon, Jack and Danny arrived at their office. The telephone was ringing as they walked in and Jack grabbed it. Lucy didn't waste time.

"It matched! The ounce you gave me to test came from the same chemist!"

"Thank God. Oh, Luce, are you sure?"

"Yup!"

Jack rushed into Louie's office where Danny caught up to him.

"I need to get authorization to make a UC purchase," Jack said.

"From who?"

"From this Red that I was telling you about!"

"Some low-level dealer that you *think* might be selling speed? Forget it! Wigmore would wipe his ass with that request."

"Lou, she is selling ounce level for sure. She supplies all the speed dealers in the bar."

"And how do you know that?"

Danny looked at Jack. *This should be interesting.*

"Managed to turn an informant. He gave me the lowdown on the place."

"Really?" Louie spoke to Jack but stared at Danny. "You came up with an informant pretty quick. Is this person reliable?"

Danny felt uneasy. *Christ, is he like Jack? What way are my eyes supposed to look?*

Jack answered for him. "We got lucky. Did surveillance like you told us. Caught a guy with an ounce of speed and managed to flip him. I haven't told you the best part yet. It's a match. The lab matched the ounce with the meth at the murder scene and the meth associated to Satans Wrath back east. They've obviously started a new connection with the club out here!"

"Sounds like a reasonable theory."

"This is a good opportunity to take a swipe at Satans Wrath. Give Wigmore the details; he's bound to approve it!"

"I'll speak with Wigmore, but first, I want you to talk with Homicide."

"I've been doing inside surveillance. This isn't the place for people in suits."

"I'll vouch for that," said Danny, glancing at his hand.

"They don't have to go inside and hold your hand. I'll call them myself."

Jack and Danny took a seat and waited while Louie called CC. He relayed the information and listened, then hung up.

"Well?" Jack asked. "Are they coming to babysit?"

"They're not interested yet. CC has worked on Satans Wrath before. She said they never talk on their phones and never rat each other out."

"So they don't want to be involved?" Jack's voice sounded upbeat.

"She appreciates what you are doing but says she's not interested unless you have something more substantial."

"She's got a point," Danny said. "How do we take on an army like that? They must have hundreds of dealers, maybe thousands."

"Have to work our way up to the multi-kilo level," said Jack. "Catch a club member who has the inside track. Someone willing to talk."

"But these guys have a reputation for never talking," replied Danny.

"We'll see about that," replied Jack. His voice sounded cold.

"Maybe get an undercover operator inside the club?" suggested Danny.

Jack shook his head. "Won't work."

Danny looked at Louie, who explained. "They test their strikers for at least two years. Make them do all sorts of things. Robberies, drug trafficking, maybe murder. Things that UC operators can't do. Jack is right. You need to turn someone on the inside."

"With proper funding," said Jack, "we'll get our informant to make bigger and bigger buys. Maybe even introduce me. Once we get high enough, the bigger fish will surface."

Louie nodded in agreement. "I'll talk with Wigmore. I'm sure he'll be interested." He dialled Superintendent Wigmore, who gave him an immediate audience.

"Turned an informant, did they? Both Taggart and that new guy? What's his name again?"

"Danny O'Reilly."

"Right ... O'Reilly. Did they both turn this informant, or just Taggart?"

"I don't know the specific details about that. Jack isn't one to take credit. It might have only been him who grabbed the guy."

"Well, it doesn't really matter. I was simply curious." Wigmore took a deep breath and slowly exhaled. "I don't mind Taggart placing that porn investigation aside. Taxpayers have more important issues. But as far as funding goes, I'm sorry to say that we're way over budget and there won't be any money available until next spring. I feel awful about it, but that's the way it is. Tell your men they can continue with surveillance, but they're not to do anything else. Even if Homicide isn't interested now, I still don't want your men trampling on something that could later turn out to be important."

Wigmore watched as Louie left his office. *Informant, my ass!*

Louie motioned for Jack and Danny to follow him to his office where he told them what Wigmore had said. It bothered him that Jack didn't protest or utter a word. He just turned and walked out of the office. That meant that he already had an alternate plan.

It also bothered him that Wigmore said he didn't remember Danny's name. Wigmore had a reputation for remembering detail. He had welcomed Danny to the office less than two weeks before. *Why does he want me to think that Danny isn't important to him?*

"So now what?" asked Danny, when they returned to their office. "Without funding we're screwed."

"I'm not going to let someone like Wigmore stop me! There are always people like him around. It's a fact of life. You have to learn to deal with it."

"You won't have enough money to keep doing this on your own."

"You're right about that. Maybe enough for a couple of ounces. I'll have to come up with more."

"How? We're talking tens of thousands."

Jack gave Danny a hard look and chose not to answer. "Let's see if we can identify Baldy. Find out who he is before scoring from Red again."

"Back to the Black Water?"

"You got it."

"Even if we do catch a member of the club with a couple kilos of speed, do you really think he would rat out?"

"How does that old movie go? I'll make him an offer he can't refuse."

Jack's voice was light and lively. Danny was learning. Jack's cold, dark eyes said that he was anything but light and lively. *Wigmore is right....*

chapter nine

It was ten-thirty that night when Jack approached the entrance to the Black Water. His timing was lucky. Baldy came out of the bar in front of him and walked away in the opposite direction. Jack heard a short squeal of tires from the parking lot and knew that Danny had seen him too.

Moments later, Danny quickly pulled up beside Jack and passed him a portable radio through the window.

"Tell me you've had the surveillance course?" said Jack.

"That, I've had," replied Danny.

Jack stayed behind Baldy on foot. Baldy was the cautious type and paused frequently to look around, but Jack remained elusive. Four blocks later, Baldy entered a dilapidated apartment building. Jack crept up the stairwell behind him and watched him unlock a door to a suite and step inside. He waited a moment, then got the apartment number and matched it with the name on the mailbox at the entrance to the building. Seconds later, he joined Danny.

"You get it?" asked Danny.

"Apartment 206. Mailbox says 'L. Waschuk.'"

At the office, Jack studied a mug shot of Leonard Waschuk. Baldy now had a name. He also had a lengthy record for drug trafficking and was currently on probation.

Jack then discovered something on the police computer that made his adrenaline pump. Leonard's last drug conviction was for a pound of cocaine. That investigation indicated that the cocaine originated from someone connected to Satans Wrath, but it wasn't known who.

"So we're two steps away from the club then?" said Danny.

Jack could feel the excitement in his body. "If I order enough to bypass Red and get to Leonard, we'll only be one step removed. It worked with Spider. Tomorrow I'll see if I can do the same with Red. I'll pick you up after lunch. This time you'll hide in the back alley to watch. If Leonard is stashing it there, I want to know where."

The next morning, Jack lay in bed and stared up at the ceiling. He had been awake for over an hour, but it was too soon to go to work. It was the time of day he hated. Being alone gave him too much opportunity to reflect upon events of the past. His telephone rang.

"Susan would like you to come over for lunch," said Danny. "She wants to meet you. I understand if you don't have time. We are pretty busy."

Jack felt a sense of relief. He enjoyed being around families — especially complete families. "I'd be glad to come. I've been looking forward to meeting your family, as long as your kid doesn't barf on me."

A few hours later, Jack couldn't help but laugh out loud as Tiffany squealed and laughed when he made blowing sounds into her neck. When he pulled his head back, her eyes flashed and she smiled and giggled in anticipation of more. He caught the sparkle in Susan's eyes as she watched. *This is a great family ... lots of love.*

Jack invited them out for dinner on Sunday night. It would be his treat. They were to include Tiffany as well. He was pleased when Susan eagerly accepted but said that she would prefer to get a babysitter.

Danny seemed less pleased with the invitation. He looked at his watch and said, "Shouldn't we be going to work?"

Jack waited until they were in the car, then said, "What's the matter? I sense there's something you're holding back. Are you upset with me?"

"No."

Jack reflected for a moment, then said, "You're worried about me buying dope without permission, aren't you?"

Danny didn't respond.

"I'm certain that nobody will find out, but if they do, I'll swear that you had nothing to do with it. If you're that stressed, then wait in the car and I'll do it myself."

"You would protect me, wouldn't you?"

Jack was taken back. "Of course. We're partners!"

Danny was quiet for a few minutes, then asked, "How much can you afford to buy?"

"Is that what's bothering you? Don't worry, I'm not that broke. I can afford dinner ... plus an ounce and a half."

"Think it will be enough to bring out Leonard?"

"Let's find out. I have to stop at my bank on the way."

"We'll stop at my bank, too. Two ounces would improve the odds."

Jack looked at Danny. "Thanks, but no thanks. You've got Susan and Tiffany to support. This is my fight."

"Look at my damned hand! I'm in this fight, too."

Jack felt good. It wasn't the money. It was having a partner he could count on and trust.

On the way to the Black Water, Danny stopped at his bank and gave Jack the money. Jack was grateful but caught the guilty look on Danny's face.

"Hey, have you talked about this with Susan? I don't feel right taking —"

"Take it!" Danny snapped.

Jack accepted it but could tell that Danny was still troubled as they drove. He looked at Danny's bandaged hand and said, "I really don't mind you waiting in the car. This den of snakes, as you call it, there's no real need for you to be there."

"Yeah, except to cover your ass. Like you said, we're partners. If you're going to wallow in that filth, then I should be there alongside you."

Jack smiled, then reached into the back seat and handed Danny a bag.

"Glad you feel that way. I got you a present."

"A present?" Danny looked in the bag. "Coveralls and a box of latex gloves?"

Taggart stood in the alley behind the Black Water and studied the pile of garbage that overflowed the Dumpster. He adjusted a green garbage bag strategically on the pile. The bag was ripped and coffee grounds spilled out. The afternoon sun didn't improve the stench.

Danny's muffled voice came from within. "That's enough! I can barely see!"

"Welcome to Intelligence work," said Jack, as he walked away.

Red sat at a table in the back of the bar with a hooker as Jack approached. An untouched hamburger and fries sat on a paper plate in front of them. He heard them talk as he got close.

"Damn it, Crystal! I'm sick of waitin' around all the time for those fuckin' whores. I want the money on time. If they can't make it, tell 'em I said to give you the hundred bucks and you can bring it to me."

"Some of the girls said that it's a lot of money to be payin' you every day."

"Tough titty. Besides, you know it ain't goin' in my pocket."

Both women quit talking when Jack sat down.

"You lookin'?" asked Red.

Jack nodded.

Crystal knew that privacy was needed and she immediately left the table.

Jack told Red what he was looking for.

"Two ounces? No problem. Wait here, I'll be right back."

Red disappeared into the lobby for a minute and then returned.

"You're gonna have to wait. Can't get hold of someone. Maybe try again in an hour."

"No problem. Let me buy ya a drink." Jack wondered how difficult it would be to convince her to introduce him to Leonard. She didn't bat an eye at selling two ounces. His chances didn't look good.

Danny watched a hooker with a customer in the back alley. The customer stood with his back to the brick wall of the hotel. The hooker undid his zipper and got to her knees. Two minutes later the alley was empty again.

It was dusk when a young girl came down the alley. Danny figured she was between ten and twelve years old. She cautiously looked around as she walked. She approached the steel door at the back of the hotel, hesitated, then rapped lightly on the door. A moment later she rapped louder.

Red opened the door.

"Hey, Marcie! You're here!" Red used a chair to block open the door, then stepped outside. She handed a hamburger and fries to Marcie and sat beside her on the step.

"Sorry it's cold. Was expectin' ya sooner."

Marcie had already started cramming the food in her mouth. "No. Thanks! It's great!" Between mouthfuls of food, Marcie said, "And thanks for lettin' me crash at your place last night. Some guy was hasslin' me in the park and I didn't want to stay there, so…"

"Don't worry about it, kid. Come on. Give me a big smile, that's all I ask."

Marcie turned her head and looked at Red. Danny couldn't see if she smiled or not, but he heard Red.

"Ya call that a smile? I've seen dogs eatin' shit smile better than that!"

Red pulled a syringe out of her purse. "Tell ya what. I'll give you a little treat. Guaranteed to make ya happy. I hate bein' around people who aren't happy."

"No, I mean I used to smoke sometimes, but…"

"Hey. Okay by me," said Red, cramming the syringe back in her purse. "Just tryin' to help. Speakin' of which, remember I told you about the guy who pays big bucks for young models? I checked and he thinks he could squeeze you in for an appointment this evening."

"Yeah, sure! That's exciting!"

"Wait here. I'll go check." Red kicked the chair out of the doorway and the steel door banged shut behind her. Danny watched as Marcie looked nervously up and down the alley. He felt sick, and it wasn't the smell of the garbage.

A few minutes later, the door opened and closed again as someone stepped outside. He recognized a hooker who frequented the hotel.

"Hey, kid, what are you doing?" he heard her say.

"I'm waiting for someone. Red. Do you know her?"

The hooker nodded, then sat beside Marcie and asked, "Is she family to you?"

"No, don't have any family. Except for my dad. Red's my friend."

"You shouldn't be down here. This isn't the place for you. Where's your dad? Bet he would be glad to come and get you and —"

"Forget that! He ain't ... touchin' me no more!"

The hooker patted her on the back and said, "Sorry, kid. Been there. Know where you're comin' from. Tell you what, after the bars close, me and some other girls meet for pizza. My name's Crystal. If you're hungry or need a place to sleep, I'll help you out."

"Thanks, Crystal. My name is Marcie, but I already met a friend who —"

The rear door opened again and Red stepped out and stared down at Crystal.

"Fuck off!"

"Hey, I'm just tryin' to look out for this —"

"I said, fuck off!"

Crystal stood up and headed down the alley. Danny heard Red tell Marcie, "You stay away from her. She's bad news!"

A silver Acura slowly drove down the alley and stopped. It was too dark for Danny to see the driver or make out the licence plate.

"Get in the car, Marcie. This guy will take ya to your appointment. When you're done, he'll bring ya back. Knock on the door again and I'll meet you."

Marcie's voice quavered slightly. "Can't you come?"

"Sorry, kid. I got business to take care of. This guy is all right. He'll take good care of you. No need to be afraid."

Red rejoined Jack at the table. "Sorry, I don't know where the fuck he is. Too bad you didn't want a quarter-pound, instead of two."

"Two is all I can afford."

"That's good. At least I know you ain't a cop. They always have enough money."

"So what difference would the extra two ounces make?"

"I know the people my friend gets it from. I'm allowed to go to them if my friend isn't around, but not for less than a quarter. You sure you can't spring for more bread?"

"Yeah, I'm sure." Jack let out a sigh. He then thought about Danny hiding in the garbage. "Listen, Red, maybe I better split. I might come back tomorrow."

"Let me try my friend one more time," she said and went to the lobby.

She smiled when she returned. "You're in luck, I connected. It'll be here in an hour."

Danny heard footsteps coming down the alley. They stopped beside him.

"It's going down," Jack whispered. "Supposed to arrive within the hour. Make damn certain nobody sees you or it will blow everything."

"Christ! It's about time! What the hell you been doing in there?"

"Just having a few drinks … a few laughs."

"What!"

"Take it easy. Red couldn't connect until now. Keep your eyes peeled for Leonard."

"Take it easy? You sit on your ass in this filth and see how easy it —"

"Keep it down. Someone might hear."

Danny listened as Jack's footsteps faded away. A moment later, another steel door opened close to the Dumpster. Danny heard the sound of a busy kitchen. Moments later, two more bags of garbage were added to the pile. The person went back inside the restaurant and the alley was silent again.

chapter ten

Wizard eyed the girl casually. She probably hadn't reached puberty yet. She had barely spoken a word in the twenty-five minutes he had been driving. Not unusual. Grown men were usually afraid to speak or make eye contact with him. He spotted The Suit's car parked two blocks away from the motel. *Always cautious, The Suit. Always cautious.*

Wizard pulled into the motel unit. It was composed of individual cabins. It was remote, which was why Wizard had chosen it. He had given The Suit the key to the room earlier.

The kid became agitated in her seat. Soon she found the courage to speak.

"What are we doing?" She said it as a question, but Wizard knew that her brain had already told her what she was afraid was going to happen. Her brain was not that experienced. Nothing in her imagination could prepare her for The Suit.

"This isn't for modelling, is it? There aren't going to be any pictures taken for —"

Wizard parked in front of one of the cabins and said, "Listen, kid. The guy in there, well he only likes to look. He won't touch ya. There could be a lot of money in it for you. He does take pictures but keeps 'em for himself. You got nothin' to worry about."

"I've heard of guys like that. He'll put them out on the Internet or something!"

Wizard chuckled. "Not this guy. He's so afraid that someone will find out about his hobby that you won't even see him."

"I won't see him?"

"He wears a mask. He's probably more afraid of you than you will be of him."

"No! I think you better drive me —"

"I didn't bring you here for nothing! Pay me fifty bucks, then I'll drive you back!"

"I don't have any money," she whimpered.

"Then you either get inside that room and have your picture taken, or you can stay in the car with me and I'll take it out on trade!"

Wizard started to undo his belt but stopped as Marcie quickly reached for the door.

"I'll wait and give you a ride back after. Don't try and fuck with me! I'll be watching! Oh, and give him this," he said, handing her a small flap of folded paper.

Marcie walked up to the cabin but glanced back at the man in the car. A street light cast shadows on his face, but she could see his goatee and knew he was watching. She knocked on the door.

She noticed the curtains move, and a man's voice said, "Come in."

Marcie opened the door and stepped in. The only light in the room was dim and came from a table lamp.

She saw the man standing at the back of the room beside the bedroom door. He was wearing a mask of President Bush and had on a jogging suit.

"Lock the door!"

Marcie fumbled with the latch and locked the door.

"You're late!"

"Sorry, it wasn't my —"

"Shut up! No talking! I don't want you to talk at all!"

Marcie swallowed but didn't speak. From the sound of his voice, she guessed he was slightly older than her own dad.

"Take off all your clothes and sit on the sofa and wait."

Marcie could feel her body shaking. She glanced toward the locked door but then thought of the man in the car.

"Hurry up! Are you trying to make me angry?" the man yelled.

"No, mister," Marcie replied.

"I said no talking! Now take 'em off!"

Marcie thought about what the man with the goatee had said. He was the type who only looks. It made sense. He didn't want her to undress in the bedroom. She placed the paper packet on the coffee table and started to take off her clothes. Her hands were shaking and she had trouble with the buttons on her shirt.

"You are a young one, that's real gooood."

She finished undressing and looked back at the man.

"Turn the light off and sit down!"

Marcie flicked off the light, plunging the room into darkness, then sat on the sofa and drew her knees up to her chest. The man grunted something and went into the bedroom.

She could hear him muttering. A few minutes later she heard the bedroom door open and close, then he walked in and turned on a lamp. Her eyes widened and her mouth dropped open as she gawked up at him.

He was wearing only socks, shoes, and his plastic mask. He was a thin man with wavy black hair. There was no hair on his chest and his skin was creamy white. When she saw what he was carrying in his other hand, she bit her lip and began to tremble.

It was a leather leash attached to a choke-chain collar — the kind used to control large dogs.

"Don't worry, I'm not going to touch you," he said in a quiet, soothing voice. "Let me move the hair back from your pretty face a bit." He gently stroked her hair with his fingers.

Marcie quivered and drew her knees tighter to her chest.

"There, that's a good little bitch. Sit still … that's a girl."

Without warning, he slipped the chain over her head.

"Mister? What —"

Her words were choked off as he savagely jerked the end of the leash and wrapped a loop of it around his fist. The chain bit deep into her neck as he dragged her onto the floor.

"Bad bitch! I told you to keep quiet!"

He squeezed the collar tight while whipping the end of the leather leash across her body with his other hand. She twisted and turned, her legs writhing as she clawed at the chain. Her fingernails broke and the jagged remains gouged her throat as she frantically fought for air.

The pain started to go away. She realized she was still lying on the floor and the collar had loosened. Her lungs sucked in air and she gulped it down like water. She began to sob, but the air exploded from her lungs as the toe of his shoe struck deep into her stomach.

"You're not at all trained, are you? You need lessons!"

He jerked on the leash and began to walk and drag her behind him. She started to get to her feet but he yanked down on the leash, bringing her to her hands and knees.

Her scream was cut short by a kick to the side of her rib cage. The pain tore through her chest. Each breath she took caused more pain. She stayed on her hands and knees, looking down at the floor. She opened and closed her eyes, trying to see through her tears.

This isn't happening! It's my body, but it isn't me! It's only a dream! It has to be! He's moving again … I have to keep up. It hurts so much to breathe ... this isn't a dream!

"That's right, bitch! Walk on all fours!"

He started walking her back and forth and around the coffee table, then stopped.

"Heel!" he said, barking out the command.

Marcie stayed quivering on her hands and knees. He slapped her thighs with the leash and said, "On the floor!"

Marcie sat back on her heels.

"Keep your hands on the floor," he snarled.

Seconds later, he started walking again, leading her on her hands and knees.

Marcie was breathing deeply. She could taste the dust rising from the carpet as it found its way into her eyes and down her nose and throat. Her arms and knees burned from being dragged across the rug. Then he patted the floor beside the sofa and said, "Lie down!"

He sat on the sofa for a few minutes, only to get up and jerk her around the room on the leash again and again.

Eventually he seemed to tire of the ritual and turned on the television. He sat on the sofa to watch. Marcie stared blankly out into the room. Her brain seemed to be turning off and on. *This is all a nightmare. Wake up!*

She watched him open the paper packet on the coffee table and tap out two lines of sparkling white powder. He got down on his knees beside her and turned his back to her and slid his mask up on his head. She could hear the sound, like a pig, as he placed a finger alongside his nose and snorted the cocaine. She turned her head as his bare ass touched her face. He then pulled the mask down and turned and patted her on the head before settling back on the sofa. She sensed that he was smiling at her from behind the mask.

She could feel the swelling in her throat and the burning sensation where the sweat running down from her head found its way into the open wounds around her neck.

He stood up and lightly tugged on the leash. Without thinking, she got up on her hands and knees.

"That's a good bitch! You're young enough to teach!"

He walked around the room once more, then led her into the washroom. He stopped in front of the sink and poured himself a glass of water. She stared down at the tiled floor. It felt cool and soothed her bloody fingertips and the burning sensation on her knees. She could hear him swallow slowly and smack his lips.

"You've been a good bitch," he said quietly.

His voice sounded gentle. Her mind started to come back to reality as she grasped at the hope it would soon be over. *At least he hasn't touched me…*

"Do you want a drink of water? Well, do you?"

She sensed that to say no would make him angry. She looked up and nodded her head.

"Okay, drink then!" He flung open the toilet lid and pointed inside.

"No!" she replied, shaking her head.

"You don't tell me no! You stupid bitch!"

The chain tightened around her neck; her fingers instinctively clawed at her throat. She kicked out with her feet as he dragged her across the floor. He didn't loosen his grip on the collar while grabbing her hair with his other hand and shoving her head inside the toilet bowl. Down into the water ... out ... down again.

Briefly, she thought the water was full of small black bugs, but realized it was only her vision clouding over. Seconds later, darkness engulfed her.

He loosened his grip and she became conscious and blinked her eyes as water dripped from her face into the toilet bowl.

"Drink, you bitch! I said drink!"

She felt him grab her hair as he dunked her head into the toilet again, before letting go. She lowered her face and touched the water with her lips.

"Lap! I want to hear you lap!" he shouted.

She made a lapping noise with her tongue. She felt his legs on each side of her rib cage as he stood straddling her. Pain shot through her side where he had kicked her. Automatically she squeezed closer to his opposite leg.

"Lap, you bitch!"

A condom wrapper fell in the toilet beside her face. "No DNA for you, bitch," he muttered. She glanced back and saw him masturbating.

"Lap, I said!"

She turned her head back into the bowl and felt his legs grip her body while his hand twisted and pulled on her hair. Moments later he relaxed. She could hear the sound of her own breathing in the bowl.

Without warning he yanked on the leash, pulling her backward onto the floor.

She scrambled on her hands and knees to keep from being choked as he half-dragged her across the hall and opened the bedroom door, hauling her inside. Then she heard him say, "Okay, Cutesy! Come here, boy, it's your turn. Now ... be a good little bitch and lick him off. Go on! Blow him!"

For a second Marcie didn't understand. Then she felt something cold and wet touch the back of her leg. She turned around and looked directly into the eyes of a German shepherd.

"No! Oh, God..."

The collar tightened, choking off her screams. She fell on her back and started kicking. The dog lunged at her, biting her fingers and then knocking her skinny arms aside to sink its teeth into her chest.

Moments later she could breathe again and started to sob. He ignored her as he led the dog up to straddle her face.

"Mister ... please ... don't, please ... I'm bleeding..."

He picked up a camera and there was a blinding white flash of light.

His words started to fade. "Okay, okay. That's enough. He's ready! Get on your hands and knees. Now! You don't think I'm going to fuck you, do you?"

Wizard sat in the car and watched the flash of the camera on the cabin's curtain. He thought about Damien and chuckled out loud. Damien despised The Suit and had no stomach for this. *Being a family man with two young daughters has made him weak. The Suit is the key to success. Big mistake for Damien to let me control that key.*

Wizard watched as The Suit eventually left the cabin. The Suit avoided eye contact with him and hustled down the street with his dog.

Wizard took a syringe out from under the dash of the Acura and walked toward the cabin.

chapter eleven

Danny saw a figure moving down the darkened alley toward him. Light from a dirty bulb farther down the alley briefly identified the bald head. Leonard Waschuk!

Leonard paused near the rear of the Black Water and looked around. Danny held his breath and watched. Leonard bent over and Danny heard the sound of a brick scrape as it was moved out of place. Moments later, Leonard hurried off down the alley.

Jack saw Red glance behind him toward the front entrance of the bar. She put her beer down and casually made a thumbs-up sign with her fist, while pretending to scratch her chin with her thumb. Jack pretended not to notice Leonard as he walked by. Leonard made a circle around the pool tables, then walked out the front of the bar.

Red looked at Jack and said, "Okay, sit tight and get your bread ready. It's time."

Jack nodded to the group of men playing pool and said, "Do you want me over there?"

Red grinned. "Naw, sorry about that. First-time customers. You know how it is."

Red went to the rear door and pushed it open. Seconds later, she was back. Jack passed her the money under the table. She discreetly counted it, then passed him two baggies of powder. As Jack took it, Red said, "Shit!"

"What's wrong?"

"Bart and Rex."

Jack turned around and saw two large men slowly moving through the bar. They were scruffy-looking and wore jeans. Even the bouncer, who himself was a giant of a man, quickly stepped aside as they approached. One man was casually tossing a ring of keys into the air with his hand. They made a jingling sound each time he caught them. The noise in the bar died off to a few whispers and the sound of jingling keys.

"Who are Bart and Rex?"

"City narcs," she whispered. "Bart's the one with the keys."

With his back to the two men, Jack slowly tucked the two baggies of powder in the elastic tablecloth under the table, then glanced behind him. He saw looks of fear and hatred on the patrons' faces as Bart and Rex walked past them.

Jack heard the jangling of keys come closer, then stop behind him. He stared at Red, trying to read her eyes, then slowly took a sip of beer. He could see Spider sitting at another table with a junkie. The junkie let out a dry cough and put his hand to his mouth.

The jangle of keys started again, but on the second toss, Bart missed them and they fell beside Spider's table. Bart stooped down to pick up the keys, but as he did, he grabbed the junkie by the throat with his other hand and hurled him backward off his chair onto the floor.

Rex immediately pulled out his gun while Bart sat on the junkie's chest and choked him.

"Open your yap!" Bart yelled. "Spit it out!"

The junkie shook his head and gritted his teeth.

Without letting go, Bart used his other hand to take out the handcuffs hanging from the back of his belt. He flipped one cuff open to expose the serrated clasp, then jammed it into the junkie's mouth. A small bundle of dope, wrapped in a condom, spit out from between the junkie's bloody lips. Bart then dragged him out the front of the bar while Rex tagged along, his gun still drawn.

"Christ, I hate those fuckin' guys," muttered Red.

"Too damn close, if you ask me," said Jack, retrieving the two baggies from under the table. "Think I'll sit and have another beer and make sure those two gorillas are gone before I leave."

"Yeah. Good idea."

Danny had seen Leonard return to his stash and then hand the drug to Red. He waited for Jack to exit. *What the hell is taking him so long?*

A car came down the alley and stopped. Someone opened the trunk, and Danny cursed silently as he felt the weight of more garbage being thrown on the pile.

The waitress came over to Red and said, "Someone called and said to tell ya your package is here."

"Yeah? Thanks. Send a cab around back for me, will ya?"

Red sipped her beer. A moment later she stood up and said, "Gotta go. See ya around." She walked out the back door into the alley.

Jack wanted to leave as well. Danny would be fuming, in more ways than one. He decided to give Red a few minutes to clear the alley. She was paranoid enough without him walking out right behind her.

Danny watched Red enter the alley. She looked around, then strolled over to where he was hiding as a taxi rolled to a stop behind her. *Has she seen me?* She reached her hand toward the garbage. *Should I pretend I'm drunk?*

She shook the garbage and said, "Hey! What're ya doin' in there?"

What the hell should I say?

A girl moaned loudly. *Someone is lying on top of me!* Red shook her again and she started to wake up. Red stood back and said, "Oh my God, Marcie, it's you!"

She half-lifted and half-dragged Marcie out of the Dumpster and into the alley.

"It's a good thing I came along! Come on, get in the cab. What happened?"

Red got in the taxi with Marcie and the car disappeared down the alley. Danny was able to get the taxi's number.

The door opened again. It was Jack.

"It's about bloody time!"

Jack helped Danny stagger out of the garbage. He had sat for so long that his legs had gone numb. "Did you see Leonard?" Jack asked.

"Yeah, I saw him. But that's not all that happened. Red set up some young girl by the name of Marcie. Only about ten or twelve years old. She's really hurt. They just left in a cab. I got the number."

"So did he stash it?"

"What are you talking about?"

"Leonard. Did you see where he stashed it?"

"Yeah, there's a loose brick over on the wall, but this kid —"

"Where? Show me!"

Danny found the loose brick and pulled it out. There was a small empty cavity in the wall behind the brick.

Jack was pleased. "This is great! I've got an idea. With the amount I scored tonight, we better stay away from here for about a week. After that —"

"Forget the fuckin' stash for a moment, will you!"

"What's wrong?"

"This kid! I got the number of the cab that took her away. I think we —"

"You're worried about someone in this 'den of snakes'?"

"This is different! This is just a kid!"

Jack gestured toward the bar with his thumb and said, "Everyone in there was a kid once. We can't let ourselves get sidetracked over —"

"Damn it, Jack! Aren't kids what this is all about? The girl that Red set up tonight … she's about the same age that Maggie was."

Natasha Trovinski treated her last patient of the night. She saw the child to the door and watched her leave in a taxi. Her patient left against her advice, but she was used to people ignoring her advice in this clinic. She returned to her office, straightened up the papers on her desk, and shut off her stereo. She was looking forward to going home and having a long hot bath. *Considering this last patient, I'll probably have a long cry at the same time.* She took her coat off the rack as her receptionist walked in.

"They're back. The two Mounties who were here earlier in the week."

"He's too early to have his stitches out."

"It's not about that. They want to talk to you about the girl who just left."

She put her coat back on the rack. "Send them in."

Dr. Trovinski quickly located *The Marriage of Figaro* and turned the stereo back on.

"Gentlemen! Come in and have a seat." She looked at Danny and said, "How is your hand, officer? I hope you haven't been ... falling on any more glass?"

Danny grinned, then said, "No. My hand is fine, thanks."

"Jack, I want to thank you for the CD. I also want to apologize for lying to you about being married."

"Don't mention it."

"How did you know I wasn't?"

Jack smiled, then said, "Trade secret."

"What CD?" Danny asked.

"The one she put on as we were walking down the hall," said Jack. He caught her blush and added, "We want to ask you about a young girl who just left here."

"Her name is Marcie," said Danny.

"I told you gentlemen before, I don't talk about my patients. I extended that courtesy to you. The same goes for my other patients."

"But we're police officers...," protested Danny.

"Most of my patients are not on very good terms with the police. If I talk, *especially* to the police, some of them would risk dying rather than come in for treatment."

"I'm sorry," said Danny, letting out a sigh. "I guess you're right. Besides, she saw you, so I'm sure she's okay now."

Okay? That damned kid is far from okay! She watched Danny get to his feet. Jack remained seated, staring at her.

"She's not okay, is she, doctor?" he finally said.

She stared back. She didn't need to speak. The tears that flooded her eyes said it all.

"I deal with victims in my work," Jack said. "You and I, our objectives are not all that different. You treat the victims. I try to eliminate those who turn people into victims. We just go about it from different angles. You have my word. Nobody outside of this office will ever know that we have talked to you. I really would like to know what happened to her. Maybe I can do something to help or to prevent someone else from getting hurt."

Danny looked at Jack. *What did he really mean when he said eliminate?*

The doctor stared at Jack for a moment, then quietly said to Danny, "You better sit down. This will take a few minutes.

She waited until Danny sat down and then looked at Jack. "Marcie has recently become a street kid. Except for a grandmother in a nursing home, the only relative she has is her father. Although she wouldn't come right out and say it, I strongly suspect that her father carried on an incestuous relationship with her. Tonight she told me that she went to sleep under someone's porch when she was attacked by a dog and repeatedly bitten. She said that the dog's chain got wrapped around her neck and she almost strangled. She said she got her hands on her first fix of heroin tonight, to ease the pain."

"So that's what happened," said Danny. "And someone dropped her off in an alley after she fixed."

Her reply was laced with anger. "That is not what happened! There was a woman with her. Long dyed red hair and tattoos. I wanted to speak to Marcie alone, but she insisted that her friend had to be with her."

"I'm acquainted with her ... companion," said Jack.

"Marcie was coached. She looked at her so-called friend for every response."

"Did you treat her for *animal* bites?" asked Jack.

"It was evident from the eye teeth that they were animal bites. I treated her for bite marks on her fingers, breast, and thigh, but her clothes weren't punctured or torn."

"Sexual perversion with a dog," said Jack quietly.

"That's my guess. And you can bet she didn't inject herself, either. The injection site was on her right arm. She's right-handed, so the likely location should have been on her left arm."

Danny felt nauseous. He thought of Tiffany. *If someone did that to her...* He waited until they left the clinic before turning to Jack and asking, "What can we do about this?"

"There is nothing we can do right now."

"She's just a kid, for Christ's sake. We've got —"

"There's lots of kids like Marcie. Social workers are always on the street trying to convince them to accept help. It's not easy. Even if we take Red out of the picture, there will always be someone else to take her place. All we can do is wait for an opportunity."

"What kind of opportunity?"

"I don't know yet, but as far as Red goes, she told me that she can deal with Leonard's connection if he isn't around. Providing the quantity is a quarter-pound or more."

"So?"

"So for now it would be better if we dispose of Leonard."

"Dispose of Leonard? What do you...?"

Danny was interrupted when Dr. Trovinski caught up to them and said, "Excuse me, gentlemen, but I'm off shift now. Would you mind walking me to my car?"

They walked in silence to her car. She unlocked her door and then looked at Jack and blurted, "Would you like to have dinner with me? I'm off on Sunday. I know it's short notice, but that's the only day off I have for a while."

"I'm sorry," said Jack. "I already have a commitment for Sunday."

"Bring her along!" said Danny. "Make it a foursome."

"I was taking Danny and his wife, Susan, to a little Italian restaurant. A family-run place. The food is excellent. If you would like to join us..."

"You don't mind?" she asked.

"Doctor, I don't mind at all!"

"My name is Natasha. Please, no more 'doctor' bullshit."

Danny noticed that their eyes came more alive as they looked at each other. *Jack is right. If you pay attention, you can tell a lot from people's eyes. Wished I paid more attention to Jack's eyes when he talked about disposing of Leonard....*

chapter twelve

Marcie locked the bathroom door and eased herself into the bathtub. Steam rose from the water. She closed her eyes for a moment and gritted her teeth. In the other room, Red turned on the stereo, and it blasted out heavy metal. Marcie could feel the vibrations of the music when she laid her head back on the ceramic tiles.

She sat up and with a facecloth gently scrubbed her body with soap and rinsed in the hot water. Then she scrubbed herself again, rubbing harder.

Then she felt it. Slowly at first. Like lice, crawling over her body. She examined her skin. There was nothing there.

She started over, using a hand brush, feverishly washing herself. Her skin became raw and red. The bandages on her fingers became soggy and fell off. Blood seeped through the dressing on her chest. She stopped washing. She didn't feel any cleaner. She sat for a moment with her arms at her side, and then she cried.

She stayed in the bathtub until the coldness of the water brought her back to reality. Then she wrapped the damp bandages back over her fingers and went to her room and put on jeans and a loose-fitting shirt. She eased herself down on a mattress on the floor. There were no sheets and the mattress was dirty and badly stained. She started to shake and curled up in the fetal position.

Moments later, Red walked into the room. She sat down on the edge of the mattress and gently brushed the hair back from Marcie's eyes.

"I'm so, so sorry, baby. I had no idea this guy would hurt you. You've got to believe me."

Marcie didn't respond.

"I'll tell you what, you won't have to do this kinda stuff ever again. You just stay here and rest for as long as ya want. I'll take good care of ya! You'll see!"

She closed her eyes and drifted in and out of sleep. Suddenly, he was back! Wearing the same mask and holding the leash in one hand. He was naked, except for his shoes. He walked toward her, rattling the silver chain on the end of the leash. "Okay, Cutesy..." His dog was at his side.

She tried to yell, but no sound would come out. The dog's lips pulled back over its gums as it snarled, its hot breath on her face. Then it shook its head, flinging saliva across her cheek and mouth. Claws scratched her skin. She screamed and sat up.

"It's okay, baby, it's okay," said Red, sitting on the edge of the mattress, hugging her tight. "You're just havin' a bad dream. It's okay."

She opened her eyes. There was daylight in the room. She looked at the bandages around her fingers. "It's not a dream!" she cried.

"Just lie here, baby, everything will be okay," said Red, easing her down on the mattress. "I'll get ya somethin' that'll make ya forget. You'll feel better," she added, as she left the room.

Seconds later, Red was back. She smiled as she kneeled down beside her. A small piece of surgical hose dangled from her hand, along with a syringe. Red put them both on the floor.

"Just lie still," she said softly. "Close your eyes. Soon you'll feel real good."

Red tied the hose tightly around her arm, slightly above her elbow. Marcie lay there, staring up at Red's face. Red picked the syringe up off the floor, then smiled at her while gently brushing the hair back from her face. "This ain't gonna hurt a bit, baby, you'll see. It'll help ya."

Marcie watched Red put the needle over a vein in the crook of her elbow. Her skin resisted slightly before relenting. Marcie turned her head as the needle entered her body. Instantly she felt warm all over. Then she felt sick and scrambled to the washroom.

"It's okay, baby!" yelled Red from the bedroom. "Lots of people puke the first time or two. Don't worry, ya get use to it real quick. After that, it feels good, you'll see."

Marcie woke up in her bedroom. She felt so tired. She tried to get up off the mattress but couldn't. She slept some more. Red came in and sat beside her, smiling, brushing the hair back from her eyes. She felt the hose around her arm again and shook her head.

"No, Red," she murmured, "it makes me puke."

Red smiled, shaking her head. "Not this time, baby, not this time."

She felt the needle slip under her skin. It didn't hurt this time, and she didn't feel sick. Red was right. She felt like she was floating on air. Her whole body felt good, really good. For the first time in her life she was truly happy. No pain. No dog. No Daddy. No more anything.

*

The restaurant was crowded, so Danny stood up and waved to Jack and Natasha when they arrived. They were both laughing and laughed louder when they looked at him.

Danny introduced Susan, and the two women greeted each other warmly.

"So what was that all about?" Danny asked. "When you came in, I had the feeling that the two of you were talking about me."

"We were," said Jack.

"Jack! That was supposed to be confidential!" said Natasha.

"Okay, out with it!" said Danny, flicking his fingers to emphasize his demand.

Jack grinned, then said, "Well, I'm sure that Natasha here, being a doctor, had the utmost professional concern when she asked me if I had ever spoken to you about your problem."

"His problem?" Susan leaned forward. "You mean about his hand?"

"No, not that," said Jack. "She asked me if I had ever spoken to him about his BO."

"BO?" asked Susan.

"Body odour," said Jack. "She's only met your husband twice before tonight. The first time he smelled of urine. The second time he smelled like garbage!"

"Hey! That's from working with you! I don't smell...."

Danny's protest was drowned out by the laughter of his three dinner companions.

"Think what I have to put up with," said Susan. "I have to sleep with him!"

Jack ordered the cannelloni. Natasha and Danny

did likewise. Susan ordered linguini of the sea. It came with scallops, prawns, and clams.

The food was delicious, and the evening went by quickly. Perhaps too quickly, thought Danny. *Tomorrow I have to call Wigmore.* He waited until Susan and Natasha went to the ladies' room before talking work.

"So, what's next? Are we going to the Black Water tomorrow?"

"No. Give it a few days. Make them think I'm busy selling the speed I bought."

"What about Marcie? I think I should try to convince her to go to Social Services."

"Do that and you'll blow your cover. If what she has just been through doesn't convince her to leave, nothing you say will."

"Maybe I should call them myself. It bothers me thinking about her."

"I feel the same way, but now is not the time. With what she has been through, she probably won't be downtown for a week or so. She'll be going through the honeymoon phase with Red, or someone else she thinks is her friend."

"Honeymoon phase?"

"Someone will be extra nice to her and try to earn her trust, or at least get her to be dependent upon them. Once we dispose of Leonard I'll figure out how to bypass Red. Then we won't be at the bar and you can take your chances with Marcie."

"How the hell do you expect to come up with the money to buy quantity? Not to mention *disposing* of Leonard?"

"I'll figure something out," said Jack. He then changed the subject as Susan and Natasha returned. Danny had the feeling that Jack had already figured something out.

A couple with two children sat at a nearby table. Natasha caught the silent reflection on Jack's face.

"You come from a big family, Jack?"

"No. I just have a sister and brother-in-law who live on a farm outside the city."

"Sounds nice. Do they have children?"

"No. Would you please pass the garlic toast?"

"You still have some on your plate. I take it you're the private type and don't like to talk about your family?"

"Not tonight." Jack quickly looked around the room and said, "Excuse me, I have to go the men's room." The table shook, slopping wine from their glasses as he stood up. He didn't stay to apologize.

Natasha looked at Danny and Susan's faces. Danny was expressionless and stared down at his plate. Susan looked like she was about to burst into tears.

Natasha was shocked. "What did I say?"

Susan's voice was a whisper. "Jack's sister did have kids. A boy and a girl. They were murdered less than a month ago in an abandoned farmhouse up the Valley."

"Those kids in the news? They were his niece and nephew?"

Jack washed his face with cold water. The solace he sought in the men's room vanished as Natasha strode in.

A man at a urinal said, "Hey lady, this is —"

"I'm a doctor," she snapped. "You look like you're done."

"I — I guess so." He left without washing.

Natasha then approached Jack and put her arm across his shoulder. "I'm sorry," she said softly. "Susan just filled me in. I'm so, so sorry."

"It's not your fault." He squeezed the rim of the sink with both hands, then splashed more water on his face. "It's not your fault."

She grabbed him by the shoulders and made him turn and look at her. His hair was askew and his face dripped water.

What happened next came without warning or reason ... and shocked them both. Two people who had walked through that valley of death too often had, within themselves, suddenly unleashed a primal lust for life. They kissed each other hard and passionately on the lips. Passionately enough, for a moment, to block out the world around them. It was their first kiss.

chapter thirteen

Monday evening came, and Danny told Susan that he needed to go to the store. He used a payphone to call Wigmore.

"I made a mistake. Jack isn't breaking the rules. I know I —"

"What the hell are you talking about! You told me last week that Taggart left his gun in the car and went in the bar to buy dope! Bullshit, O'Reilly! What are you trying to pull?"

"Nothing, sir. I saw him take off his holster, but I later discovered that he has two holsters. He switched his gun into an ankle holster. I just didn't realize it at the time."

"You also said he went in the bar alone. What have you got to say about that?"

"He had an informant in there and was just catching the person's attention so they could meet outside. His informant is a little paranoid and Jack wanted to meet alone to start with."

"The story I heard was that the so-called informant came about as a result of being caught with drugs — *after* you started working down there."

"That's someone else. That's who Jack's first informant tipped us off about."

"Is that a fact?"

"Yes, sir."

"I see. Well ... all the more reason for you to keep me posted so that I fully understand what is going on. Dealing with informants is acceptable, but you are aware, aren't you, that you and Taggart are not to do anything other than surveillance down there?"

"Yes, sir."

Wigmore paused, then said, "Don't wait until Monday night to call me anymore. It will be up to you to call me as soon as possible if Taggart is not obeying orders or following policy."

"I'll do that, sir."

"Keep up the good work, Danny. I expect to hear from you soon."

Danny felt a sense of relief flood over him when he hung up the telephone. No more weekly calls needed — as long as Wigmore didn't find out what Jack was up to.

It was 8:15 Tuesday morning when Superintendent Wigmore called and spoke to the inspector in charge of Internal Affairs.

"Yes, we need to meet," he said. "We now have two rogue officers to discuss."

Mid-week, Jack and Danny started making periodic visits to the Black Water, but there was no sign of Red or Leonard. Marcie was not around either.

It was not until the following Saturday night that Red showed up.

"Where ya been?" asked Jack. "I've been lookin'."

"I had other business to take care of. You want another two?"

"How long would it take to get me three? I don't want to wait around all day like before."

Red went to the lobby and then returned a few minutes later. "It'll be here in about an hour, maybe an hour and a half."

A few minutes later, Jack had a quick visit with Danny in the men's room.

"Make your anonymous call," said Jack. "I don't have the money for this!"

Leonard cautiously made his way down the darkened alley. He took three ounces of speed out of his boot and carefully slid the brick out of position. Then he saw two shadows appear on the wall in front of him and he darted to the left.

Leonard had about as much chance as a baby lamb being jumped by a grizzly. Bart's large, muscular hands compressed his throat while the force of his body simultaneously smashed him down into a puddle of water.

"Police! Open your mouth! Open your fuckin' mouth or I'll rip your throat out!"

Leonard automatically tried to pull at the hairy hands holding his throat. The grip tightened. He was stunned and blinked his eyes. A smear appeared on his lips. He had bitten the end of his tongue when the back of his skull bounced off the wall. His legs jerked a little as his brain told him to run before realizing it was impossible.

Bart sat on his chest, choking him. Water in the puddle slopped around his ears and up his back. His eyes bulged as his lungs fought for air. He blinked, then obediently opened his mouth.

"Move your tongue around so I can see if you're hidin' somethin'!"

Leonard moved his tongue.

"Never mind, Bart, it's in the wall."

Bart released his grip, and Leonard made a gasping, gurgling sound as air rushed back into his lungs.

Leonard was jerked to his feet and slammed back against the wall. He didn't realize until later that the warmth he felt in the crotch of his jeans was from his own body.

Leonard was completely soaked, and a combination of fear and cold made him shake.

Bart barked, "Put your hands on your head and don't fuckin' move, asshole!"

Leonard watched silently as Rex removed three small plastic baggies from the hole in the brick wall. He squirmed a little when he heard Bart's deep voice comment on the putrid odour.

"Oh, Christ, Rex! He shit himself! So help me, this job makes me wanna puke sometimes! An' my jeans are wet from the knees down!"

Rex turned his head slightly away so Bart wouldn't see him grinning.

"Next time, you do the honours. I'm gettin' too old for this bullshit. What've we got?"

"I'd say about three ounces." Rex waved the baggies in Lenny's face and said, "Care to confirm this for us? We're going to have it analyzed anyway."

"I want my lawyer!"

Their moment of silence as they went through the papers in his wallet gave him a little more courage.

"Besides," he added, "I don't think you got reason'ble and proper beliefs to grab me in the first place! You'll be lucky if my lawyer don't sue you or somethin'."

"Shut up, asshole, or I'll make you eat your shorts," growled Bart.

Leonard paled and stood quietly, looking down at his feet. Minutes later he was half-dragged down the alley and tossed unceremoniously into the back of an unmarked police car. His pale face became whiter yet when he was driven to an underground parking lot several blocks from the hotel.

"Where ya takin' me? This ain't no police station!"

"Relax, Lenny. We're just going to have a little talk, is all," said Bart. "But we'll do it outside the car. You stink too much, even with the windows rolled down!"

The three men got out of the car before Bart continued. "You're goin' to tell us who you got this from."

"Fuck you, I am." Leonard looked around at the empty parking lot and said, "What are you going to do? Beat me? Go ahead!"

"Don't be impolite," said Rex. "I get real pissed off at people who are impolite!"

The conversation was interrupted when the police radio informed Bart and Rex that Leonard was still on probation for trafficking in drugs.

"How about that, Lenny!" said Bart. "Caught again while you're still on probation. You're lookin' at doin' some serious time!"

"Don't care. I ain't rattin'."

Leonard leaned and stretched his head forward as Bart and Rex whispered to each other, then jumped nervously when Bart unexpectedly laughed.

"Okay, Lenny, you can go. We'll keep the dope, but go ahead, fuck off!"

Leonard stood with his mouth gaping, looking back and forth at the two faces in front of him. "You're gonna shoot me for escapin'!" he said, his eyes nervously darting back and forth.

"Naw, I ain't gonna shoot you," replied Bart.

"I can just walk away?" said Leonard in disbelief. "Just like that?"

"Sure, Lenny, just like that. I'd suggest you use what little time you have left to wash out your shorts so you won't smell so bad at your funeral."

"What do you mean?" asked Leonard suspiciously.

"Well, the way I got it figured is you've got three choices."

Leonard stared at Bart without answering.

"Number one is you can tell everyone about the two nice narcs who relieved you of a few thousand dollars worth of dope but didn't arrest or charge you."

"I won't do that! Everyone would think I was a rat! My life —"

"If we find the prints of your supplier on these baggies, we'll tell 'im you ratted!"

Bart let this message sink in and then continued.

"Number two is you could just say you lost it or were ripped off. But I got a feeling that a low-life like you doesn't have enough money to pay for this up front. So I think you still owe money ... which means someone will be awful pissed off at you. In fact, they'll probably think you ripped them off."

Lenny's head drooped down. "You guys have pretty well got it all figured out, don't you?" he mumbled.

"It's our business. Do you want us to spell out your third option?" asked Rex.

Lenny raised his head. "No, I know how the game is played. But if someone finds out I squealed ... I'm dead!"

"We won't tell if you don't. But make up your mind fast because I don't plan on hanging around here all night!" said Bart gruffly.

Leonard swallowed, and then said, “All right, I’ll talk. It’s speed. I get it from a biker by the name of Halibut. I don’t know his real name,” he said nervously, looking at Bart, “but he’s got a glass eye,” he added quickly.

chapter fourteen

"What's the scoop, Red?" asked Jack as he sat down. "Last night was a waste of time."

"My guy almost got busted last night."

The word *almost* bothered Jack. "What are you talking about?"

"He said there were narcs all over. Bart and Rex in the alley and more of 'em out front. He saw them and split. We're gonna lay low for a few days until the heat is off."

"There's always narcs. We just gotta be cautious or go somewhere else."

"I don't call the shots. Who knows? There could be some narcs in here right now watchin' us. Best for everybody to tap it cool. Give it a week or so."

"Maybe I'll find somebody else. Maybe at a better price."

Red laughed. "Don't try and scam me. My stuff is the best there is, and I'm still sellin' it to you the cheapest. If you have been lookin' elsewhere, you know that I'm not shittin' ya."

Jack grinned and said, "Yeah, I know your stuff is the best."

"I sometimes wonder why I'm lettin' you have it so cheap. I think it's only because of them big blue eyes of yours. Tell ya what. To make up for last night I'll buy ya a beer. You can sit and chill with me for a bit."

Marcie sat on her mattress and looked at a small swollen lump on her arm from the last needle taken an hour ago. With her fingernail, she scratched off a little piece of dried blood.

It had been two weeks since ... the motel. If she could go thirty seconds without thinking about it, it would be a relief. She thought about her grandmother. *She's the only one who really loves me.*

She heard the door open as Red arrived home. A moment later, she stuck her head into the room to check on Marcie.

"Red, I've been thinking," Marcie said. "I'm gonna split out of here. Go live by my grandma in Regina."

"What? What are you talkin' about?"

"Well ... I kind of miss her. I think I'll go live there so I can visit her."

"You ungrateful little slut! You think you can just walk out of here like that?"

"What do you mean? Why not?"

"What about all the money you owe for clothes an' dope?"

"Money?"

"Yeah, money! You retard! Where is it? Go ahead; cough up with what you owe! Then I don't give a rat's ass what you do!"

"I thought, like, the speed was free?"

"Free? Like fuck it was free! Sure, I lent you some out of the goodness of my heart, but you damn well better pay me back! It cost me money! Besides, it's not speed, you twerp. It was the big H. An' that stuff is fuckin' expensive!"

"Well, like, I thought I didn't have to go to work, you know, since, because, you know..."

"You still mopin' about that? It was only a dog! He couldn't have had that big of a dink! You think you can just fuckin' hang out here all day, while I pay the rent, buy your clothes, and put juice in your arm? Who the fuck do you think you are that you can just rip me off like that?"

Marcie looked up with her mouth gaping open.

"You want to leave? Fine!" said Red, shaking her fist. "Get up and get the fuck out there! Start earning me the money you owe! It'll cost ya a hundred bucks a day for protection. What you owe me is above that."

Marcie's voice was barely audible. She started to get up and said, "I'm sorry. I wasn't thinkin'. I know I owe you, but..."

Red grabbed her by the front of her shirt and pulled her close enough for Marcie to feel the hot breath on her face.

"You're damn right you owe me!" said Red, shoving her back down on the mattress. "And now is payback time!"

Marcie wiped some spit off her face with the back of her hand. She could feel Red's burning glare as she slowly stood up and walked over to the closet. She trembled as she took off her jeans and put on the new clothes that Red had given her earlier. Mesh nylons, a miniskirt, and a tank top. The she slipped on a pair of high heels.

"Marcie! You better not be thinking of screwing off and rippin' me for what you owe!"

"I won't," she squeaked, looking down as she spoke.

"Better not, because all you got for family is that grandmother of yours. Unless of course you want to go back to Daddy! What do you think dear old Grandma would say if she got all those cute little pictures of you and the doggie in the mail?"

Marcie's face turned white. Tears streamed down her face, but she didn't utter a sound.

Red's voice softened. "Look, I'm not hard to get along with. I just don't like the idea of anyone rippin' me off. The guys I pay for protection? They're all with Satans Wrath, and now you owe them, too. If you tried to fuck off on them, do you know what they'd do?"

Marcie shook her head, staring tearfully at Red.

"First they'd kill your grandma, 'cause she'd be easy to find. Then they'd track ya down and rip the guts right out of ya. There's no place ya can hide. They got guys all over the world!"

Marcie didn't answer. She stood, looking straight ahead, tears dripping from her cheeks.

It was late Friday afternoon, but Sid Bishop waited patiently and smiled warmly when Bart and Rex walked through the doors of the Department of Justice. Most people had gone home, but Sid was the group head of the department. He hated drug traffickers with a passion and was more than willing to wait and review the wiretap application.

Sid refused to admit it, but he actually feared drug traffickers. And the more he feared them, the harder he worked to deny that fear. It was a vicious circle. The harder he worked, the more he had to fear. He was also starting to drink more.

Bart tossed a large manila envelope on his desk. Sid waited until both men sat down before talking. "You said on the phone that this involves Satans Wrath."

"It's all in there," said Bart. "Rex and I turned an informant. We've had him make a couple of buys while we watched to verify everything. He's been buying quantities of speed from a guy who goes by the name of Halibut. Through our guy, Halibut has been supplying all the speed to the Black Water Hotel."

"This Halibut is a member of Satans Wrath, is he?"

"He's been striking for the club for two years. He's still on probation, but I expect he'll be getting his full colours soon."

"Colours?"

"Yeah, his patch. The cutoff jackets they wear. Right now he only has British Columbia written on the bottom. It's what they call the bottom rocker. Once he's done strikin', the full name of the club and their skull emblem gets sewn on, too."

Without so much as a glance at Bart and Rex, Sid opened a large drawer on the side of his desk and removed three glasses and a bottle of Courvoisier. He told Bart to pour while he opened the envelope.

Eventually Sid looked up. "Nobody has caught any of these miscreants for a long time. If you're successful, I'll take you both out salmon fishing."

Bart and Rex smiled and clinked glasses. It was no secret that Sid's parents were extremely wealthy and had left him with a fortune when they died. Sid enjoyed life to the fullest. He lived on an acreage of oceanfront property northwest of the city and owned a cabin cruiser. Sid welcomed guests, and parties at his place were notoriously good. The haunt was secluded enough that police and prosecutors alike could unwind without facing the disapproval of a critical public. Bart was more than glad to be invited.

Last year Sid had contributed $20,000 to the Heart and Stroke Foundation. When asked why he still worked, Sid would say that it was for the sheer pleasure of putting bad guys in jail — a trait that Bart both respected and admired.

Sid told them that there would have to be some grammatical changes and rewriting of a few paragraphs concerning the reliability of the informant, but overall it looked good.

Sid was scheduled to start a trial on Monday but promised to burn the midnight oil and assured them that he would work on it over the weekend. If all went as planned, they should have it before a judge by Monday or Tuesday. Sid stared at the bottle of Courvoisier when they left. It occurred to him that he was beginning to despise alcohol as much as drug traffickers.

Damien sat at a table outside, overlooking the marina. He nodded for Wizard to sit down, and the waiter hurried over.

Wizard ordered a Grandview Island Stout. It was a local beer, one he preferred over the imports.

Damien waited until the waiter left before asking, "So what's The Suit's problem?"

Wizard shrugged indifferently. "Not a big problem. Just a rodent."

"In-house or out?"

"Gnawing outside one of the striker's houses. Halibut's place."

"Take care of it personally and be sure to advertise why."

"Why me?"

"Involves The Suit. The fewer who know, the better. Use Rolly as well."

"I want a driver."

"That's fine."

"I'll use Lance. He's —"

"Shut the fuck up. I don't need to hear all the details."

chapter fifteen

Danny walked toward the Black Water and saw Crystal talking to Marcie in an alcove. He stopped and pretended to tie his shoelace.

"You haven't eaten yet, have you?" said Crystal, sounding angry.

"I had a burger last night at suppertime," she whined.

"A burger! That's no good for ya! Ya gotta start lookin' after yourself better. Go an' get yourself a decent meal, for fuck's sake!"

"I can't. I haven't made any money yet. Red's gonna be real pissed at me."

"Fuck Red! She's a bitch. You should move out and come live with me."

"I can't. Red won't let me go until I pay up what I owe her. She would find me and —"

"Yeah, I know. I owe her too. But you're only twelve years old, for fuck's sake. You shouldn't be out here."

"I'm almost thirteen. My birthday is a week tomorrow."

"Like that makes a big fuckin' difference. They got ya hooked yet? Are ya usin'?"

Marcie looked down at her feet as she spoke. "I've tried it a few times, but I'm no junkie. I can handle it. I only use it, like, maybe two or three times a week."

"Goddamn it! You *can't* handle it. Believe me, I know! My little sister died with a spike in her arm. She told me she could handle it, too!"

Danny couldn't hear Marcie's reply, but he had no problem hearing Crystal.

"Bullshit! Soon it'll be two or three times a day, then six times a day!"

Marcie didn't respond. Crystal grabbed her by the arm and said, "Come on, I'm takin' ya to buy you some dinner. You're as small as a mouse. In fact, I think that's what I'm gonna start callin' ya. Mouse!"

As Crystal led Marcie away, she glared at Danny. He quickly stood up and entered the tavern. He saw Red sitting near the pool tables and took a seat where he could discreetly watch. He saw Leonard walk over and say something to her. She laughed and slapped him on the arm. Leonard then walked over to the rear door and disappeared outside.

Red stared after Leonard as he left. When the door banged shut, she held up her hand and cupped her fingers to her palm a couple of times as she waved goodbye. It was how a little girl would wave. It didn't suit her.

Minutes later, Jack entered the bar as the sound of sirens came to a screaming halt in the rear alley. A crowd spilled out of the Black Water to see what the commotion was. Jack glanced at Danny, who gave him a subtle shrug. They joined the crowd in the alley. A police officer gestured for everyone to stand back while her partner radioed for assistance.

Leonard was sprawled on his back behind her. A profuse amount of blood had pooled by his mouth and the end of his tongue lay on his chest. More blood had run down from his forehead where the word *RAT* had been carved. Jack saw that the blood had stopped running. *His heart isn't pumping. He's dead.*

The crowd eventually started to disperse down the alley. Red caught up to Jack and tugged on his sleeve.

"Let's take a walk," she said. "Gotta talk to ya."

"What was that all about?"

"Looks like he musta been a rat. Good thing someone offed him."

"Right on. So what do ya want to talk to me about?"

"There's gonna be some changes around here. Spider's gonna be handlin' most of the inside stuff from now on. He'll be workin' for me."

"Spider? I won't deal with him. Someone at his table got busted just the other night."

"Relax. That's why I'm talkin' to ya. I'll still come down here sometimes. With the amount you been scorin', I'll deal with you direct. I got a pager now. If I'm not around, you can give me a buzz. It's the type that vibrates. Think I'll keep it in my crotch, so call me often."

They rounded the corner toward the hotel and saw Crystal and Marcie walking ahead of them. Red called Marcie over.

"What are you doin' with Crystal?" she demanded. "You're supposed to be workin'!"

"She just bought me some food. I was hungry."

"Yeah? You got what ya owe me?"

"No. I just got here when she came along, so..."

"Next time work first and eat later."

Marcie nodded her head, then looked nervously at Jack.

"Ain't interested, girl," he said, then looked at Red and added, "This kid looks pretty young. With what just happened out back, there's gonna be a lot of heat around here."

Red thought for a moment, then replied, "You're right. You should be an investment consultant or somethin'." She turned to Marcie and said, "Someone carved up a rat out back. Fuck off home now. Give ya a few days off before comin' down here again."

Jack poured Danny another shot of Jose Cuervo and then leaned back on his sofa and put his feet up on the coffee table.

"So Bart and Rex must have rolled Leonard instead of busting him," said Danny.

"I hadn't counted on that, but it's good police work. They were working their way up."

"Yeah, but it was us who set him up. What we did got him killed."

"That was a bonus. Except now we better give things a few days to cool off. His murder could attract some heat from the City."

"Getting someone killed was a bonus?"

"Took out a rung in the ladder. Red is dealing direct with Wrath now. I'll start buying more until I get to the kilo level. It'll just be a matter of time before we find someone to roll over."

"Yeah, like Leonard?"

"Somebody a lot smarter and somebody with more to lose. Someone on the inside. Leonard was small-time. He probably had a loose tongue."

"Yeah, real loose. The end of it fell out on his chest. And where the hell do you plan on coming up with the money to buy quantity?"

"Thinking of Leonard gives me an idea. I still have those two ounces I bought from Red last time. I'll use that to get money. All we have to do is —"

"You're not! Tell me you don't plan on selling that shit."

"Christ, Danny!" Jack slammed his drink down on the end table. "You don't know me at all, do you?"

No, I don't. And that's what scares the shit out of me!

chapter sixteen

Louie Grazia hung up the phone and pursed his lips while straightening his tie. Why did Assistant Commissioner Isaac want to see him? Isaac had a reputation for being both fair and firm. But he also had the power to make or break a person's career at the snap of his fingers.

Maybe it wasn't really serious. Had someone been in his office again? Isaac did have a quirk about his personal office. Louie recalled several months earlier when Isaac came in to work and found a small sticky mark on the glass top of his desk. No doubt someone drinking in the officer's lounge the night before had gone in to use his phone and put a drink down. Isaac was furious and threatened harsh punishment if it ever happened again.

"Go on in, Louie, he's waiting for you."

Louie smiled cordially at the secretary, then walked across the plush carpet leading into Isaac's spacious office. Isaac was seated behind a large oak desk.

Directly behind him was a stuffed buffalo head mounted high on the wall. The curved black horns and shaggy head gave it a majestic appearance as it stared out over the room. The men under his command had presented it to him years earlier as a gift when he was transferred out of the Yukon. Below it were two lances crisscrossed on the wall.

Isaac looked formidable. He was a big man who had a bushy grey handlebar moustache, thick grey eyebrows, and a horseshoe pattern of grey hair around a bald head. He liked to canoe, and his large, muscular arms handled this hobby with ease. His eyes were a deep brown that at times looked black. He was a no-nonsense type who expected nothing short of excellence from his subordinates. Those who didn't measure up were transferred or forced to retire.

Beside a Bible on his desk was a picture of his wife. Several family pictures lay flat on the table under the glass. In front of his desk were several overstuffed brown leather chairs.

The curtains on the large windows were open, giving an unobstructed view of the mountains. The sun shining in cast a reverent glow over the room.

Louie recognized the long, serious face of Inspector Ted Nash. He was in charge of the Vancouver City Police Vice Section. Beside him sat Wigmore, whose much smaller office was across the hall.

"Good morning, Louie. Have a seat. I believe you and Ted know each other?"

"Yes, sir, we met once before, thank you."

"Read this report Ted brought over and tell me what you think."

Louie took the report. It outlined the murder of a Leonard Waschuk, who was found behind the Black Water Hotel three days ago. *Damn it! What the hell has*

Jack been up to? Louie silently read on. Leonard was shot upwards through the lower jaw with a .22-calibre pistol. The end of his tongue had been cut off and placed on his chest. The word *RAT* had been carved on his forehead. Louie glanced at a colour photograph of the victim before reading further. A potato was visible beside Leonard's head.

"A .22-calibre slug," remarked Louie. "Professional hit. Very little noise and just enough power for the bullet to ricochet around inside the skull and turn the brain to mush. The potato was used as a silencer to make the weapon even quieter. With Ted being here, I presume the victim was a City informant?"

Isaac smiled briefly at Nash before answering, "You've hit the nail on the head! He was a methamphetamine dealer who purchased the drug from a probationary member of Satans Wrath Motorcycle Club. Someone who goes by the nickname of...?"

"Halibut," said Nash.

"Ted tells me there were a few people in his office who knew he was an informant."

"That's right," said Nash. "The two detectives who turned him in the first place, and maybe three or four others."

"Why should this involve us?"

"Ted's men had read a bulletin put out by our Homicide Section saying that they were interested in cross-matching methamphetamine. They called them to let them know what they had and that they were planning on running wire."

"We'd just obtained a wiretap order on Halibut when it happened," said Nash. "That was a couple of days ago. There's been nothing on the lines to help us yet."

Louie looked at Nash and said, "You think someone on Homicide let it leak? Would your men have given them Leonard's name?"

"They didn't give out his name to anyone, not that it would take a rocket scientist to figure it out. That's not why I'm here, and I'm definitely not accusing anyone. This Leonard wasn't the sharpest needle in the pile. My guess is he probably blabbed to his girlfriend or someone. I'm here because your Homicide Section said that your office is doing some work in the area. I was wondering if you had any sources that could give us a lead on the murder?"

"I would think Halibut would be a pretty good suspect."

"He would," replied Nash, "except he pissed on the side of one of our uniform cars that day at about noon."

Louie caught the frown that Isaac gave Nash. He did not condone swearing, and there was little doubt that if Nash didn't work for another agency, Isaac would have reprimanded him.

"The murder happened around suppertime," continued Nash. "Halibut was locked up in the drunk tank then. He wasn't released until the following morning."

"How convenient," replied Louie.

"This informant was involved in trafficking in methamphetamine," said Isaac as he looked at Louie. "Your office does have some sort of ... intelligence probe concerning methamphetamine in that vicinity. Correct?"

"Yes, sir. Project 13. Taggart and O'Reilly have been working on identifying the source of methamphetamine coming into Vancouver. We suspect that Satans Wrath is behind it."

Wigmore smacked his hands together and sat forward in his chair. "Precisely," he said, looking pleased. "And I understand that Taggart has an informant around the Black Water Hotel who recently supplied him with an ounce of speed. At least, I think that's what his report said?"

"Yes, sir. That's correct."

"Taggart," mused Isaac. "I've read several of his reports over the years. There's something about him. He seems rather ... intuitive."

Grazia caught the eye contact between Isaac and Wigmore. There was little doubt as to who had sparked Isaac's curiosity about Taggart.

Isaac sat back in his chair and smiled as he spoke. Grazia knew he was anything but relaxed. It was a simple ploy. To appear relaxed when you're fishing for information. This makes other people relax, and sometimes things just slip out in casual conversation.

"Sir?" asked Grazia.

"I just can't quite put my finger on it." Isaac glanced at Nash and said, "It's uncanny. He accurately predicts internal problems that criminal organizations will be having well in advance." Isaac looked at Grazia, gave a small chuckle, and asked, "So what's his little secret?"

"He is exceptionally astute, sir. Definitely the best man I have. He's unique, innovative, a hard worker and —"

Isaac leaned forward, slapping his hands down on his desk. "Yes, yes, but there's something else! Why is it that major criminal groups suddenly start killing themselves off once he starts to investigate?" His dark eyes studied Grazia's face.

"Well, sir, it is easier to investigate a group that is suffering internal problems. Naturally a good investigator would strike while the iron is hot, so to speak."

Isaac's gaze remained riveted on Grazia for a moment, and then he leaned back in his chair and said,

"Well, I'm sure you know your men. In any event, if this Project 13 uncovers any information that will assist Ted here, I expect you to cooperate fully."

Wigmore smirked and said, "Well, considering that a homicide just took place, I think it would be prudent for Taggart to provide us with the full name and address of his informant. Perhaps the ... informant is somehow involved."

"Sir." Louie looked directly at Isaac. "As a matter of policy, we don't disclose the names of informants to anyone. It's just not —"

"I really don't need to know," said Nash.

"Nonsense," said Wigmore. "It would be good for at least you to know just in case the name surfaces in your investigation."

"It is unusual," said Isaac, "but under the circumstances, I fully agree. Who is the informant?"

"I'll check with Taggart and get back to you on that, sir. I think he only used the source once because we couldn't get funding."

Wigmore coughed loudly, then said, "I just saw Taggart at his desk a few minutes ago. With your permission, sir, why not have Louie use your phone and call him now."

Isaac gave a nod of approval and Louie called Jack and briefly explained where he was and what had transpired.

"No problem," said Jack. "Hang on while I get the name from out of my desk."

Jack ripped off an envelope taped to the back of his desk drawer and then held the telephone in the crook of his neck while sifting through multiple pieces of identification.

"We're waiting," said Grazia, with a noticeable edge to his voice.

"Sorry. Here's a name. I mean here's the name. Edward Trimble."

Grazia relayed the information to Ted Nash, who assured everyone that he would never disclose it but would keep it in mind in case it surfaced in the murder investigation. Wigmore also wrote down the name and address in his own notebook.

Later that afternoon Bart and Rex spotted their target. It wasn't difficult; he was wearing exactly what the tipster had told them. He also appeared to be watching everyone around him when he left the phone booth. Rex stuck the plastic radio receiver in his ear and followed on foot, while Bart remained nearby in the car.

Rex watched his quarry duck down an alley and retrieve something from an empty takeout coffee cup lying in a window well.

Bart's radio crackled. "Bart, I think he just picked up. Ditch the car. Let's grab this mother before we lose him."

Moments later, Rex and Bart saw their target walk down another alley. Bart covered off one end of the alley while Rex hid and waited at the other end.

Rex crouched close to the wall. His muscles bulged under his shirt as he tensed in anticipation. All at once, his target loomed in front of him. Rex lunged for his throat. The victim's eyes widened in panic and the mouth gaped open, but then he disappeared!

It was Rex's turn to look surprised when the man ducked and left him grasping at air. He looked down as he sailed over the man and received a jab in both eyes with a pair of fingers.

Rex sprawled on the pavement, skinning both elbows. His target was doing an Olympic dash back down the alley. Rex clambered to his feet and stumbled after him, while wiping his eyes with his fingers.

Bart, peeking around the end of the alley, waited silently. There was no grab for the throat this time. Bart stepped quickly into the alley and buried one meaty, knuckle-bound fist deep into the man's midriff. A belch of air escaped the man's mouth and he collapsed to the ground as two baggies fell from his hand.

"Ya got 'im," panted Rex, still wiping his eyes with the sleeve of his jacket. "Jesus, he's fast!" he said, giving the man a solid kick to the ribs.

"He sure got you dancin' in the alley like a wounded prairie chicken!" said Bart, picking up the baggies.

"The bastard poked me in the eyes! I couldn't see!" he said, kicking once more.

Danny, parked down the next alley, held the binoculars to his eyes with one hand while eating an apple. He stopped chewing and chuckled when he saw Bart slam their quarry back against a wall.

Minutes later, Bart and Rex drove into an underground parking lot. Their quarry, whom they identified as Edward Trimble, lay slouched in the back seat. He was more than willing to cooperate in exchange for not going to jail. He admitted that he bought the speed from Red, who used to buy it from Lenny. He said Red now bought it from someone in Satans Wrath. Fast Eddy, as Bart called him, was willing to make more purchases from Red if they supplied the money. He thought he might soon be able to deal with Satans Wrath directly if Bart and Rex wanted him to. They did.

Danny leaned over and opened the car door and watched as Jack eased himself inside.

"You took a few good licks there," Danny commented.

"Had to make it look real. They bought it. Money shouldn't be a problem now."

Danny started the car and said, "Where to?"

"My ribs are sore. Maybe stop by the clinic to check things out."

"Check things out? What things?"

"Shut up and drive."

"Oh, those things."

chapter seventeen

During the next couple of days, Jack purchased another order of speed from Red. Bart and Rex were pleased. They were able to follow Red to a restaurant where they saw her meet with John Dragonovich, another striker for Satans Wrath, who went by the name Dragon.

Bart and Rex were delighted when Fast Eddy said that Red was becoming receptive to introducing him to her connection in the event she wasn't available, providing that Fast Eddy was buying quarter-pounds or more. They told him they wanted two more small purchases from Red, then they would have him make larger purchases.

Marcie warily walked toward the car as it stopped by the curb and peered through the open passenger window at the man who was driving. The sun was low in the sky, and she squinted as she tried to make out his face while checking him out.

"Hey, mister! Looking to party?"

"Maybe."

"Think maybe you'd like to party with me? I could show you a good time." She tried to put some enthusiasm into her voice.

"Sure, little girl, you'll do just fine."

"You got your own place?"

"No."

"Well, that's okay. We can use my place." Marcie held up a key to a room at the Black Water. A room Red told her to share with two older hookers.

"You look like you're just a kid!"

Marcie shrugged, forcing a smile. "So? Do you want to party with me or not?"

"I don't know. I guess you'll do. But if I'm not getting a real woman, I'm not payin' more than thirty."

"Hey! Get real! The room cost me that much!"

"Take it or leave it. You look like you could use the money. Aren't you hungry for a little food, or maybe somethin' to get high?"

"Not that hungry!" Marcie turned on her heel and walked away.

"You'll be sorry, girl! Next time my offer won't be so good!" he yelled, speeding off.

She watched the car drive out of sight. Then she waited, pacing back and forth. She tried to make eye contact with the drivers of various cars as they drove by. Some would slow down to gawk. One car with three young men pulled over to the curb. They laughed and quickly drove off when she approached. She wondered what other girls were doing on their thirteenth birthday.

*

Danny watched Jack say goodbye to Red and slip out the back door of the Black Water. He ordered another beer. Jack would be meeting with Rex and Bart so there was no hurry. An hour later, he went to the car on the second level of the parking garage. Jack was peering through the binoculars as he arrived.

"How did it go?" Danny asked.

Jack put the binoculars down and said, "Good. Scored from Red again. Bart asked me if I would be willing to testify. Explained the witness protection program to me."

"They'll be pissed if they ever find out who you really are."

"I played along. Bart said just one more small score and they'll start funding larger transactions."

"Great. The sooner we're out of here the better I'll feel," said Danny, while unconsciously massaging his jaw. It ached from grinding his teeth in his sleep.

"I know," said Jack. "You don't like working in this den of snakes."

"Who are you watching?"

Jack passed the binoculars to Danny and he saw Marcie on the sidewalk a short distance from the hotel. He heard someone yell from directly below where they were parked.

"Hey, Mouse!"

"Cyrstal!" Marcie yelled back, then crossed the street.

Jack and Danny got out of their car and peeked over the edge at Marcie and Crystal.

Marcie was pleased that Crystal gave her a hug.

"So, Red has got ya back out on the street," observed Crystal.

"Just started."

"How much ya usin' now?"

"I sort of did what you told me."

"Sort of?"

"I only used twice this last week."

"Twice is twice too much! Damn it, Mouse, if you can't quit now, you won't be able to by next week. Then you'll be here until ya die! Which won't take long."

"Yeah. I gotta get to work. I need to make some money." Marcie started to walk away.

"Hold it! Don't go yet. I got somethin' for ya!"

Danny watched Crystal reach in her purse as Marcie walked back to her. He couldn't hide his sarcasm when he whispered, "Bet the bitch is giving her some dope just to help her out a bit!"

Marcie examined what Crystal gave her and said, "Oh, Crystal! It's beautiful! A little glass mouse! Look! It's got little beady eyes and black whiskers! It's really cute!"

"Yeah, well, I wanted to give ya somethin' for your birthday. It's made out of crystal, just like my name, so you'll think of me."

Danny was shocked. "A birthday present?" he whispered.

"A real den of snakes," commented Jack, as they quietly got back in the car.

Danny sat quietly.

"They should all be shot," added Jack.

"Up yours. I get the point."

"Good. We'll soon be out of this neighbourhood. You can take a crack at her then. Doubt that she'll listen to you, though."

Wigmore received a call back from Vital Statistics. He wasn't surprised. Yes, they had a record for Edward Trimble. He died of a drug overdose two years ago.

Wigmore reached for a file he had marked "Project Hotshot."

It was Friday night when Jack paged Red and arranged to meet inside the Black Water within the hour. It was to be the last small purchase. Red said her connection didn't trust her enough to handle large quantities yet. If Jack wanted a larger amount, she would have to bring in her connection. It was what he had hoped for. Bart and Rex assured him that they would have the authority next week to provide the money to make bigger purchases.

Jack and Danny parked in the parking garage and Jack went to the hotel. Danny waited a discreet amount of time before walking down the ramp toward the street. He had reached the ground level of the parking lot when a voice spoke behind him.

"Good evening, officer!"

Danny spun around as Crystal walked up to him.

"I'm not a cop!"

Crystal laughed and said, "Damn right, you are! I've been watching. The way you swing your arms says you're a Mountie. City cops don't take that much drill marching, or whatever it's called. Not to mention," she clicked her teeth before continuing, "you're on a dental plan."

"You're mistaken. I used to sell cars."

"Yeah, right! Don't worry about it. I'm not going to tell. I'm leaving tomorrow."

"Taking your yearly holiday to the Mediterranean?"

"Don't I wish. Naw, I'm goin' back east. I finally saved up enough to do it. I'm gonna go back to school. I want to be a social worker. Bet that surprises the shit out of ya, huh?"

Danny was momentarily stunned.

"Told ya it would shock the shit out of you!"

"Crystal, to tell you the truth, I think that's great. I wish you all the best, I really mean it."

"Thanks."

"Why spend your last night down here?"

"Just hoping to convince someone to come with me."

"Marcie?"

"Yeah." Crystal looked at Danny and smiled before continuing. "I saw you spyin' on us that day when you were pretendin' to tie your shoelace. That was the same day that Lenny got whacked. You should have been in the alley catchin' them instead of spyin' on me and Marcie."

Danny didn't know how to respond and said nothing.

"It still pisses me off that you don't arrest kids like her and get their sorry little asses off this street. Nobody seems to give a shit about kids."

"I care, but —"

"Yeah, I know. Nothin' you can do. It just pisses me off, is all."

"You said it was 'them' who whacked Lenny. Who is 'them'?"

Crystal thought for a moment, then glanced all around before saying, "I'll tell ya what. I'll give ya a tip, but promise you'll wait until tomorrow before doin' anything."

"I'm really not a cop. I'm just curious. I won't say anything to anyone."

Crystal chuckled, then said, "God, you're a horrible liar, but I'll tell ya anyway. Red is the key. She knows who did it. She fuckin' works for them."

"Who is 'them'?"

"I'm not that stupid. You'll have to find that out through her somehow. Now, I gotta go. Nothin' personal, but talkin' to you makes me feel nervous."

Crystal sauntered across the street. O'Reilly stared after her, then started to walk toward the hotel. After a few steps he realized he was swinging his arms. He shoved his hands in his pockets and glanced back at Crystal. She gave him the thumbs-up sign. Danny took one more look at Crystal when he reached the door. She was standing on the sidewalk looking around. Marcie was not in sight. Danny entered the bar and sat at his usual table.

A few minutes later, Crystal found Marcie working the street at the end of the alley that came out from behind the Black Water. Heat escaped from a large vent on a building and Marcie huddled close to it.

"Hey, Mouse! What ya doin' workin' back here?"

"It's warmer."

Crystal looked down the alley. "Yeah, also more dangerous. Come on. I got somethin' to show ya!"

Marcie walked with Crystal over to the parking garage. Her wide eyes and open mouth revealed her astonishment when Crystal held up a set of keys.

"Crystal! Is it yours? You actually bought a car? Or is it...?"

"No. I bought it! Get in! It's mine!"

Marcie quickly got in. "It looks great! I can't believe it!" She giggled.

Crystal smiled while nodding her head. She started the car and backed out of the stall.

"Where we goin'?" asked Marcie, sounding excited.

"Just around the block." Crystal drove down the street before glancing at Marcie and saying, "I want to talk to ya. I'm leavin' tomorrow morning. Goin' back to Ontario."

"You're leaving?" Marcie looked like she was going to cry.

"You can come with me! I'll either drop you off with your grandma or you can come and stay with me.

We'll get straight jobs."

Marcie stared wide-eyed at Crystal and shook her head. "No, oh no, I can't!"

"Why not? Because of Red?"

Marcie looked down and didn't answer.

"That bitch! Fuck her! You don't want to live with her! You can stay at my place tonight. I got a lot of stuff to pack but there'll be room for you. We'll leave first thing in the morning."

"But what if they come after us? They know where you live!"

"Fuck them!"

Marcie thought briefly, then said, "No, Crystal, you go, but I better stay. Thanks anyway."

"Why not? Look what they make you do! Those bastards! Get out now while you can!"

"Maybe in a few weeks I'll leave. But right now … like, I still owe them money."

"You owe them money? Bullshit! They say I owe them, too, but fuck 'em. Do you have any idea how much money I've paid them already? They always say you owe them!"

"But they're everywhere! They'll find you, and then somethin' will happen to…"

Crystal arrived back at the parking garage and looked for a place to park.

"Come on, Marcie! Please come with me. Now! Before it's too late. I'll just find a place to park and we'll talk about it. I don't wanna be burnin' up gas."

"See? That's just it. I don't have enough money to pay you for taking me."

"I'm not askin' ya for any bread! I've got enough to get us there. It'll be tight. We won't exactly be eatin' three meals a day, but we can still do it."

"So, like, we could just go? Right now?"

"Right fuckin' now!"

The car stalled and rolled to a stop. Crystal tried repeatedly to start it. Eventually the battery became weak and the engine wouldn't turn over.

Marcie quietly got out of the car and walked away.

Danny caught a subtle nod from Jack. It was time to go. Jack had said they had the weekend off. He was looking forward to it.

Danny left the bar first. He heard Crystal crying when he walked into the lower level of the parking garage. She was trying to push her car into a parking stall. Danny helped her. She tried to start the car again. No luck. Danny checked the battery cables. They were well connected and the battery looked new.

"What happened? It sounds like it's out of gas."

"It's got half a tank. It just fuckin' quit," she sobbed.

"Did you find Marcie?"

"Yeah. I think she was gonna come with me until this piece of shit...!" Crystal kicked the side of the car and then cried louder.

"Maybe it's nothing serious," said Danny.

"Yeah, nothin' serious if ya got a regular fuckin' paycheque," she yelled.

"Give me your keys," Danny demanded.

"Why? It won't fuckin' go! Marcie won't fuckin' go! I can't fuckin' go, either!"

"Give me your keys and I'll give you my cell number. Call me tomorrow morning."

Later, Jack listened closely as Danny told him what happened.

"Why not have her take the bus?"

"I suggested that. She says she has too much stuff that she wants to take with her."

Jack sighed, then said, "Okay, I'll pay half."

"I wasn't asking you for money."

"If it gets her out of here, it'll be worth it. The sooner the better. I'm meeting Natasha for lunch tomorrow. Call me later in the day and let me know if they can fix it and what it costs."

"A second date with Natasha?"

Jack smiled, then said, "What? You keeping notes on me, Danny?"

It was dinnertime the next day when Crystal met Danny at a garage. Her car, equipped with a new fuel pump, was running smoothly.

She hugged him and gave him a kiss on his cheek and then said, "I hope your wife doesn't mind."

"My wife?" Danny asked.

"The lady watching us from that car over there. She is your wife, right?"

Danny chuckled, then waved at Susan. "Yes, she's my wife."

"She's pretty."

"Come on. It's against policy, but I'll introduce you to her and Tiffany."

Susan gave Crystal a hug and wished her luck, then Danny walked her back to her car.

"What about Marcie?" he asked.

"I phoned her. She won't go."

"You phoned her? I thought you wanted to be a social worker! You've got to try harder than that! Go see her. Don't take no for an answer!"

*

Marcie answered the knock on her apartment door. Her look of surprise at seeing Crystal was quickly overtaken by fear.

"What do you want?" she whispered. "Red's just gettin' out of the tub."

"It's fixed. It was just a gas thing. Runnin' good now."

"I told you on the phone that I'm not going."

"I'm not taking no for an answer."

"Crystal, I can't. You're my best friend and everything, but I can't."

"Come on! It's stupid to stay here!"

Marcie thought about Red and the big man with the goatee. She thought about her grandma and the pictures. No, she could never go back. She looked at her friend and slowly shook her head as tears streamed down her cheeks.

Crystal lowered her voice but the intensity of her words was clear. "Come on, Mouse! Walk out right now. Don't worry about your things. Just leave. Come with me now."

"I can't. I'm afraid they'll ... I just can't! You go."

"I really want you to come with me!"

With a quivering smile she said, "Thanks, Crystal, but no. Except maybe for my grandma, you're the only real friend I've ever had. Good luck."

"You won't change your mind?"

Marcie stared down at her feet, then shook her head. She felt Crystal's hand on her shoulder and turned to look her in the face. Crystal was crying too.

"This is silly," said Crystal. "Everything will work out, you'll see! I'll get hold of ya real soon! We're friends for life, right?"

"I'll always keep the mouse in my purse to remind me of you," she replied.

Red, wearing only a towel wrapped around her, appeared behind Marcie. "What the fuck is goin' on?" she asked.

Crystal was defiant. "I'm movin' back east. Leavin' tomorrow morning. Just seein' if Marcie wants to join me."

"Leavin'? Like fuck you are! You owe me money! So does this little bitch here! You're not going anywhere until I tell ya you —"

Crystal's punch caught Red high in the stomach. She buckled and gasped for air. Crystal shoved her back inside and slammed the door shut.

Red swore at Crystal from inside the apartment, but she didn't open the door.

"See?" said Crystal. "She's not so fuckin' tough if she doesn't have any of her goons around. Come on, let's split. The both of us!"

"I can't."

"Marcie! Listen to me!" pleaded Crystal. "Ya stay here, and you're gonna die! Believe me, I know what I'm sayin'."

Red's voice came through the door, "Marcie, you better get back in here, right now!" Seconds later, they heard the sound of cutlery as Red rummaged in a kitchen drawer.

Marcie looked at Crystal, then said, "I'm gonna go back inside now."

Crystal grabbed her by the shoulder and said, "I'll tell ya what, kid, in a month or so, when I get settled, I'll phone ya. If you change your mind, I'll send ya bus fare or whatever, okay?"

They wrapped their arms around each other and said a quick goodbye.

Marcie reached for the door, but Red yanked it open. She was naked and held a butcher knife in her hand. She pushed Marcie aside and stepped into the hallway. Crystal was gone.

chapter eighteen

The sun cast a crimson glow as it came up behind the Rocky Mountains. Crystal lugged her last garbage bag full of clothes out to her car. Her car was already packed, but she found room to wedge it behind her seat. She never looked back as she pulled out into the morning traffic.

She didn't see the orange van that wheeled in behind her. Axle, a striker for Satans Wrath, drove the van, while his only passenger, Nails, sat beside him. Nails had been a member of the club for six years. He earned his nickname because nails were a tool of his trade.

Crystal pulled into a gas station and filled her car. She saw the orange van in the reflection of her car window as it slowly drove by behind her. Minutes later, she paid for her gas and was walking back toward her car when she saw the van drive by again. The two men inside stared back at her.

She fought to control her fear. *Probably some past trick who recognizes me...* She spotted a cellphone on the seat of another car. The driver was inside paying for gas.

Moments later, Crystal pulled back out into traffic. There was no sign of the orange van and she felt foolish for being afraid. By the time she eased her car off the on-ramp and onto the eastbound lane of the Trans-Canada Highway, the sun was glistening down the western side of the mountains, sparkling off the snow on the peaks.

The sun was directly in her eyes, but it was Sunday morning and the traffic was light. She accelerated and passed a semi-truck before switching back to the slow lane. Seconds later, she saw the orange van in her rear-view mirror.

"Thanks for dropping by." Danny closed the door behind Jack and gestured to one of two sofas in his living room. "This is the new one. The other one needs to go upstairs. It's a hideaway bed. Weighs a ton. Susan and I would never get the damned thing up there by ourselves. Have you had breakfast yet? We've still got the coffee on."

"I've eaten. Let's move this and then I'll have a coffee before heading out to the farm. What about Crystal? What do I owe you?"

"The bill is in the kitchen. We can figure it out over coffee."

Danny led the way up the stairs while Jack wrestled with the lower end of the sofa. Halfway up the stairs the sofa became wedged on a landing. Both men paused to rest.

"Did she leave yesterday?" Jack asked.

"No. She called me last night and said she was heading out this morning." Danny's voice sounded glum.

"You did a good thing by helping her. Why the long face?"

"I was hoping she would take Marcie with her."

"You said she tried. What more did you expect her to do?"

"I told her to go over to Marcie's and talk to her direct. She did, but Marcie wouldn't go."

"Doesn't Marcie still live with Red?"

"Yeah."

"Was Red home when she went over?" There was concern in Jack's voice.

Danny chuckled. "That was the good part. I was going to tell you over coffee. Crystal gave her a knuckle sandwich and she backed right off. Too bad she didn't do it a long time ago." Danny saw the furrowed look on Jack's forehead and said, "You don't think that's funny?"

The conversation was interrupted when Danny paused to answer his cellphone.

"Danny! I think I'm being followed!" The fear was evident in Crystal's voice.

"Where are you?"

"Two guys in a van. They could be bikers. They watched me gas up and now they're behind me on the freeway."

"Where are you?" Danny yelled into the phone.

"I'm on a cellphone. Just coming up to the Willingdon exit. What should I do?"

"Keep driving. Don't get out of your car and don't hang up. I'm on my way. You're less than ten minutes away from me!"

"Crystal's in trouble!" Danny yelled to Jack, while jumping over the railing. The glassware in the dining room vibrated, knocking into each other.

Seconds later, the tires squealed as Jack drove through the quiet residential street. Danny sat beside him and tried to talk calmly with Crystal. She said that she was driving in the slow lane but explained that she had changed her speed a few times and each time, the van had matched her speed.

"Danny! They're pulling alongside me now! What should I do?"

"Can you see them in your side mirror? Is the passenger window open? What about a sliding door?"

"Side mirror? The fucking passenger is practically beside me. His window is closed. The van doesn't have a sliding door!"

"Then they're probably not going to shoot at you. We're only five minutes away. What does the van look like? Can you see the plate?"

"Oh, Danny." Crystal started to giggle. "They drove right past! Didn't even look at me."

Danny heard Crystal laugh out loud, then she said, "I'm so stupid. I'm sorry. I shouldn't have called. I was just scared after seeing Red yesterday. Christ! I even ripped off some guy's cellphone..."

Nails turned in the passenger seat and looked out the rear window of the van. He held a small radio transmitter bought from a hobby shop. The kind intended for small remote-controlled airplanes. He nodded at Axle and then thumbed the control. Axle didn't slow down as the explosion sounded behind them.

The bomb, wrapped in nails, had been placed to blow the gas tank up into the interior of the car. Normally death would have been instant. Nails hadn't counted on the bags stuffed with clothes that Crystal had placed inside the car.

Danny heard the roar of the blast over his phone and the uninterrupted screaming that followed as Crystal's car came to a stop in the ditch.

A fire truck, returning from a small garage fire, witnessed the explosion as it drove in the westbound lane of the freeway. The driver cut across the meridian, but the truck became stuck in the middle. It was close enough that the firemen were at Crystal's car in less than a minute. The interior of the car was ablaze.

The firemen were using the jaws of life to cut open her door as Jack and Danny arrived. She gazed up at Danny for a few seconds, then died.

It wasn't the smell of burnt hair and flesh that would forever haunt Danny. It was the look in her eyes. They didn't express anger or fear. Only acceptance of death — and a look that asked him why he did this to her.

Jack put his hand on Danny's shoulder and said, "Come on. Let's get away from here before the media arrives."

Danny felt numb as he threaded his way past onlookers who were getting out of their cars. The sound of sirens could be heard approaching in the distance. He waited until getting in the car before turning to Jack and asking, "Why?"

"If Satans Wrath let her go they would start losing control of the others. That's why they didn't kill her with an overdose or something. This is the same as Lenny. They wanted to advertise. Make sure everyone knows what happens if you cross them."

"I killed her."

"What?"

"I killed Crystal. I told her to go see Red. If she hadn't, she would still be alive."

"It's not your fault. You didn't know."

"It is my fault ... and you know it!" Danny's voice cracked as he spoke.

Jack's anger showed in his voice. "You didn't know! If anything, it's my fault."

"Your fault?"

"I brought you into a world that you didn't even know existed. The rules are completely different. Crystal knew the rules and took her chances when she went over to Red's place."

"But I sent her to Red's! Looking back on it, I should have seen how scared she was."

"You didn't kill Crystal. She had her doctorate in street smarts! You're still in kindergarten. She knew that. Ultimately, it was her decision to do what she did."

"I feel sick, oh Jesus!" Danny said, while opening the car door and leaning out.

Jack put his hand on Danny's shoulder, and when he finished vomiting, Jack gently pulled him back into the car.

Jack pointed out the window and said, "Uniform is arriving. Homicide will be here soon. You've got to make a choice."

"About what?"

"You could tell them what you know about Red. Then they'll interview her."

"She'll just tell them to fuck off."

"I know. It would also heat her up. The narcs expect me to meet her and arrange a big score. They've probably got her phone and pager tapped."

"What choice do I have?"

"Find out who did this ourselves."

"What can we do that Homicide can't?"

"Homicide plays by society's rules. If you play by the rules of the world I work in, we might have a chance to get whoever did this."

Jack noticed that Danny was starting to shake, so he started the car and turned on the heat. "I'm going to drive you home. You can call Homicide after."

Danny didn't respond as Jack pulled out into the line of traffic and slowly drove past Crystal's body. It was on a stretcher and being covered with a yellow emergency blanket.

When Jack pulled into Danny's driveway, Susan ran from the house. Jack saw Danny speak to her, and then they held each other. He thought about calling Natasha but knew he wouldn't make very good company. *Same goes for Liz and Ben.* He would go back to his apartment and stare at the fish in his aquarium.

His thoughts were interrupted when Danny got back in the car.

"What are you doing?" Jack asked.

"I want you to teach me."

"Teach you?"

"The rules. I want to know the rules."

"Today's not the day. You need time to clear your head. Go back to Susan. You're lucky to have her."

"She'll be okay. Come on. Let's go."

"Go where?"

"I don't know!" Danny yelled. "Just find out who did it! Go over and rip Red's face off if we have to!"

"That wouldn't work. You have to look at the big picture. Today's not the day to —"

"What big picture?" Danny screamed at him.

Jack sighed, then said, "Sit here. I'm going to talk with Susan."

Jack walked over to Susan and asked, "How are you doing?"

"I'll be okay," she replied. "Worried about Danny. He's hurting."

"I know."

"He's angry. I'm a little afraid he'll do something stupid right now."

"I'll look after him. We won't work. I'm going to take him back to my place for a talk."

"You mean you're going to get drunk."

Jack grimaced. *This woman has seen this picture*

before. "Possibly. He needs to vent. I've got a pullout bed in the living room if he needs to stay over."

"He snores," she said, then turned and walked back into her house.

Susan understood, sort of. She recalled the time Danny and a group of policemen had shown up at her house after the funeral of a murdered comrade. She had watched the alcohol slowly eat away at the tough facades on their faces. Everyone was polite, but the conversation was stilted, and she knew it was because she was there. She made an excuse to go to bed, and not long after she heard their emotions pouring out. Despite being a wife, she was still an outsider.

Right now, she felt angry and hurt. Why did he shut her out of his life at a time like this? She wanted to be with him, to make sure he was all right. This brotherhood of policemen that he belonged to ... sometimes it seemed like others knew him better than she did. She wanted to tell him how much she loved him and listen to him say they'd always be together. She looked at Danny's portrait and felt so alone.

The new bottle of Jose Cuervo was half empty. Danny knew it was the booze talking, but he said it anyway. "I want to kill whoever did this to her."

Jack shook his head. "I know how you feel, but you've got to look at the big picture."

"What the fuck is the big picture?"

"We're not dealing with one rotten animal. This is organized crime. They've got about nine hundred professional criminals in our area alone. Do you think it would really make any difference to Satans Wrath if you killed a couple of them?"

"It would make a difference to me!"

"You're damn right it would. You could end up in jail. Susan, Tiffany — gone! And for what? Satans Wrath will keep on going. There will still be other kids like Marcie and Crystal getting killed. You could lose everything and not change a thing."

"So what are you saying? That we give up or put whoever did this in jail?"

"Putting one or two in jail doesn't help either. In fact, it only helps *them*."

"Helps them?"

"Jails are a great place for them to recruit more trusted comrades. Instead of getting weaker, the club becomes stronger."

"Then what the hell can we do?"

"You either have to put dozens of the hierarchy in jail, which our laws aren't geared for, or you need to gain control of the club. Crime will continue, but if you can control the higher echelon, you can make the club less effective."

"And how do you expect to do that?"

"Turn someone on the inside. Once you have one informant, it's easier to get more. Then you penetrate the higher echelon. The fact that they're vicious killers is something we can use. That's why we have to find someone in the club who is like you."

"Like me?"

"Someone with a family who has too much to lose."

"I don't understand."

"You will when the time comes."

"I can't see any of them ratting out, unless maybe we put them in protective custody."

"Their rules don't usually allow that."

"What are you talking about? Their rules? We use our rules, and that includes the Witness Protection Program."

"For them, to break their rules is to lose respect. To lose respect means to lose one's life. If that life is not available to take, then the rules allow for other lives to be taken. Every son, daughter, wife, uncle, aunt, cousin, and close friend would have to be protected."

"That's impossible!"

"I know."

Danny thought for a moment, then said, "I'd kill them if they ever came near my family."

"So would I. You have my word on that."

Danny studied Jack's face closely. "You mean it, don't you?"

"Messing with a cop or his family is against the rules. I guarantee that the coroner would run out of body bags."

"You'd do that for me?"

Jack became exasperated. "What the hell do you think? If you're not prepared to do that, then the bad guys don't respect you. You're looked upon as being weak. It's the law of nature. If you're weak, then you die — or someone close to you does!"

"The bad guys know this?"

"The real professionals do. It's not something that's spoken about. If they respect you they should take that for granted."

"Others feel this way?"

"Most long-time UC operators do. What we know, what we have been through, it's like we're all family. Organized crime can afford to lose a few soldiers on the bottom. The only thing keeping a lot of us alive is that they know we would seek revenge against the executive level for authorizing the hit. I don't care if it's some poor cop on the other side of the country that gets whacked; it's a declaration of all-out war. Otherwise you won't survive."

"That's one of them rules?"

"That's one of them rules."

Danny thought it over. What would Wigmore think if he heard this? He thought of Crystal's eyes. He looked at Jack and said, "So this same rule doesn't apply to someone like Crystal?"

"No. The rules allow them to get away with killing her."

"Why?"

"She's not family. Think what you said earlier, you would kill them if they ever came near your family."

"What about your niece and nephew?"

Jack stared into his aquarium. He imagined that the eyes on the fish belonged to Maggie and Ben Junior. They were silently looking at him. They knew his promise. That was enough.

It was suppertime when Susan answered her door. She was surprised to see Natasha standing on her porch with a small bouquet of flowers and a bottle of Riesling wine.

"Jack called," explained Natasha. "Said he thought you could use some company. I would have come sooner but I had to work. Thought we could order in dinner if it's not too late."

Susan hugged Natasha harder than she expected to. She felt like her body was about to overflow with emotion.

Jack crushed the empty pizza box and put it in the garbage, then cleaned up the coffee table and put the glasses in the sink.

Danny lurched back from the washroom. "I'm beat. Don't feel so good," he mumbled.

"I'm not tired, so sleep in my bed," said Jack. "I put clean sheets on this morning and it's closer to the bathroom. Think you might need it."

"Where will you sleep?"

"The sofa pulls out if I need it. Get some sleep. I want to hit the street by noon."

"Why so early?"

"I want you to borrow a car from GIS and talk to Marcie as soon as she hits the street."

"After what happened to Crystal?"

"Especially after what happened to Crystal."

"She didn't listen to Crystal, she sure as hell won't listen to me!"

"Use Crystal's death to convince her. She'll end up dead if we let her stay there."

"She's liable to tell everyone I'm a cop. I wouldn't be able to cover you then."

"I'll only meet Red one or two more times. Then I'll be doing business elsewhere."

Danny mumbled in agreement and then wandered off to Jack's bedroom. Moments later, Jack knew that Susan was right. Danny did snore.

He turned out the lights and turned the television on to the news channel. He watched as the news of Crystal's death continued to recycle itself through the broadcast. He turned his attention to the paper fish. The light from the television cast an eerie glow on the aquarium. *What if I never find out who killed you?*

Perhaps it was the broadcast or the alcohol, or both, but he realized that his mind and body were spent. He could no longer focus and realized it was because of the tears filling his eyes and running down and dripping off his cheeks.

Eventually he drifted off to sleep.

chapter nineteen

It was dusk when Marcie arrived at the Black Water. She leaned against an air duct leading into the ally and watched indifferently as the four-door grey car with a microphone hanging from the dash pulled up to the curb.

Danny leaned over from behind the steering wheel and gestured with his finger for Marcie to approach the car. She sauntered over and opened up the passenger door.

"Good evening, officer, what can I do for you tonight?" she asked, giving a cocky smile.

"Get in the car, Marcie."

She groaned audibly. "Vice? How do you know my name?"

"No, I'm not Vice. My name's Danny O'Reilly. I just want to talk to you. Get in."

"Are you arresting me?"

"No."

Marcie glanced quickly up and down the street.

"Don't worry if someone sees you. Cops talk to hookers all the time. Hurry up and get in. We'll sit right here."

"You got no proof I'm a hooker."

"Get in!"

Marcie sat in the front seat and closed the door.

"So what's this all about? How come you know my name? If you're not Vice, what are ya, a narc?"

"No, I'm not a narc. I'm on an intelligence-gathering section with the RCMP. We've learned something that could save your life."

The smile masking Marcie's face was replaced by fear. She looked like the scared little girl she really was.

"Save my life? What are you talking about?"

Danny took a deep breath and slowly exhaled. "We know a lot about you, Marcie. Who you're involved with, what type of people they are."

"I'm not involved with anyone."

"What can you tell me about Crystal? Who killed her? Who was she involved with?"

Marcie gave a small, dry cough. "Crystal?" her voice cracked. "Is that the person who got killed on the freeway yesterday? I heard something about it on the news. I think she hung out down here sometimes, but I don't really know for sure."

"She was your friend, Marcie. Don't you care about what happened to her?"

"I said I didn't know her!"

"Three nights ago she met you here and wanted you to leave with her. Two nights ago she went to your apartment and asked you."

Marcie's face paled. "How do you know about that?"

"We know a lot of things. We also believe the same people who killed Crystal think you know too much. They're going to kill you too."

Marcie's mouth twitched, then she shook her head and replied, "I don't believe you! You're just saying that!"

"Marcie! Please! Think about what I've said! Talk to me and I'll make sure nobody hurts you. We'll look after you. Think about what happened to Crystal!"

Marcie was silent for a brief moment, then slowly shook her head.

"If you won't help me with who murdered your friend, then at least save your own life!"

"I can look after myself." Her wide eyes and trembling lips revealed she knew she couldn't.

"Come on, Marcie! Use your head!"

"I'm gettin' out," she said, opening the door.

"Marcie!" shouted Danny, grabbing her arm. "Believe me! I know what I'm saying!"

"Let go!" she wailed. "If I'm not under arrest, you can't do this!"

"Look, think about what I've said. I want to help you, I really do. Take my card. It's got my cell number. If you change your mind you'll know how to reach me."

Marcie reluctantly put the card in her purse and then got out of the car.

"Marcie," said Danny, before she closed the door, "I hope you saved the little glass mouse Crystal gave you, 'cause there's not much else left of her."

Marcie's eyes started to water, then she slammed the door and walked back to the mouth of the alley.

The hours slowly ticked by. Marcie stared at her watch to make sure it hadn't quit. She kept thinking about Danny. Was he telling the truth? How did he know so much?

His face looked familiar. She was sure he had been coming and going from the BW. *Should I tell Red? What if she thinks I squealed?*

She took his card out of her purse and looked at it before stuffing it back inside. *He said he'd look after me ... but look what happened to the guy in the alley when he ratted out!* She looked at the crystal mouse in her purse, then quickly closed it.

Almost midnight and still no customers. Typical Monday ... when things are dead.

She saw headlights coming down the alley from behind the hotel. A dark-coloured pickup truck came to a stop. The headlights partially blinded her, but she could make out the silhouette of a figure gesturing to her from behind the steering wheel. She walked around to the passenger side, putting one foot on the running board as she stuck her face up to the open window.

"Hey, mister, looking to party?" she asked with a smile. Her smile vanished when she saw that the man was wearing a ski mask that hid all but his eyes and mouth.

She stood transfixed as the barrel of a shotgun rose toward her face. Abruptly, the shotgun jerked to a stop when it caught in the seatbelt harness.

The man pulled it free and Marcie screamed and turned her face as she started to tumble to the ground. The roar from the shotgun echoed up the alley as the truck careened wildly out into the street and disappeared.

•

Danny answered his cellphone. Two minutes after that, Jack and Danny pulled up to the curb a few blocks away from the Black Water. There was a telephone booth nearby, but it was empty. Seconds later, a figure crawled out from under a parked car and ran toward them.

Jack watched her yank open the back door of the car and clamber inside. She was saturated with urine, rain, and mud. Jack noted her face around her eyes. It was dry.

The dirt and dust hadn't been stained. As scared as she was, she hadn't cried.

How hard has she become? Is she already like so many others down here whose brains protect them from their world by shutting out any emotion that causes pain? Completely incapable of any real feelings?

She looked out the back window of the car and then glanced out the side windows.

"You're safe now, Marcie," said Danny. "This is Jack Taggart, my partner."

Marcie turned to stare out the back window.

"Marcie! You're safe! You really are," said Jack. The gruff tone of his voice caught her attention. She looked at him for the first time, then said, "I know you! You were with Red a couple weeks ago! When that guy who ratted got killed in the back alley!"

"I was. Red doesn't know who I really am."

Marcie paused for a moment, then said, "You said somethin' that made Red take me off the street for a while."

"I tried to help. Sorry there wasn't anything else I could do."

Marcie stared briefly into his eyes, then her body relaxed and she held her head in her hands and wept.

Jack looked at Danny and said, "Let's go to my apartment. She can have a shower and warm up while I wash her clothes. Then we'll talk."

"We could take her to my house. Susan wouldn't mind."

"No," replied Jack quietly. "If things don't work out, I don't want anyone knowing where you live. It's easier for me to change apartments than for you to sell your house."

"Are we going to call Social Services?" asked Danny.

"I'm not going with them!" wailed Marcie. "They got people in there who tell them stuff. I know, 'cause

Red told me! You make me go there and I'll just run away. I mean it!"

"Take it easy," replied Jack. "Who do you mean when you say 'they'? You said, 'They got people in there.'"

"Bikers," she sobbed, "Satans Wrath."

He looked at Danny and whispered, "I believe her."

It was two hours later when Marcie stepped out of a warm shower, wrapped a towel around herself, and peeked out the bathroom door.

"Your clothes are on my bed," yelled Jack from the kitchen. "I didn't iron them, but they're clean. I just took them out of the dryer; they're probably still warm. I also put one of my shirts on the bed. Put it on, too."

Minutes later, Marcie walked into the kitchen. She looked flustered and gestured with her arms. She had rolled up the sleeves several times, but they still hung down to her wrists. The tail of Jack's shirt hung to her knees.

"Don't worry about it," said Jack. "It looks better than the tank top."

Marcie's face flushed and she sat down at the table.

"How do you like your eggs?" asked Jack, opening the refrigerator.

"I — I'm not hungry," she replied, sitting down at the kitchen table. "Thank you for washing my clothes. I was so scared I pissed ... I mean wet myself."

"So who tried to kill you, Marcie?" asked Jack, while dumping a package of bacon into a frying pan. "You said somebody took a shot at you. Do you know who it was? Did you see their faces or get a licence number of the car?"

"It wasn't a car, it was a truck. It was just one guy. He was wearing a ski mask. I didn't see any licence plate, but I think it was a black truck, or maybe blue."

Marcie drew her feet up onto the chair and wrapped her arms around herself as she started to tremble. "I don't know how he missed me. It was really close! It must have gone over the top of my head, just as I turned and fell."

"Do you have any idea who it was?" asked Jack.

"No, but it was a biker."

Jack and Danny exchanged a quick glance. Jack asked, "How do you know? You said you couldn't see him too well."

"Well, I just know. That's who killed Crystal, 'cause she was runnin' out on them. Red told me I was lucky I didn't go with her or they'd have killed me, too."

"Do you know who killed her?" asked Jack.

Marcie shook her head. "I don't know. I hardly ever saw them. Just one guy. He's really big and has a grey goatee. Red told me we all work for Satans Wrath. They charge all the girls a hundred bucks a day. She said they'd kill us if we try to leave owin' them money."

Marcie looked over at Danny and said, "Crystal did want me to go with her."

"She liked you," said Danny.

"She was my friend," admitted Marcie, starting to weep.

"Try to relax," said Jack. "I want you to tell us everything from the beginning. Why you left home. Who your relatives are. How you met Red. I want to know everything that's ever happened to you, including things you've heard or saw. How much dope you're using … everything. Understand?"

Marcie wiped the tears from her eyes. "It's gonna take a long time."

"That's okay," said Jack. "We want all the details." He looked at the frying pan and knew the smell of bacon wafting through the apartment would be hard to resist. "Are you sure you won't change your mind on some breakfast? It'll help warm you up."

"Well, okay, thanks. Maybe a little," replied Marcie, giving Jack a quick smile.

It was one o'clock in the afternoon before Marcie finished telling everything she could about herself, including what happened the night she was taken to a motel and what she knew about everyone else.

Danny went to the office and returned with two large photo albums.

"I want you to look through these pictures very carefully," said Jack. "They're photographs of every known member of Satans Wrath living in British Columbia. I want to see if you can recognize if it was one of them who drove you to the cabin."

"If he's in here, I'll know him."

Marcie turned just two pages before sitting up rigidly in the chair.

"That's him!" She stabbed at the picture with her finger. "That's the guy right there!"

"Are you sure?" asked Danny.

Marcie glared at Danny. "Of course I'm sure! I'll never forget his face. Never!"

Jack took the book and looked at the picture. "Randy Bennett, alias Wizard. He's the president of the west-side chapter."

He thought about the significance of this. An executive member of Satans Wrath wouldn't act as a pimp for some young girl or supply drugs to anyone who wasn't a club member. Those jobs would be left for more expendable members. Whomever Wizard drove Marcie to meet in the cabin must be so important, or secret, that he wouldn't delegate the job to someone else.

Jack looked at Marcie. *How small and pathetic she looks. Life has dealt her a pretty dirty hand ... yet there is still a spark of stubbornness in her. She's not the type to give up easily.*

"Good going, Marcie. I'm proud of you."

"You're proud of me?" She looked surprised.

"Yes, I am. You're a fighter. You've been through a hell of a lot. Right now, though, I think you should go in there and get to bed. You've been through enough for one day!"

"What are you goin' to do with me? Like, I can't stay here. You've only got one bedroom. My grandma's in a nursing home, so I can't stay with her."

"Trust me," replied Jack, trying to give her a reassuring smile. "We won't toss you out on the street. We are your friends. Real friends. I want you to remember that."

Marcie smiled. "Thanks. For cops ... I mean police, you guys are really nice."

"Get some sleep; we'll figure something out."

An hour later Jack peeked in the bedroom and saw she was asleep. When he returned to the living room, Danny asked, "Do you think she's honest about only using dope a few times?"

"I saw her arms when you went to the office. She pushed up her sleeves to wash the dishes. She didn't have much in the way of needle marks. She told us about everything else, so I don't think she would lie about that."

"You made her wash the dishes after what she's been through!"

"She insisted on washing while I dried. I think she wanted me to see her arms, to show she was telling the truth."

"She's a spunky kid. Most adults would be in a psych ward by now if they'd been through what she has."

"She's a tough little character. Pretty sharp, too. I also asked her if she told anyone about you being a cop. She said she didn't. She was too scared."

"Do you believe her?"

"Yes."

"Maybe I can still give you inside cover."

"I'll meet Red tomorrow and try to arrange to meet her source later in the week."

"So Eddy Trimble rides again."

"A little longer, then he'll disappear."

Danny pointed toward the bedroom and said, "I still can't help but wonder how she would have turned out if she had been raised by a real parent instead of a monster. I hope she's not so screwed up now that it's too late."

Jack nodded in agreement.

"Too bad she doesn't know who is supplying Red or who planted the bomb under Crystal's car. Maybe it's that Wizard guy."

"I'm definitely going to take a personal interest in him," said Jack. "But before *justice* is served on Wizard, I'm going find out who molested her in the cabin. From her description, it didn't sound like a biker."

Danny wondered what Jack's definition of justice was. He cleared his throat and said, "She said something, that he called her cutesy, or something about, 'Cutesy, it's your turn now.' Was he talking to her, or was he talking to the dog?"

"I don't know. I don't think she knew. The guy was smart enough to avoid DNA."

"Probably been busted before."

"Maybe." Jack leaned forward and whispered to Danny, "I don't want to leave her here alone, so I'll get you to return the truck. Don't forget my ski mask. It's under the seat."

"Will do."

Jack got to his feet. "Hand me that piece of paper with the name of her grandmother's nursing home. I'm going to make a call."

Moments later, Jack returned to the living room and looked at Danny without speaking.

"What is it? You look upset?"

"She no longer has a grandmother. She died in her sleep two weeks ago."

Danny paused as the message sank in, then replied, "The poor kid. As if she hasn't been through enough. We'll have to call Social Services!"

Jack closed his eyes for a moment while massaging his temples with his hands, then he walked back to the telephone.

chapter twenty

Jack politely declined to join Ben and Liz for dinner but did accept a cup of tea while they ate. He knew that they could tell by his demeanour that he had something to say, so he said it.

The blood pressure immediately rose in Ben's face. He shoved his plate back and stood up from the kitchen table. "You brought her here? Damn it, Jack! I told you on the phone that we couldn't do this!"

He went to the kitchen window and looked out at Jack's car, then turned to Liz. "She's sitting in his car, right now." He looked at Jack and said, "I want you to leave. You've got no right to be asking us to do this after what happened. Get her out of here!"

Jack stood up from the table and said, "I'm sorry. I thought maybe if you just met her..."

"What did you think you were doing?" asked Liz, wiping tears from her face. "Trying to replace Maggie?"

Jack sighed, then said, "This isn't about you or Ben. It's about Marcie. She's been sexually abused most of her life by her father. She ran away from that only to be attacked by another pervert. She just turned thirteen and is living on the street and chipping heroin. If she doesn't get a break now, she's dead. It might already be too late."

"Call Social Services," said Liz.

"As I told you on the phone, it's too risky. If you heard the news about the young woman blown up on the freeway two days ago, that was her friend."

"The news said that was a prostitute," said Ben. "You're telling me that her friend was a prostitute?"

"Yes. Marcie has been working the street, too."

"What? You expect us to take in a drug-addicted prostitute? You're out of your mind!"

"I said she was chipping. It means she's just starting — an occasional user. I don't think she's addicted … yet. That's another reason why being way out here on a farm would be better for her. It won't be so easy for her to get a fix."

"But she's a prostitute!" said Liz.

"She's still a child. Since she was an infant, the only person she had to protect her was her father. All that bastard did was use her for his own sexual perversion. Now she's on the street. Is it any wonder?"

Liz went to the kitchen window and peeked out at Marcie, who was getting out of the car. As Liz watched, Marcie approached a pair of geese. The gander felt protective of his mate and honked and flapped his wings as he charged toward her. Marcie ran back to the car.

"Doesn't she have clothes?" asked Liz. "That looks like your shirt, Jack."

"She's wearing all her clothes underneath. Miniskirt and a tank top."

"Has she eaten?"

"Not for a while, but..."

"You're not bringing her in here," said Ben.

"Ben! If she hasn't eaten..."

"Liz! No!"

Liz thought for a moment, then said, "We'll give her some of Maggie's clothes. It's the least we can do. She looks to be the same size."

Minutes later, Ben and Jack each carried a box of clothes out to the car and put them in the trunk. Liz watched from the kitchen window.

Ben looked at Jack and said, "Sorry, it's just..."

"It's okay, Ben. You're right. It is too much to ask. We'll take our chances with Social Services."

"Our emotions are really eaten up right now. She's the same age and size as Maggie. It would be a constant reminder. Even their names are similar. We just can't handle..."

"It's okay, I understand. You're right. I should have listened to you on the phone."

Jack got in the car and slowly drove away.

Ben watched as Marcie absent-mindedly used her finger to draw a big unhappy face in the condensation on her window. He wondered if she liked to doodle. His eyes brimmed with tears. He turned and looked at Liz. She had seen it too. Their eyes met; Liz gave a slight nod.

It was late in the evening when Red walked into the Black Water. The music was vibrating from the stage, and she looked up at the young stripper.

Red yelled, "Hey, little girl! Why don't you take off and come back when you can grow some tits!"

A few laughs from the crowd didn't drown out the girl's response. "Fuck you! I don't see you standin' up here!"

Red paused until she had the crowd's attention before pulling her black singlet T-shirt up over her head to expose her bare chest to the crowd. "Because if I did get up there, cupcake, I'd put you out of a job!"

Red soaked up the applause for a moment, then replaced her T-shirt and strutted to the rear of the tavern. She casually looked around before sitting at a table with Jack.

"It took you long enough," said Jack.

"Yeah. Sorry, Eddy. I got your page but had some business to take care of. Took me a little longer than I thought. So, are ya lookin'?"

"As a matter of fact, I am. Business has been going good. So good, I'm lookin' for half a pound."

Red let out a low whistle. "That's a lot! When? Right now?"

"Not now. Tomorrow afternoon or the next day at the latest."

"I don't usually handle that much."

Jack shrugged his shoulders. "Too bad. I'm done fuckin' around with this small shit. Maybe I'll have to find someone else."

"I can check with my man. Maybe he'll front me four ounces at a time. Do it in a couple of deals."

"Naw, as I said, I don't want to be fuckin' around. Two deals means twice the risk. Tell you what, put me in touch with your man and I'll make it worth your while."

"How much worth my while?"

"Enough. Depends how smooth things go and what I gotta pay for it."

Red thought for a moment, then said, "Wait here, I'll make a call."

Red went to the lobby and then sprinted upstairs and knocked on a door.

"Who is it?" asked a gruff voice.

"Wizard! It's me, Red," she whispered.

Seconds later, Red was inside the room. Wizard, with his goatee and muscled arms covered in large tattoos, towered over her. Rolly was lying on the bed. In the corner of the room sat a third biker. A light behind him cast shadows down over his face. His forehead had a large circular scar from an incident years earlier when someone had caught his attention with the broken end of a wine bottle.

"Well?" asked Wizard.

"Yeah, he's here right now," said Red.

"Did he hit you up?"

"Oh yeah! Wants half a pound. I told him I'd make a call." She looked at her watch. "And that was, like, not even five minutes ago."

"Good," replied Wizard.

"I think maybe I'll cut his balls off instead of his tongue," said Rolly. "We were too easy on Lenny!"

"Shut your trap!" hissed Wizard.

There was a brief silence in the room before Wizard continued, "So what's he wearin'?"

"You can't miss 'im," replied Red. "Jeans and a red sweatshirt with a big white band around the chest and arms."

"Okay, you know what to do," said Wizard. "Give us twenty minutes to set up." He flashed her a roll of money and said, "When you're done, go home. I'll drop over after."

"Thanks, Wizard," replied Red, casting one more quick glance at the man sitting in the corner. He hadn't spoken a word the whole time. Then she turned toward the door.

"Red! One more thing. Make sure you keep your yap shut about this!"

"About what?" replied Red, smiling as she left the room.

When she was gone, Wizard turned to the biker in the corner and said, "Lance, you get the car and cruise the block until you see Red, then hit the alley."

Minutes later, Red joined Jack back in the bar.

"You're in luck," she said. "My guy is a little nervous, but he said he's willin' to meet you, just to check you out."

"Good. He's got nothing to be nervous about. When can we meet?"

"In about twenty minutes. He wants to talk to me out front first. Give me about five minutes just to reassure him, then I'll get him to drive me around back and you can meet us in the alley."

A few minutes later, Jack gave Danny a subtle nod and they met in the men's room. Jack explained what was happening, and Danny said, "Just in case they want to take you for a little drive, I'll get the car and stand by."

"Good idea."

"Think it will be Halibut?"

"Maybe. Or some other striker. We'll soon find out."

Jack returned to the table. Red left on time and headed out the front door. Jack looked at his watch and waited five minutes.

Danny sat in his car and watched from the parking garage. He eventually saw Red walk out the front door of the bar and approach a green Volvo parked nearby. The Volvo drove to the end of the block and turned into the alley. He caught the plate number and noticed Red walk back toward the bar.

Danny drove in the opposite direction and parked on the street at the end of the block to cover off the other end of the alley. If the Volvo did take Jack for a ride, this was the direction it would drive out. He radioed in the plate number. The name that came back wasn't one he recognized.

An arc of light briefly cut into the back alley when Jack opened the rear door to the alley. He stood in the doorway for a moment before stepping out. His red sweatshirt blended into the darkness, but the white stripe stood out like a beacon. He saw a car drive slowly down the alley toward him, then stop a short distance away. He walked toward it, using his hand to shield his eyes from the headlights.

As Jack approached a Dumpster, Rolly silently moved in behind him, unsnapping a leather thong and removing his hunting knife from its scabbard while quickening his pace.

Rolly was in striking distance when Wizard stepped out from the Dumpster and said, "Hey! Eddy!"

Jack felt the adrenaline rush to his limbs as his brain told him to run. He tried to act calm and said, "Yeah? Do I know you?"

"Pest control!" Rolly snickered when Jack spun around to look.

Rolly brandished the knife at throat height and gave an evil grin when the lights from the car reflected off the knife and into Jack's eyes. Wizard stepped forward and pointed a .22-calibre pistol at the back of Jack's head. The headlights cast dark shadows on Wizard's face as Jack turned and found the barrel of the pistol entering his nostril.

"Goodbye, rat!" hissed Wizard, as his finger slowly squeezed the trigger.

Jack chopped the inside of Wizard's wrist with the edge of his hand, flinging the gun from Wizard's grasp. It bounced off the side of the Dumpster with a loud clang. Rolly immediately plunged the knife toward the back of Jack's neck, but Jack ducked while shoving two fingers into Wizard's eye, and the knife glanced off his shoulder blade instead. Jack darted past Wizard toward the car.

"Get him!" yelled Wizard, scrambling to pick up his gun. Rolly ran after him while Wizard wiped his eye with one hand before raising his gun with the other hand. Then he hesitated, fearing he might hit Rolly.

Lance lurched the car forward, smashing the passenger side fender into the alley wall. The interior light went on as he stepped out of the car, blocking the alley. The snarl on his face further accented the scar on his forehead as he moved around in front of the driver's door. His face didn't look any prettier when his mouth gaped open as Jack ran up over the hood of the car.

A bullet ricocheted off the car's windshield as Jack dove over the roof and continued running.

"Out of my fucking way!" yelled Wizard, running up to the car. He fired four more shots at the crouched figure zigzagging down the alley. His target ran faster.

Wizard held the gun with both hands and rested his arms on the roof of the car, aiming toward the end of the alley. Briefly, his target was silhouetted in the light at the end of the alley. Wizard fired one more shot and watched as the body crumpled and fell.

"Got 'im! Quick! Get in the car!" he ordered, grabbing Rolly by the arm and shoving him inside. He looked at Lance and said, "Back down the alley fast! Drive right over the rat-fucker! Make sure he's dead!"

Lance stepped on the throttle, and the tires squealed as the car hurtled backwards down the alley. Sparks flew off the side of the car as it briefly scraped along the side of a brick building, knocking the mirror off the passenger side door.

Wizard and Rolly grabbed the dash as they tensed, waiting for the crunch of broken bones and the thump of a mangled body as the car bounced out of the alley.

As Danny waited, he saw Red walk across the intersection. *Why isn't she meeting with Jack?*

His question was answered by the sound of gunshots from the alley. Adrenaline slammed through his body like a tidal wave. His car leaped out of his parking space, but the traffic was heavy and he had to slam on the brakes to avoid a collision. He fumbled under his seat to retrieve the red light to toss on the dash. He cursed as the cord for the light became entangled in the seat springs. Seconds later, he yanked it free and plugged it into the cigarette lighter. He reached for the hidden switch to turn on the siren.

Lance slammed on the brakes and brought the Volvo to a stop facing the sidewalk and entrance to the alley. The headlights picked up a puddle of blood and the smear of tire tracks where he had backed through it.

"I didn't feel nothin'," said Lance. "He ain't hung up underneath."

"You fuckin' missed him!" yelled Rolly, clenching his knife.

"Out of the fucking car!" screamed Wizard, waving his gun in all directions.

The three men scrambled from the car and looked at the blood.

Wizard pointed to a trail of bloody marks along the sidewalk. "He's gone this way, and you can bet he hasn't gone far." He stepped out on the street to look behind some parked cars.

"He's got to be right here somewhere," said Lance. "He hasn't had time to make it to the end of the block," he noted, while following splatters of blood to the edge of the curb.

The piercing scream of a police siren cut the night air, followed by screeching tires. The flash of a red light reflected off the wall as it approached the opposite end of the alley.

"Let's get the fuck out o' here!" yelled Wizard.

All three men scrambled back into the car and sped off in the opposite direction. Five minutes later, they pulled into another alley.

Lance retrieved a container of gasoline from the trunk and doused the car. He lit the rag on a beer bottle half-filled with a mixture of gas and oil and threw it on the car. Seconds later, the three men drove away from the blaze in another car.

"Get hold of the boys," said Wizard. "I want someone at every hospital and clinic there is. If this rat-fucker doesn't die first, I want him dead before some fucking doctor gets his hands on him!"

"Will do," replied Rolly.

"You and Lance cover off the nearest hospital and clinic. Get reinforcements. Try and whack him before he enters. Be less witnesses to take care of."

"Where ya goin'?" asked Rolly.

"Red. She's a loose end. If the rat makes it to the cops, they'll know she helped set 'im up. I'll let The Suit know what happened, too. Just in case he hears anything."

chapter twenty-one

The tires of Danny's car screamed as he rounded the corner into the alley. There were no other cars in sight and he realized that the Volvo had backed out the other side.

He stopped briefly by the Dumpster and was relieved not to see Jack's body. He jumped back in his car and continued on. At the end of the alley he saw a fresh patch of blood smeared by tire tracks. Fear ravaged his body as he slammed on the brakes and leapt from the car. His knuckles were white as he gripped his gun.

Seconds later, Jack crawled out from under a parked SUV. Danny helped him into the car, and Jack fell over on the seat and hit the switch under the dash. The siren stopped instantly. Jack yanked the light off the dash.

"What the fuck are you doing?" yelled Danny, scrambling into the driver's seat. "You're hurt! I'm taking you to the hospital!"

"No! I'm okay. They think I'm a rat! Let them keep thinking that."

"You're bleeding like a stuck pig! I'm taking you to the hospital." Danny hit the gas and the car shot out of the alley and onto the street.

"It was Wizard and two others. I recognize their faces from the pictures but can't remember their names. If you take me to a hospital or clinic they're liable to finish the job. I don't want them to know what happened to me."

"Jesus Christ! I knew this would happen! You keep usin' the fuckin' alley — how am I supposed to protect you? Now you're telling me not take you to the hospital! Goddamn it!" Danny hit the brakes and pulled over to the side of the road. "Turn around, I'm takin' a look!"

Danny pulled up Jack's sweatshirt and he yelped in pain.

"You've been stabbed in the back!"

"Did you teach them that?"

"Jesus Christ! Your arm! Looks like a bullet hole! You've been shot, too!"

"Went clean through. Lucky break."

"Yeah, you're real fuckin' lucky," said Danny sarcastically. "I'm taking you in. Then I'm calling in the troops and we're going to find Wizard."

"The hell you are! Putting him in jail won't help!" Jack grabbed for the cellphone.

Natasha Trovinski looked in the mirror and quickly brushed her hair. She was pleased that Jack had finally called, asking if he could drop by.

She hurried into the living room, grabbed some books from the coffee table, and replaced them on the bookshelf. Would she have time to vacuum before he arrived?

The apartment security buzzer answered her question.

Moments later, she tried to hide her disappointment. Jack hadn't mentioned that Danny would be with him.

"What a pleasant surprise! Come on in, you two. I'll put some coffee on."

Natasha looked again. *They're arm in arm. Jack is staggering.... Have they been drinking? Jack's sweatshirt — it's stained with blood!*

"My God! What happened? Get him in here!"

"I just want to make it clear that I did not fall on broken glass," said Jack.

"He's been shot and knifed," said Danny, as soon as she closed the door behind them.

"You fools!" said Natasha harshly. "I'm calling an ambulance. You should have gone to the hospital!" she added, rushing to the telephone.

"No! Don't do that! It's not that bad," Jack insisted. "I don't want anyone to know I've been shot. At least not now. I need time to figure this —"

"A hospital or clinic might not be safe!" interjected Danny. "It might be a policeman responsible for Jack getting shot! Please! You've got to help him!"

Natasha stared at the two men, then hung up the phone.

"Okay, let me take a look," she said calmly. "Sit on the kitchen chair."

Natasha quickly retrieved a first-aid kit from her bathroom vanity. She used scissors to cut off Jack's sweatshirt, then she examined his wounds closely.

A purplish line bored its way from near the centre of Jack's back up across his rib cage, where it disappeared. A small puncture hole in the back of his arm looked black, but the flesh had closed in around the wound and there was little bleeding. Natasha gently raised his arm to expose an exit hole on the opposite side that was still oozing blood.

"It looks like you were only shot once. I think the bullet reflected off the left side of your rib cage before travelling up through the biceps on your arm. I take it you were bent over at the time or in a prone position?"

"I tried to make as small a target as possible, while running like hell."

"There's another injury, exposing part of your left shoulder blade. You were slashed with a knife."

"That happened first. I didn't really feel it much then, but I do now."

"So it's not too serious? He's going to be okay?" asked Danny, sounding hopeful.

"Have you been coughing up or spitting up blood?" she asked, ignoring Danny.

"No, but it hurts like hell to talk. Even breathing causes pain."

"You should be x-rayed. I'm sure you've got some fractured ribs. The humerus, too, but it's your ribs I'm concerned with. A fractured rib could puncture your lung. The slice across your shoulder blade is going to require quite a few stitches. How long has it been since it happened?"

"About half an hour," replied Danny.

"It was a policeman who did this?" asked Natasha, as she cleaned the wounds in preparation for the dressings.

"Not exactly," replied Jack. "I set up a couple of City narcs to think I was an informant. Three bikers tried to kill me, thinking I was an informant. They don't know I'm a cop. Someone is leaking information. Could be one of the narcs, or maybe a secretary in their office.

They were also dealing with our Homicide Unit, so it could be someone out of our building."

"You should be taken in and x-rayed."

"No. The guys who did this belong to a big organization. They'll have every hospital and clinic covered. Even if they don't finish the job, we'd never find out who's behind the leak. If you will just patch me up, I'll be on my way."

"I have to report all gunshot wounds to the police."

"Now you decide to talk to the police!" said Danny angrily.

"You didn't let me finish, Danny. You're a policeman, so consider yourself informed. I won't inform anyone else, *providing* Jack stays here where I can keep an eye on him for a few days. If his condition worsens, I will call an ambulance," she said firmly.

"I can't do that to you. I'm sure I'll be fine once I —"

"You're not going anywhere until I say so! I'll sleep on the sofa and you'll use my room. I'm going to start you on antibiotics. Have you had a tetanus shot within the last ten years?"

"Uh, no, I guess I haven't."

"I'll go to the clinic and pick up what I need. Danny, I want you to hold this compress tight to his back until I return."

"These people are really dangerous," said Jack. "We can't trust anyone. I probably shouldn't even be here. I think I should leave as soon as —"

"You'll leave when I tell you to! Tomorrow is my day off. We'll see how you are then."

"I think you should listen to her," said Danny. "It's not safe for you to go home like this."

Jack moved slightly, and the pain caused him to clench his teeth. "Perhaps you're right. I don't feel like travelling very far tonight. Sorry, Natasha. I'm sure that being a doctor on your day off wasn't what you had in mind. Be careful. We don't know who we can trust."

"You said they were bikers?"

"Satans Wrath."

Natasha arrived at her clinic twenty minutes later. She walked past a car in the parking lot parked near the front entrance. Two men were inside. The driver was drumming the steering wheel with a nervous energy. Natasha noticed the numerous rings across their fingers. *Oh, shit!*

She found a plastic bag in her office left over from buying a new pair of shoes. She filled it with what she needed, but her mind was still on the two men outside. She took a scalpel and held it in her jacket pocket as she walked to the car. She needn't have worried. The two men paid her little attention and continued to stare at the front door of the clinic. She drove away from the clinic and breathed a sigh of relief when the other car remained where it was.

It was three o'clock in the morning when Natasha ushered Danny out the door.

"Don't worry about him. I'm sure he'll be fine," whispered Natasha. "I gave him some medication to ease the pain and help him sleep. Say hello to Susan."

Danny nodded solemnly and said, "I'll drop back around noon to see how he's doing. And Natasha ... thank you!"

It was noon when Jack woke up to the aroma of fresh coffee. He groaned as he eased over to the edge of the bed and put his feet on the floor.

"How's my star patient this morning?"

Natasha stood in the doorway. She was backlit by a beam of sunlight.

"I hurt!"

"Pain is a common consequence of being shot and stabbed. Does this happen often?"

"No, I just thought it would make a good excuse to see you again."

"Next time try phoning and inviting me out. It's easier."

"Thanks for the suggestion." Jack saw a clock in the bedroom and said, "Hey, it's late! I can't believe I slept this long. Especially with this sling on my arm."

"The medication helped you sleep. You needed to."

"Well, at least I'm not spitting up blood, so my lungs must be okay. If I can borrow your phone, I'll have Danny drop by and pick me up."

"You're not out of the woods yet, buster! Infection could still set in, or a fractured rib or bone fragments could still cause serious problems."

"Well, I'll take it easy and I'm sure I'll be —"

"First thing I want you to do is get in the tub and I'll give you a sponge bath. Then we'll take a look and change those dressings again. Your sweatshirt has had it, but I'll wash the rest of your clothes while you're soaking in the bath."

"That's not necessary. I'll phone Danny and then —"

"Just do it and quit giving me a hard time!"

"Some bedside manner you have! Are you this rude with all your patients?"

"Only those patients who think they know more than the doctor."

Jack eased the sling off his left arm but gripped his right shoulder with his fingers as he stepped into the warm bath. Moments later, Natasha entered and used a sponge to gently wash his back. Jack hunched forward in the water, hoping not to embarrass himself, or if he did, to make sure that Natasha didn't notice.

"Sit up straight, I'll wash your front," she said.

"No! That part I can do myself!"

Natasha seemed amused. "An undercover cop who's bashful. Interesting. Okay, soak in here for a while and I'll wash your clothes."

Jack relaxed when Natasha left the room. He had to admit the bath did feel good, and the warm water seemed to ease the pain. He heard Danny arrive so he got out of the tub and carefully patted himself dry and replaced the sling. When he was finished, he wrapped a towel around himself and walked into the kitchen where Danny and Natasha were having coffee.

"How do you feel?" asked Danny.

"A little like they succeeded in driving over me last night, but I'll be okay."

"They tried to drive over you, too?" Natasha asked.

"Yeah, don't you hate nights like that?" replied Danny with a grin.

"Danny, I'm sorry. I never even thanked you last night. If it hadn't been for you, I wouldn't be standing here. I owe you one, brother."

Danny's expression became sombre. "After hearing the shots and seeing the blood on the road, I figured they had taken you to either finish you off or dispose of your body. You don't know how relieved I was to see you! I wasn't thinking that you would use Marcie's trick."

"Marcie's trick?" asked Natasha.

"He hid under a car."

"I knew they would find me pretty fast," said Jack. "I saw their feet as they followed the blood up to the curb. It wouldn't have taken them long to find me."

"You mentioned Marcie," said Natasha. "Is this the same Marcie I treated earlier? You've seen her again?"

"Seen her!" said Danny. "Jack's got her living with his sister and brother-in-law out in the Valley. We were concerned that Social Services might have a leak too."

"She's been there less than two days," said Jack quietly. "I don't know if it'll work out."

Natasha looked at Jack. *This guy is pretty special.*

Jack flinched as he eased himself into a chair.

"Pansy," said Danny.

"I'm impressed you were able to convince her to leave her life on the street," said Natasha. "Most street kids I've met are either too addicted or too caught up with the excitement of this whole new world to ever be convinced to leave."

"Uh ... well, actually, it was Danny who took a chance and talked to her. It was a shot in the dark, but it appears to have worked out well." He turned to Danny to change the subject. "Did you talk to Louie this morning? Does he suspect anything?"

"I told him you decided to take a few days off and go fishing."

"Fishing! God, you're a lousy liar."

"So I've been told, but he didn't say anything."

"I don't think I could stand any of his lectures right now. I'll wait a few days and then let him know we've got a new game plan."

"A new game plan?" asked Danny.

"Time to take the gloves off," said Jack. He gave Danny a hard look. Danny caught the message and didn't pursue it.

An uncomfortable silence followed. Everyone took a sip of coffee, then Natasha got up and said, "Well, let's take a look at you."

Jack felt her fingers gently remove his dressings.

"The wound across your shoulder blade and the hole punched through your biceps look good, but infection could still set in. I'm still worried about damage to your rib cage. You're definitely not going anywhere for a day or two."

Jack waited until she finished placing clean dressings on him before standing up. He saw Danny give Natasha a knowing look.

"Well, thanks, Natasha," said Jack. "I really appreciate what you've done for me, but I need to be going. Don't worry, I'll be careful!"

"I told you he would be like this," said Danny.

"So, if I can just have my clothes back I'll be out of your hair. I'm sorry for the inconvenience I've caused. I'd like to call you in a day or two. I owe you at least one dinner, not to mention new sheets. I bled on them during the night."

Natasha scowled and didn't respond for a moment. Then she said, "Your clothes are in the bedroom, but you're a fool for not listening to me!"

"I probably am," he admitted, slowly making his way to the bedroom.

Moments later, Jack returned to the kitchen where Natasha was sitting alone.

"Did you say my clothes were in the bedroom? I couldn't find them."

"Danny has them."

"Where is he?" asked Jack, glancing around.

"He's not here. He left."

"He left! I'm supposed to go with him!"

"No."

"What do you mean, *no*?"

"What part of that statement don't you understand?"

Jack looked down at the towel he was wearing, then back at Natasha.

"Now, I'm going to make you breakfast and then you're going back to bed. You lost a lot of blood last night and I'm going to see to it that you get some rest."

"But ... what about my clothes?"

"If you behave yourself and do what I tell you, then I'll let you keep the towel."

Jack paused to think about the predicament he was in.

"Are you angry?" she asked, out of idle curiosity.

He paused, then said, "I'm being held hostage by a beautiful woman who's stolen my clothes and is demanding I sleep in her bed. I think I can live with it for now."

Later that afternoon, Jack wrapped a blanket around himself and plodded out to the kitchen. Natasha was preparing dinner, so he sat at the kitchen table.

Their conversation was light, which relieved him. She wasn't the type to be nosy and ask many questions, although he knew she was probably curious as hell.

After supper they sat on the sofa and Jack talked about Marcie and how great Ben and Liz were to look after her. He said that the four of them had a long talk. Ben and Liz agreed to take her in on a trial basis. Marcie agreed to start seeing a psychologist and go to school.

He also told her about Maggie and Ben Junior. He confessed he was having nightmares where they were calling out to him for help and he all he could do was sit there, unable to move.

"Do you always have the same nightmare?"

"Lately, I do."

"Often?"

"Quite often."

"Does it bother you to talk about it?"

"Not with you, for some reason. Maybe because you're a doctor. It feels good to be able to talk to someone about it."

"You were talking in your sleep last night. You repeated the word *dirty*."

"I said that?"

Natasha nodded. "Sorry, I didn't mean to be listening in on your private dreams, but I was concerned you might be getting an infection and I was checking to see if you had a fever."

"No, it's okay. I didn't realize I talked in my sleep. *Dirty* was what Maggie printed in the last page of her sketchbook, just before she was murdered. It's been bothering me ever since."

"Maybe whoever killed her was dirty or perhaps was using foul language?"

"I don't think so. She was really talented. You should see some of the drawings she did. They're incredible. She could really draw what she saw."

"Meaning?"

"She was too talented just to print the word *dirty*. I think it has more meaning."

The security buzzer announced Danny's arrival, and Natasha let him in.

"Well, big guy, are you going to tear a strip off me for leaving you here this morning?" asked Danny, while placing two photo albums on the coffee table.

"I don't know whether to yell at you or thank you." Jack stole a quick look at Natasha and added, "But I think maybe I'll thank you."

"I should be home by five tomorrow," said Natasha. "I'll check on you then. If you're okay, you can go, provided you take some time off and don't go back to work for a while."

"Maybe by then I won't want to go." Jack caught the sparkle in her eye and thought how good she was for him — and not just as a doctor.

"So what's this? Your family photo albums?" asked Natasha.

"Pictures of Satans Wrath," replied Danny. "See if Jack can put names to who did this."

Jack opened the binder to the picture of Wizard. He knew it well but wanted to look again. After turning a few pages, he recognized another picture.

"That's the driver. His forehead looks like someone performed a frontal lobotomy." Jack looked at Natasha. "Your work?" he asked.

Natasha snickered and lightly squeezed his leg.

Danny took a look. "Lance Morgan. Okay, that's two out of three. See if you can recognize fat boy."

Jack took a few more minutes to identify him. "His name is Roland Leitch."

Natasha went to the kitchen and Danny whispered, "We got a computer kickback on Red this afternoon. She's dead. The landlord found her body. Looks like an accidental overdose. The needle was still hanging off her arm and there was a deck of heroin nearby."

"That was no accident. She was a connection to them. Dig up everything you can on my three friends from the alley."

"Will do. Also got a response on the Volvo."

"Stolen?"

"Yup. The owner was out of town. He reported it stolen last night when he returned."

"Speaking of returning home. Come back in the morning and bring me some clothes! It's time I got out of here. With this blanket I'm beginning to feel like a monk!"

"Don't give me that!" replied Danny. "I saw how you two snuggled in with each other when you were looking at the pictures! Besides, you've been through those pictures a dozen times. It should only have taken you seconds to find them!"

"Well ... I had to make sure I picked the right person."

"Oh? Well, I hope she is the right person," retorted Danny.

Jack didn't respond, so Danny asked, "What did you mean when you said the gloves were coming off?"

Jack's face hardened. "I've got a plan. Might get a little violent."

Natasha saw Danny out the door and then returned to sit with Jack on the sofa. Earlier, she had studied his face as he spoke. He seemed intense, yet he was quick with a smile. She had watched his eyes as he related his past experiences. His long, dark eyelashes made his blue eyes take on a deeper shade, but at the same time he had a boyish, wide-eyed look of innocence. The type who had freckles as a kid, she decided.

Considering his experiences, she knew he was far from naive. Briefly she felt irritated to think other women had probably fallen for his boyish charm. Still, he was compassionate. He hadn't become hardened and callous, like so many people who deal with life and death.

Maybe it was the intensity and openness of his conversation, or the realization that they both dealt with grief and sorrow, but it occurred to her that she felt closer to this man in the short time she had known him than any other man she had ever met.

Right now, with a blanket wrapped around him, he looked cute. But earlier today, when he was wearing only a towel, she had felt aroused. There was no denying that. She had only ever kissed him once. That was in a men's room. There was no denying what she had wanted to do then, either.

Enough fantasizing! I'm a professional. I've got to behave like one.

"Okay, you're still my patient. Turn around on the couch and lower the blanket so I can have a look under those dressings again."

Jack did as he was told. She carefully removed the dressing covering the wound across his shoulder blade. She gently ran her hand over the smooth skin on his back, lightly probing with her fingers. She felt his muscles tense under her hand and noticed he held his breath.

"I'm sorry, does it hurt?"

"No," he replied softly, "it feels good."

Neither spoke as Natasha put on a fresh dressing.

"Turn around and let me take a look at your arm."

His eyes were intensely fixed on her face. She pretended not to notice as she peeled off the dressing.

"This looks fine, too! You're really doing well." She picked up a fresh roll of gauze and wrapped the dressing around his arm. The closer she came to the end, the slower she wrapped.

When she finished she said, "There! All done," in a voice she hoped would sound perky.

He stared at her eyes, their faces almost touching. He didn't move or speak. She tried to smile but felt her lip tremble and quickly looked away.

She felt his other hand on her back, guiding her toward him. She closed her eyes and felt his warm lips on hers. It was much different than their first kiss. This was long and gentle. She felt herself drawn against his naked chest, where she remained a moment before pulling away.

She cleared her throat. "Get in there and get some rest. I'll see you in the morning before I go to work."

"Are you going to sleep on the sofa?"

She stared at him for a moment without speaking, then answered, "Yes ... but I want you to kiss me once more before you go."

chapter twenty-two

It was mid-morning when Jack let Danny inside Natasha's apartment.

"Louie wants to talk to you!" said Danny, handing Jack a bag containing his clothes.

"I'm not surprised. We'll go back to my place and I'll call him from there."

"I was supposed to wait until Natasha looked at you. Maybe we should leave a note."

"She's working until four-thirty. I found a spare key on top of the fridge, so I'll be able to lock up. I'll talk to her later."

Danny stared at Jack, then said, "She's a smart girl — and damned attractive."

Jack looked at Danny, then said, "I noticed. Now take me home. We've got work to do!"

*

Back in his own apartment, Jack looked at the information that Danny had found on Wizard, Rolly, and Lance. Wizard was forty-five years old and had four convictions for trafficking in drugs: fines on the first two, thirty days in jail for the third, and six months of house arrest for the last time. A month later he was charged with armed robbery, but it was dismissed. Jack pointed to the report and said, "Why?"

"Lack of evidence," said Danny. "The only witness was killed in a hit-and-run accident. Wizard is also a suspect in three murders. Those victims were all drug dealers."

"Probably a little tardy in their payments."

"He changes addresses and girlfriends about as often as you'd change your shorts."

"Speak for yourself."

"He maintains a pretty high lifestyle," continued Danny. "Most of his apartments have been penthouse suites. He also drives a Ferrari."

"Does he work?"

"Fisherman. He owns a crab boat out in White Rock. It's paid off, too."

Jack looked at Rolly's file. "Thirty-seven years old. Convicted for drug trafficking, break and enter, armed robbery, assault causing bodily harm, extortion ... a regular pillar of society."

"He owns an older-style house on a double lot in North Van."

"Mortgage?"

"Nope. He paid it off one year after moving in. Lists his occupation as a mechanic. Spends two days a week at one of the bike shops owned by the club. He's been living with some stripper for the last two years."

"Another boy not smart enough to hide his money."

Jack then picked up the file on Lance Morgan. "This is interesting: he's thirty-nine years old and his record is mostly for auto theft, fraud, false pretences, impaired driving, and one charge of trafficking, which was dismissed."

"He was caught with two kilos of cocaine in a rental vehicle," Danny explained. "He took the stand and gave the usual story that someone who rented the car previously must have left it in there. The judge said it was enough for reasonable doubt and dismissed the case."

"He only served a one-month sentence for auto theft, strictly provincial. He's never seen the inside of a federal pen."

"He's still a badass," said Danny.

"By the looks of his record he's not as violent as his partners."

"Or he's just smarter and hasn't been caught."

"I'm looking for someone smarter. What else do you have on him?"

"He's married to some waitress, and they've got four kids. He owns an arcade, and they've got a modest home just outside of Vancouver. I think it's in..."

"Surrey," said Jack, studying the report.

"Yeah, it's just an average house with a big mortgage."

Jack slowly sifted through the file again.

"So? What are you thinking?" asked Danny.

"I want to know more about Lance Morgan. See if he owns any companies or whatever. An arcade is a good business for laundering money. It would be tough to prove how many kids are dropping how many quarters into all those machines. Lance may be a lot smarter than his cohorts. He also has a family. This could be our chance."

"Our chance to do what?"

The telephone interrupted Jack's reply.

"All right, Jack! What the hell are you up to?"

"Oh ... Louie! How are you?" replied Jack, catching the worried look on Danny's face.

"Don't give me that crap! What are you up to?"

"Didn't Danny tell you? I took a few days off to go fishing."

"Bullshit! I didn't say anything to him in case he believed it. But I sure as hell don't!"

"Well ... I'm fishing for bad guys."

"Jesus, you drive me nuts sometimes. I've been listening to the news, reading the papers — even the obituary columns — trying to figure out where you were or what you were up to. I've been phoning for two days. If you've been down to the States again, so help me I'll —"

"No, no, Louie! Relax! There's nothing to worry about. I've been spending a lot of time on the street. Only at home to sleep."

"So everything is okay?" asked Grazia suspiciously.

"You bet."

"Did you catch any?"

"Catch any?"

"Bad guys. You said you were fishing for bad guys."

"Had a few nibbles. Nothing solid, but I've got a feeling in my bones that we're on to something."

Natasha was in a grim mood as she drove home from work that evening. Usually she enjoyed a warm autumn rain. It made her feel cozy when she sat beside her fireplace with a glass of wine. Today was different. The rain only served to accent her feelings of despair, along with a dyspeptic stomach that gnawed at her like a disease.

She had picked up sandwiches at the deli and rushed home at lunchtime, hoping to surprise him, only to find her apartment empty. *The ungrateful swine could have at least written a note to say thank you!*

She felt the tears well in her eyes as she tried to force her office key into her apartment door. She changed keys, unlocked the door, and stepped inside.

She looked on the counter as if by magic there might be a note, but there was nothing.

But something had changed. She looked again. Her kitchen felt warm, and her stereo was playing quietly in the living room.

"Hi," Jack said softly, appearing from the living room.

He was clean-shaven and dressed in a navy blue suit accented by a burgundy tie and handkerchief. He held a solitary long-stemmed red rose in his hand.

He looked at her face and dropped the flower on the counter, stepping forward.

"What is it? What's wrong?"

"Absolutely nothing," she said, then kissed him and let him hold her tight before pushing him away and picking up the long-stemmed rose. "Is this for me?"

"No, I thought it was Danny coming in."

She saw the grin on Jack's face and smiled back. "Where's your sling?"

"I'm okay as long as I don't jar it."

"You can cook?" asked Natasha, while retrieving a vase from her china cabinet.

"I've taken a few courses. French, Italian, Thai, but being a one-armed gourmet is something new. My repertoire is small, but I like to think it's good."

Natasha noticed that the gas fireplace was on. Her table had already been set, with two new candles alongside her dishes. Romantic music drifted softly through the room. "Give me a minute to change," she said.

Natasha liked the look on Jack's face when she

reappeared wearing a black chiffon dress, a pearl necklace accenting her long dark hair.

The candles had burned to the bottom by the time dinner was over. Crab-stuffed mushroom caps were followed by a beef roulade accompanied by mushroom gravy. The wine was a pinot noir. It was a good match for the food. The main course was followed by latticed chocolate rum pie. Natasha found the whole meal a sensual experience.

After dinner, Natasha sat on the sofa while Jack went to the kitchen. He appeared moments later carrying a silver tray, upon which were two glasses of flaming liqueur.

"Sambuca," he said, putting the tray on the coffee table and sitting down.

She moved closer to him on the sofa and watched the rain running down the outside of her patio doors. The glass caught the flickering reflection from the fireplace. The rain seemed beautiful again and gave a feeling of intimacy.

She felt his arm wrap around her bare shoulder, coaxing her body closer. The musky, haunting smell of his cologne aroused her senses. She enjoyed the feel of his warm hand on her shoulder as she snuggled in.

She raised the sambuca to her lips and watched as the clear liquid picked up the light from the fire, shimmering like diamonds. Three coffee beans floating on top glistened below the blue flame dancing above. She marvelled at it for a moment, then caught the shine in Jack's eyes as he held his glass up, giving a silent toast.

She gave a small breath to blow out the flame and let the licorice flavour of the liqueur explore her mouth before warming its way down her throat. She looked intently into his eyes, then put her glass down and took him by the hand and led him to her bedroom.

*

She felt his naked body next to hers as he lay on his side, softly touching her face before gently kissing her on the temple. She felt his hand gently glide up the inside of her thigh and then slowly trail up the rest of her body. The underside of his arm brushed her nipples and she felt them harden to his touch. His scent filled her lungs and she could almost taste him, wishing he were inside her.

Finally he kissed her again. She responded with a lustful hunger but felt him pull away.

"I'm sorry," she murmured. "I keep forgetting you're injured. Did I..."

His placed his finger lightly on her lips, shaking his head. "No, you didn't hurt me," he said softly. "I just want to remember this moment forever."

Their mouths found each other again and her passion grew with intensity until it exploded when she felt him inside her. When they were finished, she lay with her head on his chest, enjoying the feel of his hand as he continued to caress her body.

She was not totally unaccustomed to making love, but it had never felt so good and so right in all her life as it did tonight. Her body tingled again under his touch and soon she was aroused to a passion that, until now, was something she thought existed only in books and the fantasies of others.

chapter twenty-three

Lance Morgan locked the public door from inside his arcade and walked to his office in the rear. It was mid-week, and business had been slow. He flicked off the lights and opened the rear door leading into a small parking area behind the arcade.

The barrel of a shotgun rammed deep into his belly below the rib cage. He doubled over, his lungs paralyzed as his knees sunk to the floor. Danny stepped forward and with his free hand grabbed Lance's hair and sent him sprawling backwards. Jack followed and flicked on the light to the office as the door swung shut behind him. He also carried a shotgun with a metal folded stock.

Lance looked up from the floor, still trying to catch his breath, and gasped, "Take it, guys, no need to hurt me. It's only about four hundred bucks. Mostly coin. I'll open it for ya," he said, waving his arm toward a small safe in the office.

"You don't remember me, do ya?" Jack barked out the words while stepping closer and sticking the barrel of the shotgun into Lance's crotch.

Lance used his hands and feet to edge himself backwards on the floor. He stopped when Jack pushed the shotgun deeper into his crotch. His eyebrows furled as he stared up at Jack.

"One week ago, behind the Black Water," Jack added.

The blood drained from Lance's face. He whispered, "You're Eddy!"

Jack smiled down at him. "So, how does it feel to be on the receiving end?"

"You ought to know," said Lance bitterly. "Live by the gun, die by the gun. Just do what you came here to do, man. I had nothin' against you personal, so just kill me an' get it over with."

"Tell you what," snarled Jack. "Tell me why you tried to kill me and maybe I'll consider letting you live!"

"Yeah, sure you will," said Lance sarcastically. "Besides, you know the answer to that yourself!"

"I want you to tell me!"

"You're a rat!"

"Who says so? Who told ya I was?" snapped Jack.

"I don't know, I was just carrying out orders," replied Lance defiantly.

"From who? Who were the two guys with ya? Fuckin' talk, man, or I'll blow ya away right now!"

"Fuck you. You're gonna do me anyway. I'm not sayin' nothin', so you might as well get it over with!"

Jack raised the shotgun and pointed it directly at Lance's face. Lance glared back. When he saw Jack's finger slowly squeeze down on the trigger he closed his eyes. The seconds ticked by. When he opened his eyes he saw that Jack had lowered the shotgun.

"I got some news for you, Lance. I'm not going to kill you. But I might arrest you!"

"You what?" asked Lance, looking confused.

Jack and Danny produced their badges.

"You guys are cops!" A nervous laugh escaped his lips.

"Yes, I'm a police officer. My real name is Jack Taggart. For attempting to murder me, you could be looking at a long time in the crowbar hotel."

"Oh, man," said Lance, shaking his head, "I didn't know you were a cop! I thought you were just a rat."

"Well, this could be your lucky night, Lance, because if *you* become a rat, we'll forget the whole thing!"

"What? You'd let me off tryin' to kill ya? Just for me to rat out?"

Jack nodded. "Yeah, but you'd be working for us for the next ten years. I think that's fair. You'd be ours, body and soul. You lie to us just once or try an' hide something from us and we feed you to the wolves!"

Lance reflected on the proposition, then gestured to a picture on his desk of his wife and four children. "I can't. Go ahead and bust me. I got them to think about."

"You've got my word. I will never arrest anyone or do anything if I think it will jeopardize your position. Once we haul you out of here it's too late to change your mind. You could be looking at life in prison. You won't be any good to your family in there."

"Thanks, man, I appreciate what you're sayin', but no, I'm still not turnin' in my brothers." He gave a weak smile, then added, "As they say, don't do the crime if you can't do the time!"

Jack picked up the picture of Lance's wife and children. "I'm no psychic, but I have a feeling that if you don't cooperate, you'll be a widower soon."

"What are you talking about?"

"If you don't cooperate, I'll arrest you now and charge you with stealing the car. Considering your record, you'll probably get about six months in jail. I'll put in a good word for you so you'll be out as soon as you're eligible."

"You're only going to charge me with stealing the clunker?" Lance gave Jack a puzzled look.

"Later tonight," continued Jack, "we'll pick up Wizard and Rolly and charge them with attempted murder. They'll end up getting life. Especially with the parole reports I'll do on them."

Lance gawked up from where he sat on the floor. "What do ya mean? You already know who they are? I tried to kill ya just as much as..." He stopped talking when he saw the grim smile creep across Jack's face.

"You can't! They'll think I cut a deal with ya! That I gave 'em up to save myself!"

Jack nodded. "Life's a bitch, ain't it! Your own brothers, as you call 'em, will do you just like Lenny. Except with you, they'll probably take it a bit more personal. I doubt they'd kill you as quickly as Lenny."

Lance sat in a stunned silence, slowly shaking his head. Jack knelt down so they could look at the picture together.

"Nice family. Tell me, I'm curious to see what will happen. You know your bros better than I do. If we see to it you serve your time in protective custody, where they can't get at you ... what do you think they'll do?"

"You fucking bastard! You know what they'll do!"

"Oh, well," said Jack, standing up. "What did you say? Live by the gun, die by the gun? Well I have one you can tell your family: If you fly with the crows, expect to get shot at."

Lance's face turned pasty white, and for the first time his trembling body betrayed his fear. He looked up and his voice quavered. "Okay, you guys win, but I gotta tell ya, you got someone on your side who's talkin'. Someone big."

Jack and Danny looked silently at each other for a moment, then Jack turned back to Lance. "We know there's someone. Who is it?"

"I don't know, man. I really don't know."

"Don't give us that shit!" said Danny. "If you cooperate, you go all the way!"

"I am fuckin' cooperating! Do you think I'm gonna fuck with you two, with what you'll do if I lie? I really don't know! Look at me, I'm shakin' I'm so fuckin' scared. If I knew who it was, I'd tell ya, just to make sure I stay alive! I told you I'd cooperate, and I will. I'm just sayin' you better fuckin' watch who you tell, 'cause I'm puttin' my life in your hands!"

"We'll be very selective on who knows," said Jack.

"If you're not, I'm dead." He nodded toward the desk and asked, "Can I get up now and sit down?"

"Got a piece in your desk?" asked Jack.

Lance smiled briefly. "No, it's not in my desk. It's fastened in a holster under the drawer. I wasn't gonna do you guys. I bet someone knows you're here?"

Jack ignored the question as he retrieved the pistol from underneath the desk drawer. "Not a bad piece of hardware: 9 mm," he said casually, before returning the pistol to where he had found it.

"You're not takin' it from me?" asked Lance.

"No, it would only inconvenience you until you got another one. We don't want to change how you operate. We just want to be informed. So have a seat. We have a few questions."

Lance got up off the floor, and after a few nervous glances at Jack and Danny, he pulled out the chair from the desk. He was careful to place his hands flat on top of the desk as he sat down. Jack sat on the edge of the desk, looking down at him, while holding the shotgun in one hand with the barrel pointing toward the ceiling. Danny stood to the side and held his weapon with both hands.

"So why, Lance? Why'd they try to kill me?"

"It wasn't you! We thought you were a rat!"

"Who told you?"

"Wizard an' Rolly. They have someone on the inside who lets them know what's goin' on. They call 'im The Suit. I don't know his real name and have never seen him. He likes young broads. I heard Wizard and Rolly laughing about him one day. Does sort of a power trip on 'em. I think he uses a dog, too. Rolly used to handle the whores. I think that's how they met the guy."

Jack thought about Marcie. He became conscious that the bullet wound in his upper arm hurt and realized that his fist was clenched. He took a deep breath and slowly exhaled.

Lance continued, "This guy has been talkin' for years, but except for maybe Damien, the rest of us don't know who he is, just in case."

"In case what?" asked Danny.

"In case you guys infiltrate the club somehow. Only a select few know what's goin' on."

"Last week in the alley, how did Wizard and Rolly know what I looked like?" asked Jack.

"Wiz knew some bitch who knew you. Red's her name. You must know her; she said you'd been buying from her."

"I knew her."

"She met us in a room at the BW about half an hour before we tried to do ya. She told us what you were wearing. Don't think she could help ya now. Wiz had her pegged as a loose end. Said he was gonna take care of her."

"She died of an overdose," said Danny.

"I'm pretty sure Wizard gave it to her," replied Lance.

"That's what we figured," said Jack. "How about Lenny? What happened with him?"

"It was the same way as you, except with Lenny, we didn't have any problems. I drove. Wiz shot 'im with a .22. It was the middle of the day and people were around, so he used a potato for a silencer. Rolly carved him up after. If somehow he got past them and ran, then I was supposed to drive over him." Lance looked at Jack. "Just like with you, except I didn't expect ya to run toward me. I couldn't drive over ya because that dumb, fat Rolly was right on your ass."

"Does Wizard still have the gun?" asked Danny.

"Naw, he probably threw it in the ocean. He never keeps it once he's done a job."

"So tell me, Lance, who was it that blew up Crystal?" asked Jack.

"Crystal? Was that the whore on the freeway who tried to skip out?"

"Yes, that one," said Jack, glancing at Danny. The knuckles on Danny's hands turned white as he gripped the shotgun.

Lance took a deep breath and exhaled slowly. "Oh man, I just don't know," he mumbled, putting his elbows on the table and holding his head with his hands.

"What do you mean, you don't know?" yelled Danny.

"That's not what I mean," muttered Lance, shaking his head. "I just don't know if I'm doin' the right thing by talkin'. I didn't mind about Lenny, 'cause I knew you had that one figured out, but…" His voice trailed off and there was silence as Lance grappled with his uncertainty.

Jack picked up the family picture. Lance eyed him nervously as he laid the picture down on the desk between Lance's elbows. Lance looked down at his family. They disintegrated before his eyes as Jack smashed the butt of his shotgun into the glass. Splinters of glass sprayed out while other pieces tore into the faces on the portrait. Lance fell back in his chair. His eyes were wide and his mouth opened and closed. Fear and anger made him speechless.

Jack reached for the telephone and said to Danny, "I'm calling the office. We'll have Wizard and Rolly arrested tonight."

"It was Axle and Nails! Don't call, man! I'm tellin' ya, it was them!"

Jack was silent for a moment, then said, "There's no going back now."

Lance looked at the picture and sighed, then said, "Yeah, I know."

Jack replaced the telephone receiver and asked, "What role did you play?"

"I had nothin' to do with that one! Nails was in some special branch of the army. He knows all about makin' bombs an' booby traps."

"Who besides Axle and Nails were involved?" asked Jack.

"The hit would have been sanctioned by Wizard or Damien, but I don't think anyone else was involved. It's not the sort of thing you normally talk about, but a few of the boys were called out to watch hospitals and clinics the night we tried to whack you. Axle was paired up with me. He's still striking and he told me all about how Nails planted a bomb on her car. He wanted to know if I thought he would get his patch for what happened."

"What role did Axle play?" asked Jack.

"He stood six while Nails planted the bomb."

"That's all? He was just a lookout?" asked Jack.

"He also drove and followed the whore until Nails detonated the bomb. Axle supplies us with hot cars when we need 'em. Whatever he was drivin' when they followed the whore would have been stolen. It was Axle who got me the car we used on Lenny. The same goes for the Volvo I used for you."

Jack leaned over, close to Lance's face. Lance felt uncomfortable and started to roll his chair back, but Jack gripped the armrest. "What other murders do you know about?"

Lance swallowed, then said, "Well, two others for sure."

"Start with the most recent one," said Jack.

"They were both killed together, not too long ago."

Jack found himself holding his breath, listening to every sound to come out of Lance's mouth. *This is it!* His grip on the chair and shotgun became intense. His muscles rippled and the knife wound on his back oozed blood. He could see every blemish and pore on Lance's face.

"It was a couple of Vietnamese guys," continued Lance. "I don't know their names, but they were brothers. They were startin' to move a lot of speed on the west side. Real good stuff. Ice. We warned them to go someplace else, but they didn't listen."

"When was this?" Jack relaxed his grip and struggled to keep tears from appearing.

"It would be a year ago next week. I remember it because it was the Thursday before the May long weekend. Wizard has a boat out in White Rock. A big one, for fishin' an' crabbin'. My job was to bring a couple of oil drums an' a wheelbarrow full of bricks out to his boat. We stuffed one guy in each drum, popped holes, weighed 'em down, and rolled 'em overboard."

"You killed them on the boat?" asked Jack.

"Naw, actually I didn't see who killed 'em and I didn't ask. Wizard, Rolly, and I were already out on the boat. Wizard didn't want to take a chance on haulin' the bodies down the pier in White Rock. It's too long and there's lots of tourists. We left the dock an' four of the guys delivered 'em to us in a speedboat. They were already dead. Shot once in the head. Wiz didn't want to make a big deal out of it. There's too many of them Asians, an' they don't give a fuck who they kill. Wizard decided it would be better if they disappeared, so we wouldn't be startin' any wars or anything."

"Who were the four guys who delivered the bodies in the speed boat?"

"It was all guys from our chapter. Sparrow, Pan-Head, Halibut, an' Rockin' Ronnie. I think it was Rockin' Ronnie who did 'em, but he's dead now. Some old lady hung a left turn in front of 'im when he was ridin' his bike this summer. He piled right into her."

"What makes you think it was Rockin' Ronnie who shot them?" asked Jack.

"Yeah, it's kind of convenient," said Danny, "the guy you say did it is now dead."

"I didn't say he fuckin' done it, I said I *think* he fuckin' done it!" replied Lance, glaring at Danny.

"Why?" asked Jack.

Lance looked back at Jack. "Well if Halibut had done it, he'd have probably gotten his patch soon after. But he's still strikin'. That leaves Sparrow, Pan-Head, and Rockin' Ronnie. I noticed that Rockin' Ronnie had a fresh lookin' DD tattoo about a week later. Sparrow and Pan-Head still don't have one."

"What tattoo?" asked Jack.

"The Dirty Dog. It first started about four or five years ago. You can earn it by doin' a hit that's sanctioned by the executive. It's got to be verified, too."

"The Dirty Dog," Jack repeated. The words replayed through his brain.

"Yeah," Lance replied. "I know he didn't have it before, so I'm presumin' that's how he earned it."

"How big is this tattoo?" asked Jack abruptly. "What does it look like? Could you see it, say, from across a room?"

"You could, if the lighting was good. I don't have one, or I would show ya. It's just the words *Dirty Dog* tattooed over the head of a pitbull. Most guys get it on their biceps, but if they already got a tattoo there, then they usually put it on their forearm."

"Names!" Jack demanded harshly. "I want the names of everyone who has them!"

"I don't know everyone for sure," said Lance, nervously. "It's not somethin' most guys run around showin' off right away, either. At least, not if they're smart. Just off the top of my head, I'd say I know about six or seven guys who got it."

"Write down their names!"

Lance slowly pulled open the desk drawer and retrieved a pen and a sheet of paper. A minute later, he pushed the list toward Jack. "There may be others, but these ones I know."

Jack looked at the list: Wizard, Nails, Rockin' Ronnie, Thumper, Whisky Jake, and Two-Forty Gordy.

"Who are Two-Forty Gordy, Whiskey Jake, and Thumper?"

"Just guys in the club. Different chapter than me. They're from the east side. Two-Forty probably weighs three-forty now."

"This is all of them?"

"All I can remember."

"If you remember any more names, call me on my cell!" said Jack, ripping off a piece of paper and writing his number down. He stared intently at Lance's face and asked, "The two Vietnamese brothers are the only other murders you know about?"

"Yeah. Them and Lenny and the whore on the freeway. I guess Red, too, if she was hit."

"I don't suppose the club, or the executive, keeps any list of who gets a Dirty Dog tattoo and when they get it?"

"Naw, are you kiddin'? Would be too risky in case it fell into the wrong hands."

"Who does the tattooing?"

"A friend of the club owns a parlour down near the waterfront in Vancouver. He does all the club tattoos. It's called Popeye's. He's had the place for years."

Jack nodded, then asked nonchalantly, "By the way, who handles the speed coming in from Montreal?"

"Hey! I'm impressed! You know about that already? We only got that started a couple of months ago!"

"Tell us what you know about it. When's the next shipment due?"

"Not much to tell. We either pay cash or swap blow for speed with our brothers in Montreal. Someday we'll get our own labs out here, but for the moment, the French shit is excellent. Wizard went to Montreal and set up the original connection. I think we've only done one deal so far. Fifty keys is what Rolly told me."

"Rolly is handling it?"

"He picked up the first shipment to make sure everything went smooth. It came by train. I think another shipment is due this Friday. They'll probably get one of the strikers to handle it now. Likely either Halibut or Dragon."

"No problems with the first shipment?" Jack studied Lance's face carefully.

"Not as far as I know. That's some of the same stuff you were buying from Red."

"You guys got any heavy connections an hour or so drive out in the Valley? Someone that Rolly may have dealt with on that first shipment?"

"Nobody that I know of. I don't think he would make a big delivery out there. Maybe some of the strikers got some people. I don't know everyone."

"Would it draw any heat on you if this next shipment gets taken down?" asked Jack.

"Don't think so. Especially if it's a striker. They might think the heat came from Montreal."

Jack stood up and said, "Stay in touch. We'll talk again in a couple of days."

"I won't be around if it's this coming weekend."

"Why not?"

"We're taking our hawgs out for one last run before winter. Headin' up to the interior for a big bash. Leavin' Friday afternoon and comin' back Sunday. Pretty well the whole club is going. Taking our ol' ladies along too."

"Then go. But if we find out you're holding anything back on us, you're dead meat."

Lance didn't respond, so Jack said, "Did you hear me?"

"I've got ears," he replied sullenly.

When Jack and Danny were at the door, Lance asked, "So tell me, man, how close did we come to doin' ya? I thought Wiz plugged ya."

Jack yawned, then said, "Got me once, but it ricocheted off my back and through my arm. Rolly slashed my back with a knife. It did more damage than the bullet did."

Lance nodded. "Yeah, I guess a .22 is okay if you got it stuck in someone's ear or the base of their neck, but I figure if they'd been usin' a 9 mm, you wouldn't have been so lucky."

"Yeah, you're probably right. See you around."

Lance sat and stared at the broken picture after Jack and Danny had left. He thought about Jack's response to his last question. *Tough motherfucker. Seems to tell it straight.* For a moment it made him feel safer, then a wave of fear and shame overtook his brain.

Danny waited until they were in the car before turning to Jack. "You did it! Just like you said you would. You got somebody on the inside!"

"We did it. The two of us."

"So, the guy they call The Suit has to be the one who molested Marcie."

Jack nodded.

"And now we know who murdered Crystal! Let's haul their asses in! Maybe Homicide can match something from the bomb on Crystal's car to Nails' and Axle's houses."

"No."

"No?"

"I gave Lance my word. Arresting them would jeopardize his position."

"Busting Axle and Nails is more important than worrying about that piece of shit!"

Jack looked sharply at Danny. "Always keep your word!"

"What the fuck is wrong with you? They murdered Crystal! You were there! Did you see her eyes? She was —"

"I was there."

Danny drove the car out of the lot before saying, "You're waiting to get information about Maggie and Ben Junior, aren't you? That makes sense, except Lance doesn't know anything about that, so let's arrest Axle and Nails. Maybe they do! One of them might talk!"

"I gave Lance my word."

"This is bullshit! I don't believe you!"

"You better believe me, because it's true. It's about respect."

"You're telling me that you respect that asshole sitting in there!"

"It's about us having respect, not him. And actually, yes, I do respect him."

Danny's face reddened. His nostrils flared and his lips curled down, exposing his teeth. "He's a sleazebag! Kept referring to Crystal a whore! How can you respect him?"

"In Lance's world you use derogatory names. If you dehumanize them, it's easier on your conscience. What was he supposed to refer to her as? The young woman who was being sexually victimized?"

"Crystal was a good person."

"I know she was. I respect her for what she tried to do."

"But Lance is nothing but scum!"

"How would you respond if someone shoved a shotgun into your nuts? Would you have the guts to stare them in the eye and refuse to talk? Think about it! He expected to die! No whimpering, no pleading. The only reason he did cooperate was to protect his family. Yes, I have some respect for him too."

"He tried to kill you!"

"Hey! I respect that he's dangerous! He could still flip back to the other side. Which is why I didn't give him your name or cell number."

"Why not?"

"You have a family to look after. As I said, I respect the fact that he's dangerous."

"That's bullshit! I'm your partner. Susan knows the risks. She married me —"

"That doesn't mean *you* have to take risks if you don't need to."

Danny shook his head. "I guess it doesn't really matter. If you're not going to do anything, then we're no further ahead. Not when it comes to your sister's kids."

"We're a lot further ahead. This is the first phase in gaining control."

Danny drove another two blocks, then said, "So now what do you propose we do?"

"Keep quiet about Axle and Nails. Verify what we can about what Lance told us, then concentrate on Wizard and Rolly. They were involved in the original speed connection. Find out if they have contacts up the Valley and find out who the leak is."

"How? Lance didn't know of any —"

"They're leaving on a ride this Friday. Search their places. Maybe turn up an address book or phone numbers."

"You figure we have enough to get search warrants?"

"No. Even if we did, we don't know who the leak is. I'm not jeopardizing Lance. Speaking of which, from now on, we don't use his name. No slip-ups — anywhere!"

"What do you plan on calling him?"

"Just refer to him as our friend."

"*Your* friend, maybe, not mine. And now you're talking about doing illegal searches."

"Damn it, Danny! Do I have to spell everything out? You sound like you're wearing a wire and working for Internal, for God's sake."

Danny squirmed in his seat and glanced out his side window.

"I appreciate that you have a family," continued Jack. "I'll understand if you don't want to take risks. If you want to work on something else, talk with Louie and get reassigned. But make a decision. I need someone I can trust and depend on."

"With what we've been through, don't you feel you can trust me yet?"

Jack looked at Danny and sighed. "I'm sorry. I owe you my life. I know I can trust you. But you do have Susan and Tiffany to think about. I've done enough searches in my life; I don't really need you to come along."

"Yeah, right. In the space of a month, my hand was slashed with a knife and I stabbed a junkie in the back. You've been shot and stabbed. Lenny, Crystal, and Red murdered..."

"It does sound like we could be on to something."

"It's not funny! I'm waking up at night seeing Crystal's eyes, asking why I got her killed."

"You see what you want. I see her eyes, too. I see her asking for justice."

"Whatever! But that's what I see and I'm not bailing out now! I may not agree with you, but I'm still your partner."

"Glad you feel that way. There is something else." Jack paused as the memories of an abandoned farmhouse interrupted his thoughts.

"Something else?"

Jack swallowed, then said, "The last thing Maggie did before she was murdered was print the word *Dirty* in her sketchbook. Tomorrow night I'm going to take a look at Popeye's. See if there is any record of who has the Dirty Dog tattoo or when they got it."

"You think she saw that word tattooed on someone?"

"It's possible."

Danny shook his head, then mumbled, "What the hell. After what's happened so far, what are a few break-ins going to matter. Speaking of which, how do you plan on getting in?"

Jack took a leather case out of his jacket pocket and flashed Danny an array of lock picks.

"Where did you get those? Do you know how to use them?"

Jack smiled, then said, "Some locksmith must have dropped them. Yes, I know how to use them. Believe me, with *my* new friend helping, nothing will stop us. It's just a matter of time. I'm also going to revive Eddy Trimble and give the City narcs a present."

"Bart and Rex?"

"Can't use our narcs. We're only doing surveillance, remember?"

"What if one of them is the leak?"

"*My* friend didn't think he would draw any heat if it was taken down. If it was one of the narcs, they wouldn't have turned me into an informant in the first place. I trust them. Wish I could say the same for the rest of their office — or our own people."

"Enough emphasis on *my* friend already! I'm your partner. He can be *our* friend."

"Good. Welcome aboard. Hope you enjoy the ride!"

An hour later, Danny arrived home in time to pick up his telephone. He recognized the harsh voice immediately.

"This is Superintendent Wigmore. Meet me at the Oceanside Lounge. Immediately!"

chapter twenty-four

Danny spotted Wigmore sitting alone in the lounge. Wigmore scowled at him and nodded toward a chair. Danny sat down as the waiter approached the table.

"Bring me another Glennfiddich on the rocks," commanded Wigmore. "This time, bring the Scotch on the side." He gestured toward Danny and said, "Nothing for him; he won't be staying."

Wigmore waited until the waiter left, then said, "Tell me, O'Reilly, why do men pay prostitutes money?"

"Sir?"

"A simple question." Wigmore's voice became sarcastic. "Surely you've been a policeman long enough to have heard about prostitutes."

"Men pay prostitutes money in exchange for sex," said Danny.

"Any other reasons?"

"Not that I can think of."

"Do you think it conceivable that a man who has engaged a prostitute would murder her if she was perhaps going to spill the beans on him, so to speak?"

"Yes, sir. I guess that is conceivable."

Wigmore stared smugly at Danny while the waiter returned with his order.

"Ice in your glass, with the Scotch on the side," said the waiter, somewhat contemptuously.

Wigmore waited until the waiter left before continuing. "So, O'Reilly, you've answered why you paid a prostitute — Miss Doyle — money."

Danny was shocked. "I don't know what you're talking about! I don't know any Miss Doyle!"

"Come come now, O'Reilly. You paid Miss Christine Doyle's bill for her at a garage. With the tow bill it came to over $800."

"Crystal! I didn't know her real —"

"Oh, of course. You would have known her by the name she uses for customers."

"I wasn't a customer!" The edge to Danny's voice revealed his anger.

"We've got your credit card receipt! An auto mechanic identified your photo as being the man who paid her bill! He also saw you and a woman hugging her in the garage parking lot."

"That woman was my wife."

"I see. You and your wife are into ... group activities, are you?"

Danny seethed with anger. He opened and closed his fists under the table to control his rage. "We were simply helping her out! Her car broke down. She needed help!"

"Forget the charade, O'Reilly! Homicide traced the cell number! You just told me you couldn't think of any reason a man would pay a prostitute except for sex. She was talking to you on the phone the next day when she was murdered! What have you got to say about that? It appears to me that you may have been involved in her murder!"

Danny fought to keep his composure. *This son of bitch wouldn't have called me here if he really believed what he was saying.* Danny glared at Wigmore and said, "Right! Let's forget the charade! What do you really want?"

"Don't get snarky with me, O'Reilly! I know Taggart is involved! I warned you before about him! People dying around him is nothing new. Think about it! Since you've been his partner, there was this Leonard character in the back alley. Now a hooker is murdered while talking to you, and you not only don't inform me, you also don't report it to Homicide!"

Danny started to protest, but Wigmore held up his hand to silence him, then continued, "Just for argument's sake, even if you did help this hooker with her car and happened to introduce her to your wife, it's against policy. However, as a police officer, not reporting what you know to Homicide is obstruction of justice! And that's a criminal matter! You're already in trouble for neglect of duty in regards to the PM. Now this!"

"I — I didn't report it because I just thought the phone went dead. She just phoned to say goodbye. I thought she was moving back east."

Wigmore shook his head. "Get it through your skull, O'Reilly. I warned you not to get sucked into Taggart's world. I even understand that you're scared and that's why you just lied to me. It's Taggart I want, but if you continue to act dumb and not cooperate, then you'll both end up in the same cell."

"It's not that I'm not cooperating, it's just that he isn't doing anything wrong."

Wigmore chuckled, shaking his head, then said, "So there would be no problem with me scheduling you to take the polygraph? Start off with about a dozen questions concerning policy matters, then look at criminal matters. Questions like: did you intentionally hinder the investigation into Christine Doyle's murder?"

Wigmore picked up on the look of fear on Danny's face. *Or is it guilt?* It triggered a response like a shark to blood. He leaned across the table until his breath was in Danny's face. "Perhaps question if your actions contributed to her murder?"

Danny stared back at Wigmore. He didn't know how to respond. He wondered what he would say to Susan.

Wigmore leaned back in his chair. He had made his point. "I'll be out of town for the next two days. I expect to hear from you on Monday. With the weekend, that gives you four days to think about it. By then, if you decide not to spill the beans, I'll demand a full Internal. Starting with slapping you on the polygraph!"

It was noon when Danny walked into the office. Jack was already there, and by the amount of paper piled up, he had been at work for a while. Danny plunked himself down.

Jack looked at him and asked, "What's wrong? You look like you've been up all night."

"Nothing's wrong."

"If you're that upset about these searches, I told you, I'll do them myself!"

"I'm just tired. A lot happened last night for me to think about."

"It was a good night. I've got more good news. I found a report from Vancouver City on Asian gangs. Two Vietnamese brothers who were controlling speed distribution in Chinatown, as well the west side, disappeared last year around the May long weekend, leaving their cars, money, and homes untouched."

"It looks like our friend is telling the truth."

"I think we can chalk them up as crab bait. I also wandered into Popeye's this morning. No sign of an alarm system. We'll do it tonight and Rolly and Wizard's places tomorrow night. Go in a couple hours after midnight. Shouldn't be anyone around."

Danny silently nodded his head. *Three break-ins. Wigmore would be happy with that. Or would he still wait for Jack to get caught with the ultimate crime? As Jack said, it's just a matter of time....* Wigmore's words lit up the closets of his mind like neon lights. *Don't get sucked into his world! Breaking the law ... murders ... Jack's world.* He saw Jack studying his face and turned away. He had to make a decision.

"Jack, if we're going to be that late, then I've got some personal business to take care of this afternoon. Do you mind?"

"No, go ahead. I'm going to meet Natasha for dinner. Let's meet back here at midnight."

"What is it, honey?" Susan asked. "I didn't expect you back so soon."

"I have to talk to you."

"Sounds serious."

"It is."

Danny sat at the kitchen table with Susan. The words suddenly spilled out of him. He confessed about his meetings with Wigmore and that he had been ordered to spy on Jack.

If Danny was looking for sympathy, he didn't find it. "And you waited until now to tell me?" Susan shouted.

"I was following orders. I couldn't tell anyone."

"You're my husband! You call this a marriage? We're supposed to talk with each other!"

"I am! Telling you and defying orders!"

"So, why now?" she yelled. "Are you hoping to unload your bundle of guilt on me? Are you hoping I'll say that you're doing the right thing? What?"

"I'll carry the guilt for this all my life. It's my load to carry, but what I do now could affect *our* future. Not just mine. Yours, mine, and Tiffany's."

"And Jack's."

"And Jack's."

"So why now? What's going on that you decided to tell me?"

"Jack and I have a new informant. We just found out who killed Crystal. It might not be long before we find out who killed Jack's niece and nephew."

Susan's face brightened. "Well, that's good!" She paused and added, "Isn't it? This Wigmore fellow will be pleased with that!"

"I don't think so. Jack's not supposed to be involved with the investigation. Besides, as far as Crystal goes, we could never prove it legally."

"So what will you do?"

Danny shrugged. "I don't think there's anything I can do. It's just ... I'm worried about what Jack might do. Especially if we find out who killed his niece and nephew."

"What do you mean? You think he'll..." Susan stared at Danny, waiting for an answer.

Danny didn't reply.

"You better not do anything you shouldn't!"

"That's why I'm talking to you! I want to do what's right, I just don't know what that is."

The concern in Susan's voice was evident. "Danny, what has happened to you? This isn't like you. We used to talk, remember? You've really changed since we moved here. I look into your eyes and you're not the same person."

Danny took a deep breath and slowly exhaled. "You're right about that. When I shave in the morning ... I don't see my own eyes looking back at me."

"What do you mean?"

"I see Crystal's eyes. I see them all the time. Now I'm being haunted by your eyes and Jack's eyes as well."

Susan sat quietly. Moments later, Danny caught the frightened look on her face as she stood up. "I'm going upstairs to vacuum. You do what you think is right."

Her voice sounded tired and empty. Danny sighed. *What is right?*

Susan started to walk away, then stopped and asked, "Will you ever be haunted by Wigmore's eyes?"

"No, not that asshole. Why?"

"You're the policeman, you figure it out."

Danny stared after Susan when she left. He realized he loved her very much.

Jack stood in the doorway, shivering in the darkness as a moist, cool breeze blew up from the ocean. His fingers worked the pick and he felt the lock start to turn as the tumblers slid into position. The building had been painted green, but most of the paint had peeled, exposing the wooden structure to the elements.

Above his head, a sign hanging from a wrought-iron pole squeaked as it waved slightly back and forth. The word *POPEYE'S* was hand-painted in red ink on the sign, over a faded emblem of a ship's anchor.

Danny stood behind him, staring out at the empty street before risking a glance back at Jack. "Do you want me to hold a flashlight for you?"

"No, it's okay," whispered Jack. "I go more by feel than I do by sight."

"You're sure it's not alarmed?"

"Not from what I could tell this morning. I wouldn't think there'd be much for someone to steal, but we're about to find out."

Jack opened the door and they stepped inside.

The front office was small, and Jack quickly searched for business records but didn't find any. He made his way to a room at the rear, which was only slightly larger. The beam from his flashlight revealed another open door leading into a washroom. He fanned the beam around the room. There wasn't much to see. A table, couple of chairs, a barstool, a cot, and a shelf with tattooing supplies.

He pulled out a book from under the cot, along with two other dust-covered books he found further back. They contained pictures and sketches of various types of tattoos. The Dirty Dog tattoo was not among them, nor was it on any of the walls.

He shone his light across the calendars on the wall. "Danny! I found it."

Danny came up beside him, and Jack turned and smiled with satisfaction. "Take a look," he whispered. "These are his appointment books!"

Danny shone his light on the block numbers below the pictures. Names and times were lightly penciled in on a couple of the dates.

"Look!" said Jack excitedly, pointing to one entry. "Look at the date here, it's got *1 p.m.* and the names *Sheila, Rose.*"

"Two women getting tattoos!"

"Or someone by the name of Sheila was getting a tattoo of a rose," whispered Jack. He flipped through the calendar to August. He could feel the tension grip his heart and lungs. His eyes met Danny's and he slowly shook his head. He turned the page to September.

"It's here!" shouted Jack, jabbing at an entry with his finger. "Only two weeks after Maggie and Ben Junior were murdered! Take a look!"

Danny looked down at the notation on the calendar. The words *Rolly-DD* were printed above a brief narrative in brackets, *conf Wiz.*

"This is it!" Jack said. "Dirty Dog, confirmed by Wizard!" He grabbed Danny by the shoulder. "Remember? Our friend said a hit had to be verified and sanctioned!"

The intensity of Jack's voice made Danny feel uneasy. He cleared his throat. "The timing seems right, but with the number of murders these guys do, we can't be positive."

Jack's voice was laced with anger. "It's them, all right. Explains why Rolly isn't bragging about it. Not much respect for killing children. I bet Wizard was with him."

"So what do you plan to do? We can't use any of this as evidence. We've got no grounds to get a search warrant."

"It's evidence for me!" Jack paused for a moment, then said, "But you're right, we can't be positive. We'll keep digging until we are."

"Then what?"

Jack let the pages fall back to their original position and walked out the door.

*

Once inside the car, Jack looked intensely into Danny's eyes and said, "I know it's Wizard and Rolly. The timing is right. Rolly got his tattoo ... it all falls into place. Our friend said a murder had to be confirmed and sanctioned. Maggie was shot through the door. Until then, they wouldn't have known that Maggie and Ben Junior were there. Rolly would have never risked phoning anyone to sanction the hit. Wizard had to have been with him."

"Or someone else who was executive. That's if it was Rolly who did it."

"Wizard arranged the original shipment and Rolly handled the delivery. The two of them killed Lenny and tried to kill me. I know it's them. We'll do their places tomorrow night."

Jack hadn't raised his voice, but there was no mistaking the cold look in his eyes and the venom in his voice.

Danny wondered if Jack would wait until tomorrow night to look for more evidence. He cleared his throat and said, "If it was Wizard and Rolly who were there, it's still possible that they were with another dope dealer. Someone else might have murdered them as well."

"When I get my hands on them, I'll find out!"

Danny knew that the time had come. "Jack, let's go to the seawall. We need to talk."

"I don't feel like drinking right now."

"You might when you hear what I have to say."

Jack jumped down from where he was sitting on the seawall and took a couple of angry steps in the sand before turning to confront Danny. "I should have known from the first time I worked with you! You stabbed someone in the back that night! Now you're stabbing me!"

"I'm not stabbing you in the back! I've never told Wigmore anything, except for that first night about you going in the Black Water, and I covered for that later."

"Well you sure as hell didn't tell me anything, either! I thought we were partners! You're supposed to talk with your partner! Why the hell are you telling me now? Do you expect me to forgive you? Tell you I'll understand? What?"

"Jesus. You sound like Susan," muttered Danny. "That's what she said." He then looked up to the sky, holding his hands to the heavens, and yelled, "I'm not asking for forgiveness!"

"Then what are you asking for?"

"I'm just telling you so you know what's going on. You do anything rash and Wigmore will be all over the both of us. I'm trying to protect your ass as much as mine! I told you because you are my partner and I'm not ratting you out!"

"When did you tell Susan?"

"This afternoon."

"You waited until now to tell her?"

"Yes, and now she's scared. I knew she would be."

"Worried about her family," said Jack, his voice calming down.

Danny nodded and said, "Yeah. That and she's really pissed at me."

"So am I. You should have told me sooner."

Jack walked back to the car and got in as Danny reached for the passenger door. It was locked. Jack gestured at Danny with his middle finger and then drove away.

Danny waved his fist and shouted, "You son of a bitch!"

It took Danny an hour to walk out of the park and find a taxi to the office. It was another forty-five minutes before he arrived home.

He was shocked to see Jack's car blocking his garage door. He parked on the street and got out of his car as the front door to his house opened. He saw Jack putting on his coat. Susan, holding a glass of wine, laughed at something he said. She gave him a hug and kissed him on the cheek. Jack walked toward his car.

Danny stood in the driveway with his mouth hanging open. Susan looked at Danny and yelled, "Hi, honey! Glad you finally made it home!"

Jack unlocked his car and glanced across the roof at Danny. "See you at the office at ten tomorrow night. Let me know if you're bringing an arrest team so I can get a lawyer." He then drove away.

Danny went inside his house. "What's going on? Do you know that the son of a bitch dumped me in a park tonight? I had to take a cab..."

"I know," snickered Susan. "Want some wine? Oops! Guess there's none left."

"What's going on? Why are you so happy all of a sudden?"

Susan turned to face Danny. Her voice became serious and she said, "Jack told me that he would always protect you and our family — even if you are a bonehead. He said I had his word on that."

Danny didn't respond.

"Do you think Jack's word is good?"

"Jack's word is good."

"I thought so. I respect him. Trust him, too, to do what he says."

Danny sighed, then said, "It all sounds nice, but how do you protect yourself from someone like Wigmore?"

"That bastard! You hadn't mentioned that he accused me and you of having a threesome with Crystal!"

"Jack shouldn't have told you that part."

"I'm glad he did. He has a plan. He said I could help. I'm looking forward to it."

"What do you mean? He's got a plan? You're not getting involved with this shit."

"Wigmore tried to fuck with my family! You're damn right I'm getting involved!"

"What plan? What does he want you to do?"

"Talk, talk, talk. I'm horny. Let's go to bed."

"Tell me about the plan!"

"It starts off with the two of us having sex."

"What?"

"That's what Jack said I'm to do. Oh yeah, and tell you I love you because he says you really love me."

"Jack said that?"

"Yup. Then we fuck Wigglemore after."

"That's Wigmore. And I don't like it when you swear."

"It's your fault. I swear when I'm horny."

chapter twenty-five

Jack listened to the news on Friday afternoon. "Vancouver City Police recorded the city's largest ever seizure of methamphetamine around noon today. Fifty kilos of the drug were seized at the train station. Police attribute the seizure to an anonymous tip received by the police in Montreal. A juvenile from Montreal was arrested, along with a local man known in the underworld by the unusual name of Halibut. His real name…"

Jack's telephone rang a minute later.

"You hear the news?" asked Danny.

"Sounds like the narcs will be happy with Eddy Trimble. Bet I could get them to buy me a beer."

"No kidding! You were right about Bart and Rex. They're trustworthy."

"They even threw in the bit about the anonymous call in Montreal. They're not only trustworthy, but they're doing their best to protect me."

"Or Eddy Trimble."

"Whatever. It's good news. This is just the beginning. I told you there would be no stopping us now. How's Susan?"

"Her head hurts a little, no thanks to you, but she's fine. We had a good talk last night. Thanks. I really owe you."

"Talk? That's not what I told her to do to you!"

Danny paused, then said, "Right. She fucked some sense into me, too."

Jack chuckled and Danny continued, "Susan said you have a plan to get Wigmore off my back?"

"I haven't worked out all the finer details. We'll have to wait until Monday when he returns, but trust me, by then I'll have it together. Need a woman to help us, though."

"Susan's primed. She wants to help."

"Good. See you tonight at the office."

"This time I'm driving!" yelled Danny. He was too late. Jack had hung up.

Danny checked his watch. The search of Wizard's penthouse apartment hadn't taken long. All they had found was a .357 magnum revolver stuck in a holster fixed to the back of a bedside table. None of the phone numbers they located had prefixes for outside the city.

"That was quick," whispered Danny. "Took us less than fifteen minutes. Do you still plan on doing Rolly's? His place is an old house; it's going to take a lot longer."

"Yes, I plan on doing Rolly's! Just give me a minute."

Jack took the .357 from its holster and stuck the barrel of the gun deep down into the dirt of a houseplant. He then tamped the dirt in the barrel with his pen, wiped off the outside of the gun, and replaced it in the holster.

"Maybe if we get lucky it'll blow up in his face," said Jack bitterly, ushering Danny out the door.

Danny's silence as Jack drove to Rolly's house betrayed his troubled thoughts.

"You're quiet," said Jack.

"Thinking about what you did with the piece back there."

"Think it's wrong? If he shoots at you it won't seem wrong."

"If we do find out Wizard and Rolly killed your sister's kids, what do you plan to do?"

Jack parked a block down the street from Rolly's house and they walked the remaining distance. It was in an older district that was heavily treed. A few street lights lit up the street, but the neighbourhood appeared to be asleep.

Only the top half of Rolly's two-storey house was visible in the moonlight. It was completely surrounded by large cedar trees and was set back from the road. An eight-foot chain-link fence encircled the property at the edge of the treeline. Three strands of barbed wire stood out at an angle from the top of the fence, adding more height. A gate across the driveway was padlocked shut and bathed by floodlights.

Danny looked at the chain-link fence and then at Jack. "Well?"

"The gate's out in the open." Jack looked up at the fence and added, "My back and arm are still a little tender, but I can make it. It'll be safer than picking the padlock. These trees should give us enough protection from the street."

Minutes later, Danny was at the top of the fence. He flung his jacket over the strands of barbed wire before making his way down the other side. Jack eased himself over the top and climbed down to join him.

A low growl caused both men to leap for the fence. Danny reached the top as Jack yelled in pain. The German shepherd had its teeth clenched on a torn strip of his pants and he was slowly dragging the dog up the fence.

"He's got me! Do something!" said Jack, gritting his teeth as the snarling dog shook its head in a frenzy while dangling from the torn cloth.

"I bet this is the dog the pervert used with Marcie! What do you think?"

"Christ! I don't know! Do something!"

"Shake him off!"

"It's all I can do to hang on! If I fall there won't be enough of me left to make a stir-fry!"

"Want me to shoot 'im?"

"No. The noise will wake up the neighbours! If Rolly sees his dog dead…"

Danny watched as Jack tried to shake his leg. The cloth tore a little more, but then held fast at the seam at the bottom of his ankle. Danny eased back down the fence and kicked the dog squarely on top of the head. The dog didn't let go, but Jack's fingers slipped a notch.

"Don't! Watch … Oh, great! Lights!"

Across the street a neighbour's upstairs light had come on. Jack tossed his gun, keys, and one ankle boot over the fence as another interior light came on. Then he undid his belt. Seconds later, he clambered down the fence as the front porch light was turned on.

The door opened, and a man in a housecoat stepped out onto the porch and walked over to the railing and stood looking toward the fence.

Jack and Danny lay on the ground while Danny peered at the man from behind a tree.

On the other side of the fence, the dog took out its frustration by shredding Jack's pants and grinding them into the dirt.

"What's he doing? Did he see us?"

"I don't think so. He's just standing there," whispered Danny, glancing back at his half-naked partner. "What should we do if he comes over?"

"Pretend we're gay."

Danny's silent prayer was answered when the man went back inside.

"He's gone. Now what?" asked Danny.

"Wait a few minutes to make sure he's not still watching, then get the car and take me home. We've still got tomorrow night to come up with something."

They watched as the dog quit growling, picked up Jack's pants, and trotted back toward the house.

"Just like he's bringing home a trophy," said Danny.

Jack's reply was inaudible as he limped over to pick up his gun, keys, and boot.

Jack glanced back inside the compound. The dog had returned, without the pants, and was standing over his other ankle boot, staring back, as if daring him to try to retrieve it.

A short time later, Danny eased the car over to the curb in front of Jack's apartment, and Jack hobbled inside. With the interior light on, Danny saw the blood seeping through Jack's fingers as he held his leg.

"You're hurt!"

"He took a chunk out of my calf, but I don't think it's as bad as it looks," said Jack, easing his hand off.

"You might need stitches."

"Damn it!"

"Natasha?" asked Danny.

Jack groaned. "I guess I'd better. I'm not going to Emergency like this. She's home now."

"Great!" replied Danny enthusiastically.

"What do you mean, great?"

"I want to see how you explain losing your pants."

Danny chuckled. "Almost makes up for dumping me in the park last night."

"Slow down and make sure we don't get stopped for speeding," grumbled Jack.

Twenty-four hours later, Jack and Danny sat in a brown four-door sedan. It belonged to a Highway Patrol unit. There were no markings on the car, but with a thick Plexiglas shield between the front and back seat, most people could easily identify it as a police car. They slowly drove up the alley behind Rolly's house.

They got out of the car and walked up to the fence. Jack picked up a handful of gravel from the lane and tossed it over the fence. The dog appeared instantly, pressing its jaws up against the fence to reveal a snarling, salivating mouth full of teeth.

"Good," said Jack. "Keep him here for about ten minutes while I pick the lock, then bring him around front. Don't stumble!"

"You don't have to tell me," responded Danny.

Ten minutes later, Danny made his way around to the gate while the dog, emitting a deep, low growl, stalked him on the other side of the fence.

Jack had positioned the car alongside the gate. Both back doors of the car were open and Jack waved to him from the front seat.

"God, I'm fucking crazy to be doing this!" Danny took off his jacket and swatted it against the fence. The dog snarled louder, leaping at the fence. Danny then raced over and crawled partway into the back of the police car.

"Okay, go for it!"

From the front seat, Jack leaned out the partially open window and shoved the gate slightly open. Danny, looking out the open car door across from him, shook his jacket once more as the dog lunged into the car after him. He immediately backed out, slamming the door. Jack slammed the door from the other side. Seconds later they drove off as the dog, realizing it was trapped, went into a frenzy and started shredding the upholstery with its teeth.

They parked the car a short distance from the house. As both men got out of the car, chunks of upholstery and stuffing rained down within.

"It looks like it's snowing in there!" said Danny. "HP is going to be pissed!"

"Makes up for the ticket they gave me last year. Hope he doesn't eat his way into the front before we get back."

They crept up the steps leading into the back of Rolly's house. A spiked dog collar tied to a heavy chain lay on the porch. The chain led down the steps and was wrapped around a tree in front of a large doghouse. Two empty aluminum dog dishes lay upside down in the dirt. Both had holes chewed through the rims. The remnants of Jack's pants were hanging out of the doghouse.

"This is a good omen," whispered Danny. "We've already found your pants."

"Wonderful. Next week is Halloween. I'll go dressed as dog food."

Danny heard the door open and saw Jack step inside.

"Christ, you're fast! You're going to have to teach me someday," said Danny in amazement.

"Thanks. But it wasn't locked."

Danny glanced at the dog collar. "I can see why."

They started their search in the three bedrooms upstairs. The furnishings in two of the bedrooms consisted only of dirty mattresses lying on the floor. There was a dresser in the main bedroom, and Jack searched through the drawers. Danny spotted a shotgun leaning against the wall and carefully picked it up.

"Loaded?" asked Jack.

Danny nodded, putting the shotgun down.

It was an hour and a half later when they finished their search. They found a few telephone numbers in a kitchen drawer, but again, none were for outside the city.

"Well, at least we tried," said Jack. "Let's get out of here before the sun comes up. We've still got to return the dog."

"Yeah. Hope he leaves on his own so I don't have to coax 'im out," replied Danny, feeling apprehensive.

Outside the house, Danny watched as Jack retrieved his pants from the doghouse, then got down on his knees and shone his flashlight inside.

"Do you see your shoe?"

"What's left of it." Jack reached inside and pulled out a badly mangled ankle boot.

Danny was about to go, but Jack stayed kneeling, staring at the doghouse.

"You coming?" whispered Danny.

"This floor is thick."

Danny shrugged. "Just insulated to keep the poor little puppy off the ground."

"They'd do that for the mutt but not bother to leave it any food or water while they go away for a couple of days?"

Jack moved his flashlight beam across the floor of the doghouse. It was covered with short, dark green outdoor carpeting, which was glued down, except along one wall where it had been cut slightly too large to fit the floor.

He pulled back the carpet to reveal a plywood floor. A small grubby knothole was visible in the plywood. He stuck his finger in the knothole and pulled. The floor of the doghouse lifted like a page in a book.

A compartment underneath held a brown leather case. He carefully lifted it out and undid the zipper, shining his light inside.

"Well?" asked Danny breathlessly.

"Take a look," said Jack, holding the case open.

Danny looked in and saw some handguns, stacks of money held together by elastic bands, and a large brown envelope.

"Look at all the cash," said Jack. "These are thousand-dollar bills!"

"Yet he still has dirty mattresses on the floor in two of the bedrooms?"

"Guess you can't make a silk purse out of a pig's ear. Come on, let's go back inside and take a better look. There's a downstairs washroom without any windows. We can close the door and turn on the light."

Danny noticed the sky was beginning to lighten but didn't say anything as he followed Jack into the house.

Jack carefully pulled the contents of the leather case out onto the floor. There were three .22-calibre handguns.

"Do you think these have been used?"

Jack shook his head as he picked up the brown envelope. "I doubt it. Our friend said they throw them away after each hit."

"Pass me those bundles. I'll start counting. Let's see how much he's got."

Jack didn't respond as he stared into the brown envelope. His face became mottled.

"Jack? ... Jack? What is it?"

Jack silently passed Danny the envelope.

It was stuffed with newspaper clippings. For a moment, Danny didn't understand, until he saw the bold lettering of one caption: *GRISLY MURDER OF TWO CHILDREN — Discovered by mother...*

Danny pulled the newspaper clippings from the envelope. Most of the clippings were about the children's murder. One clipping was different. It was about another murder that had taken place three days ago. The article said: *Bobby Singh, a 29-year-old man who police believe was involved in the drug trade, was found shot to death in his home Wednesday night by relatives who...*"

Jack pointed his finger beside the man's name. Someone had written "2" in ink.

"Look at Ben Junior's name," said Jack.

Danny flipped back the pages and looked. Beside Ben Junior's name, someone had written "1" in ink.

"Rolly murdered Ben Junior," said Jack. "He's even keeping score! Bobby Singh was his second victim. He didn't put a number beside Maggie's name. Probably because Wizard killed her."

"We can't be sure," replied Danny.

"Can't we? Then you give me another explanation for it!" yelled Jack.

"How can you be sure it was Wizard?"

"He's the one who vouched for Rolly's tattoo! And he already has the Dirty Dog tattoo. That's what Maggie was drawing when she was killed."

"It still doesn't confirm he killed her."

"You're saying you don't think he did it?" asked Jack incredulously.

"I didn't say that, but it would never stand up in court."

"Court! What the hell does court have to do with anything? None of this will stand up! We can't use this! We don't even have grounds for a search warrant! Who's talking about court?"

"So what do we do then?" asked Danny, his voice cracking. "Do you set yourself up as judge, jury, and executioner? What if it wasn't Wizard? Okay, I'll admit Rolly had a hand in it, but what if it wasn't Wizard? It's just ... could you live with there being any doubt as to who did kill Maggie? Wondering if a third person was there, maybe another dealer, and Wizard only saw what happened."

Jack didn't respond for a moment. He sat on the floor, breathing like he had run a marathon. Eventually his breathing returned to normal. "Okay," he said. "You want more proof? I'll get it for you!"

The sound of birds chirping outside told Danny that now was not the time to ask how.

Jack picked up one of the handguns and walked out of the bathroom and over to a plant in the living room. He looked back at Danny. "Are you going to help?"

Danny looked down at the remaining two guns. *This is wrong. Everything I'm doing is wrong.*

"Forget it, I'll do it myself," said Jack, plunging the barrel of the gun into the dirt.

chapter twenty-six

It was daybreak when Jack pulled alongside Danny's car in the office parking lot.

"So we take tonight off? That's what you said."

Jack nodded. His face looked grim.

"You're not going to do anything…?"

Jack shook his head and said, "In my heart, I know you're right about needing more proof. I'm convinced about Rolly, but Wizard, or whoever they were meeting, is another story. Our friend gets back from the ride today. We'll meet him first thing tomorrow morning."

"You've already got a game plan, don't you?"

"I know what I'd like to do, but I don't think you'd want to hear about it."

Danny sucked in a deep breath. "Christ, Jack, we're supposed to be cops, for God's sake."

"So what do *you* suggest?"

"We've got a good informant. Let's get a wiretap for

drug trafficking. It might lead to some dealer up the Valley that we don't know about."

"Then what? They're not dumb enough to say anything over the phone. If we run wire we'll have to bring more people into it, which means more risk for our friend."

"What's your plan, then?" asked Danny nervously.

"Turn up the pressure on our friend."

"Too much pressure and he's liable to do something stupid."

"I've decided to chance it. I'll call him tonight and set up an early morning meet. I'll pick you up at five-thirty tomorrow morning. If he hasn't received any heat over those fifty keys, then I'm going to put the screws to him."

"Hope you know what you're doing. This could get pretty hairy."

"Hairy is okay. It's bloody that you have to watch out for. But you're right, so let's take today off. Do something special with Susan. You owe it to her. She's a great lady."

"I know."

"We've got almost twenty-four hours. I plan on spending it with Natasha."

"That's right! Today is the big day," Danny said, lightly punching Jack on the arm.

"She's just meeting Liz and Ben."

"Don't be nervous. They'll like her. Susan and I do."

"I'm not nervous. Good night!"

It was noon when Natasha walked into her bedroom and gently shook Jack's shoulder. "Come on, sleepy-head, breakfast is ready."

Jack groaned and looked at the clock on Natasha's dresser. "Why so early?"

"It's not early. Besides, I'm keyed up. Think I need to expend some energy," she said, reaching under the sheets and running her hand up the inside of his thigh.

"It's only my sister and her husband."

"Oh? So it's not a big deal?"

Jack reached for Natasha's head and pulled her face close to his. He smiled and said, "Yeah, it's a big deal. At least Liz thinks so. Speaking of which, you better have an appetite. Her Sunday dinners are always great."

"Is that the way to your heart? Through your mouth?"

Jack grinned, then said, "Not necessarily. Your hand may have found another way." He kissed her as her bathrobe fell to the floor.

As they finished breakfast and started clearing dishes, Jack thought about their visit to the farm … and about Marcie. What type of image did The Suit portray to others? What would his profile consist of? He decided to tell Natasha about The Suit. How he provided the bikers with secret police information and the ugly details of his attack on Marcie.

Natasha's face expressed her horror. "Give me a minute to think about it." She was quiet as she slowly collected her thoughts. She saw the grim look on Jack's face as he stood drying the same dish over and over again. Finally she said, "He's sick. Really sick."

"All those years of medical school and you tell me he's sick? Incorrect answer, doctor! I want something more professional. A psychiatric profile to help identify him."

"I know. Just hang on." She drained the kitchen sink before taking the towel from Jack's grasp and tossing it on the counter. "Hold me a sec." She wrapped her arms around his waist. He saw that she had tears in her eyes.

"I'm sorry," he said softly. "I shouldn't be talking to you about my work, let alone this."

"No, it's okay. I knew something appalling had happened to her. I just didn't know how awful." She wiped her eyes with her fingers, then continued, "Psychiatry is not my field of expertise, but considering what he did to Marcie, I would say you're looking for someone in a position of power or authority."

"Like a policeman?" Jack said it as a question but meant it more as a statement.

"Perhaps. It's no coincidence that the mask he wore was of the president of the United States. This is a guy who wants absolute power. He likely portrays a perfect, strong image, yet deep down inside he is very insecure. He would detest feeling like anyone had any power over him. The type of person who would strongly object to something as benign as, say, a seat belt law, because he would feel that it implies that someone has power over him by telling him what to do."

"So I'm looking for a guy who doesn't wear a seat belt?"

"He might wear it, only to present a perfect image, but would despise the nuance of power that he believes it holds over him."

"Ah, that makes it easier," said Jack bitterly.

"I'm sorry. I'm just telling you what —"

"No. Don't be sorry. I appreciate what you're telling me, it just upsets me that I don't know who he is. I wonder if he's ever sought treatment?"

"He might have if he had been caught and thought it would keep him out of jail. In reality, I suspect that he is so twisted that he doesn't see himself as the perverted, sick animal that he is. He has a psychopathic personality. Someone without a conscience. He would stridently defend his belief that it is okay to molest children, except he knows it would tarnish his image or perhaps get him caught."

"So your final diagnosis is...?"

"He's like a rabid dog. I don't believe there is any cure for someone like that."

"Maybe a bullet."

Jack cringed as soon as he said it. *She's a doctor. She saves lives.*

Natasha's face was without expression. She chose her words carefully. "Killing him would be like eradicating an infectious disease. You would be doing society a favour. The risk is contamination — that you could become infected and be viewed as having rabies yourself."

The meaning of her words was not lost on Jack, but a more important issue crowded his brain. He realized he was afraid of something that had never bothered him before. He thought about what he was going to do tomorrow — and became afraid of dying. The prospect of not being with Natasha... He felt a strong desire to tell her how much he loved and admired her, but the timing wasn't right. Talking about murder and molestation ... it wasn't a topic for love.

"What are you thinking?" she asked.

"I'm thinking that my ethics could never become infected, as long as I have you as my guiding light. Having you makes me think that I would never want to face ... quarantine."

"Good. Promise me you'll keep it that way."

"I promise."

Natasha hugged him. He felt her warm face on his neck and held her there for a long time.

*

Late that afternoon, Jack watched as Natasha, Liz, and Ben chattered like long-time friends. Marcie sat in the living room as well, but she was mostly silent, keeping her thoughts to herself. When Liz excused herself to check on dinner, Jack followed her into the kitchen.

"Need a hand with anything?" he asked.

"No, I was just checking. Everything is under control."

Jack stayed and looked at his sister.

Liz smiled, then whispered, "I think she's great. Intelligent, beautiful, charming. Witty with a good sense of humour. Yes, I like her. Is that what you came in to find out?"

Jack grinned.

"She also seems open and honest. I can tell that Ben likes her, too."

"Thanks, sis, it means a lot to me that —"

"Anything I can do to help?" Natasha asked.

Jack spun around quickly. "Uh, no. Liz and I were just coming back to sit down."

"Oh? Talking about me, were you?"

A laugh escaped from Elizabeth's lips, then she said, "Add perceptive to the list!"

Liz and Natasha took delight in announcing that Jack was blushing when they returned to the living room to join Ben.

Jack changed the subject by asking, "Where's Marcie?"

"She went to the barn to toss a couple of bales down for the animals," Ben replied. "She shouldn't be long."

"How are you all doing? It's been two weeks."

Ben and Liz exchanged glances, then Ben said, "She's a really good kid. A hard worker. Maybe working too hard. It's like she's always underfoot."

"Sounds like she's trying to please you."

"She's been volunteering for everything, from helping Liz in the house to wanting to help me on the farm. On top of that, she's doing about three hours of homework every night."

"She's a bright kid," said Liz. "I've been checking with the school. She's missed the first six weeks, but they said that at the rate she's going, they expect her to catch up soon."

"What about the psychologist?"

"She's had two meetings so far. Now she's scheduled for one a week." Liz looked at Natasha and said, "I talked to the psychologist; she said that Marcie has post stress disorder."

"PTSD," replied Natasha. "Post-traumatic stress disorder. Yes, I'm sure that diagnosis is correct. Considering her history, she may need a lot of counselling."

"That's what we were told."

"So what's the problem?" asked Jack. "I feel like you're holding something back."

Ben and Liz exchanged another glance, then Liz said, "Don't get me wrong on this. We both think she's a really great kid."

"That's what you've been telling me on the phone. What's changed?"

Ben cleared his throat, then said, "Last Thursday … maybe I overreacted, but Liz was pretty upset."

"It's not Ben's fault," said Liz. "I was the one who overreacted. I went in her room and she was drawing pictures on sheets of paper. Not nice pictures. Pictures of people crying and sticking needles in their arms. Then I realized that the sheets of paper were ones that Maggie had drawn pictures on. On the other side. I started to cry and that's when Ben came in."

"I yelled at her. Told her to keep her damn hands off stuff that wasn't hers. I apologized to her later, but she acts like she doesn't hear. Not rude. More like her mind is elsewhere. She's hardly spoken to us since. Not working much anymore, either. Stays in her room a lot."

"She was expressing her feelings through the drawings," said Natasha. "It's actually a good sign. The therapeutic value of art is well recognized and respected."

"Maybe, but not on Maggie's pictures," said Ben.

"I know she feels really bad," said Liz. "This morning she gave me a little glass mouse. She used to have it in her room. I told her to keep it, but she just acted indifferent. It's there ... on the fireplace mantle."

Natasha saw the cute crystal mouse peeking out from the mantle over the large stone fireplace. "Why don't you buy a big scrapbook for her to use?" she suggested.

"I did," said Ben. "I gave it to her yesterday, but I don't think she's used it."

Jack looked at Natasha and she gave a slight nod of her head. "We'll go talk with her."

"We're not upset with her now," said Liz, "but she's been real quiet ever since. I'd appreciate it if you would tell her that we're not angry. She acts like she doesn't believe us."

A few minutes later, Jack and Natasha climbed a ladder inside the barn leading to an open trap door in the loft. Marcie was batting a rope back and forth that was hanging from the open doors at the end of the loft.

"Hey, Marcie! What ya doin'?" asked Jack.

Marcie looked startled. "Just playing," she said.

"You looked like you were in pretty deep thought," said Natasha. "Is there something bothering you?"

"No."

"What were you playing?" asked Jack, as he gave the rope a slap and watched it swing out the open doors at the end of the loft.

"I don't know. I was just thinking it would be fun to swing out in the yard ... but if I fell and hurt myself, I guess it wouldn't be good."

"Jack could tie a big knot at the end of the rope. You could stand on it and it would be safer."

Jack caught the rope in his hand and spoke to Marcie while tying a large knot. "It wouldn't be good if you hurt yourself. I would be upset. So would Liz and Ben."

"No, they wouldn't. They're mad at me. I did a stupid thing. But what else is new," she mumbled.

"They told us about that, but they're not angry with you at all," said Natasha. "As a matter of fact, they were just bragging to us about how much help you've been and how hard you've been tackling your school work."

"Listening to them," said Jack, "makes me really proud of you. They're really happy with you. They're definitely not angry with you. In fact, I think the three of you help each other much more than you realize."

"That's nice they said that." She looked at her watch. "I bet dinner is ready. We should go."

Natasha found out that Jack had not exaggerated how great the meal would be. The simplicity of the roasted free-range chicken, scalloped potatoes, and broccoli with hollandaise sauce made for a homey, mouth-watering meal. She wasn't surprised at the freshly baked apple pie with ice cream for dessert. The aroma of the pie had greeted her when she first arrived.

Supper conversation was easygoing, which she appreciated. The occasional friction of Jack's knee rubbing against her leg brought on fantasies of a primal nature. More intellectual conversation would have been difficult.

After dinner, she insisted on helping Liz clean up in the kitchen, while Ben went to get wood for the fireplace.

She saw Jack and Marcie escape the work detail as they headed outside to walk off dinner. She didn't mind; it gave her time alone with Liz. Time to squeeze any stories out of her about Jack. Either as a child, or as a man.

Liz told her about Ben's heart attack and how Jack spent every spare minute he had working on the farm until Ben slowly regained his strength. She said something else. Jack was really good with Maggie and Ben Junior. He'd been like a second dad to them.

"In case you wanted to know that," said Liz, with a smirk on her face.

Natasha smiled. "It's good to know," she replied.

Later, they had coffee in the living room. Marcie seemed happier and joined in on the conversation. At nine o'clock, Marcie announced that it was her bedtime, and Natasha realized that it was time to go.

They said good night at the door. Jack gave Marcie a hug first, then Liz. Natasha saw Ben standing back. He looked shy. She smiled and gave him a hug. His arms were huge and strong. She felt like a child in his grasp.

Liz hugged her and whispered, "You take good care of my little brother."

"I will," she whispered back.

It was then she noticed Marcie in the living room, standing on her tiptoes at the fireplace. She picked up the glass mouse and took it with her as she headed down the hall to her bedroom.

Natasha glanced at Jack. He looked pleased. She felt good too. She liked Jack's family, and she knew she loved Jack. Her only disappointment for the day was that Jack wouldn't spend the night with her. He had an early morning engagement — one that was important enough that she could not convince him to stay.

chapter twenty-seven

It was six-thirty on Monday morning when Jack and Danny finished their coffee in a small restaurant adjacent to a large cemetery.

"Time?" asked Danny.

"It's time," replied Jack.

Danny punched the numbers into his cellphone. Superintendent Wigmore was getting dressed for work when he answered the call.

"Sir? It's Danny O'Reilly."

"O'Reilly! Well, well. Aren't you the punctual one. What have you decided?"

"Sir, I've only got a few minutes. I'm at a coffee shop. Jack is here, too, but he just went to the washroom."

"So you've decided to come clean? Tell me what Taggart is up to? Or, should I say, what the two of you have been up to?"

"Yes, sir, but a lot has happened this last week.

Taggart thinks he knows who killed his niece and nephew. Two bikers from Satans Wrath."

"How does he figure that?"

"We turned a good informant. Someone inside the club."

"Turning an informant in Satans Wrath? Just like that? Come on, O'Reilly! What's been going on?"

"Sir, it's a long story, and I can't talk right now. Basically, I'm afraid of what Jack will do to the men who did this. He trusts me completely and tells me everything. He said that he's thinking of getting them. Wants to take a week or two and plan how to do it."

"A week or two? This is good.... We have time. Meet me tonight at the Oceanside and we'll go over everything. Then I'll take it to Internal and we'll come up with a plan."

"Tonight isn't good, sir. Jack wants me to work surveillance with him the next couple of nights. If I slip away, he might get suspicious. Wednesday night would be better." Danny's voice suddenly became more official and he said, "Sorry, no. You've got the wrong number."

"Taggart is back, I take it?"

"Yes, that is this number," said Danny.

"Okay, no problem. Call me at home Wednesday night to set up a time to meet."

A few minutes later, Wigmore left his apartment and walked to his car. He was irritated when he saw that someone had left an empty liquor bottle standing on the roof of his car. He picked the bottle up and looked at the label. *Glennfiddich ... my brand. Too bad someone hadn't left a full one!* He set the bottle by the curb before driving off.

At the same time, Jack and Danny walked up a grassy knoll in a cemetery. The ground was soaked from an overnight rain and the air was crisp. Leaves had already fallen, exposing black branches to the grey sky. Some of the upright grave markers were silhouetted on the crest of the hill. The business towers and high-rise apartments on the horizon were still lit up.

"Whose idea was it to meet here?"

"Mine. If our friend doesn't cooperate, I'm going to send you back to the car to get some stuff from the trunk."

"What stuff?"

"A blanket and —"

"Over here!" Lance yelled.

Jack and Danny had reached the crest of the hill and saw Lance sitting on a marble tombstone.

"How's it goin'?" asked Jack. "Are you taking any heat over Halibut getting busted?"

Lance shook his head. "Naw, they figure it was one of two things. Either the heat came from Montreal like they said on the news, or else the cops threw that out as a red herring and were really following Halibut all along. If they decide the heat was on Halibut, it will look bad for Rolly."

"Why Rolly?" asked Jack. "Come on, we can walk as we talk," he added.

Lance stood up and joined Jack and Danny as they slowly walked through the cemetery.

"Wizard gave Rolly shit this weekend," continued Lance. "He told Rolly that he should have used Dragon because the heat had been on Halibut before, when we whacked Lenny. Not much else was said about it, but Damien is pissed off. It's caused a bit of a stink in the club."

"Why is that?" asked Danny.

"This was only the second shipment. Now the guys back east are pointing fingers at us, saying we screwed up, and we're pointing fingers back at them."

"Speaking of Damien," said Jack, "how come you're not an executive officer? Maybe not national pres, but you've got more brains than Wizard. You could be president or vice-president of your chapter. You've got a lot of years in."

Lance shrugged. "Wizard is smarter than he looks. He's got a good chance of beating Damien out for national pres. The election takes place in a couple of weeks. Presidents from all the chapters in the country will be flyin' in to vote."

"You think Wizard is in the running?"

"Definitely. He's fluent in French and has a lot of support from the guys back east. He's been down there schmoozing with them. It was him who set up the speed connection."

"Still doesn't explain why you haven't made executive level."

"It's a lot less hassle just being one step removed from executive. Less work, but you're still respected and not stuck with a lot of the shit jobs."

"Start campaigning. We want you to be an executive officer."

Lance nodded. "Yeah, I could see that comin'."

"Anything else going on?" asked Jack.

"Don't know if you're interested, but I heard Damien telling Wizard that he was flying down to the Grand Caymans for a week. Damien said that if they couldn't reach him for any reason when he was gone, then Wizard would act as national president. He left last night and is coming back next Sunday."

Jack stopped walking and stood beside a fresh grave. He prodded the dirt lightly with the toe of his ankle boot and said, "Doing a little banking, is he?"

Lance chuckled, then said, "Yeah, probably. Doesn't say and I don't ask."

"Speaking of asking," Jack flashed a glance at Danny, then continued, "I've got something for you to ask Rolly."

"Yeah? What's that?"

"Did you hear about those two little kids who were killed in a farmhouse up the Valley? Eight weeks ago?"

"Yeah. Is that when it was? I only know what I heard in the news."

"Rolly killed the little boy."

"What? You certain?"

"I'm positive. I think Wizard did the little girl. I want you to talk to them about it. Find out if they were with someone else."

"You don't ask questions like that! Forget it!"

"You will ask! I'm not giving you any choice in this!" yelled Jack.

"Fuck you! I'm not doin' it!"

Jack flung his car keys at Danny, then tackled Lance by the throat.

Shortly after arriving at work, Wigmore received a call from a man with a nasal voice.

"Superintendent Wigmore speaking."

"Yes, is this Superintendent Wigglemouth?" came a somewhat mumbled, nervous-sounding reply.

"It's Superintendent Wigmore!"

"Yes, Superintendent Wigglemore?"

"Wigmore," he replied, enunciating the name carefully.

"Wrigglemore," the voice repeated carefully.

"For Christ's sake! It's Superintendent Wigmore! W-I-G-M-O-R-E!"

The caller hung up.

*

It was dusk when Lance walked along a path in Stanley Park. The street lights came on and he nervously looked behind him, didn't see anyone, then walked up to Wizard and Rolly, who were sitting on a bench eating popcorn.

They stood up as he approached. Wizard jerked his head toward the path, indicating they should walk as they talked.

"So what's the deal?" said Wizard gruffly. "How come ya want to meet us out here?"

"The deal is," said Lance, his voice trembling, "I got a real nasty visit from two cops this morning."

"What the fuck did they want?" said Rolly with a higher than normal laugh.

"They wanted me to become a rat is what they fuckin' wanted!"

"What!" said Wizard incredulously. "What were they, two rookies tryin' to give away a handful of cash?"

"These weren't fuckin' rookies," said Lance. "One guy is fuckin' crazy. Maybe both of them are, but one for sure. They took me to a graveyard and the crazy one jumps on me and starts chokin' the shit out of me until I black out. When I come to, he's still sittin' on my chest!"

"Are you fuckin' serious?" said Wizard.

"That ain't all. Then I see that the other fucker has got a blanket spread out on the ground and is shovellin' dirt onto it out of a new grave. Pretty fuckin' obvious what they were plannin' on doin' with me!"

"You're sweatin' just talkin' about it! You are fuckin' serious, ain't ya?"

"You're fuckin' right I'm serious!"

"Why? What the fuck did —"

"The crazy one said I tried to kill him two weeks ago."

"What?"

"Remember Eddy? Behind the Black Water?"

"Yeah. Did he rat out on us?" asked Rolly.

"Whoever told you he was a rat fucked up real bad. Because Eddy was the crazy one who attacked me this morning! He's an RCMP officer!"

"Fuckin' Eddy is a cop?" Wizard looked astonished. "Can't be!"

"I saw their badges. The crazy one said he'd let me live if I cooperated with them."

"So what did you tell 'em?" growled Wizard. "How come he didn't kill ya?"

"Fuck, I was in a bad situation! Then the crazy one says he wants me to testify about Lenny and also wants me to find out what Rolly did with the shotgun he used on some kid!"

"What?" yelled Rolly. "They know about me?"

"I told them I needed a couple days to think about it. I knew if you used a piece to whack someone that you would have tossed it, but I wasn't gonna tell them that!"

"What made them think I whacked some kid?" spluttered Rolly.

"They know all about you two," said Lance, while nervously looking around.

The three men stopped talking as a couple jogged towards them, then passed by.

"What do ya mean? What'd they say?" asked Wizard.

"They told me things I didn't even know. Like they said that Rolly killed a little boy out in some abandoned farmhouse. They said you were with him when he killed the boy and popped the kid's sister first."

Wizard immediately grabbed Rolly with both hands around his throat and pinned him back against a tree. "You fuckin' idiot! Who you been blabbin' at?"

"Fuckin' nobody, Wiz, fuckin' nobody!"

"Then how could they have known?" yelled Wizard. "There was only the three of us there! The Suit wouldn't have said anything! They even know which one of us did which kid!"

"No way! I haven't said a fuckin' word! I swear, not a word!"

Lance looked at Rolly and said, "They told me that you also whacked a guy last week. Someone by the name of Bobby Singh."

"You stupid, stupid fuckin' cocksucker!" screamed Wizard, pinning Rolly's head against the tree and choking him with one hand while punching him in the face. Rolly's nose crunched like a piece of celery and two teeth slid down the back of his throat like wayward Chiclets.

Rolly screamed out, more in fear than in pain. "Don't, Wiz! Please! I haven't said a word! I swear on my mother's grave!"

"Well, how else could they have found out?" seethed Wizard, slowly releasing his grip. "How the fuck could they have known that unless you've been talking?"

Rolly shook his head, spraying blood across his shirt and Wizard's face. "I haven't been! No way! Maybe it was The Suit!" Rolly looked at Lance and said, "He's the one who ordered us to kill the kids. 'Cause they saw him. They was loose ends!"

Wizard slapped Rolly across the face with the back of his hand and said, "The Suit didn't know about Bobby Singh! How the fuck do you explain that!"

"I don't know. I just don't…." Rolly wiped his face with his hands and then wiped his bloody fingers on his pants.

Wizard spun around to face Lance. "So how come they haven't arrested us yet?"

Before Lance could reply, Wizard continued. "I'll tell you why! They don't have enough evidence on anything, or else all three of us would be sittin' in the slam. It was pretty dark the night we tried to do 'im in the alley. You're probably the only one the pig can really identify. That fuckin' scar of yours. Plus the interior light of the car came on when you got out. I bet he's only guessing about Rolly and me."

Lance shrugged and said, "I don't know, but it sounds like they're thinkin' of doin' somethin' real quick."

"So who are these two pigs? When did they say they'd get hold of you next?"

"They didn't say, but the crazy one said he'd be in touch soon, and if I didn't cooperate he'd either kill me or put me in jail."

"Are these pigs the narcs from hell, or what?"

"No. They belong to some Intelligence thing, but I don't know what it's called."

"What's their names?"

"I only know the name of the crazy guy. The guy we thought was Eddy. His real name is Jack Taggart. Don't know the other guy, but he does what Taggart tells him."

"See if they'll give ya their home numbers. Get licence plate numbers, anything to help us find out where they live."

"I'll work on it."

"Yeah, do that. And hurry before they decide to scoop us!"

"Who's this fuckin' bozo who told you he was a rat in the first place? It seems to me he's the one who set us up," said Lance heatedly.

Wizard reflected for a moment, then said, "I don't think so. He's always been right on in the past. Besides, he'd have too much to lose, what with me lining him up with little girls. Not to mention free powder. Naw, our problem lies with these two fuckin' pigs. I'll get you to call them … tell 'em you got to meet them. If we whack them, our problems will be over. Especially this Eddy … or Jack, or whatever the fuck his name is."

"Yeah, but they're cops!" said Rolly.

"Fuck, what's the difference? They're just a couple of guys, same as everyone else."

"Where and when?" asked Lance.

Wizard slowly looked around. "Why not right here? It would be nice if they're both together. But if not, just make sure we get the pig from the back alley. He's the only fucker who could point a finger at us!"

"Yeah, I agree with ya there," replied Lance.

"One more thing," said Wizard. "Who else have you told about this?"

"Nobody else knows."

"Keep it that way. Keep your mouth shut about everything! That means the bros, too. No need for anyone to know about the kids — or the pigs — for now."

"Fuck, *I'm* not stupid," said Lance, looking at Rolly.

"Hey! Wait a minute —"

"Shut up, Rolly!" yelled Wizard, before looking back at Lance. "No, I know you're not stupid. In fact, before today, I was gonna ask ya if you were interested in somethin'."

"Interested in what?"

"If I make national pres, what say I back you to replace me as president?"

"You would do that?" Lance noticed the scowl that Rolly gave Wizard.

"Yeah, I'll do that. We just gotta take care of a few loose ends first."

"Let me shoot Taggart. He was gonna kill me, so let me return the favour! I wanna pop one in each eyeball. You owe me that!"

Wizard chuckled, then said, "Anxious to get your DD, are you? Yeah, no problem. You can kill 'em both if you want."

"The fuckin' heat's gonna come down real bad," said Rolly.

"I can handle the heat," said Wizard. "Nobody should be runnin' this club who can't!"

Jack glanced impatiently at his watch. What was keeping Lance? The harsh cry of a seagull over the ocean caused him to look up, but too many trees blocked his view.

Danny sat on the park bench beside him, with his head back and his eyes closed. It looked like he was sleeping. Jack knew better. Stress had reduced both men to silence.

Two children zoomed by on skateboards, but Jack only caught a partial glimpse of them through the trees and shrubbery.

A rustling sound in the bushes behind him told him a squirrel was probably storing food for the winter. It would be peaceful here, he thought, if it weren't for what they were doing. More comfortable than waiting in a cemetery and thinking about the dead.

Lance walked through the trees toward them. Jack nudged Danny, who sat forward in anticipation.

Lance stood an arm's length away, staring down at them. For a moment, nobody spoke. The glow of a street light illuminated beads of sweat on Lance's forehead.

"Well?" asked Jack.

"I've got something for ya!" replied Lance, reaching inside his black leather jacket and pulling out a tape recorder. He handed it to Jack and said, "You were right! Wizard wasted the little girl and Rolly did the boy. It's all here for ya to listen to."

Jack took a deep breath and slowly exhaled. He gripped the recorder tightly to try to stop his hands from trembling.

chapter twenty-eight

Jack unlocked his car and Danny got in beside him while Lance sat in the back. He rewound the tape and pushed "play." When it reached the place where Wizard admitted that he shot Maggie, he subconsciously ran his fingers across the grip of his pistol. *This is it. Time for justice.*

He stopped the recorder and looked at Danny. "You wanted proof. Well, we just got it!"

Danny silently nodded.

Jack started the recorder again. Seconds later, he knew he wasn't done. *The Suit! The goddamned Suit ordered them killed!* "No! Jesus Christ!" he yelled, slamming his fist into the dash. His eyes brimmed with tears and he bit his lip. He looked in the rear-view mirror and briefly locked eyes with Lance before looking away.

Minutes later, the voices on the tape ended. Danny reached over and shut it off.

Jack sat in silence for a moment to regain his composure, then turned in his seat and spoke to Lance. "You did good. In fact, better than I expected."

"I've never been so fuckin' scared in all my life. Do you have any idea what they'd have done if they decided to search me and found the recorder?"

Jack nodded.

"So what are ya gonna do with the tape? Use it as evidence?"

"That's not going to happen. I told you I would protect you and I will."

"You call today protecting me? Man, this is gonna be a long ten years!"

"It worked out good. I told you that Rolly would get the heat."

"Yeah, you're right about that. Wiz smacked him a few good ones. The dumb bastard looks uglier than ever now!"

"I wish I had seen it," said Jack, "but I didn't want to take the chance of them spotting any surveillance."

"So what do we do now?" asked Lance. "These guys are gonna ace ya, and I don't want any of your buddies thinkin' I had a part in it."

"We can stall for the time being," said Jack. "Tell them we called you and said we're going out of town for a while. Keep them on the hook. We have to find out who The Suit is!"

"Then what?" asked Lance.

Danny looked at Jack for a reply. Their eyes met briefly, then Jack turned back to Lance. "That's none of your concern. We'll look after you. Just make certain you look after us!"

"I hear ya."

Jack looked at Danny and said, "There's something personal I need to talk to him about. Wait here." He took off his gun, put it on the seat beside Danny, and got out of the car.

Moments later, Jack and Lance strolled into a heavily wooded area in the park.

"You got a problem with me from this morning?" asked Jack. "We can deal with it now."

Lance looked around. There was nobody else in sight. He turned to face off with Jack and said, "I figure I got about three inches on ya, and maybe forty pounds. Plus I notice you still favour your left side. You really think you could take me?"

Jack shrugged and said, "Probably not. That's why I jumped you by surprise this morning. But that's not the point."

"I saw you leave your piece behind."

"Forget the badge. This time it's just you and me. You can look at it as payback time."

"That's not the only thing I saw back there."

"What do you mean?"

"This is personal for you, ain't it? You knew those kids, didn't you?"

Jack paused for a moment. His stomach muscles had been constricted, expecting to receive a boot or a fist from Lance. He slowly exhaled, then took another breath before replying. "They were my niece and nephew."

"I figured it was something like that." Lance was silent for a moment, then said, "If it was any of my kids that got whacked, I figure I would go crazy too. Naw, it's okay. I don't have a hard-on for what you did."

"Glad to hear it."

Both men continued to walk and Jack asked, "Why didn't you just go along with them and have us killed?"

"I was wearin' your recorder. Hard to deny what was said."

"Yeah, but you could have made an excuse, said you forgot to turn it on or something."

"I know, I thought about it, but..."

"But what?"

"It wasn't that it would really bother me to kill you two. It's just that I'm more upset with guys in the club like Wizard and Rolly."

"What do you mean?"

"Things have changed. When I was a young fucker, without brains, I used to think it was exciting. Sometimes it was. But not now. Lookin' back on it, I wish I'd quit years ago."

"Why?"

"The club's not what it used to be when I first joined. We used to have good times ... go on rides ... things were different. Sure, we were a bunch of badasses sometimes, but not like it is today. When I first joined, you'd have never gotten a tattoo for knockin' off some kid! Fuck, we'd have knocked you off! Now, we hardly ever ride. It's all about makin' money. We've become a bunch of fuckin' businessmen. The guys in power just use the club as an image, for protection to make more money."

"A lot of people like making money."

"Yeah, but they're not real bikers, at least, not what we used to be. It just ain't worth it now. It'll only be a matter of time before the Vietnamese, the Russians, the Indos, or some other group takes over the business. Being a biker used to represent freedom to do whatever the hell you wanted. Where's the fuckin' freedom when you're always lookin' over your shoulder wonderin' when the competition is going to put a slug into ya!"

Jack nodded that he understood.

Lance looked at Jack and said, "Then there's the heat, but you guys are the least of our worries." He smiled briefly and added, “Well, I used to think that until I met you.”

“I guess I have put a burr up your ass.”

“You’ve done that, all right.”

“You did good work today. I heard you on the tape, pumping Wizard for information about The Suit. Remember when I said you would be working for us for ten years?”

“How could I forget? Now it’s nine years, fifty-one weeks and two days.”

“Make it five years now.”

“No kiddin’?”

“No kiddin’. If you find out who The Suit is, I’ll say we’re even. If I find out first, then you’re still looking at serving your country for another five years.”

“Deal!” said Lance, sticking out his hand.

Jack felt his firm grasp.

As they shook hands, Lance said, “One more thing,” and buried his left fist deep into Jack’s midriff. Jack buckled over. His already battered ribs were racked with pain as his lungs gulped for air.

Lance said, “Guess I did have a bit of a hard-on for you over this morning. Now we’re square on that!” He released his handshake.

Jack managed to give a thumbs-up sign, and Lance smiled and walked away.

It was 2:10 a.m. when the telephone shattered the silence in Wigmore’s small apartment. It took four rings before his sleepy voice answered hello.

The voice on the other end was that of a man. Feminine, but definitely a man. A man with a slight lisp.

“Hi! I’m the one who’s been admiring you down at

the Oceanside Lounge. You know who. I'm the one you winked at the other night, you cheeky devil."

"I never winked at anyone! Who is this? How did you get my number?"

"You're a policeman, aren't you? I'd just love it if you would show me your gun. I'm home now, all alone, or would you like me to come —"

"Listen! Whoever you are, never phone me again!" Wigmore slammed the receiver down.

Seconds later the man called back.

"Hi, big boy! As you can see, I don't take no for an answer. I live in the pink house across from the Oceanside. I think it would be just divine if —"

Wigmore roared into the phone, "You fucking fag! You don't know who you're messin' with! Now I know where you live! You bother me anymore, and so help me, I'll take my gun and ram it up your ass and pull the trigger! That's after I rip your face off and shove it up your ass too!"

Louie Grazia sat at his desk and slurped his morning coffee as he listened to Wizard and Rolly talk on the tape. When it ended he sat with pursed lips, staring across his desk at Jack and Danny.

"What do you think?" asked Danny, feeling uneasy.

Louie stared hard at Jack. "I take it they tried to kill you behind the Black Water when Danny told me you had gone fishing?"

"It wasn't all that serious. Danny was right there to cover my ass."

"Yeah, right," replied Louie sarcastically. "It wasn't too serious. That's when you didn't come to the office for a few days. Which means you got hurt!"

Jack nodded.

"I knew it! Goddamn it, I knew it! You could have told me, instead of keeping me worried about what the hell you were both up to!"

"It was my idea not to tell," said Jack. "If you know about it and I screw up, then you're in trouble too."

"You still should have told me," he said, harshly. "So tell me," he continued, his voice softening a little, "how close did they come?"

"It was close," admitted Jack. "Got my arm drilled and needed a few stitches from a cut on my back, but —"

"Jesus Christ! You were shot?"

"As they say in the movies, it was just a flesh wound. Nothing serious. Finding out who pulled the trigger on Maggie and Ben Junior ... it was worth it." Jack paused and his face became angry and red. "Now we need to find out who ordered them to do it."

"Have you told your sister and her husband?"

Jack shook his head. "I won't until it's over. When I find The Suit. Then it will be over."

"You've done more than enough already. No evidence to arrest, but at least we can point Homicide in the right direction."

"Homicide? Who's talking Homicide? It'll be over when Wizard, Rolly, and The Suit are buried! Not left to some —"

"Damn it, Jack! Cool it! I don't want to hear that kind of talk. You're on an Intelligence Unit. Try using some! You've gone way beyond what you were allowed. Back off. Give Homicide a chance!"

Jack locked eyes with Louie for a moment, then quietly said, "I apologize. You're right. I was just letting off steam."

Jack sounded calm. Too calm, thought Louie. It was the demeanour that a professional would use. *A professional killer.*

"The problem is," Jack continued, "we don't know who the leak is. It could be someone in Homicide. Letting others know means jeopardizing our source, and it could also tip off the leak so that we never find him."

"Any ideas who that is?" Louie asked.

"I was inclined to think it came from one of the City narcs, but that was just my own bias. I didn't want to think it was one of ours. The narcs talked to our Homicide Unit about Lenny and me, or Eddy Trimble, each time before things got hot."

"You think the leak is from Homicide?" asked Louie.

"It's the secret identity that makes me wonder. City narcs don't usually wear suits. Homicide do."

"It could be someone higher up in City. Their bosses wear suits, including Ted Nash."

"So do our bosses. Finding out may not be easy, but I will," said Jack with bitter determination.

"What did that kid ... Marcie ... say The Suit looked like?"

"She didn't see his face, but described him as slim, with collar-length dark wavy hair."

"Doesn't help much. That fits you. What about CC? Do you trust her?"

"As far as I would trust most cops, why?"

"You know she's not the leak. Tell her that a reliable source said that Wizard and Rolly murdered the kids on instruction from someone who is leaking information. Tell her that they also killed Lenny and tried to kill someone by the name of Eddy Trimble. If that isn't enough to get a wiretap, mention that they're also responsible for running a speed connection out of Montreal. Maybe it will lead to The Suit. If she needs a partner, tell her to make sure it's someone chubby who she trusts completely."

"These guys would never contact The Suit from their home phones."

"I agree, but maybe Homicide could get a room bug in or something. Maybe bug their cars. It wouldn't hurt."

"These guys don't talk inside and they change cars like you change shirts."

"What have you got to lose? Wizard and Rolly already know that you're on to them."

"It wouldn't hurt, except I'm not supposed to be involved in this." Jack glanced at Danny before continuing. "Wigmore is acting kinky. If I start ducking questions from CC or anyone about who Eddy Trimble is, it won't be good. Especially if CC does end up bringing the City narcs on board."

Louie nodded that he understood, then said, "Danny, you pass on the information and take responsibility for any questions or meetings. No need for them to know who Trimble really is. This is only Tuesday. If CC hustles her ass, she could have wire on by early next week."

Danny squirmed in his chair, then said, "I guess that's not lying."

"You're not lying," said Louie. "You're just not disclosing everything."

"What about Axle and Nails?" asked Danny. "They killed Crystal."

"That's a card we could use later. See how this plays out first. We don't have the manpower to be everywhere at once. Concentrate on Wizard and Rolly. They're the ones who want to kill Jack. If they make a move we need to know immediately!"

"Understood," said Danny.

Louie pointed his finger at Jack and said, "You stay in the background! Especially where Wizard and Rolly are concerned! We're going to have to figure out a way to cover your ass and make sure —"

"I've thought of that. I told our friend to tell them that we'll be out of town for a while. That should give us breathing room enough for us to find out who The Suit is."

"And how do you expect to do that?" asked Louie.

"You're right about running wire. When it's on, we'll run surveillance on Wizard and Rolly. I'll get our friend to meet them and say he just heard from me that I found out who The Suit is. With luck, they'll either panic and say something, or they'll go warn him and we'll follow them and find out."

"And if Wizard and Rolly decide to find you first?"

"We rattled their chains good last night. They'll be so paranoid that they'll be looking over their shoulders at everyone. We'll lie low the rest of this week. Give them a little time to cool off and for CC to get the wire up and running. Then do it. Once we find out who The Suit is, I'll arrange for Wizard and Rolly to find me. I'll pick the time and place."

Louie shook his head. "That's not a good idea."

"Don't worry. When the time comes, I'll make sure that both you and Danny get an invitation. It will be a formal affair. Dress in black and bring sniper rifles."

"Damn it, Jack! That's not —"

"Hey, Louie! Lighten up! I'm just joking."

Louie looked at Jack's eyes. Jack stared back and didn't blink. He was supposed to think Jack was telling the truth. He knew better.

chapter twenty-nine

Later that afternoon, Wigmore was putting his work away when his telephone rang.

"Superintendent Wigmore," the young woman said, "my name is Linda. Are you Jack Taggart's boss?"

"Indirectly. What can I do for you?"

"I used to go out with Jack, but he doesn't think I'm good enough for him now."

"I'm sorry, miss, but I'm not responsible for personal issues that —"

"I understand that! But he shouldn't be allowed to break the law, even if he is a cop."

"What do you mean?"

"Well, when we were going together, he once told me about something he did to some big-time bank robber. A Frenchman, I think."

Wigmore gripped the receiver and reached for a pad of paper. "What did he say?"

The woman paused, then said, "I don't like discussing this on the phone. Would it be okay if I met you? I could be there in two hours, say 6:15."

"Please do! Just come to the front counter and ask for me. I'll wait."

"But what if Jack comes in? I don't want him to know. Maybe this isn't a good idea...."

"Do you want to meet someplace else?"

"I'd still feel safer at your office. Do I have to come to the main entrance?"

Wigmore paused, then said, "No, you don't. Come to the fire escape door at the rear of the building. I'll let you in and sneak you up the back stairs. Nobody will see you, I promise."

"Well ... that sounds okay. I'll be there at 6:15 sharp."

At six o'clock Wigmore called the Communications Office. He told them to ignore the alarm system at the back door at 6:15 while he let in a "special person."

At 6:05 the woman called Wigmore again. She would be just a couple of minutes late and would call him from her cellphone when she reached the parking lot.

A young man in Communications watched the security camera as the woman approached the rear of the building. Her wide-brimmed hat hid her face, but her tight suit jacket and skirt revealed a good figure with long legs. Her blouse was pinned at her neck by a broach. He glanced at his watch. It was 6:15. She was right on time. The alarm buzzed briefly indicating that the fire escape door had been opened. He watched the camera as the woman stepped inside, and then he reset the alarm.

Wigmore received another call from the woman at 6:30. She sounded scared. She said that she was about to walk across the parking lot when she saw Jack Taggart drive away. She wanted to wait an hour to make sure that it was safe before coming in. Wigmore glanced at his watch and reluctantly agreed to await her next call.

At 7:25 the security alarm notified the Communications Office of another breach at the back door. The young man watched as the same woman left the building. She carried her suit jacket loosely over her shoulder, and her blouse was unbuttoned enough to show her cleavage. She did a little pirouette in the parking lot, swinging her purse in an arc around herself, then staggered before regaining her footing and walking away. Yes, she looked like a "special person."

Moments later, Wigmore grabbed his telephone on the first ring. The woman said that she was tired and didn't want to meet him tonight. Maybe some other time.

The security tape in the Communications Office recorded that Wigmore left through the front door of the building at 7:35 p.m.

Jack put his binoculars on the dashboard and smiled. Tiffany let out a squeal, so Jack picked her up. "It's okay, sweet pea, Mommy will be here in a minute."

It was not yet seven o'clock in the morning when Assistant Commissioner Isaac arrived at work. As usual, he was well ahead of the rest of his office staff. He didn't need to pull back the drapes to know the sanctuary of his office had been violated. The smell of Scotch permeated every corner of the room. A large, wet stain spread out from an empty bottle of Glennfiddich that was lying on the carpet, along with the picture of his wife, his bible, his pen set, and his brass business card holder. His business cards lay scattered across the carpet.

Isaac also didn't need to look at the brassiere hanging from the horn of the stuffed buffalo head to figure out what had taken place on his desk.

Isaac made two telephone calls. The first was to Internal Affairs. "You find them!" seethed Isaac. "I want to know who's responsible for this! And I want to know now!"

His second call was to a carpet-cleaning company.

Two hours later, the Identification Section announced that they had found fingerprints on the empty bottle of Scotch.

Late that afternoon, Wigmore fidgeted with his hands as he entered Isaac's office. He denied being responsible. He denied knowing the woman on the tape of the security camera. Yes, he had received a call from someone, and yes he had called Communications, telling them to ignore the alarm. Yes, he drank Scotch. No, he didn't have a drinking problem. Yes, he could explain how the bottle with his prints got there. He was framed by Jack Taggart!

Isaac listened to Wigmore's raspy voice plead his innocence and wondered if it was a set-up. After all, a commissioned officer ... it just didn't seem possible. And the brassiere hanging from the buffalo's horn ... it did seem like overkill. He told Wigmore, who was begging for a chance to take the polygraph, that he would accommodate his request before the week was over.

It was 10:30 p.m. when Danny called Wigmore at home. Wigmore was furious but listened to Danny's plea that he didn't know anything about Jack framing him. Wigmore said that he was looking forward to seeing Danny in person. The Oceanside, in one hour!

It was 11:45 when Jack and Danny parked with Susan and Tiffany at a payphone near the office, about a forty-minute drive from the Oceanside Lounge. Susan used the payphone to place her call.

"Oceanside Lounge," said the bartender.

"Yes," purred Susan. "Is Marvin Wigmore in there? Big guy, brush-cut, drinks Scotch."

"Yes, he is."

"Tell him I left my bra in his office and I want it back."

The bartended suppressed a snicker and said, "I think you better tell him that yourself. Hang on." Susan heard the bartender shout, "Mr. Wigmore! Telephone!"

Susan passed the receiver to Danny.

"Yeah, this is Wigmore. Is that you, O'Reilly?"

"Yes, sir."

"Where are you? Why aren't you here? I've been waiting!"

"You're nothing but a jealous, pompous, vindictive little man with the brain a size of a rat's and probably the balls to match!"

"What?" screamed Wigmore. "You think you can talk that way with me? You're finished! Do you understand? Finished! When I see you I'll rip your face off and —"

"Sir, sir, sir!" interjected Danny. "It's not me that said that!"

"What? What are you talking about? You said I had the balls of —"

"Sir, no, you misunderstood. I was reading from my notes. That's what Jack said about you tonight. I was just telling you."

"Taggart? He said that?"

"Yes, sir. I made notes of it. Sorry, I should have explained that first."

"Where are you? You could have told me that when you got here."

"That's why I'm calling. It's Jack. He's really freaked out tonight about you. I don't know why. He's been drinking and calling you all sorts of names. I think I should stick with him. He's talking like he wants to shoot you."

"Shoot me? That son of a bitch! Okay, listen O'Reilly! You stay close to him. Tomorrow morning we'll meet at the office. I want you to tell Assistant Commissioner Isaac every detail."

"Yes, sir. I'll be there. Good night, sir."

At 11:58 Wigmore walked out of the lounge and went home. One minute later, the bartender looked up at a new customer.

"Do you have a phone I can borrow for a local call?"

"At the end of the bar. Help yourself."

It was exactly midnight when Assistant Commissioner Isaac mumbled an apology to his wife while leaning across to answer the telephone on the bedside table. He recognized Wigmore's raspy, angry voice immediately.

"It's Superintendent Wigmore! W-I-G-M-O-R-E! Listen, you fuckin' faggot! You don't know who you're messin' with! You bother me anymore and so help me, I'll take my gun and ram it up your ass and pull the trigger! That's after I rip your face off and shove it up your ass too!"

The line went dead. Isaac was shocked, but he still thought like a policeman. He checked his call display and then called the Communications Office. He demanded to know where Jack Taggart was at this exact moment.

One hour later, a policeman interviewed the bartender. Yes, Mr. Wigmore had been in. He was certain. Left around midnight, right after he used the phone. Some woman called him. Said she left her bra in his office. It's not the sort of thing you would forget. Wigmore might have made another call after. He was really angry. Yelling at someone on the phone.

*

Wigmore left for work earlier than usual and cautiously looked around as he walked down his apartment hallway and pushed the elevator button. He was wearing a bulletproof vest under his shirt and carried a pistol — something he hadn't done since being commissioned.

The elevator door opened and Wigmore did an imitation of a freshly caught bass, blinking his eyes while opening and closing his mouth. Three members of the Tactical Team leapt from the elevator and ordered him to the floor. Four more officers appeared on each side of him in the hall, also dressed in black and also carrying automatic weapons. They too screamed for him to hit the floor.

"Go on in."

Louie Grazia nodded to the secretary, then walked across the fresh-smelling carpet and sat down in front of Isaac's desk.

"Good work on Project 13 so far, Louie," said Isaac. "This new informant your section has cultivated is proving very valuable. I gather there is still no indication who is supplying the bikers with information?"

"No, sir, not at this time. We're working on it."

"Well, if you hear anything, let me know immediately!"

"Yes, sir."

Isaac glanced at the picture of his wife and looked back at Grazia.

"You heard about Wigmore this morning?"

Grazia nodded.

"It's a shame. I just heard from the hospital. Preliminary examination indicates he may be suffering from paranoid schizophrenia. The doctor thinks he truly doesn't know reality from fiction. He was wearing a bulletproof vest and carrying his sidearm when they took him down. He's afraid that policemen are trying to kill him. Also said that Taggart and O'Reilly framed him and that O'Reilly called him last night at some lounge and set him up."

"Oh?"

"It was actually a woman friend of his who called him there. She spoke to the bartender first. Somehow it triggered Wigmore. He went berserk and called and threatened me right after. I haven't told you this, but Wigmore made accusations yesterday saying that Taggart framed him for the ... indiscretion in my office. After Wigmore threatened me at home, I immediately called Communications."

"Do you think Taggart was involved?"

"Taggart was with O'Reilly. Communications proved that the both of them entered our building only minutes before Wigmore called to threaten me."

"I'm glad my men weren't involved, sir."

"I know. I think Wigmore snapped under the pressure of being commissioned. He's looking to point his finger at anyone rather than take a good look at himself. The sad thing is, he really believes it."

"It sounds pretty serious."

"It's serious, but they don't think he's actually dangerous. They expect to release him shortly and treat him as an outpatient."

"Will he be coming back to the job?"

"No. I'll see to it that he goes to pension as soon as he's released." Isaac leaned back in his chair and said, "Well, enough about that. Let the men know I'm pleased with how Project 13 is progressing and keep me abreast of any new developments."

"Yes, sir," replied Grazia.

*

It was eleven o'clock on Friday night when Jack and Danny stepped up on the darkened porch and Jack rapped on the door. A few minutes later, the porch light went on and the door opened a crack.

Jack stuck his foot in the doorway and said, "Police! We've got an arrest warrant for Jose Cuervo! Open up! We got a tip that he's hiding in your kitchen!"

"Come on in," said Louie. "I'll lead you to him."

Louie led Jack and Danny into the kitchen. Louie took his pistol from his housecoat pocket and placed it on the kitchen table, and then retrieved the bottle of tequila and three glasses.

The three men gave a silent toast and drank. When they were finished, Louie pointed a finger at Jack and said, "Pour another. I'll be right back."

Jack did as he was told, and Louie returned a moment later with a tape recorder. He spoke with a lisp and said, "Lithen to thith, big boys!"

Jack, Danny, and Louie howled with laughter when the tape of Wigmore's voice was played. When it was finished, Louie became sombre and looked at Jack and said, "He might be vengeful. Keep your eyes open for a while."

"We've talked about this before. As I said, the man's a bully, which makes him a coward in my eyes. He wouldn't have the guts to try anything."

"I agree, but just be careful all the same. Now, time to burn this," added Louie, reaching for the tape.

Danny pleaded with Louie to play it one more time while he refilled the glasses.

By 2:00 a.m., the tape had been played several times before being destroyed.

chapter thirty

CC sat in the passenger seat flipping through her wiretap application while her partner, Charlie Wells, drove the car. She looked up and said, "Take the next left."

They parked in front of Bishop's estate and had barely gotten out of the car when the sound of three rapid gunshots came from behind the home. CC and Charlie both reached for their pistols and ran to the back of the home.

A long pier led into the ocean. A large cabin cruiser was parked at the end of the dock, opposite a small boathouse. Sid Bishop stood near the boathouse and watched a clay pigeon fly into the air. Three more blasts followed, but he missed again and silently cursed the bottle.

A few minutes later, Bishop invited the police officers into his home. He poured them each a cup of tea while he sat and browsed through the wiretap application.

"This information came through a Daniel O'Reilly," mused Bishop as he read the pages.

CC reached for a scone and said, "His informant."

"I may need to talk to him later."

"No problem, I'll give you his cell number. O'Reilly works with Jack Taggart on the Intelligence Unit. They probably both run the informant. Taggart's pretty experienced; I'm sure the informant is reliable."

They were interrupted by the sound of the door chimes. Sid left momentarily, and CC saw that it was a catering company making a delivery.

Sid returned and said, "Sorry about that. Having a bit of a social here tonight. Now, back to this, why isn't Taggart's name on this application?"

"The two kids that were killed were his niece and nephew," CC replied.

"His niece and nephew?"

"Yes."

"It would be prudent for him to remain in the background. Less chance of defence claiming that the information is biased."

"You're right, but there's more to it than that."

"Oh?"

"The superintendent who was recently in charge of the Intelligence units told me that he considers Taggart dangerous — a loose cannon. He ordered him to stay clear of this investigation. I have the feeling that Taggart is really involved, maybe holding something back."

"Holding something back? This application alludes to the fact that someone is divulging classified information. How classified? Would this person know where I live, for example? What about Taggart? Does he know who it is? Damn it! This shouldn't be taken lightly!"

"There is no indication of anything to be concerned about in regard to anyone's safety. As far as Taggart goes, I'm certain he doesn't know anything in that regard."

"What makes you certain of that?"

"Two things. One is they provided me with the grounds for this application." CC paused, trying to formulate her words.

"And the second reason?" Bishop asked impatiently.

"From what I heard about Taggart, Wizard and Rolly wouldn't still be alive."

It was almost midnight when Nails spoke with Axle.

"Just heard from Wizard. We got a job to do tomorrow morning. Need to vaporize a couple of pigs."

"Pigs!"

"You got it. I expect you're about to earn your patch."

It was Saturday evening, and Jack was helping Marcie clear the dishes from the table when Danny called. Elizabeth answered and passed the telephone to Jack.

"Just got a call from a prosecutor," said Danny. "Some guy by the name of Sid Bishop. Must be dedicated. Wants to meet me at Willy's Restaurant tomorrow morning at ten for coffee and go over Homicide's wiretap application. Also wants you there."

"CC must have put two and two together. Like I need that!" said Jack, sarcastically.

"I can try it alone. It's at a mall, and Susan wanted to pick up some things. I don't mind."

"I'll bring my own car and wait nearby. If you don't think the prosecutor will push the application through without talking to me, then call and I'll join you."

"Will do."

"Depending upon what happens, we should meet our friend right after and prepare him to do his bit."

"No problem. We could meet him in your car and Susan can drive ours back home."

chapter thirty-one

Rolly parked near the restaurant parking lot. He watched as Danny arrived. His wife was with him, pushing a baby stroller. She entered the mall while Danny headed for a restaurant.

He pulled up alongside Axle and Nails, who were parked in a van, and gave them a detailed description of O'Reilly's car before calling Wizard on his cell.

Wizard waited impatiently at the airport. Damien's flight was to arrive in ten minutes. It would be some time after that before customs was cleared.

Wizard answered Rolly's call.

"Bad news," said Rolly. "Just one pig. Not the main one."

"One is better than none."

"I guess. The pig also brought along a sow and a piglet. Your call. Now? Or some other time?"

"Do it now! It's our asses on the line!"

"Understood."

"Cover the delivery, then get the hell away from there."

Rolly watched Nails carry his package in a paper shopping bag across the parking lot. He disappeared for a few seconds behind the pig's car. Rolly felt a few tense seconds as a woman parked nearby. Nails stood up quickly and walked back toward the van. He was still carrying the shopping bag, but it was swinging freely and Rolly knew it was empty. He then drove and parked a block away.

Minutes later, Axle and Nails drove out the restaurant exit to park far enough away that they couldn't be identified but would still be able to see when O'Reilly's car approached the exit. Then they could easily detonate the bomb and leave unnoticed while everyone else was distracted by the explosion.

Neither Axle nor Nails knew what Taggart looked like, but their faces were ingrained into his memory. He arrived in the lot as they passed him in the opposite direction.

Danny knew by Sid Bishop's abrupt tone that he was less than impressed that Jack wasn't with him. He fired several questions about the reliability of the informant, but Danny was able to answer them all. Their informant was a member of Satans Wrath and had been proven reliable. There was no reason to call Jack. Sid spent more time discussing personal safety than he did the actual investigation. Danny also noted that Sid loved his coffee. Lots of it, black.

When the meeting was over, Danny shook hands with Sid and went into the mall to look for Susan and to call Jack. He didn't need to call. Jack was inside the mall entrance.

"It went well," said Danny. "All he had were the basic questions. I could handle it myself. He said we should have the authorization signed by tomorrow or Tuesday."

"We need to talk," said Jack.

"Are we meeting our friend?"

"Yes, in about an hour, but..."

Jack's attention was diverted by a gentle poke in his ribs. "Hi, Jack!"

He smiled politely and then said, "Hi, Susan. Done your shopping already?"

"Afraid so. This cheapskate keeps us on a tight budget."

Jack looked at Danny and said, "With all the overtime you make?"

"Yeah, right! And when do *I* get time to spend it? I'm always working!"

"A cheapskate *and* a complainer. I don't know, Susan. It must be rough."

"It is. I just live in quiet desperation and bear the pain." She grinned and said, "He is pretty good in the sack, though."

"Only pretty good?" said Danny, wrapping his arm around her and pulling her close.

"Okay. You're great!"

"That's better!" He kissed her and Tiffany each on the cheek. "See ya, hon," he said, passing her his car keys. "I should be home around twelve-thirty."

Damien and his family cleared customs faster than Wizard had hoped. Buck entered the public part of the terminal first, followed by his two sisters. Wizard was just hanging up his cell as Vicki and Damien appeared.

"What's going on?" asked Damien.

Wizard tried not to smile as he stuffed his cell back in his pocket. "Had some business to take care of. Tried to reach you but couldn't."

Damien checked his cell. "It's been on."

"Must not work down south or on the plane."

Damien partially covered his mouth with his hand. He was always conscious of the possibility of someone pointing a directional microphone at him. His voice was quiet, but the tone was angry. "What is it? What have you done?"

Wizard partially covered his own mouth and gave Damien an update on what happened during the last week. He saved telling him about killing O'Reilly and his family until last. When he was finished, he added, "Just one pig to go. Jack Taggart. We'll have his address today or tomorrow."

Wizard expected Damien would be furious, but it wasn't his ass on the line. Besides, the election for national president was only eight days away. Showing enough class to off a pig, or two pigs by then, would prove that he had the balls to do the job. He looked at Damien. *You've only got a few days left. You know it and I know it!* By the look on Damien's face, he knew that Damien was thinking the same thing.

"This is my fault," Damien said. He didn't sound angry, but calculating and matter of fact.

"What? What do ya mean?"

"I should never have left you in charge. You don't have the ... capacity to handle the position. I see that now."

"Bullshit! I did right! It's easy for you to talk! The cops aren't about to bust you for —"

Damien stabbed a finger into Wizard's chest and said, "You have no idea what you've done! Do you really think there won't be retribution over this?"

"They'll never pin it on us!"

"You dumb fuck! I didn't say that they'd be looking for evidence! I'm talking retribution!" He then turned and walked back to his family.

Wizard watched as Damien herded his family to an airline counter and bought them all tickets to Mexico. *Yeah, well, if you're worried about your family, you shouldn't have one.*

Danny rushed out of the mall as Susan was putting the stroller in the car. "There's been a change of plans," he said, glancing around the parking lot.

"Aren't you going with Jack?"

"No, we're going for a drive right now. Jack is going to follow us. Hurry up and get in."

Susan could tell by the look on Danny's face that he was either angry or scared. Or perhaps both. "Danny, what is it? What's going on?"

Danny waited until he had backed out of the parking stall before saying, "Jack saw two bikers arrive shortly after we did. He's been watching them. They're parked in a van watching this parking lot."

"You think they're here because of you? That they followed you?"

"Looks like it."

"Where are they? I don't see anyone!"

The words were barely out of her mouth when there was a horrendous explosion in an adjacent parking lot. Susan saw the back of a van lift off the ground before bouncing back down. An orange fireball of flame filled the inside and she could see the silhouettes of two people in the front.

The passenger instinctively grabbed at his blown eardrums before slumping over. The driver clawed at his door, but the van had buckled from the explosion and the door wouldn't open. His body writhed inside the van and then fell from sight.

"My God!" Susan screamed. "Danny!" she said, pointing to the van.

"That's them!" he replied. "They blew themselves up!" He gazed at the van momentarily and then sped out of the mall lot. "They were planning on killing us! You, Tiffany, and me!"

"What are you saying? I don't understand! What's going on?"

"They're the same two guys who murdered Crystal. One guy is a bomb expert."

"A bomb expert? But why?"

Danny glanced in the rear-view mirror and said, "Guess he wasn't an expert, but you can bet it was intended for us."

"Why aren't you waiting for the police? Why —"

"I'm getting you and Tiffany the hell away from here! There could be others! You're going to pack, and I'm putting you on a plane. Call your brother in Calgary and stay with him."

"But why? What are you going to do?"

"They probably know where we live! Jack told me to move in with him while we sort things out. He's going to make a few calls."

"To who? What for?" said Susan, starting to cry.

"This is against the rules. The bastards have just declared war and they're going to get it."

Wizard answered his cellphone.

"We've got a problem!" Rolly's voice was high-pitched.

"What the fuck are you talking about?"

"Find a television! It's on right now!"

Wizard and Damien went into one of the airport's lounges and saw live coverage of a breaking story on television. An explosion had ripped a van apart. Two bodies were recovered, but the broadcast said they were burned beyond recognition.

"I don't get it," said Wizard. "Rolly saw them put the package on the pig's car!"

Damien looked at Wizard for a moment, then said, "This being the same Rolly who the cops know killed the little boy and later the Indo? Who else knew he whacked them two?"

"He said he hasn't told anyone."

"So only you know ... and the police."

Wizard didn't respond.

The two men walked back to where Vicki and the children were waiting.

"You gonna cancel their flight now?" asked Wizard

Damien shook his head. "There could still be retribution. The fact that you failed won't make a difference."

"But..."

"Shut the fuck up and listen! We've got a rat in-house! It could be Rolly or someone else in your chapter."

Wizard was about to defend Rolly, but Damien gave him a long, hard look, and he decided it was in his best interest to stay quiet on that subject. "What about the two pigs?" he asked.

"Unfortunately, because of your stupidity, now I have to deal with them immediately before any more shit hits the fan. Then we'll find out who the rat is. In the meantime, nobody in your chapter is to go anywhere near them. It'll strictly be the east-side boys. Understood?"

"Understood."

"And that means you, too!"

chapter thirty-two

Jack and Danny made sure they were not being followed, then checked the area around Danny's home. Nothing aroused their suspicions. Six hours later, Danny kissed Susan and Tiffany goodbye and watched them go through security at the airport to board their flight. Jack had taken another car and followed them to the airport.

Jack and Danny were walking back to their cars when Danny's cellphone rang.

"Danny! It's Sid Bishop. I just saw the news! Did you hear what happened?"

"About what?"

"Two bikers were blown up in a van this morning near Willy's Restaurant! It had to have happened right after we left. That's no coincidence!"

"Oh, that. Yes, I heard." Danny covered the mouthpiece on the phone and whispered to Jack, "It's Sid Bishop!" He then held the phone so they could both hear.

"What do you mean, oh, that? How did they know we were there? They tried to kill us! Christ, I don't want to go home!"

"Sid, relax. If they wanted to kill you, they could have shot the both of us when we were leaving."

"That's not very comforting! I called Marvin at home and —"

"Marvin?" asked Danny.

"Sorry, Superintendent Wigmore. He gave me the home number for Assistant Commissioner Isaac. He's not home yet; I keep calling. I want to hear what he says about this!"

Jack rolled his eyes, then took the phone from Danny and said, "Sid. This is Jack Taggart, Danny's partner. I'm positive that your life is not in danger. If you think about it, the bikers would have nothing to gain by killing you. In fact, they would have a lot to lose. We don't think this is connected to us. We have intelligence that a drug war is starting. Getting the wire hooked up is the best thing we can do right now."

Sid sounded surprised. "You think it's a drug war? That it was a coincidence?"

"I'm certain of it. We heard that Satans Wrath killed a speed dealer by the name of Bobby Singh. This is probably retaliation for that."

Sid paused, then calmed down. "So you don't think I'm in danger?"

"No."

Jack heard Sid turn away from the phone and say, "Oh, God, thank heavens." He then spoke to Jack: "I must admit, this incident has shaken my composure. I'm glad to hear you say that. It took me a long time to get through on Danny's cell. He should get a new phone!"

"There's no need to panic."

"I don't panic! I was just concerned."

"I'll give you my home and cell numbers. Danny will be staying with me for a couple of days, so if you need to, you can reach either of us there."

"Why is he staying with you if there's no need to panic?" said Sid, his voice rising.

"Just coincidence. His wife is out of town and we decided to bach together. By the way, how well do you know Superintendent Wigmore?"

"Not well. Just socially on occasion. He didn't speak very highly of you."

"Oh?" said Jack, feigning surprise. "He's had some emotional problems lately. I won't hold that against him. I'll call you as soon as we know something further."

"Now what?" asked Danny, after Jack hung up.

"If Isaac thinks our lives are in danger, he'll transfer the both of us so far north we'll need a dogsled team. If that happens, I'll quit and stay here to finish this on my own."

"After what happened, how can you convince him otherwise?"

"Play up that it's a drug war. I'll have a report on his desk first thing tomorrow morning saying our informant told us a drug war is starting. Convince him that today was a coincidence."

"Isaac will want to know who is dumb enough to take on Satans Wrath."

"I'll say it's conflict within Satans Wrath. That way when more of them start dying, it'll make sense."

"You think he'll swallow that?"

"I hope so. Otherwise you and Susan better develop a taste for whale blubber."

"Speaking of our friend?"

Jack glanced at his watch. "This should be interesting. When I cancelled the meet with him at noon, he sounded like he didn't know anything yet. Since then he's left half a dozen urgent messages for me to call him."

"Why not call him?"

"I will, but I want to see his face when we talk."

Jack called Lance's number. His message was brief. "Cemetery! Two hours!"

Jack then said to Danny, "Tell me you've got your vest on?"

"It's on."

Two hours later, Lance made sure that his jacket covered the handle of the 9 mm tucked in the front of his jeans before quietly making his way into the cemetery. He didn't approach from the normal direction, but circled around and came in from behind instead.

Minutes later, he heard whispering and saw Jack and Danny standing near a grave marker. Their backs were toward him and they continued to whisper as he approached. Lance stopped behind them and said, "Glad to see you guys didn't bring a shovel with ya!"

Jack and Danny turned to face him. "It's not that far away," said Jack.

"How come ya didn't get back to me? I've been phonin' and leavin' messages all day!"

"Why didn't you call before it happened?"

"I swear to fuckin' God I didn't know about it! The first I heard was when Wiz called a meetin' around noon. That's when he let everyone in the chapter know that Nails an' Axle got blown up. He said that they were takin' care of business when somethin' happened. It was after the meetin' that Wiz and Rolly let me know that it was supposed to be for you guys."

"What did they say?"

"Wiz apologized for not lettin' me in on it but said that there wasn't time. I asked him what happened." Lance looked at Danny and said, "Rolly was there. He thought he saw Nails put the bomb on your car and then drove about a block away and waited. He mentioned that some broad had driven in when Nails was doin' it. At the time, he thought it had been planted but realizes now that it wasn't."

"Who else was there besides Rolly? Wasn't Wizard around?" asked Jack.

"It was just the three of them. Wiz was at the airport meeting Damien. He was just getting' back from the Grand Caymans."

"Did Damien sanction this?"

"Don't know. But they do know that someone in the club is rattin'. The heat is really on."

"They had to figure that out once you let them know that we knew who Rolly and Wizard murdered. This doesn't really change anything as far as you go."

"Yeah, I guess not, but it's getting' pretty damn uncomfortable."

"We'll look after you."

"So now what?" asked Danny. "What are they going to do next?"

"I asked. Wizard said we're not to do anything right now. He promised to let me know if that was going to change."

"You're sure about that?" asked Jack.

"That's what he said. We got orders to sit tight. Wiz did say that things will change after the election. He's confident that he'll beat out Damien." Lance looked at Jack and asked, "There was somethin' you were going to get me to do?"

"I was going to get you to put more pressure on Wizard and Rolly this week, but things are too hot right now. We better wait a week or so and see what happens."

"You're fuckin' right things are hot! Waitin' is fine by me."

Lance agreed to stay in touch and was walking away when Jack said, "One more thing!"

"Yeah? What's that?"

"Just out of curiosity, are you packin'?"

Lance lifted his jacket slightly to expose the handle of the 9 mm. "You're fuckin' right I'm packin'! If I'd seen another shovel I would've used it to bury you both!"

Jack smiled, then said, "Take care of yourself, Lance."

Jack and Danny stood in the cemetery and watched Lance drive away. Moments later they heard the metallic sound of a bolt sliding in a rifle.

Jack turned and said, "Louie, you look like a bloody ninja. Except for the white socks!"

Louie looked quickly at his feet. "You asshole! They're black!"

"You weren't sure, though, were you? I don't know, Louie. I think you're getting old."

"Not so old that I couldn't kick your ass!"

Danny interjected. "Listen guys, if it's okay with you, I want to get going. I told Susan I'd call her and Calgary's an hour ahead of us."

Jack gave Danny an extra key to his apartment and told him to go ahead. He said he wanted to make sure that Louie didn't get lost in the graveyard and then stop at the office to put in a quick report for Isaac to read in the morning.

Danny let himself in through the main entrance of the apartment building and walked across the lighted lobby to the elevators.

From across the street, Damien and The Suit sat in a car looking out through the tinted windows. The Suit lowered his binoculars and said, "That's O'Reilly!" Damien took a quick glimpse through the binoculars, then picked up a portable radio.

"Pork chop number two just entered through the main entrance."

Whiskey Jake, who was the president of the east-side chapter, sat in a van parked in the underground parking lot of the building. With him were Sparks, Thumper, and Two-Forty Gordy.

Whiskey Jake thumbed the radio and said, "Copy that."

A couple of minutes later, Damien gave another message: "Lights just went on. He's in the apartment. It's up to you guys now."

"No problem," replied Whiskey Jake.

Damien glanced at The Suit and said, "I'm taking you to your car."

"No, I want to see it," said The Suit. "I want to see them beg for their lives!"

Damien grabbed The Suit by the front of his jacket, jerking him halfway across the seat. "You put my family and everyone in the club at risk today! I'm not selling ringside seats here! This isn't a fucking game you're watching!"

Twenty minutes later, Damien stopped a block from where The Suit's car was parked. Neither man had spoken a word. The Suit got out and slammed the door as he left.

Two hours later, Jack drove into the underground parking lot and parked in his stall. A minute later, he opened the metal door leading to the alcove where the elevators were. He stepped inside and saw that he wasn't alone. The man facing him was wearing a ski mask.

Jack's adrenal glands instantly electrified his body, but it was too late to prevent the solid kick he received to his groin. His knees wobbled as two more men grabbed each of his arms from behind. The pain made him want to vomit.

He was slammed face down on the concrete floor. He could see the square-toed boots of the man who had kicked him. A small piece of leather was curled back off the end of one of the boots. He wondered, briefly, if it was the result of someone being kicked in the teeth, then thought it ironic that he would think of that when he was about to die. A hand jerked his pistol out of his holster, and he braced himself for the shot.

Seconds later, his eyes and mouth were plastered with duct tape. He hands were bound behind his back and his ankles were also wrapped. They found the knife he carried for undercover duties and slid it out of its scabbard. He was then lifted off the ground by his arms and dragged out the door. He heard the sound of a sliding door and was tossed inside a van. Perhaps he had been optimistic, thinking that his life would end so quickly. *They want to know who the informant is first*, he realized.

He felt someone remove his keys from his pocket. Nobody had spoken a word. He heard the sliding door again as some of the men left the van. He had a sickening feeling that he knew why they had taken his keys.

His body rolled against a metal bar under a seat as the van sped away.

Danny was sitting on the sofa watching television when he heard the sound of the key in the apartment door. "Good, you're back!" he hollered. "I feel like a drink."

He heard the footsteps behind him and said, "I talked with Susan. She's scared but she's okay."

Danny felt the cold barrel of a pistol in his ear. He snapped his head around, and the barrel of the pistol obscured the vision of one eye. The man holding the pistol was wearing a ski mask. He looked past him and saw two other men. They were also wearing ski masks — and they were also pointing pistols at him.

chapter thirty-three

Jack estimated an hour had passed before the van came to a stop. During the trip, he vowed that he would never release Lance's name. He would quickly give them a few names, then hold out for as long as possible — and finally give them Rolly.

He thought of other things. He wished that he had a chance to tell Natasha that he loved her one more time. He wished that he could apologize to Susan for failing to protect her husband, and somehow to Tiffany, for giving her a life without a father.

The sliding door of the van opened and he was hauled out by the arms and dragged across rough ground before being placed in a kneeling position.

The minutes ticked by and all he heard was the engine noise from a couple of vehicles. He started to lose his balance and felt himself falling forward, but a hand grabbed him by the hair and jerked him back into position. The duct tape was unwrapped from around his eyes.

Jack blinked and strained his eyes to see. Headlights behind him cast light and shadows across a construction site. He stared down at a hollow wall of rough planks interwoven with metal bars. He was kneeling in front of a large pit that had been dug out of the ground to build a basement. The construction was at the stage where the forms had been prepared for the pouring of the cement floor.

Jack looked behind him but was blinded by the high-beam headlights of a van and a car. He glanced down at the feet of a man standing beside him. He could make out the same square-toed boots and realized that his groin still ached. The man was no longer wearing a ski mask and sneered down at him. He recognized him from photographs of the east-side chapter as someone who went by the nickname of Thumper. Two more men approached from out of the headlights, and one of them used Jack's knife to cut the tape wrapped around the back of his neck before peeling it off his mouth. Jack recognized him as a striker from the same chapter. The striker handed the knife to the third man, who commanded, "Leave us!"

Thumper and the striker walked back and disappeared behind the headlights. Jack recognized Damien's face as he stepped closer.

"Do you know who I am, Officer Taggart?"

Jack looked up at his face. "Sure I do, Damien. Please, call me Jack. I hate formalities. Excuse me for not shaking hands."

Damien did not appear to be amused. "Let's get to the point. What do you think the point is, Jack?"

"The point is, you fucked up this morning by trying to kill my partner and his wife and baby. Now you're fucking up again!"

"I can understand why you would think that. Tell me, why do you think you ended up out here?"

"You want me to give you the name of someone. Good luck. Let the games begin! What will you start with? Water and a cattle prod?"

"Interesting tip. Tell me, Jack, just out of curiosity, what name would you yell out first?"

"Yours!"

A wry smile flashed across Damien's face, and then he said, "That's what I thought. I know we've got a rat in our club. I accept that. It happens, and it is something that will be dealt with. Unfortunately for you, others don't accept it quite as easily as I do, which brings us to the point of our meeting here."

"The point being?"

"The point being that sometimes large organizations have internal problems that need to be dealt with. You referred to an incident this morning. I had no knowledge about that incident until after it happened. I admit that someone in my organization may have been impetuous. I have since rectified the situation."

"Impetuous! Is that what you call committing murder? I don't care if you sanctioned it or not. You're in charge, and that makes you responsible!"

"I agree. I must, and do, accept responsibility for what happened. However, it would hardly be fair for other ... innocent people to get hurt simply because someone acted foolishly."

"What are you implying?"

"You're hardly the person to ask what I'm implying! You know full well what I'm saying! You and I are in different clubs, but we're very much alike."

"Alike? That's bullshit! I don't kidnap and murder people!"

"Kidnap? Murder? I brought you here to save lives! That's the whole point! You need to know that if I wanted you dead, you would be."

Damien then took the knife and slashed the tape from Jack's ankles and wrists.

Jack got to his feet and asked, "What about my partner?"

"He's okay. Probably relaxing in a tub right now."

"So you don't plan on committing any murders today?"

Damien leaned close and hissed, "Don't you, of all people, stand there and accuse me of murder! You're only alive because the others didn't figure it out!"

"Figure what out?"

"The switch! When you get home, wash your jacket. You've got an oil stain on the back from crawling under vehicles!"

Jack found himself at a loss for words.

Damien scowled and said, "I bet you and your partner had a good laugh over that one."

"He doesn't know. He thinks it was an accident."

"Loose lips?"

"I prefer to call it a need-to-know basis. He didn't need to know."

"Just as well. Do you give me your word that we're even for what happened this morning?"

Jack thought for a moment, then quietly said, "Yes."

Damien handed him his knife and pistol. Jack checked the pistol and saw that it was fully loaded.

Damien then yelled, "Thumper! Take him home!"

Jack glanced down at Thumper's square-toed boots as he approached. The man was slightly shorter than Jack and sneered up at him as he got close. Without warning, Jack kicked him hard in the groin and watched as he buckled over and staggered back.

Jack then turned to face Damien and said, "Now we're even for tonight, too."

Jack felt a tap on his shoulder and was surprised to see that it was Thumper.

"Ya want a piece of me, pork chop?" Thumper asked.

Jack had two months of rage burning inside him. He was eager to release some of it. He handed his gun and knife back to Damien and said, "You're damn right I do!"

Damien and the third man both laughed. Damien whispered something to Thumper, who nodded, then looked at Jack and said, "Okay, pig, let's see how tough ya are!"

Thumper opened with a side kick to Jack's ribs. Jack blocked the kick with his forearm and landed a fist on the end of Thumper's nose. Thumper stepped back, his eyes watering and blood gushing down across his lips. Jack stepped in close to deliver a karate punch to the solar plexus, followed by another punch to the throat. He didn't connect with either. He found himself sailing though the air, and then he landed in the pit dug for the basement.

He scrambled to his feet as Thumper jumped in beside him and planted a boot squarely across his chest. He staggered back, then lunged forward with another punch. Thumper grabbed his wrist and spun him sideways while delivering another kick to Jack's armpit.

Jack felt his arm go numb, and for a moment, so many fists and feet were slamming his body that he believed he was fighting all three men. He realized he wasn't when he was lying barely conscious, face down in the dirt, and heard Damien from above ordering the striker to go down in the hole and help Thumper carry him back to the van.

Jack was still winded and dazed as he was tossed onto the floor of the van.

Damien dropped Jack's gun and knife on the floor beside him and said, "I think I figured out who the rat is, so we really don't have a problem."

Jack didn't respond.

Damien then said, "Also, for your information, Thumper teaches kick-boxing, karate, and tae kwon do. You should sign up for lessons."

"Too late. My body just declared bankruptcy."

Damien chuckled, then softly closed the sliding door and walked away.

The striker hopped in the van and drove, while Thumper sat in the passenger seat. During the trip, Jack heard the striker say, "This has got to be a first, Thumper. Never seen anyone smack ya in the face before, let alone a pig."

Thumper replied, "Damien said he didn't want any other pigs getting excited. Told me I couldn't hit him in the face and to try not to break any bones. It's hard to fight when you're only playin' with someone like that."

Jack groaned.

When they pulled up to his apartment, Two-Forty Gordy came to the van with Jack's apartment keys and Thumper tossed them back to Jack. A few minutes later, Jack entered his apartment.

He found Danny wrapped in duct tape and lying face down in the bathtub. It took him a few minutes to take the tape off.

"Christ! Am I glad to see you," said Danny, blinking and wiping his eyes as he stepped out of the bathtub.

"Likewise," said Jack.

"What took you so long? I've been lying in this tub for hours!"

"I was detained."

"Detained? You're filthy! You look like you crawled out of a grave!"

"Close guess. I had the crap beat out of me by a guy who could have won with both hands tied behind his back."

"What happened? How come we're alive?"

"Grab the medicine. I'm too sore to reach the cupboard. I'll have mine on ice. We'll talk in the living room."

Danny poured drinks while telling Jack how he was grabbed and tied up like a Christmas turkey.

"Why did they dump you in the tub? Why not leave you on the rug?"

"Maybe they wanted me to think that they were going to drown me. When they dumped me in the tub, that's what I was afraid was going to happen."

"Did they run any water, just to scare you?"

"They didn't need to. I was already scared shitless. How did they grab you?"

Jack explained how he was kidnapped and brought to see Damien. He explained that Damien was making the point that he wasn't involved in the bomb incident and that he could have killed them tonight had he wished.

Then he said, "After I had the crap beat out of me, Damien told me that he thinks he knows who the rat is in their club."

Whiskey Jake and Sparks sat in the back of a van parked a block from Jack's apartment. Sparks turned the volume up on the speaker and said, "Here it is!"

They listened as Danny's voice came over the speaker.

"Damien knows who our friend is?" he said.

"I'm not so sure," said Jack. "If he really knew who it was, why let me know?"

"I don't know, but maybe we should warn him."

Sparks swore and said, "Come on, pigs! Give us a name!"

Whiskey Jake put his finger to his lips and Sparks became silent.

"He doesn't need warning," said Jack. "He knows the heat is on."

"So what do we do now?"

"At least we know that The Suit isn't with the City narcs," said Jack.

"Yeah, I've been thinking about that. CC said she would keep this on a need-to-know basis. She couldn't have told too many people."

"I've been thinking the same thing. We shouldn't forget Department of Justice, either."

Danny thought for a moment, then said, "There can't be that many guys who knew. If we get pictures of all the possibilities, maybe Marcie could point him out to us."

"Possibly. Either way, I figure we'll find out who this bastard is before the week is over!"

Sparks turned and looked at Whiskey Jake. "Who is this Marcie? Think we should let Damien know?"

"Fuckin' right!"

chapter thirty-four

Assistant Commissioner Isaac accepted the call from Wigmore, who had heard the news about two members of Satans Wrath being blown up. He sounded more deranged than before when Isaac mentioned that Taggart had submitted a report saying that an informant indicated that it was the result of internal strife within the club.

Wigmore said he had been building a file on Taggart and asked Isaac to look in his desk drawer. He said the documentation would prove that another one of Taggart's so-called informants, Edward Trimble, had been dead for years.

Isaac felt that Wigmore was psychotic, but that didn't mean there weren't any fibres of truth to his allegations. He spoke with Inspector Burg, who was filling in as a temporary replacement for Wigmore. Inspector Burg rifled through the desk and found a folder marked "Project Hotshot" and handed it to Isaac. Edward Trimble had been dead for over two years.

Late that afternoon, Inspector Burg examined the contents of a computer disc that he found in Wigmore's desk. He called Isaac, who took one glimpse, then called GIS. A search warrant would be obtained immediately.

Early in the afternoon of the next day, Jack called Natasha to make arrangements to pick her up. Liz was holding a surprise dinner party for Marcie for receiving an excellent report card. As he hung up, his cellphone rang.

Sparks, sitting near the apartment in his van, nudged Whiskey Jake and said, "Piggy's got another call. It's on his fuckin' cell so we'll only get his half of the conversation."

Louie was quick and to the point. "I've got some news. Are you and Danny sitting down?"

"Danny went home to pick up his mail," replied Jack. "He'll be back in an hour."

"You missed an interesting event last night. I just found out myself."

"I'm so damn sore I just about need a wheelchair to move around in. Mental note: never fight with a guy named Thumper."

Sparks smiled and gave Whiskey Jake the thumbs-up sign.

"I had planned on coming in tomorrow," continued Jack. "What's up?"

"I just talked with Isaac. We may have found the leak!"

"You think you know who The Suit is? Fantastic! Who?"

"Wigmore!"

"What?" Jack felt dumfounded. "Why? Why would he do that?"

"They found something in his desk. He's a goddamned pervert. Into kiddie porn. They seized a computer out of his apartment last night. It was loaded with the shit. Explains why he wanted your ass so bad."

"Explains the bomb at the mall. He talked the bikers into doing his dirty work for him!"

"You working on that porn file scared him."

"Find anything with bestiality?"

"I don't know yet. They're still downloading his computer."

"It makes sense," said Jack. "He was certainly in a position to know everything."

"They didn't find a George Bush mask in his apartment and he doesn't own a shepherd, but the bikers could be holding that for him."

"Is he in jail?"

"Not yet. They're assigning a special prosecutor to review everything. You know the system. It'll take months."

"Damn it! What if he skips out? Satans Wrath could send him anywhere in the world!"

"Why would they bother? Child pornography is all we can prove. We'll be lucky if he gets a hefty fine."

"I don't care about proof! As long as there's enough proof for me!"

Louie didn't respond. His silence was more powerful.

Jack felt like a fool. *Unprofessional.* "I was about to pick up Natasha and go to the farm," he said, changing the subject. "I want a photo of him to show Marcie. See what she says."

"She didn't see his face," Louie said thoughtfully, "but Wigmore has a mole on his neck."

"Exactly. She was still terrified when she described him to us. Easy to forget stuff. It wouldn't hurt for her to take a look. Might twig a memory. Even to see if it's his build or hairstyle."

"I'll get you one from Staffing. We should talk about all this. Let's meet for a quick coffee and I'll give you a picture."

"I need to be positive. If she can't identify the picture, how the hell do we find out?"

"They're still downloading his computer."

"Yeah, but I wouldn't expect they'll find evidence, unless he ordered the mask online. Meet you at Starbucks?"

"Be there in forty minutes."

Jack met Louie, then picked up Natasha later. He glanced in his rear-view mirror. He'd had a feeling that a green van and maybe a car had been following him when they left her apartment, but he hadn't seen them in the last hour.

He drove down the side road toward the farm and crested a small hill and stopped. Anyone following wouldn't know he had stopped until they were practically upon him.

"Mind if I ask what you're doing?"

Jack glanced at Natasha and said, "I'm probably a little paranoid. Just making sure that I'm not being followed."

"You told me that you thought it was coincidence that those bikers blew themselves up. A drug war. With the way you're behaving, I get the feeling that there's more to it than that."

"There probably isn't. I'm just the cautious type."

"Is that why Danny sent Susan and Tiffany to Calgary?"

"As I said, it doesn't hurt to be cautious."

"Is that why you didn't come over and see me last night?"

"I felt that I should stay with Danny. We needed to talk."

"And today?"

"What do you mean?"

"You know what I mean. I was feeling … amorous when you picked me up. You treated me like I had leprosy. You really hurt my feelings, until I realized that you're moving like someone who is hurt. I take it you don't want me to see any bruises?"

Jack sighed. "Okay. You're right. I was in a scrap late Sunday night. Work related. I came in second. Yes, I am feeling a little sore."

"Why didn't you tell me?"

"I'm feeling a little tense, okay? I'm really close to knowing who was responsible for killing Maggie and Ben Junior. Sometimes my work is secret. I try to keep things on a need-to-know basis. It's as simple as that."

Natasha didn't respond, but Jack could tell by the look on her face that she wasn't happy.

He put the car in gear, and they remained silent for the rest of the drive.

Marcie was delighted that everyone congratulated her on her good grades. Later, Jack found a moment to take her aside and show her Wigmore's picture. Marcie didn't think it was him. Jack told her not to worry about it. He would soon find out for sure.

Jack thought that Natasha had warmed up to him by the time they were leaving. Ben, Liz, and Marcie came out on the back porch to say goodbye.

Marcie gave Jack a hug, then said, "I'm sorry that I couldn't say the picture you showed me tonight was the guy who hurt me in the cabin."

"It's okay. I'll find out."

Natasha gave Jack a hard look but kept silent until they were driving home. "Marcie is linked to the guy who ordered the bikers to kill Maggie and Ben Junior, isn't she?" she asked.

Jack nodded.

"So you're using her to find out who it is."

"Sort of, but —"

"She's just a kid! How could you do that to her? Hasn't she been through enough?"

Jack sighed, then said, "I know she's just a kid. But I still have to identify the guy."

Natasha made no attempt to keep the anger out of her voice. "So you're keeping her on ice at your sister's until you need her to help you!"

"No! That's not why! But if she can help, then I'm still going —"

"You think she might be in danger now! That's why you were checking to see if we were being followed tonight!"

"I'm only being cautious. I told you...."

"Drive me home, Jack. I really don't want to talk with you. Ever."

It was midnight when Jack arrived back at his apartment. He told Danny that Natasha had broken up with him. Danny was sympathetic.

Two hours later, the bottle of Jose Cuervo was three-quarters empty. Jack told Danny to pull out the sofa and go to bed. Whiskey Jake and Sparks heard a bedroom door close, and a few minutes later Sparks turned the speaker down to cut out the sound of Danny's snoring.

Jack lay in bed as he thought about Natasha. Love, anger, sorrow, and self-doubt ravaged his brain until the pain became physical and gripped his stomach and chest like a vise.

An hour later his thoughts were interrupted when he heard a bottle fall and roll across his coffee table. He got to his feet and padded barefoot into the living room. Danny was snoring on the sofa with one foot dangling beside the coffee table. The bottle of tequila was emptying the last of its contents on his rug. He picked up the bottle and was about to return to his bedroom when he stepped on something. He checked the bottom of his foot and found a small shiny screw. It looked like it came from his stereo.

chapter thirty-five

Lance hung up the phone and went back to eating his breakfast. He tried to figure out what Jack was up to. Who in the club was Rolly's favourite friend, besides Wizard? That was easy. Stallion and Rolly were like brothers. Real brothers. Where could you find Stallion alone without any club members being around? That was easy, too. Stallion fit his ethnic roots and, being single, dined at his favourite restaurant most nights after work.

Lance mulled it over in his brain. Jack had told him they would meet in person soon. Maybe Jack would explain then.

Whiskey Jake and Thumper watched as Damien reviewed the pictures. They were using a computer monitor at the apartment of one of Thumper's girlfriends. She had been sent shopping. Damien zoomed in on the digital imaging of Marcie saying goodbye to Jack on the porch.

Whiskey Jake said, "So what do ya think? I don't know who this little bitch is, but from what we heard, it sounds like she can identify The Suit. Too bad we didn't see the picture that the pig showed her."

Damien zoomed in on Jack's face and watched quietly for about a minute, then said, "The copper doesn't look too happy. My guess is that he either isn't sure or doesn't know at all."

"Should we get Wizard over for a look?" asked Whiskey Jake.

"No. Even if this girl can't point a finger at The Suit, it won't make much difference. With what's happened, the coppers will soon piece it together, if they haven't already. I'll tell Wizard that The Suit is hot and to never deal with him again. If the cops roll him, they'll try to use him to get at us. Wizard's judgement has been clouded lately. I don't want him knowing about this kid and making another mistake. Once we find out who the rat is, make sure you clean the pig's apartment. It wouldn't be good if they found the bug."

"Not a problem. We cut a spare key and he hasn't changed the locks yet."

"I'm sure the rat is in the west-side chapter. I'll get Wizard to call a chapter meeting and pass on something juicy. Something that will make the rat want to meet with the coppers."

"It's church night tomorrow for them. He could do it then."

Damien nodded in agreement. "I'll meet with Wizard today and tell 'im what I want, so keep your ears tuned to that bug."

"Sparks is doin' that as we speak."

Damien gestured to the monitor and said, "Good job with this."

Whiskey Jake appreciated the compliment and said, "Yeah, turned out pretty good. Didn't want to get much closer. On a farm like that, they could have a dog."

"Stash it someplace safe."

Whiskey Jake nodded to Thumper, who disconnected the camera from the monitor.

Thumper waited until Whiskey Jake and Damien left the apartment before making a telephone call to his friend in Montreal. The election was only five days away. Did his friend think that Wizard would become the new national pres? *Oui!*

Thumper smiled to himself as he dialled another number. He was about to become a close friend of the future boss.

It was late afternoon and Sparks sat in the van reading a magazine while the sounds over the speaker told him that the pigs were putting groceries away. He sat bolt upright when he heard Danny yell from the kitchen, "Hey! Aren't we supposed to pay our friend tonight?"

Jack was in the living room, and his reply was easily heard. "Yeah, I'll slip out in an hour and do it. I have to go to the bank first. It won't take long. Why don't you stay and cook dinner?"

"Sounds good to me."

Sparks was already using the portable radio. The timing was perfect. Within an hour they would have a complement of eleven vehicles. More than enough to follow this porker!

An hour later, Jack drove out of his underground parking stall and onto the street. The traffic was heavy, forcing him to drive slowly. The bikers followed him from a distance and watched him take money out of a cash machine.

Jack signalled a left turn but quickly changed lanes and turned right. Sparks squeezed the button on the microphone and said, "Did ya see that? Piggy is paranoid!"

Whiskey Jake's voice replied, "Everybody stay cool. We've got lots of wheels."

The bikers watched as Jack made a variety of moves, including parking for a few minutes and watching traffic pass him before pulling back out onto the street.

After about twenty minutes, Jack's driving returned to normal and they followed him and watched him park.

"You got an eye?" asked Whiskey Jake.

"No problem," said Sparks. "He's out and going into a restaurant called Giuseppe's. There's a place right out front where I can park."

Seconds later, Sparks swore under his breath and kept his binoculars to his eyes as he radioed again. "I can see who he's meeting — but I don't believe it!"

Jack entered the restaurant and saw Stallion sitting by himself at a table. Jack walked over and sat down with him.

"Who the fuck are you?" said Stallion. "Get your own fuckin' table!"

Jack bent down and pretended to scoop something up off the floor and said, "Hey, buddy, I think this is your lucky day!"

"What the fuck you talkin' about?"

Jack held a rolled wad of money in his hand and said, "I saw this on the floor under your table. I presumed you dropped it."

"What? Oh! Yeah! That's mine! Must've fallen out of my pocket when I sat down." Stallion grabbed the money and said, "Thanks, man!"

"At least you could buy me a beer! Looks like quite a bit of cash there."

Stallion thumbed through the money. *What a chump!* He chuckled and said, "Yeah, no problem. I'll have one too."

Later that night, Lance anxiously hurried up to Jack and Danny in a small park near the pier where Wizard kept his boat.

"What's up?" Jack asked casually.

"I was hoping you would tell me! I'm supposed to meet Wizard on the dock in thirty minutes and bring a barrel. I've seen this picture before! Either I'm getting whacked or else they're gonna whack somebody else."

"Trust me. You're not getting whacked," replied Jack.

"And if they want me to kill someone? What should I do?"

"Do what you must to survive. We won't bust you for anything you need to do, but you also have to understand that you don't have immunity from any other cops."

"Puts me in a fuck of a spot."

"It's better than being in the spot of whoever's getting whacked."

"You're sure it's not me?"

"It's not you. Meet us at the cemetery as soon as you're done."

Danny passed the binoculars over to Jack and said, "I can make out Wizard and Rolly. Our friend is still sitting on the barrel by the gate to the marina. Looks like they're just talking."

Jack peered through the binoculars for a moment, then said, "Here comes someone else pushin' a wheelbarrow. Looks heavy. It's ... Stallion who's pushing it."

Moments later, the four men boarded the boat and it slowly chugged out of sight. It was two hours later when the boat returned and three men got off.

Jack and Danny met Lance at the cemetery. His pale face shone in the moonlight as he leaned against a tombstone and folded his arms across his chest to try to stop the trembling.

"Was it quick?" Jack asked.

Lance slowly shook his head, then paused and said, "I guess it was quicker than it was supposed to be. Stallion didn't have a clue. He figured we were makin' a meet to whack someone else. When we were about forty-five minutes out, Wizard came up behind him and busted out half his ribs with a bat. I then hog-tied him. It was bloody awful. Rolly started blubbering like a baby and kept sayin' that he hadn't told him anything. Wizard didn't believe him. As punishment, he told Rolly that he would have to finish him off after."

"After?" Jack asked.

"Wizard sat on his legs. He had a drill and started to work on his kneecap. I had to gag him after a few seconds because Wiz was worried about noise travelling over water, especially at night. Wiz barely got started again when Rolly lost it and put a slug through his forehead. Wizard was pissed off at him for killing him so soon."

Jack caught the solemn stare that Danny gave him but looked at Lance instead and asked, "How are you doing?"

"I'm not exactly thrilled about it, but at least it takes the heat off me. Might do the same for you. With what happened, I think Wiz won't be so tight with Rolly. I could see it in Wiz's eyes tonight. Rolly's got no respect now. He's lucky that Wiz didn't waste him too. I'm sure I'll be able to slide in there and find out who The Suit is. Maybe not before the election, but soon."

Jack and Danny were silent until they got back to the apartment. Danny flipped open the sofa and then said he was going to call Susan tomorrow and move back to his own house.

"Do you want a drink?" Jack asked.

"No. I'm sick enough."

Three hours later, Jack got out of bed and went to the bathroom to get a glass of water. He turned on the light and looked at himself in the mirror. He didn't like what he saw.

chapter thirty-six

Natasha was more than a little surprised at the message she got from her receptionist. A moment later she stood to give Marcie a hug as she walked into her office. Marcie stiffened and turned away, taking refuge in a chair.

Natasha sat back down and asked, "What are you doing here? How did you get here?"

"I hitched."

"Aren't you supposed to be in school?"

Marcie nodded her head.

"I bet the school has already called Liz."

"I phoned the school and pretended I was Liz. Told them I was sick and she was keeping me home."

"Why are you here?"

"Don't tell anyone. Especially Jack! He'd kick my ass. I mean, my butt."

"No problem there. Jack and I are no longer seeing each other."

"Yeah, I know. I heard Liz talking to him. That's why I came to see ya. I wanted to tell you that Jack's a really neat guy."

"I guess I see him a little differently than you."

"I don't understand why ... and I got the feeling that it's got something to do with me."

Natasha stared at Marcie for a moment, then said, "It's personal."

"I want you to know that Jack is the only guy I've ever trusted. He cares for me. Even though he wants real bad to catch the guy who murdered Ben and Liz's kids, he's told me that I would never have to get involved. Like testifying or anything. He said that he would look after it himself. The same goes for the freak who hurt me in the cabin."

"Interesting."

"You don't believe me, do ya?"

"It's sweet of you to try to do this, but I think it's best that I put you on a bus and —"

"Sweet of me! Fuck you! Don't treat me like a little kid! I wouldn't be alive if it wasn't for Jack! And you're the one who is supposed to be a doctor!"

Natasha paused for a moment, then said, "I apologize. I didn't mean to imply that you were a little child. What do you mean that I am supposed to be a doctor?"

"Jack sees things. Things that you probably should, but don't."

"Such as?"

"Such as the night you met me out on the farm. I was going to commit suicide."

"Suicide! What on earth for? You —"

"As soon as you and Jack came into the loft, he knew it right away. In fact, I think he already knew."

"I didn't see that. I thought you were just playing. What —"

"Yeah, I know you didn't see it. Maybe you should get your eyes tested. But Jack did. He's talked to me lots since then. I feel better about myself now. I would never think of doing something stupid like that again."

"That's good. You know if you ever feel —"

"If you and Jack don't click, then so be it. But if it's got somethin' to do with me, then I'm really pissed off, because I think he's a really good guy. He really cares about people. I think you're pretty stupid if you don't know that."

Thumper watched as Wizard let The Suit into the motel room.

The Suit gestured to Thumper and said, "I take it this is Lance?"

"No. I changed my mind on that. This is Thumper. He's ... better positioned than Lance. Wait till you see what he has to show ya and you'll know why."

"So now who do I contact if need be?"

"If you can't reach me, contact Thumper. Use Rolly only as a last resort. Forget Damien altogether."

"This gentleman now makes four who know me. I don't —"

"I know how ya feel. There's no need for anyone else to meet ya. Thumper is from a different chapter. Gives us more knowledge about what's going on. At least until the election. Then everyone will report to me."

"Provided you win."

"I'll win."

Moments later, Thumper hooked up the camera to the laptop computer. Wizard glanced at The Suit and said, "Take a look at who Taggart is meeting!"

The Suit's response was exactly what Wizard had expected.

"That little cunt! What's she doing with him?"

"I know. I fuckin' near had a heart attack when I saw it too. He's got her stashed out at his sister's farm. His sister is the ol' lady of the kids we —"

"I know who his sister is! What is this little cunt doing there?"

Thumper cleared his throat and said, "We think that maybe she can identify you. Taggart has got her stashed there for safekeeping."

"Jesus Christ!"

"It's good that Thumper let us know. That fuckin' Damien wasn't gonna tell us!"

"Jesus Christ!" The Suit repeated.

"Now that the pigs don't have a rat anymore, she's the only other loose end," said Wizard.

"Her and that fucking Taggart! He needs to be dealt with as well!"

"Exactly. I'll do 'em both, but we should wait until after the election on Monday."

"Forget that! We could be in jail by then! Or from what I know about Taggart, we could be dead."

"If we whack them, Damien will be pissed. If I don't win the election, he'll have me whacked for doin' it."

"And me too," added Thumper, looking at Wizard. "So you better fucking win."

"You'll win — especially if you do exactly as I tell you," said The Suit. "I've got a plan that will earn you enough — what do you call it? — class to become national president for as long as you want."

"How?"

"Simple. Grab the little bitch when she's alone someplace. As soon as you do, I'll set up Taggart and O'Reilly so they're easy to kill. If Taggart's body is never found, and O'Reilly and the little bitch are killed with Taggart's gun, it'll make it look like Taggart flipped out and shot them. Especially if there are no ligature marks."

Thumper leaned forward in his chair and said, "I can handle six guys and not leave a visible mark on 'em. Ten, if I was in a locked room with 'em."

"But how?" asked Wizard. "This will never work! They..."

The Suit raised his hand and gestured for Wizard to stop. "I have a plan. Don't you think I know how cops think? All you need is the proper evidence. This will work. If we have to, kill his sister and her hubby, too. Won't really matter. Use a shotgun on them, just like their kids. Leave it in Taggart's trunk and the police will conclude he was also responsible for murdering their children. Arrange for the appropriate evidence in his apartment." He paused, then said, "It would be prudent to have one or two others to assist. How about this Lance fellow?"

"Lance's loyalty might be with Damien. I think it would be better to keep him out of this. I'll get a couple of strikers. T-Bone and Booger. Neither one would question whatever I tell them to do. But you still haven't explained how or when."

"Tomorrow is Friday. We do it this weekend. And I'll tell you exactly how."

Late Friday night Jack lay in bed gently running his fingers through Natasha's hair. Her head lay on his chest, and Jack knew by her breathing that she was asleep.

He reflected on their evening. Natasha was a great cook. She was also coy about why she called to apologize for having doubted his sincerity. She said a good friend had opened her eyes but wouldn't say who. He had the feeling that she enjoyed keeping a secret from him.

He watched the luminous numbers of the digital clock in the bedroom as the minutes slowly flipped by into hours. He tried to sleep but his brain wouldn't shut off. He took slow, deep breaths to calm himself but had to repeat the process often. He couldn't stop thinking about two small coffins and the promise he had made to Maggie and Ben Junior.

He waited until early morning, then left a note and slipped quietly away. Leaving a note was easier than answering questions. Besides, if things went as planned, he could explain it to her over dinner tonight.

chapter thirty-seven

Jack's first stop was his own apartment. He immediately checked a voice-activated tape recorder that he had hidden under the sofa. The footage indicator was unchanged. He looked at his stereo. *Do they plan on leaving the bug in there forever?*

He showered, changed his clothes, and headed out the door.

It was just before noon on Saturday when CC and Charlie Wells entered the motel lot. The units were individual cabins well spaced from each other, but as Charlie had commented upon their arrival, they were not the type to be recommended by the travel bureau.

They entered the office and CC asked the proprietor if he was Mr. Burnside. When he said he was, she showed him her badge and introduced her partner.

"You called our office and said that you had some information concerning the murder of those two children?" she asked.

Burnside looked nervously past them. "I don't want anyone to see me talking to you."

"What are you afraid of?" asked CC.

"Bikers," replied Burnside. "Let's go in back."

Moments later, Burnside explained. "Bikers started bringing this creep to my motel," he said, nervously glancing out the door. "Then they bring him young girls. Real young. A biker would always sit outside in a car and wait. It's none of my business. I just rent the rooms."

"What does this have to do with the murder?" asked CC.

"I was warned last night by one of the bikers that I should get out of the city for a couple of weeks. Can't do that. Lose too much business."

"Why? What biker?"

"Dunno. I think he's with Satans Wrath. He told me this guy who likes little girls has flipped out. He says the guy is gonna start killin' anyone who can identify him."

"You still haven't said what this has to do with —"

"The biker says to me, you heard about those two kids in the farmhouse? I says, yeah. He says that this weirdo was gonna do somethin' to the girl but her little brother came in and he ended up killing 'em both. Guess he told the kids to stand on one side of a door 'cause he didn't want to look at their faces when he did it. Then he blasted away with a shotgun from the other side. Apparently he missed the little boy and had to do him later. Don't know if this is all bullshit or not, but thought I should tell ya."

CC exchanged a glance with her partner. The information on how the kids were killed had never been released to the public. This was the lead they had been waiting for.

"Who is this guy? Can you identify him?" she asked.

"I don't know. Only saw him for a second. Like I said, he's weird. I went past this cabin one night. I could tell he was takin' pictures because of the flash. The curtain wasn't completely closed and I saw him stark naked except for wearing a mask of George Bush."

"You sure it was a George Bush mask?" asked CC.

"Yup. And it wasn't Halloween. But this other night was different. I think that the girl he was with slashed his back with a knife. The biker wanted me to bring a first-aid kit. I only saw his face for a second when I brought the kit. I think the guy was angry that I saw him."

"How often does he come here?"

"Maybe once a month. The biker rents the room and pays cash. Another one of the Smith family. I did write the weirdo's licence plate number down once."

"You've got his licence plate number?" CC could barely conceal her excitement.

"Yeah, but it was a couple of weeks ago and now I can't find it. It might still be around someplace. I was lookin' before ya came over."

"I'll give you my card," said CC. "I want you to keep looking and call me immediately if you find it or if this guy shows up!"

Wizard waited until Burnside was alone before walking out of a nearby unit.

"They believe ya?" he asked.

"Hook, line, and sinker!"

At noon, Jack called Natasha. She was perturbed that he had slipped away without waking her. He apologized and said that there was some work he had to take care of but hoped the restaurant he had made dinner reservations at would make up for it.

"I know the place," said Natasha. "Was there once, years ago. Right on top of Burnaby Mountain. It's beautiful. Has a panoramic view of Vancouver. You're forgiven!"

Thumper crept through the bushes and then dropped to the ground. He adjusted his binoculars and saw Ben walking to the barn. An hour ticked by before he saw Elizabeth come to the door and holler that lunch was ready. Moments later, Ben and Marcie walked from the barn to the house.

Thumper went back to a small dirt road where a van was parked amongst the trees. Rolly, T-Bone, and Booger were waiting inside. All three had sawed-off shotguns on their laps.

"Well?" asked Rolly.

"All three of 'em are in the house havin' lunch right now. Give Wiz a call and tell him we're ready to rock an' roll."

Jack glanced at Natasha as he took the exit off the main highway and onto Capilano Road. She was wearing a new dress and looked particularly ravishing. "Have you ever been here before?" he asked.

"The Capilano Suspension Bridge? No, but I looked it up on the Net once. The view looked beautiful."

"You're right about that. Stretches out over 450 feet and hangs 230 feet above the river. Hope you're not afraid of heights."

"No, it sounds like a fun place for a walk. Just make sure we don't miss our dinner reservation. I've been looking forward to that all afternoon."

"The park closes at five. That gives us lots of time to get to the restaurant."

"Only gives us half an hour here, though," said Natasha, looking at her watch.

Jack didn't respond. With what he had to say, she might decide never to see him again. He parked the car and adjusted his tie and straightened his suit jacket as he walked around to open her door.

After passing a cluster of totem poles, they made their way onto the suspension bridge. There were few tourists this time of year. Jack noticed one solitary figure carrying a cooler in one hand and a large bag in the other hand as he trudged across the bridge far ahead of them.

"My God, it's high!" said Natasha, putting one hand on the railing.

"Are you scared?"

"No … not with you here. Just excited! This is absolutely breathtaking!"

Jack held her hand as they walked toward the centre. He found himself unable to appreciate or study his surroundings. He looked at Natasha and knew that her excitement was waning as she glanced periodically at his face. They stopped to admire the view from the centre of the bridge, and Jack stood with his arm around her.

"Look! Someone left a cooler," observed Natasha.

"I saw someone ahead of us leave it there a moment ago," replied Jack. "Probably heavy. Bet he plans on picking it up on the way back."

Jack glanced around. They were alone on the bridge. He didn't see the figure hidden amongst the trees at the far end of the bridge. The man used binoculars to spot his cohort hiding on the opposite side. A portable radio hanging from his belt crackled. "Got your charges set?"

"All set," he replied.

Out in the middle of the bridge, Natasha turned to Jack and abruptly said, "Okay, what is it? You're not looking at the view and when you look at me it's like you're someplace else. What happened? Something this afternoon? What's going on?"

Jack's mind went numb. His carefully planned words escaped him. He felt like someone had ripped his tongue out.

"Jack! What is it?"

He reached in his suit pocket and handed Natasha the small velvet box.

"Oh ... Jack," whispered Natasha.

She carefully opened the box and looked at the engagement and wedding rings. The engagement ring was made of yellow gold with three small diamonds imbedded in a V at the top. The V fit into the wedding ring, which had a large diamond in the centre with three smaller diamonds in an opposite V behind the centre diamond.

"I take it you're asking me to marry you?"

Jack nodded his head. He knew he had a goofy grin on his face, but he was so consumed by anticipating what Natasha's response would be that he was at a loss for words.

Tears welled up in Natasha's eyes, but she chose her words carefully and spoke firmly. "Jack, you know I love you, but I want more out of life than that. Someday I want to have children."

"I want children, too. That's why —"

"Let me finish. I want someone who will be around to be a husband and father forever."

"You're doubting my loyalty? I can't believe that you would think —"

"I'm not doubting your loyalty! I believe you keep your promises. Which is what I'm afraid of. I've seen your eyes when you talk about Maggie and Ben Junior.

It's that loyalty that scares me! I can accept that your job is dangerous. What I can't accept is you committing ... some act that would see you taken away from me. I'd make a lousy pen pal!"

Jack felt his eyes water. "Give me a minute, please." He turned and walked to the opposite side of the bridge and stared out over the abyss. He wondered if he would ever be able to sort out his thoughts. After a couple of seconds, he realized that the answer was really very simple. *The most important thing in my life is standing right behind me.*

He turned to face Natasha. "I promise you that from this moment forward, I will not do anything that ... that would jeopardize my future with you."

Natasha was silent for only a moment, and then she started to cry. "In that case, I would be very pleased to marry you."

They kissed and hugged for several moments before Jack remembered to take the champagne from the cooler.

"What? This is yours?" Natasha asked, as Jack popped the cork and filled two glasses.

Neither one had time to say a toast. Explosions at both ends of the bridge lit up the evening sky over their heads with fireworks.

"Jack!"

"Danny is at one end. A good friend by the name of Louie is at the other."

Natasha looked in awe at the fireworks and said, "This is so beautiful." She raised her glass and said, "To spending the rest of our lives together."

"As long as we both shall live."

chapter thirty-eight

On Sunday morning, Jack felt the warmth from the sun shining through Natasha's patio doors as he ate his breakfast.

Natasha smiled at him and said, "You're a man full of surprises, Jack."

Jack swallowed the last of his toast and said, "You didn't see it coming?"

"No. I didn't see any of it coming. Yesterday was like a dream."

"I'm glad it was a dream and not a nightmare. I was pretty nervous."

"You also must have been pretty busy! We barely stepped inside the restaurant last night before they played *The Marriage of Figaro*. For the maître d' to be that attentive, I suspect you must have been more than generous."

"Yesterday was a little hectic, but you know something?"

"What?"

"You're worth it."

"You're damn right, I am!" Natasha laughed.

Jack checked his watch and said, "If you're going to take Marcie out for lunch, you better get going."

"You're sure she doesn't know?"

Jack shook his head. "Marcie was in the barn when I called. Liz is really excited but she won't say anything to her until you break the news."

"Good."

"I'm really pleased that you want to do this for Marcie."

"You don't feel left out?"

"Not a bit. Especially shopping for clothes. The two of you will have a lot more fun without me tagging along. Besides, I need to get back to my own apartment and change."

From his hiding place, Thumper watched as Ben towed the fertilizer spreader around the field on his tractor. Thumper unzipped a sleeping bag as the late-morning sun sucked the dew from the ground. Then he saw Elizabeth and Marcie come out of the house and start hanging clothes from a clothesline that ran from the back porch of the house.

Thumper glanced behind him as Rolly crept through the bush to take his turn at watching.

"They movin' around?" asked Rolly.

"Doesn't look like they're goin' anywhere. Couldn't be a better time to pop 'em. The guy is out in the field on a tractor and the bitches are doin' laundry. If we whack the bitches first, farmboy shouldn't hear the noise."

"Haven't heard from Wiz."

"Give him a call. Tell 'em the three fish are in the barrel. I think it's time."

*

Jack was excited when he arrived back at his own apartment. Too excited to remember to check his voice-activated tape recorder. It was a mistake he would soon regret.

After taking a shower and changing his clothes, he reached for his telephone. There were a lot of people to call and share the news with. Danny would stand beside him as best man, along with Louie and Paul, his previous partner. He would need six more to form the honour guard.

Marcie was ready on time and got in the car as soon as Natasha arrived. They went to a mall and shopped for about an hour before having lunch. Marcie was polite and seemed appreciative that Natasha bought her some clothes, but she was not overly friendly.

Natasha took a second bite out of her shrimp croissant before realizing that Marcie was staring at her without eating. "Something wrong with your lunch?" she asked.

"What's going on?"

"Can't I buy you lunch?"

"I feel like somethin' is going on. Like you're not telling me something."

"Oh?"

"Yeah. I know you're back with Jack. Where is he? You're not breakin' up with him again, are you? Is that it? Is that why you brought me here? To tell me that?"

Natasha put down her fork, smiled, and said, "Quite the contrary. You're right, something is going on. I invited you here to ask you something that's really important and very special to me."

"What is it?" asked Marcie seriously.

"I wanted to ask you if you would be my bridesmaid."

It took Marcie a couple of seconds to grasp the situation, then she squealed and said, "You're getting married!"

"Jack proposed to me yesterday ... well, sort of proposed."

Marcie bounced around in her seat as she said, "And, and ... you want me to be your bridesmaid?"

"It was you who brought Jack and I together. After playing such an important role in my life — our lives — of course I would like you to be my bridesmaid. If you don't mind?"

"Don't mind! You bet I will! Oh, Natasha, this is great!"

An hour later, Natasha and Marcie were loading parcels into the trunk of Natasha's car when Natasha heard the door of a van parked next to her slide open. She glanced up as three men moved in behind them and stuck guns in their backs.

A voice hissed, "If either one of you talks, screams, or tries to run, we'll kill the other one."

Seconds later, Natasha and Marcie lay face down on the floor of a van as it silently drove out of the parking lot.

Natasha felt the tears roll down her face. She had never been so afraid in her life. She stared into Marcie's face. She had a look of resignation about her. It was as if she had already resigned herself to her fate.

Jack was making a list of the people who would be in the honour guard at his wedding when his cellphone rang.

"Taggart! This is Sid Bishop! I need to see you and O'Reilly now!"

"What is it, Sid? If you're still concerned about bikers, I'm sure you're not in any danger."

"It's about the wiretap application for Homicide. I just received an interesting phone call from someone about the *real* identity of a person identified in the application as an Edward Trimble!"

Jack felt his heart sink. "I don't understand. Who called you? What does —"

"I believe you understand fully! I haven't mentioned this to anyone else yet, but I will not allow justice to be put into disrepute! I suggest that you and Mister O'Reilly come to my house immediately and start telling me what is going on!"

"I'll pick up Danny and we'll be there as soon as we can," said Jack quietly. "It will probably take about an hour and a half."

Moments later, Jack called Danny and then left his apartment. He was barely a block away when Wizard and Booger entered his suite.

Forty-five minutes passed before the van came to a stop and the side door slid open. Natasha heard the roar of the ocean. She looked up and saw three bikers standing at the door, looking down at her. Then another face appeared, someone who didn't look like a biker but was definitely in charge.

"Taggart and O'Reilly took the bait. Should happen within the hour," he said.

Natasha's panic increased. None of the men had bothered to hide their faces. She also saw that at the sound of the man's voice Marcie squeezed her eyes shut and began to shake.

"Put them in the boat," he ordered. "Thumper, you stay with them, then the rest of you set up around the house." He looked at Thumper and added, "Remember the plan. Don't leave any marks on them. With the sound of the waves, even if they yell they won't be heard, but if they do try to cause any problems, snap their necks, or, if need be, slash their throats immediately. We're not taking any chances!"

"Not a problem," said Thumper, stepping from the van.

Moments later, Natasha and Marcie found themselves face down on the bunk of a cabin cruiser. The bunk was covered in plastic sheeting.

Natasha heard the men leave, except for one. She could hear his breathing and knew that he was standing close, watching over her.

CC and Charlie Wells were in the Homicide office when CC received a call. It took her a few minutes to calm Mr. Burnside down.

"I got another warning from the bikers! Told me to get out of the city now! This time I'm doin' it!"

"Why? What did they say? Did this guy meet you in person?"

"Yeah. Same guy as before. Big guy with a goatee. He said that the pervert has really gone berserk. Thinks he's murderin' people right now!"

"Who?"

"I don't know. The biker just told me that after this guy molested one of the girls, he buddied up to her later without her knowin' it was him. You know, like I told ya, he wore a mask."

"You told me."

"Yeah, well anyway, I guess he gave this girl a place to live with his sister someplace."

"Why did he do that?"

"I don't know, but now he's going to kill 'em."

"He's going to murder this girl and his sister?"

"Not quite. I guess the girl is meetin' with the pervert's lady friend. Got him paranoid that the girl has clued in and is talkin'."

"You don't have any idea who? Anything at all to help?"

"Remember I told ya I once got this creep's licence plate number?"

"Yes."

Well, I found it."

She motioned for Charlie Wells to come over to her desk. "Quick, run this! It's the pervert's plate from the motel."

Moments later, Charlie walked back into the office as CC hung up the telephone. She noticed he looked ill and appeared to be at a loss for words. "What is it?" she asked.

Charlie shook his head and waved a printout of the registration in front of him. "You're not going to believe it. The plate. You're not going to believe it."

"Damn it, Charlie! Out with it!"

"It's registered to Jack Taggart!"

"Bullshit!" CC looked at the registration, then quickly looked through her notebook.

"What are you doing?"

"I'll tell you in a sec. I'm calling the Anderson parents."

CC's worst fears were realized moments later, when she spoke with Elizabeth and learned that they were looking after a girl by the name of Marcie. A girl who was having lunch with Jack's girlfriend, Dr. Natasha Trovinski. Elizabeth didn't know the name of the restaurant, but she did know the name of the mall. CC told her that she had some routine questions. Nothing urgent. No need to bother Jack on his cellphone.

CC hung up the phone and leaned back in her chair. "Oh, God! No!"

"What is it?"

"The sick bastard felt guilty for killing his sister's kids so he found some street kid to live with them. Now he's going to kill her and some doctor that the kid's talking to!"

"So we come clean with him?" asked Danny.

"Wait to see what Sid has to say," replied Jack. "One guess as to who called him!"

"Turn right," said Danny, as he studied the map.

"Depending on what he says, I might admit that I was Trimble. He told me that he hadn't told anyone, so that's a good sign."

"You feel you can trust him?"

"I don't know," said Jack, "but how much could Wigmore really tell him without divulging stuff about himself?"

Jack parked the car in front of a triple-car garage that protruded from one end of Bishop's estate, and then he followed Danny on the slate-stone path that meandered alongside the garage and up to the main entrance. Plastic sheeting was draped over the porch and onto the steps leading up. Bishop stepped out the front door carrying a can of paint and set it down. He looked startled when he saw them approach and said, "I didn't expect you this soon. Come on in!"

Natasha turned on her side and looked at Thumper when he sat on the edge of the bunk. He leered down at her and said, "I have to admit, your pig boyfriend has good taste in women."

"You won't get away with this," replied Natasha. "Jack will find you. You hurt either one of us and I can guarantee that it will be nothing compared to what he will do to you," she said, matter-of-factly.

Thumper chuckled, then said, "I hate to break it to you, lady, but your pig boyfriend is a pussy. I kicked the shit out of him last Sunday. Took me all of about twenty seconds, and that was without really trying."

"You're the one who did that?"

"The pussy told ya? Of course! He'd go crying to you to fix him up."

"You know something? As a doctor, I've discovered that men like you, who like to fight, are really compensating for the fact that they have a penis about the size of a peanut. Jack is much more of a man than you could ever dream of being."

Thumper stood up, and his voice was menacing. "Talk like that, bitch, and you'll find out how big my peanut is!"

"Really? You think you could get it up enough for me to quit laughing!"

Thumper stared down at her for a moment, then sneered and said, "Naw, I know your little game. You figure if I drop my strides and fuck you, it will give you a chance to escape."

Natasha stared sullenly back, shrugged, and said, "Something like that."

Thumper chuckled, then considered her for a moment and said, "Maybe you're in luck. I like games." He reached inside his jacket and pulled out a hunting knife. "There is a little thing that The Suit has about DNA ... but you know something?"

Natasha stared back without responding.

Thumper reached into a pocket and held out a condom. "I'm not too worried about DNA!"

Natasha edged farther back on the bunk, pulling her knees close to her chest.

"No, don't, mister," said Marcie. "Leave us alone."

Thumper looked at Marcie and said, "I'm not talking to you, you little whore." He opened the bathroom door beside the bunk and said, "Get in there and wait. If you speak again or try to open this door, I'll kill the doc immediately and you right after!"

"Do it, Marcie. Do what he says," said Natasha quietly.

Natasha saw the tears running down Marcie's face. She slowly eased herself down off the bunk and went inside the bathroom.

"I've already searched in there, so you might as well sit quietly until I tell you to come out," said Thumper, closing the door.

Natasha sized up the situation. Even if Marcie did decide to run, she couldn't open the door without it banging into Thumper ... unless she got him completely up on the bunk with her.

Thumper looked at the bathroom door and then back at Natasha. He smiled and said, "I'll tell you how this little game will be played. I'll give ya a chance to escape. A real good chance. But if you take that chance and lose, then you fuck me and you fuck me hard. Understood?"

"You've got the knife," Natasha said. "Is that what you call giving me a chance?"

"I said I'll give ya a good chance. Here it is!" said Thumper, tossing the knife down beside Natasha's hand and stepping back.

Natasha grabbed the knife and pushed herself back on the bunk, expecting him to attack. He stood where he was, then faked a yawn and turned his back toward her and gazed toward the exit.

Natasha leapt from the bunk in a flash, lunging toward his kidneys. Thumper sidestepped with ease and grabbed Natasha. Her scream was muffled as her face hit the floor and the sudden pain in her bent wrist caused the knife to clatter onto the floor.

Thumper kicked the knife away, then picked her up and tossed her back onto the bunk. "Guess you just lost your chance, bitch. Time to see if your peanut theory is all that funny!"

Natasha got her breathing under control, then begged, "Please ... don't hurt us."

"You don't wanna get hurt? Then fulfill your end of the bargain. Or should I take it out on her?" said Thumper, gesturing toward the bathroom door.

"No ... not her. I'll ... I'll do it."

Natasha sat on the bunk, took off her jacket, and laid it beside her. Then she slowly unbuttoned her blouse and slipped it off. Thumper ogled her breasts, which were only partially concealed by her lacy black bra. Natasha used her hands to push herself slightly back on the bunk before undoing the top of her slacks. She stared at Thumper as she slowly pulled the zipper partway down, then stopped and gestured for him to come up on the bunk with her.

Thumper smiled and gave a nod toward the bathroom while taking hold of Natasha's ankles. "Not up there, sweetheart." He pulled her legs down off the bunk so that she was straddling his waist, then he undid his jeans and let them drop to the floor.

"I'll be good," whispered Natasha. "Just let us go after."

"Yeah ... sure. If you're real good, maybe I will."

Natasha sat up and slowly undid the buttons on Thumper's shirt. When he tossed his jacket and shirt on the floor, she placed her hand on the back of his head and guided his face into her cleavage as she fell back down onto the bed. Thumper felt her clutching his hair while slowly pushing his head toward her stomach.

He watched her face as he kissed and licked her navel, while pulling down the rest of her zipper before sliding off her slacks and panties. He continued to lick and taste the salt from her body, slowly working his way down to her thighs. He felt her fingers massage and scratch his head and shoulders. She took her hands off him briefly as her body twisted and she moaned. He glimpsed her fingers as she clawed and raked the bunk beside herself like a cat in heat.

"Time to put this on," he said heavily, reaching for the condom.

"Not yet," whispered Natasha. "You said to be good. Make it last. Do what you're doing a little more." She massaged his back with increasing intensity then grasped his head, urging him upwards. He licked and kissed his way back up her stomach while arching her back with one hand and pulling her bra aside as his lips searched for her nipples. He felt her fingernails rake his upper back and neck as she pulled his face deep into the side of her breast while wrapping her legs around his.

"Back off with the scratching, bitch! That…" Thumper didn't finish the sentence. He suddenly realized that he was lying in a warm sticky pool. He pushed himself upright as a torrent of blood flowed from the carotid artery in his neck like a severed garden hose. He grasped at the thin cut running lengthways up his throat and stared in horror at Natasha. She sat looking up at him, a bloodied scalpel in her hand.

"Consider yourself fucked," she said. "Fucked hard."

Spots of blackness swept over him as his brain starved for blood. He staggered back a step, then lost consciousness and fell backwards onto the floor. His heart continued to beat momentarily before it, too, accepted death.

Natasha dragged his body aside and opened the bathroom door.

Marcie saw Natasha's body awash in blood and opened her mouth to scream. Natasha clamped her hand over her mouth.

"I'm okay. This isn't my blood. The guy's dead. I killed him. We've got to be quiet," Natasha said, taking her hand away.

"What happened?" whispered Marcie. "What's going on? How did you kill him?"

"I had a scalpel in my jacket pocket," said Natasha, while putting her clothes back on. "Put it there one night when I went to the clinic to help Jack. Save the talk for later. We've got to get out of here."

"That man. The one who told them to put us on this boat. I recognize his voice. He's the one … the one who…"

"The one who molested you in the cabin?"

Marcie nodded, then said, "Why would they take us?

"I'm not sure, but they didn't hide their faces, so that's not a good sign. I'm guessing it must be a trap for Jack and maybe Danny. Come on!"

Natasha crept forward and peered out the exit. She saw two bikers standing at the back of the house. They were both carrying rifles and talking to someone through a window.

"Two of them are in the backyard with rifles. They've got their backs to us, but I can't tell if someone in the house is looking this way or not. Are you a swimmer?"

"No," said Marcie.

"See if we can find any keys to this thing."

Both Natasha and Marcie searched for keys. There weren't any.

"I've got to chance it," said Natasha. "They could come back any second. You wait at the top of the stairs while I slip across to the boathouse on the other side. Maybe I'll find something."

Natasha peeked out the exit and saw the bikers disappear, one around each side of the house. She scrambled off the cabin cruiser and scooted across the dock to a small boathouse. She cautiously opened the door and saw a high-powered speedboat parked inside. She climbed in and frantically searched for keys.

She abruptly froze when the door to the boathouse opened, then realized it was Marcie.

"You should have waited!"

"I was afraid. Did you find any keys?"

"No."

"Maybe we should make a run for it down the dock!"

"It's too long in the open. We'd never make it. I think —"

Natasha was interrupted by the sound of gunfire.

chapter thirty-nine

Sid moved the paint and stepladder to one side, then opened his front door again and gestured for Jack and Danny to come up the steps and follow him inside. They stopped when a German shepherd came out onto the porch and started barking.

"QC! Quit barking!" Sid commanded, then said to Jack and Danny, "It's okay, he won't bite. Come on in."

"You named your dog Cutesy?" asked Jack, glancing at Danny.

"Cutesy?" Sid chuckled. "No. It's QC! Short for Queen's Counsel. Cute, don't you think?"

Jack exchanged another glance with Danny. They looked at the plastic sheeting in front of them and both went for their guns.

"Do it now!" screamed Sid toward his foyer. "They know!"

Jack pumped two shots through the door. The dog lunged at him, knocking him down as a rifle shot sent a bullet zinging past him into the side of the garage. In front of him, he caught a glimpse of Rolly clutching his throat and staggering back as the door swung open. He was only partly conscious that Danny was taking aim at whoever had the rifle. His attention was focused on Booger, who appeared in the foyer carrying a MAC-10 submachine gun.

Danny saw T-Bone standing at the end of the house as he took aim to fire another shot at Jack. Danny fired three shots. Only one counted, but it was enough. T-Bone fell to the ground as the bullet tore through the centre of his chest.

A barrage of shots rang out from the foyer, along with another shot from near the garage behind them. Danny crouched beside the steps and turned to see who was by the garage.

Jack lay on his back on the path and tried to protect his face from the dog's savage attacks with one hand while firing more rounds at Booger, who let loose with a short burst of fire before leaping back out of sight. More bullets whizzed over Jack's head from behind him, and the dog yelped and fell to the ground when a rifle bullet severed its spine.

"Take cover!" Danny yelled. "Wizard's behind you!"

Jack's only place for cover was in the house, and he bolted through the door while firing rapidly. He caught a glimpse of Sid running up a spiral staircase but directed his shots toward Booger, who stood in the living room and fired another spray of bullets toward Jack.

Jack dived into a shallow pond inlaid in the floor near the bottom of the staircase. He squeezed off another shot at Booger, who darted back behind the wall. Jack barely had enough room to keep his face out of the water without exposing his head above the edge of the pond. Looking up, he could see only the lower half of the spiral staircase. Rolly's head and one arm lay in the pond. Blood from his throat spilled into the water. His other hand lay limp at his side.

Jack raised his head slightly to look toward the living room, but a rifle bullet delivered from outside by Wizard ricocheted off the ceramic tile floor and zinged past. Wizard was rewarded for his effort by two shots from Danny, who was still crouched behind the steps. Wizard quickly retreated back behind the garage.

For a few seconds, everything was quiet except for the sound of a koi gasping for life as it flopped around on the floor.

Sid then screamed from above. "Get in there! Finish them off!"

Booger yelled back, "We're at a bit of a Mexican stand-off here. I've got him pinned down. Go to a window and tell Wizard and the others to finish the pig at the door first, then we can do this one from both sides."

Danny peeked over the edge of the top step while punching the numbers into his cellphone. When he connected, he screamed the address first, then said, "It's O'Reilly and Taggart! We're at Sid Bishop's house!" A rifle bullet slammed into the cement in front of his face. Fragments of lead and cement shot into his face and eyes. His cellphone flew from his hand as he fell back. Pain shot through his head and blood gushed out of his forehead and into his eyes.

Jack heard Danny's body slam into the side of the house. He yelled out from the pond, "Danny! Are you all right? Danny!" There was no reply. He grabbed Rolly's body and slid him into a position to partially block Wizard's view, while trying to keep watch on the corner of the living room wall. He yelled for Danny again. No response. His mind felt numb.

Wizard shouted, "Booger! What's happening in there?"

"Rolly took a hit! He's bought it, but I've got the pig pinned down in the fucking fish pond. What's taking you and T-Bone so long?"

"T-Bone is down, but I shot this fucking pig in the face as he was usin' his cell. I think he's dead."

Sid hollered, "Did he get through? Do you know if he got through?"

"I heard him give your address," Wizard yelled, "but don't think he said much else before I nailed him."

Sid screamed an angry, jumbled list of obscenities while kicking a wall.

"We still got time to think of somethin'," Wizard shouted. "Booger! You sure you got that pig in there pinned down?"

Jack saw that Booger had taken a mirror off the wall and propped it out from the corner of the living room to see him. The two men stared at each other's reflection. It was easier for both of them knowing where the other one was and what they were doing.

Booger yelled back to Wizard, "No problem! This pig ain't goin' nowhere for now!"

"Okay!" Wizard responded. "Sid! I'm goin' down to the boat and get Thumper. We'll kill the bitches and use oil and gas from your boat to throw in the pond and flush out Taggart. Torch the pigs and nobody will figure out what really happened."

"You're going to burn my fucking house?"

"It was your idea to do it here! So now what? You got a better idea?"

There was a short pause, then Sid said, "Do it!"

*

CC and Charlie Wells left a team of investigators to finish searching Taggart's apartment. They were only partway back to the office when they heard the broadcast from Communications that O'Reilly had called for help from the Bishop home but was cut off by the sound of gunfire.

CC grabbed the radio and said, "Was Taggart with him?"

"Ten-four!"

"We want Taggart for at least two murders! If O'Reilly is dead, Taggart likely killed him. Make sure everyone knows! I'm on my way!"

Jack tried his own waterlogged cellphone. No surprise that it didn't work. *Danny's dead.... What did Wizard mean, kill the bitches?* A few moments later he heard Sid speaking to him from near the top of the staircase.

"Taggart! You hear me? Taggart!"

Jack didn't respond, so Sid continued, "We've got your doctor lady friend and that little bitch you had stashed at your sister's! I want you to know that they're dying at this very moment!"

The numbness in Jack's brain was replaced with terror.

"How do you feel, Taggart? You'll be joining them in a couple of minutes. Better think of something to say to them!"

Before Jack could reply, the sound of gunfire came from behind the house.

"Did you hear that, Taggart?" said Sid, letting out a high-pitched laugh. "Did you hear that?"

Jack's mind burned with rage. He glanced up the stairs, then back at Booger, watching him through the mirror.

*

Natasha peeked out the boathouse door and saw Wizard running down the dock toward her. She quickly closed the door and turned to Marcie and said, "We have to go in the water."

"I can't swim!"

"It's our only —"

"Thumper!" yelled Wizard from beside the boathouse. "Thumper!" Wizard climbed into the cabin cruiser and screamed, "Jesus Christ! You fucking bitches!"

Wizard saw bloody footprints leading to the boathouse. With his rifle ready, he kicked open the door and stepped inside. It took him only a moment to spot the blood and wet hand marks on the walkway. He knew that Natasha and Marcie were hiding under the dock.

Marcie clung to Natasha's neck. Only their heads were above water as Natasha slowly moved along under the dock. Wizard's feet sounded above their heads, and Natasha caught a glimpse of his face as he stared down through the cracks in the boards searching for them.

Wizard pumped two shots into the dock by his feet, then stepped out of the boathouse and moved slowly along the dock, firing several more shots through the boards as he went. Bullets swooshed through the water around Natasha and Marcie, but none found their mark.

"I know you bitches can hear me," said Wizard. "Want you to know that I just shot O'Reilly in the face. I'm not lettin' your boyfriend off so easy, though. Got him tied down. I'm gonna soak his fuckin' face in gas and oil and have myself a little pig barbecue!"

Wizard stopped and listened. Natasha was crying but didn't make a noise. She heard the noise of a pail followed by a glugging sound. Drops of oil and gas dripped into the water near her face. Marcie's wide eyes stared back at her.

"You girls sit tight, I'll be back for you in a minute!" said Wizard, picking up the pail and walking away.

Wizard hurried across a patio at the rear of the house, slopping gas and oil as he went. He grabbed a lighter from beside a barbecue and cursed when he heard the distant sound of sirens. He took another step but came to an abrupt stop when the bushes parted in front of him.

Danny's face was a mass of blood. One eye was shut and he used his hand to try to keep the blood out of his other eye. His gun was pointed directly at Wizard's head.

"Thought you were dead," said Wizard.

"Put the gun down," said Danny. He spoke quietly, but there was no mistaking the deadly tone of his voice.

Wizard tossed the rifle onto the ground away from his body.

"Put the pail and lighter down and lie on your belly with your hands stretched out over your head. Turn your face away from me!"

Wizard slowly did as instructed.

"You fucked up," said Danny. "You haven't been playing by the rules."

"What fucking rules?"

"Rules that say you don't involve my wife and daughter."

"Maybe you better think about them when you decide what you're gonna say in court!"

"Maybe I better explain the rules to you."

"I know my rights. Fuck off, pig."

"You lost your rights when you tried to kill my family. You need to be educated."

"What the fuck are you talking about?"

"Let me demonstrate," said Danny, kicking over the pail onto Wizard.

"What the fuck! You can't..." Wizard's last words were drowned out by the whoosh of flame when Danny clicked the lighter.

Jack heard the sound of Wizard's screams from the backyard. It wasn't long after the screams stopped that he heard the back door being kicked in.

"Jack! You still alive?" yelled Danny.

"Where the hell were you? I thought you were dead!"

"So did Wizard! For him it was fatal. What's the situation?"

"Sid is upstairs. Don't know if he's armed or not. Got a bad guy in the living room who's got me pinned down. Thumper's got Natasha and Marcie on some boat out back. That's where Wizard was going. Was that you shooting at him?"

"No, I met him when he came back from the boat."

Jack closed his eyes for a second to clear the tears. He opened them in time to see Booger start to move, then settle down again as they continued to watch each other's reflection.

Jack heard the sound of the sirens coming closer. He glanced upstairs. *I'm not letting you surrender, you bastard!* He started to climb out of the pond and saw Booger crouch in anticipation.

"Jack!" Danny yelled. "They might be okay!"

"What do you mean?"

"I saw Wizard taking potshots into the dock. There was no sign of Thumper!"

Jack fired two shots through the wall and Booger fell back from sight. Machine gun fire erupted toward the ceiling as Jack dived back into the pond.

"Jack! Where are you? What's happening?"

"I'm okay. I'm lying in a fish pond in the foyer! I might have hit the guy in the living room but he's still firing back."

"That the one with the machine gun?"

"Sure as hell isn't what I have." Jack checked his weapon and saw that he was out of bullets. He could no longer see Booger's reflection in the mirror. He glanced back at a shotgun that Rolly had dropped near the front door but knew he couldn't reach it without exposing himself to Booger. The sounds of sirens were now augmented by the sound of screeching tires. He heard Sid moving around upstairs.

"Danny! There's two exits to the living room. I got this one covered, you —"

"Got it," grunted Danny, waving to Jack from where he was kneeling. Jack saw Danny crouched behind a corner in the kitchen, past the second exit to the living room. Jack's expression when he saw Danny's face revealed his shock.

"I'll make it," said Danny. "Sounds like the cavalry is about to arrive."

Seconds later, they heard police cars screeching to a halt in the driveway.

"You hear that, Booger?" yelled Jack.

"I hear it."

"Throw out your gun and give yourself up!"

"Walk away from my bros?" gasped Booger. "Don't think so. Why don't you come in and take it from me?"

Jack heard the car doors opening out front. He thought about Natasha. *If she's dead…* He looked down the hall at Danny peeking around the corner.

"I don't have much time," yelled Jack.

Danny pointed up to the ceiling and Jack nodded. Danny dropped to his stomach and started to crawl down the hall toward the far exit of the living room.

Jack opened his mouth to scream for Danny to go back, but it would have been too late. He was already completely exposed.

"Booger!" yelled Jack. "You want me to take it from you? Here I come!" He splashed water as he half-climbed from the pond, then sunk close to the floor, waiting for a spray of bullets. None came. Then he heard a thump from the other room.

"Jack!" Danny spoke from the far exit. "You got him. He's slumped in a chair with blood all over his chest. His gun fell on the floor. Don't know if he's dead or not."

"You cover him," yelled Jack, while scrambling across the floor and grabbing Rolly's shotgun. He ran up the spiral staircase two steps at a time.

Once upstairs, Jack found himself in a hallway with closed doors leading to two bedrooms, followed by a double set of doors at the end of the hall that led to the master bedroom. He kicked open the first two doors and barged in. Nobody there. He then fired a blast through the door to the master bedroom before bursting through and diving in on his stomach.

Jack held the shotgun close to his body as he rolled on the carpet, searching for his target. Sid was not in sight. He leapt to his feet and burst into a bathroom and then a walk-in closet. A safe in the closet had its door wide open. He stepped through French glass doors leading to a balcony. Sid was on the ground below, clutching a briefcase as he ran toward the dock.

Jack fired a blast from the shotgun, but he was out of range and Sid only ran faster. He looked at a drain spout that ran from the roof and down past the balcony to the ground. Sid had left several dents in the drain spout, but it was still attached to the wall. Jack saw Wizard's rifle lying on the ground below him.

Within seconds, he half-slid and then fell the remaining distance when the drain spout broke loose from the house. He landed on his feet and grabbed

Wizard's rifle. Sid had not yet reached the end of the dock. It would be an easy shot.

"Drop it!" a voice commanded.

Jack looked over and saw a uniformed policeman crouching behind the corner of the house and aiming a pistol at him.

"I'm Jack Taggart! I'm a police officer!"

"I said drop it, asshole! I know who you are! You're under arrest for murder! One more word out of you and you're dead! I mean it! Now drop it!"

Jack reluctantly tossed the rifle aside. He was then instructed to lie face down on the ground. Soon, two more officers joined the first one. Taggart was handcuffed and brought to his feet in time to see Sid roar out of the boathouse in a speedboat. "You're making a big mistake!" he said tersely. "Check with O'Reilly inside!"

"We found O'Reilly lying unconscious in the living room. He's on his way to the hospital. He's still alive, by the way, so we will be talking to him. Did you shoot him? Or was it one of your biker buddies? Maybe the one he nailed in the living room!"

"What the hell are you thinking? It wasn't me! Get down to the dock! My fiancée and a girl by the name of Marcie are there! They could be hurt."

"Yeah, we heard. Don't know what you did to them, but we will find out!"

Jack was brought around to the front of the house and placed in the back seat of a police car. He saw the hatred in several officers' faces when they looked at him. *What the hell is going on?* He then heard an officer radio CC. Her reply wasn't comforting. "Good! Keep the piece of shit cuffed. I'll be there in a few minutes!"

CC and Charlie Wells arrived and sat in the front seat of the police car to talk to him.

"It's over, Jack. We know," CC said.

"What the hell are you talking about? Get down to the dock! I think my fiancée and a girl by the name of Marcie are there!"

"I know about Natasha and Marcie," said CC.

"Then see if they're alive! What the hell is going on?"

"We'll find them. I would like to hear what you have to say."

"Those morons out there let Sid escape! He's the leak! The one they call The Suit!"

CC turned to Charlie and said, "Get the exhibits from the car while I read him his rights."

Charlie left and CC began to read Jack his legal rights.

"CC, I know my rights, for God's sake," replied Jack. "The only lawyer I want is Sid Bishop!"

"Did you kill him, too?" asked CC, glancing at Charlie as he returned with several exhibit bags.

"He took off from here about ten minutes ago in a speedboat."

"Really? Care to explain this?" said CC, holding up a plastic bag containing a rubber mask of George Bush.

"You found the mask! Where? What..."

"Same place we found these," said CC, as she picked up another plastic bag containing dozens of sexually explicit photographs of young girls. "In your apartment!"

"My apartment!" Jack looked out at the police officers. He was no longer confused. "You get a tip this afternoon that they were there?" he asked.

"Our investigation led us there this afternoon."

Jack thought for a moment, then asked, "You also find my tape recorder under the sofa?"

"Yes, as a matter of fact we did," said Charlie, holding up another exhibit bag.

"So you admit that this stuff is yours?" CC asked.

"The recorder is mine, CC, not the rest of it. Did you rewind the tape and listen?"

"Haven't had time yet. We will."

"Do it now ... please."

CC rewound the tape and pushed "play." Soon the tape played the sound of someone knocking on Jack's apartment door, followed by a key in the lock. The sound of footsteps in the kitchen was heard, followed by a voice saying, "We're alone."

The sound of furniture being moved was interrupted by a voice saying, "Do you see what this pig listens to? What a fuckin' pussy!"

Another voice said, "Shut up and pass me the screwdriver." Moments later, the sound of furniture being moved again was followed by receding footsteps and the opening and closing of the apartment door.

"So?" said CC, flicking off the recorder. "What's that all about?"

Jack looked at CC and said, "Keep playing."

The next noise was Jack coming home, taking a shower, and then phoning several people to tell them he was getting married. CC could only hear Jack's side of the conversation. The second-to-last call caught her interest. It was an incoming call, and she heard Jack say, "What is it, Sid?" Jack later repeated Sid Bishop's address out loud. The last call was Jack calling Danny to say that Sid wanted to meet them both.

"If it actually was Sid who called you," said CC, "what did he want to meet you about?"

"Some questions about the wiretap application. It was a ruse to kill us. Keep listening."

The noise of Jack leaving his apartment was followed by his door being opened again.

Wizard's voice commanded, "I'll stand six. Put them in his bedroom someplace. Under the mattress will do."

Booger's voice was heard saying, "Have you seen these pictures, man? This guy you call The Suit is one sick fuckin' dude!"

"I've seen 'em. Hurry up! The pigs could be here to look for 'em soon!"

CC clicked the tape recorder off and said, "Oh, my God, Jack, I'm so sorry."

Jack didn't hear her. He put his hands to his face and sobbed when he saw Natasha and Marcie running toward the car.

CC stood beside the car and watched as the three of them hugged, kissed, cried, and slowly regained their composure. The police officer who brought them up from the dock gave CC a quick summary of what had happened to them. Another officer called her on the radio, and she reached in through the open window and retrieved the microphone.

"Crane, here. Go ahead."

"I'm at Emergency with O'Reilly. He regained consciousness and is being really difficult. Wants to know about Natasha and Marcie."

"Tell him they're both okay. So is Taggart."

"Who cares about Taggart?"

"We were set up. Taggart is still one of the good guys. I'll explain later. What is O'Reilly's status?"

"Don't know yet. He's going in for x-rays and a CAT-scan. Looks like he'll lose an eye."

"Stay with him. Charlie will coordinate security."

CC passed the microphone to Charlie and said, "Take care of it. The hospital and the Anderson farm until we straighten this mess out!"

Jack said, "CC, please lend me your cell. I'm going to call Susan and pick her up."

"O'Reilly's wife?"

Jack nodded.

"I need a statement from you. From what I hear, there are bodies strewn all over."

"I'll give you a statement tomorrow! I'm taking Natasha and Marcie with me right now! We're going to get Susan!"

"Sorry, Jack. You know this can't wait. I'll wait until tomorrow for formal statements from Natasha and Marcie, but I need one from you now."

"I think I'm in too much shock to remember. Give me a night to recover."

"Come on, Jack! If you're going to play that game, then you're also in too much shock to be driving! I'll put you in a hospital room under security until you're out of shock!"

Natasha put her hand around Jack's arm and said, "Jack, I need to take Marcie to the hospital. She *is* going into shock."

Jack looked at Marcie and saw that she was shaking uncontrollably.

"Tell you what," said CC. "I'll have someone drive Natasha and Marcie to the hospital. Give me a few minutes, then I'll go with you to pick up Susan. We can talk on the way."

Jack looked at Natasha, who nodded her head in agreement. He kissed them both goodbye and stared after them as they drove out of sight.

"Here's my cell," said CC. "Call Susan. I'm going to take a quick look around and then we can pick her up."

A few minutes later CC returned. Jack passed her phone back and said, "Susan insisted on driving herself. She's on her way to the hospital. I want to be there, too."

He could tell by the look on her face that something was troubling her. "Damn it, CC! Look what we've been through! Come with me to the hospital. I'll give you a statement there!"

"Tell me what happened. Nutshell version."

Jack quickly told her, then said, "Satisfied? Now let me get to the hospital. Someone can take formal statements from me there!"

"I will," said CC, taking Jack by the arm and leading him slightly away from everyone else. "You might want to talk to O'Reilly. You know, to see how he's doing."

"What are you saying? Of course I want to see how he's doing!"

"Listen to me. I've seen the bodies. Everything appears to make sense except for one."

"Which one? I don't understand."

"A crispy critter behind the house. Looks like he tossed his weapon and lay down on the ground. Then he was soaked in petroleum and torched. O'Reilly might want a lawyer. Especially if it's his bloody fingerprints all over the lighter we found."

chapter forty

It was after midnight when Jack used a payphone at the hospital to call Lance.

"Where the fuck you been?" asked Lance. "Don't you ever turn your cell on?"

"It got wet this afternoon. Doesn't work. I'll have a replacement tomorrow. Anything going on?"

"Anything going on! Christ! You call me at this time of night to ask me if anything is going on? You know fuckin' well there is! Have you seen the news?"

"You mean the part where it said that five members of Satans Wrath were killed in a shootout when police raided a home in search of an abducted woman and a young girl?"

"Yeah, that part of it. I take it you were involved?"

"The news doesn't quite have it correct at this point. The woman is my fiancée and the girl is a friend of mine. It was only Danny and I involved in the shootout."

"Oh, fuck! Wiz and Rolly! They ambush ya?"

"At The Suit's house. It was a crown prosecutor by the name of Sid Bishop."

"Damn it! I'm sorry…."

"Glad you're sorry."

"Not for you, for me. It means I still owe ya five years."

"Maybe not. He escaped. You find him before I do and the deal is still on."

"All right! I hear ya! So you and Danny are okay? What about your woman and the girl?"

"Danny is in the hospital. He might lose an eye. The rest of us are okay."

"Lose an eye? Well, I guess shit happens. He'll be a twin for Halibut. Who else was killed? I figured it was Wiz and Rolly. They take two strikers with 'em? T-Bone and Booger?"

"They did. How do you know? The names haven't been released yet."

"We've been trying to do a head count and figure out who's missing. It's tough. Damien is going nuts. We got guys runnin' around all over because of the election tomorrow. Over a dozen chapter presidents have already flown in. The rest are arriving in the morning." Lance paused, then asked, "Who was the fifth?"

"Thumper."

"Thumper! He's not even with our chapter. He's with the east side. You sure?"

"I'm sure."

"That dirty fucker! I bet he stuck his nose up Wiz's ass because he thought Wiz was gonna win the election."

"You can strike Wizard's name off the ballot."

"Then this happens in the middle of everything! It's like someone drove a car into a yard full of hornets' nests. Guys are talking revenge. Wait until they find out it was you and Danny! I bet Damien knows already."

"What's he saying?"

"Not much. Makes him look bad that he didn't know what was going on and didn't have control over his guys. I bet he loses the election now."

"Who do you think will win?"

"Probably someone from back east. Damien wants me at his house at eight in the morning. I've never been invited there before."

"Why does he want to see you?"

"Don't know. All the presidents will be meeting him there at 2:15 tomorrow afternoon. The vote will be decided shortly after."

"I'll have a working cell by noon tomorrow. Call me when you can."

"Yeah, I will if I'm alive."

"Why wouldn't you be?"

"If Damien figures I knew about the ambush, he won't be pleased."

"Want me to vouch for you?"

"Fuck you!" Lance chuckled.

"Call me tomorrow."

Jack returned to the hospital room where Danny was sleeping. Susan was standing beside the bed while Natasha held Tiffany and sat in a chair beside Marcie. Jack put his arm around Susan's shoulder and said, "You're sure you're okay?"

Susan nodded. "The nurse said she'd put a cot in the room. I want to make sure I'm here when he wakes up and before they operate again. Appreciate you looking after Tif for me."

Jack looked over at Natasha and Tiffany. "She's in good hands. Don't worry about her. I've taken the booster seat out of your car."

"I'm not worried about her," replied Susan. She then glanced at a heavily armed member of the Emergency

Response Team who was standing outside the room. "I understand why that guy is here, but what about the one hanging around from Homicide? Why is it so important for him to be here?"

"People died today. They need to talk to Danny and make sure he didn't break any rules."

"And did he?" Susan studied his face for the truth.

Jack paused, then said, "No. I talked to him earlier. He obeyed them completely."

Susan stared a moment longer, then walked across the room and gave Tiffany a kiss on her forehead before saying goodnight to Natasha and Marcie.

"Susan ... I'm sorry," said Jack.

"Yeah. I know. You better get going. Your sister will be waiting."

Jack saw that the city lights were behind them and glanced in the rear-view mirror. Marcie was leaning against the booster seat. Both she and Tiffany appeared to be sleeping.

"There's something I need to know," he whispered to Natasha. "I'll understand if you need time, but..."

"You mean, do I still want to marry you?"

"Yes. After today, I..." Jack let the words trail off. He couldn't bring himself to say it.

Natasha's eyes brimmed with tears. "I was petrified. It was all because of you."

"I know. I'm sorry. I would never have put you in that position if I'd known."

"I'm not talking about that! I'm talking about us! I was petrified that I might never see you again! Today made me realize how fragile life is and how much the future means to me. You are my future. I'm going to cherish every day of it."

Jack breathed a sigh of relief. "Good. I felt exactly the same way."

"Speakin' of that," said Marcie, leaning forward from the back seat, "bein' as I'm the bridesmaid, when are you getting married?"

"After today ... soon!" said Jack and Natasha in unison.

Natasha leaned over in the seat, wrapping her hands around Jack's arm, and said, "Besides, I think I need to keep you around for protection."

"You need protection?" said Jack, rather incredulously. "I heard you took out Thumper with only a scalpel. How did you manage that? I couldn't have beaten him if he was handcuffed and I had a gun!"

Natasha paused, then said, "Oh, I just waited until the right moment when he wasn't paying attention."

"Yeah," said Marcie. "She sort of caught him with his pants down."

Jack stopped the car at a checkpoint set up at the entrance to Ben and Liz's driveway. The officer radioed others outside the house and they were allowed to proceed. The light bulb over the porch had already been unscrewed to prevent anyone from accidentally turning it on. Light escaped from the edges of the shades and drapes that were drawn and Jack glimpsed Ben unlock the door as they made their way across the porch. Seconds later they were inside.

The only one who wasn't hugged and kissed and didn't cry was Tiffany. When they finished their greetings they sat in the living room.

"Any change with Danny?" asked Liz.

The sound of geese honking outside brought their conversation to a stop. Ben looked at Natasha and said, "That's Andrew and Martha, our two geese." He looked at Jack and said, "They'll honk all night if those officers keep moving around. I better put them in the barn."

"I'll help you," said Jack.

Several minutes later, Jack watched as Ben herded Andrew and Martha into a pen in the barn. Ben latched the door and asked, "How long do we have to put up with this? I have a business to run. We can't leave but we sure as hell can't live with these guys hanging around outside. Now I know how the prime minister must feel."

"Sorry, Ben. I'll straighten that out tomorrow. I promise."

"Tomorrow?"

"Tomorrow afternoon."

"Why then?"

"I'm going to a meeting. Don't worry. You, Liz, Marcie … everyone will be okay."

"This meeting will straighten things out?"

"I expect so."

"That's a relief. Don't get me wrong. We're grateful. It's just … we want it to be over. When you told us the two guys who murdered Maggie and Ben Junior were dead … Liz and I felt like our life was going to … well, it will never be normal, but at least it gave us some satisfaction. Then you said the main guy escaped … now we don't know what to feel."

"I *will* catch him, Ben. I promise you that!"

"Yeah, I know. That's what I told Liz. You live up to your promises. Damn it, I haven't even congratulated you and Natasha for getting engaged."

"Thanks."

Ben stared at Jack for a moment, then hugged him and said, "Thanks. Thanks for killing those bastards. I know you'll get this other guy, too."

Jack thought about his promise to Natasha, and then he thought about tomorrow. Damien was in for a surprise.

chapter forty-one

"Your men had quite a day, yesterday," said Isaac, once Louie Grazia sat down.

"It would appear so."

"I read a statement that Homicide took this morning from O'Reilly. Take a look. Tell me what you think."

Louie read the statement, then said, "I think he should receive a medal. Both of them should."

"You read the part about how he killed the one they called Wizard?"

"Yes. After being seriously injured and barely able to see, he captured him in the backyard. Made him toss the weapon and lay in the prone position. He was so weak he had to sit down to cover him. Said he started to lose consciousness and woke up in time to see Wizard with a lighter in his hand about to shove a pail of gas on him."

"That's the part that really got to me. As injured as he was, he still chased this guy down and tried to arrest him. If he hadn't had the quick reflexes to kick the pail over, it would have been him that burned to death. Says he even caught the lighter that Wizard threw. Lucky for him the gas went in the other direction. I agree, commendations are in order."

"Good. They'll be pleased to hear it."

"There is one other matter, however, that I wish to discuss with you."

"Sir?"

"It's about Taggart. The informant he had by the name of Edward Trimble died of a drug overdose over two years ago. How do you suppose that could be?"

"Typical of drug addicts. One of them dies in some flophouse and someone else who is probably wanted snatches his identification. I'll speak to Taggart and tell him to smarten up. He should know better than to be fooled like that."

"I see. Well, considering what he's been through, I don't think you should be too hard on him. Maybe give him a break on that one."

"Yes, sir. If you think so."

Isaac leaned back in his chair and gazed out the window but watched Louie out of the corner of his eye. "In some ways, Wigmore was right about Taggart."

"Oh?"

"Yes, people he works on end up dead, including the two who murdered his niece and nephew."

Louie shrugged his shoulders but didn't speak.

"Have you had a chance to debrief Taggart? How does he feel about Sid Bishop?"

"He's upset that he escaped. That he wasn't able to arrest him."

"Arrest him?"

Louie pretended that the connotation eluded him and said, "U.S. Customs found his boat on Orcas Island in the San Juans this morning, but there was no sign of him. From there, he could have easily flown to the mainland and then anywhere."

"Do you think Taggart has any idea where he is?"

"Not a clue. He asked me if we've checked Bishop's bank accounts yet."

"And have you?"

"Preliminary inquiries look like there were some off-shore transfers to the Grand Caymans. He'll know how to cover his tracks. Bet he is living under a new identity in some foreign country. Satans Wrath could help him in that regard. It wouldn't look good for them if he was arrested. They're in dozens of countries. I'm not optimistic that he'll ever be caught."

Jack's meeting with CC was brief. He had already prepared a statement and slid it across the desk to her.

CC scanned the statement quickly, then leaned across the desk and said, "I want you and O'Reilly to know something. Strictly for professional reasons. I want you to have at least a *little* respect for me."

"CC, don't worry. Sid set me up beautifully. I have no grudge against you at all."

"This isn't about that. It's what O'Reilly did! Tell him he owes me a hell of a favour."

"I don't understand."

"Bullshit! I've taken enough statements to know when someone's been coached! Not to mention that the burn marks on Wizard did not start under his arm and on his face, where they would have if he was throwing gas at Danny. They started on the back of his arm and head. He wasn't looking when he got doused."

"Danny was badly injured, barely conscious. Maybe he was a little off on —"

"Cut the crap! This is only between the three of us. I just want you to know that I do know how to do my job."

Jack stared at CC for a moment, then said, "I'll tell Danny. He'll probably want to buy you a drink."

"Tell him that, but if it arrives with a flame on top, I'll shoot him!"

Jack returned CC's smile, then said, "I need a favour as well."

"What kind of favour?"

"It's about the exhibits from yesterday."

"Your recorder?"

"No. Something else. Something that might keep some people from dying."

Jack lay in the bushes, resting his arms and chest on a sports bag as he watched several limousines pass through the electronic gate into Damien's estate. He caught a glimpse of bikers roaming around inside. Some were there to provide security and showed their respect for the bosses by keeping their distance.

At two o'clock, Jack used his new cellphone to call Natasha.

"I want you to know that I really love you," he said.

"That's nice. I love you, too," replied Natasha. "Good news about Danny."

"Yes. Good news. I have to go, but..."

"But what?"

"Just wanted you to know how much I really love you."

"Jack? What is it? Something is going on.... You're not doing anything that could put you ... away, are you?"

"Don't talk that way on the phone. I would die before I ever broke that promise."

"Okay, sorry. I love you, too."

Jack picked up the sports bag and crept to the rear of Damien's home. He scaled the stone wall surrounding the back of Damien's property and dropped down into the grounds.

A biker who had been monitoring security cameras inside the home ran into the backyard. Damien was speaking intensely to a group of over twenty men. Anger and talk of revenge was rampant. Silence descended when the biker told Damien that there was an intruder.

Jack strode toward the group. He saw two laser beams dancing over his heart and idly wondered how many more were on the back of his head. The group parted slightly as Damien walked up to him. The rest of the men exchanged glances. They sensed that Jack was an outsider and circled him like wolves around a farm dog.

"You got your fuckin' balls walkin' in here!" screamed Damien.

Jack looked at the group and said, "My name is Jack Taggart. I'm a cop. The cop who was responsible for killing five of your brothers yesterday."

He took their moment of disbelief and shock to look Damien in the eye and say, "Out of respect for you, I brought you this." He handed him the sports bag.

The wolves recovered from their shock and moved in for the kill. They stopped when Damien put up his hand before unzipping the sports bag and looking inside. Seconds later, he pulled out five sets of colours. The jackets belonging to T-Bone and Booger only had the bottom rocker. Wizard's colours were badly burned but were still recognizable.

"You pick today to commit suicide?" asked Damien.

Jack looked at the angry faces and said, "Wizard, Rolly, and Thumper tried to kill my family, my partner's family ... and then tried to kill my partner and me. Maybe the rules have changed, but I think —"

A biker grabbed Jack by the throat and said, "Guess I'll finish what Wiz started!"

"Let him finish!" Damien demanded.

Jack was released. He continued. "I think that T-Bone and Booger were following orders from Wizard. I also believe that Wizard was following orders from someone *outside* the club." He saw several of the men look at Damien, who continued to stare at Jack.

"I believe that because I know Damien," said Jack. "If he wanted us dead, we would be. He's proved that to me already, which is why I respect him enough to return the colours and take whatever you dish out. I know if Damien wants me killed, I will be. I don't want to try and lead a life and start a family, wondering every day if there's a bomb in my car. If you intend to kill me, then do it now."

Everyone stood in silence, looking back and forth from Damien to Jack. Damien nodded his head, and one of the bikers providing security approached and used an electronic wand to search Jack.

"Clean, except for this," said the biker, taking the cellphone out of Jack's pocket and handing it to Damien.

"Check the perimeter for a five-block radius and let me know," said Damien, before dropping the cellphone in the pool. "Oops," he said.

Minutes later, Jack was roughly brought into the house and hauled down into the basement, where he was placed on a stool beside a workbench. Five strikers stayed to ensure that he didn't move. Jack spotted the electric drill on the workbench and thought about Stallion. *What goes around, comes around.* He checked his watch. It was 2:30.

At 4:25, Damien came downstairs, along with two other bikers. He gave a nod of his head and the five guards backed away.

"So you did come alone," commented Damien.

Jack nodded.

"Yesterday … tell us how they died."

Jack related what happened at the front of Sid's home and in the foyer.

"How did dat Wizard die?" asked one of the bikers with a thick French accent.

Jack looked him in the eye and said, "The official version is that he caught fire on his way back to torch me."

The two bikers looked at Damien. He gestured with his head and the three of them walked away a short distance to talk privately. Moments later, they returned.

"What about Thumper?" asked Damien.

"My girlfriend slashed his throat with a scalpel."

"No shit?" said Damien, sounding surprised.

Jack said, "Yes, she's quite a woman." For a second, he almost forgot where he was as he thought about Natasha.

"If Booger had given himself up, would you have let him live?" asked Frenchie.

"I knew he was a striker who probably didn't know the rules, but at the same time I didn't know if my fiancée and the girl had been hurt. Either way, he messed with them. If given the opportunity, I would have finished him off."

The two bikers glared at him, then looked at Damien, who said, "Yeah, that's pretty well how Sid Bishop told it."

The comment was not lost on Jack. *He knows where Bishop is!*

Damien looked down at Jack and said, "Okay, sit here. It's not us three who decide if you live. We're all taking a vote on it. Get you a beer while you're waiting?"

"No, thanks."

As they were leaving, Frenchie asked Damien, "You offer dat pig a beer?"

"This is strictly business. Doesn't mean you shouldn't be hospitable."

Jack remained on the stool as the strikers moved back into position.

It was three hours later when Damien returned, this time by himself. "Leave us!" he barked. The five strikers promptly went upstairs.

"Looks like it's your lucky day," said Damien. "You're going to live."

"It took long enough to decide."

Damien shrugged his shoulders and said, "We had an election to do as well. What saved you was that Wizard took orders from someone outside the club."

"I thought returning the colours was a nice touch."

"That showed class, but it will only be T-Bone and Booger's colours that will be kept and held in respect."

"Are you still national president?"

Damien smiled and said, "Yeah, I got it. I think you turned the tide on that one. They figure that if you acted that way out of respect for me, then maybe I was doing a good job."

"Sounds like you owe me one."

"I don't owe you fuck all! I reiterated what you said, that Wizard and Rolly took their orders from someone outside the club. Thumper was a weasel. It gave everyone something to think about. If anything, my two cents' worth may have saved your life."

"How close a vote was it? On letting me live?"

"It was unanimous. Everybody out there is clear on the rules. Wizard, Rolly, Thumper ... they broke the rules."

"That's good they respect the rules. Too bad Sid Bishop doesn't."

"The trouble with guys like him is they've never been educated on the street. They don't know how to survive."

"So where is he?"

"Fuck, you think I'm going to tell you? Give your head a shake!"

"You were the boss when all this took place, and you are still the boss. That makes you accountable. He messed with the people I love. You can't ride the fence on this."

"You don't fucking tell me what I can do or what I can't!"

"Then as far as I'm concerned, if you don't tell me, you are breaking the rules, and I'll hold you responsible."

Damien stabbed his finger into Jack's chest and roared, "You have the gall to threaten me? Right here in my own house?"

Strikers immediately appeared on the stairs and Damien yelled, "I didn't call you guys! Fuck off!"

Jack waited until they were alone and said, "I'm not threatening you. Just reminding you about the rules."

Damien studied Jack closely, then shook his head and said, "Our rules say that we never help the police. You arrest him and I'd lose respect. Think you know what that means. Unlike you, I don't believe in putting myself or my family in jeopardy."

"My family is top priority to me, too."

"Then get your priorities straight! Walking in here this afternoon ... you let your emotions rule you instead of your brain. Leave now and count yourself very lucky!"

"I want to know where Sid Bishop is!"

"You don't listen, do you? I will never help the police!"

"Who said anything about helping the police? I'm talking about me."

Damien looked exasperated. "You are the police."

"Do you remember the night you met me in that construction site, when you said that you and I were in different clubs, but in some ways we were very much alike?"

"I remember."

"I was wrong to think we weren't. You've opened my eyes. Neither of us would be alive if we went by the rules that govern the rest of society."

"What are you getting at?"

"It makes me sick, but I'm admitting that you probably know me better than anyone else. You know I don't plan on arresting him!"

Damien looked at Jack for a moment, then said, "Still no reason to help you."

"I'm in a good position to return you a favour someday."

Damien paused, then said, "So you'll be Sid's replacement?"

"Not exactly. Call it rules of honour and respect. If we play by our rules, both you and I, and our families, should be around for a long time. It's wise to invest in the future."

Damien stared at Jack long and hard, then said, "You would owe me. Owe me big!"

chapter forty-two

"*Buenas noches!*" said Natasha, unconsciously feeling her wedding ring as she walked out on the balcony. The Mexican sun was touching the top of the Pacific Ocean, and the afternoon breeze was starting its daily venture from the water to the mountains behind them.

Jack was peering through binoculars but put them down before kissing Natasha warmly on her neck. "Thought you were going to take a shower," he murmured, before kissing her again.

"Came out to see if you would be kind enough to soap my back."

Jack chuckled, then said, "With pure, unadulterated pleasure."

Natasha gestured to the binoculars and said, "When you said you were bringing the binos to look for whales, I had no idea that you would abandon me to do it. You need to get your priorities straight!"

"Priorities? Who ... where did you get that from?"

"What do you mean?"

Jack paused, then said, "Nothing, just sounded like something someone else said to me."

"A woman?"

Jack chuckled. "No. Definitely not. After being your love slave all week, I needed a few moments to regain my strength."

Natasha smiled and said, "You are so bad." She looked down the mountain toward the ocean. Below the mountain in front of her were several homes with swimming pools. The homes were built in traditional Spanish style, with red tile roofs and surrounded by white plaster walls that cut through groves of palm trees. Beyond that, she could see the brilliant white crests of the ocean waves breaking out from the deep blue waters.

"It is so beautiful," she said. She waved to a Mexican family who were heading down to the ocean with small circular fishing nets to throw in the waves. They waved back.

Jack had said that the area was virtually untouched by tourists. He was right. The local populace had not become contaminated by outside influences. Everyone was friendly, but at the same time, privacy was respected. She could not have wished for a better place for the first week of their honeymoon.

Tomorrow they were to continue the second leg of their honeymoon to a more popular and festive resort in Costa Rica. She wished their honeymoon could go on forever.

"I'm glad we came here first," said Natasha, wrapping her arms around Jack. "It's so quiet and peaceful. Have you enjoyed it? Do you feel relaxed yet?" she asked, looking deep into his eyes.

"What makes you think I haven't been relaxed? Being with you makes me the happiest guy in the world!"

"You've seemed a little distant all week. Like something is bothering you."

Jack pulled her close and said, "Someone once told me I let my emotions rule me instead of my brain. Maybe he was right. All week my emotions have been telling me that I could face anything this world could throw at me — as long as we're together. I don't think emotions are such a bad thing."

"Good. I feel the same way." She kissed Jack warmly on the lips, then giggled and said, "Okay, love slave, your work is not done! Get back inside!"

The morning sun had barely started to lighten the eastern edge of the mountains when Jack quietly slipped out of the villa and made his way down the mountain. At 6:05 he waited outside the rear wall surrounding one of the homes. He stood behind some trees and listened intently, waiting for a sound from within. His concentration precluded him from noticing the light reflect off a pair of binoculars focusing in on him.

People are creatures of habit. Sid Bishop was no different. At six-thirty Jack heard the splash as Sid jumped in his pool to start his morning laps.

He crept over the wall and crouched behind some bird of paradise bushes that obscured the area near the shallow end of the pool. He watched as Sid swam toward him before stepping out to the edge of the pool.

Sid came to an abrupt stop, standing with his head and shoulders out of the water. He wiped his eyes with his fingers and said, "Who are..." He didn't finish the sentence when he recognized Jack glaring down at him.

"Taggart!" Sid blurted. His eyes and mouth opened wide as he looked around in fright. He tried to yell but his words became bubbles in the water as Jack tackled him.

Sid kicked with his feet and jerked his knees while trying to pull at the hands around his throat. He gulped in water but managed to twist out of Jack's grasp and grabbed the side of the pool to climb out.

Jack lunged on him again, grabbing the back of his head and smashing his face in a frenzy against the concrete edge of the pool. Sid's nose broke and he gurgled and tried to scream as broken teeth cut his lips and tongue. His scream was cut short when his head was submerged once more. He tasted blood and felt splinters of teeth in his mouth as his lungs craved for air before giving in and gulping down more water.

Jack stared down at Sid's eyes in the water. He tried to think of Maggie and Ben Junior as he watched Sid struggle in a futile attempt to reach the surface. The image of the children's faces was hard to hold on to. A memory of Natasha kept appearing ... facing him on the suspension bridge while he gave his promise...

Sid started to vomit as Jack brought his head to the surface.

Jack wanted to scream out at the world in rage. Rage over the grief that this man had caused ... and frustration that even with his death, this man could affect his future with Natasha. He eased his grip and saw the colour return to Sid's face.

Sid read the hesitation in Jack's face and became emboldened. "You will die for this," he spluttered. "I will see to that!"

"Wrong thing to say," said Jack, jerking him by the throat back into the pool. Sid grabbed at his arms and twisted his body like an eel, but Jack held on firm. He stared into Sid's wide eyes and watched as frothy red bubbles parted his lips. He waited until Sid went limp before pulling him out of the water and laying his body along the edge of the pool.

A shadow appeared over Sid's body and Jack spun around.

"Natasha! How...?"

She bent down to check Sid's pulse and said, "I don't know much about whales, but I do know you don't spy in people's swimming pools for them." She looked up at Jack and said, "He's still got a pulse. What had you planned on doing with him?"

"I was going to kill him, but then I started thinking..."

"About what?"

"Priorities ... my promise to you ... letting emotion rule my brain..."

"You'll never ... correction, *we'll* never be happy as long as this bastard is alive. Besides, the promise was not to do anything that would land you in jail. This won't." Natasha then rolled Sid face down into the pool.

Jack was dumbfounded. "What?" was all he said.

"As a medical practitioner, I would surmise that this man slipped on the edge of the pool, hit his face, then fell unconscious into the water and drowned. As a policeman, what would you say?"

Jack blinked, then looked at Natasha and replied, "I would say that I love you more than life itself."

"Correct answer, officer."